An Unproven Concept

Kraken Edition

By James Young

Hope you enjoy the Con!

Happy reading!

[signature]

Dedication

"Play it again, Dad!" "Okay Jamie. Last time." For my father, a man of preternatural patience who was always willing to put on the *Star Wars Radio Drama* record one…more…time.

Foreword

The idea for this version of *An Unproven Concept* came about in a conversation with several of my reviewers. The overwhelming consensus was that the novel needed to include "Ride of the Late Rain" despite that short story being published over a year before . In addition to including "Ride of the Late Rain," I have also included artwork from Justin Adams (http://variastudios.squarespace.com/), Jon Holland (http://desuran.deviantart.com/), Christos Karapanos (http://amorphisss.deviantart.com/), Gabriel Nagy (http://surk3.deviantart.com/), Steven Sanders (www.studiosputnik.com), Eric Weathers (http://www.ericweathers.net/), and Anita C. Young (http://snowsong2000.deviantart.com/). I hope that these illustrations will not only aid in the reading of the work but also be enjoyed on their own merits. I found all of my illustrators easy and enjoyable to work with, and highly recommend them for anyone looking for art simply to enjoy. If you like the artwork, it should be available on both Redbubble.com and Cafepress.com with the keyword searches *An Unproven Concept* or "Vergassy."

I have employed standard naval definitions and terminology from the present day. For those who are not familiar with terms such as "port," "starboard," or abeam, I have included several helpful diagrams after this foreword. Times are given in Standard Spacefarer's Time (SST) throughout this book. In many cases, this is intended to orient the reader on events that are happening simultaneously, if several hundred thousand kilometers / light years apart. In cases where you may find yourself saying, "Wait, that couldn't have happened that quickly…", odds are it's happening at the same time on a different vessel.

Shipboard Diagrams and Terminology

(All Drawings Anita C. Young)

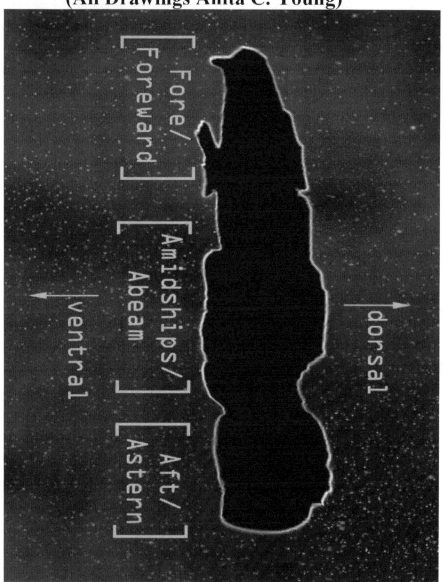

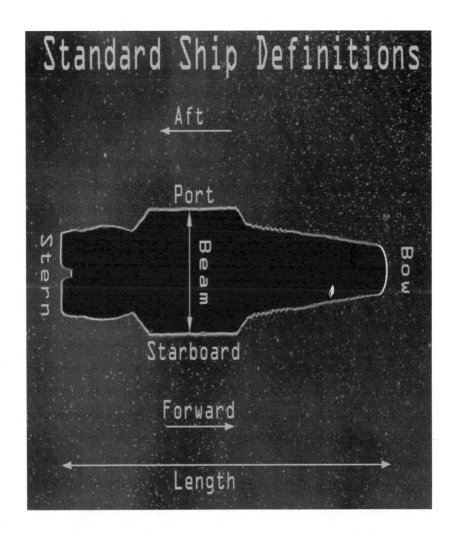

System Maps (Anita C. Young)

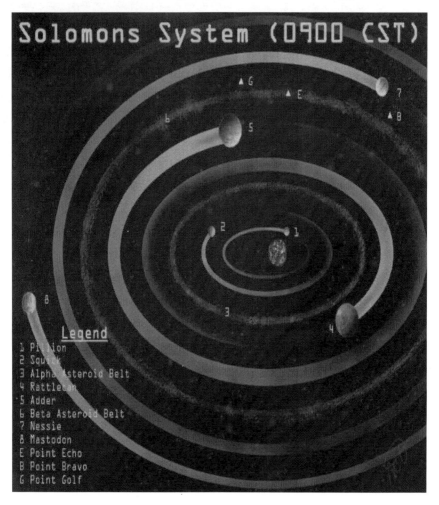

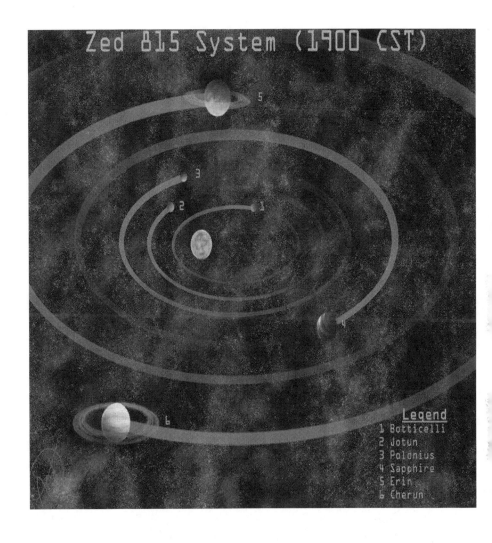

Zed 815 System (1900 CST)

Legend
1 Botticelli
2 Jotun
3 Polonius
4 Sapphire
5 Erin
6 Cherun

Prologue

Bridge
Spacefaring Starship (S.S.) Titanic
1725 Standard Spacefarer's Time (SST)
21 June 3050

Captain Abraham Herrod returned to consciousness and swiftly regretted his change of status. He was floating in mid-air, his mind immediately realizing that the lack of gravity was a very bad sign. An even worse one was the broken, clearly dead body of his helmsman arcing by. The man's head was split open like a cloven watermelon, the detritus that had been scalp, hair and brain surrounding his skull like a surreal, nightmarish halo. His dark blue uniform did not reveal all other violence that had been done to his person, but several spreading dark stains were strong indications that the impact which vented his skull had also rent his torso.

We were hit by something, Abraham thought, fighting through the fog that was clouding his thinking and preventing him from completely remembering what. I've got a concussion. Looking down, he saw his command chair roughly eight meters below him.

I must get back down there, the grizzled old captain thought, narrowing his blue eyes. Turning, Abraham saw that he was drifting towards the bridge's starboard bulkhead and attempted to bend his body in half so he could "kick" off from the ivory shaded structure. The movement made him cry out involuntarily, the sharp sensation of pain telling him that there was something seriously wrong with both his legs. Before he could react to this new information, the half-completed maneuver slammed him into the compartment's side. He had a split second to register the sickening crunch of bone before white-hot pain gripped him. Blissful unconsciousness ended his agony before he could scream again…

Abraham came to strapped into the *Titanic*'s command chair with Mr. Coors, the *Titanic*'s sensor officer, attempting to set his right leg. The fact that the man was attempting to do it with both his own legs gripping the dais seemed to be adding a degree of difficulty. Again Abraham's brain was fogged, but this time he realized that it was pain medication rather than shock. The captain felt slightly detached, as if he was watching the tall, thin man place someone else's leg, gray hairs matted in blood, into a splint from the bridge's aid station. With a start, Abraham realized that Coors' stance, the bodies still floating in midair, and splatters of other organic debris floating across his field of view meant artificial gravity still had not been restored across the deck. Abraham took a deep breath and instantly regretted it, the slaughterhouse smell hitting him like a physical blow.

"Sir, you're awake!" Coors said, relief making his Australasian accent stronger. Abraham tried to respond, his tongue thick and mouth sticky. Swallowing, he managed to creak out a single question.

"What happened?" Abraham rasped then, stronger, "Why did the cruisers fire on us?"

Coors looked up at him in bewilderment.

"Sir, those weren't Confederation cruisers," the sensor officer replied slowly.

Chapter 1: Of Airlines, Buggy Whips and Corded Phones

Solomon System
0700 SST
20 June 3050

With a bright flash, the Confederation Star Ship (C.S.S.) *Constitution* exited hyperspace and entered the Solomon system at a ninety degrees to the ecliptic. One thousand meters in length, two hundred fifty across at her beam, and two hundred fifteen from the top of her sensor array to the bottom of her keel, the *Constitution* resembled a spearhead hurled through the vacuum by some malevolent god. That being, of course, if gods hurled spears with six engines forming a circular, dark blue flaming flower at their rear.

"Helm up forty-five degrees! All astern full!" Captain Mackenzie William Bolan barked from his seat at the rear of the vessel's bridge, his face going almost as pale as the compartment's bulkheads. Tall and fit, the man's full head of black hair combined with his rugged features made to make him appear a decade younger than his forty-five years, An impressive figure in his navy blue space suit, Bolan would have looked right at home on a recruiting poster.

What in the Hell was Nav thinking?! Bolan thought disgustedly as he looked at the viewscreen that dominated the bridge's forward bulkhead. The *Constitution*'s captain found himself fighting disorientation as his brain tried to convince him he should be "falling" towards the Solomon system's Alpha belt. So designated due to it being the closest asteroid cluster to the massive neutron primary off *Constitution*'s starboard bow, the field was composed primarily of large planetoids. Planetoids that, if impacted at their current speed, would shatter the 300,000-ton battlecruiser like an insect against a cockpit.

"Aye aye, all astern full!" his helm officer, Lieutenant Commander Saburo Sakai, replied from his station directly in front of Bolan's own chair. The wiry Eurasian pulled back on the engine order telegraph to the left of his chair, then pulled back on the yoke in front of his chair. A moment later, inertia simultaneously attempted to fling Bolan forward against the viewscreen and down through his chair. Grunting, he turned left in order to give his Navigation Officer a well - deserved tongue lashing.

9

"Contacts! Three contacts, bearing oh nine oh, range eighty thousand kilometers, minus forty-five degrees!" Lieutenant Naomi Boyles sang out from the bridge's starboard rear. The short, attractive blonde was staring intently at her screen, the image a computer generated representation of what the *Constitution*'s sensors "saw" out in deep space.

Okay, I stand corrected--Nav brought us out right on top of them! I'll have to give her an attaboy after this, Bolan thought as he looked towards the Navigation station. A slight, wasp-waisted brunette, Lieutenant Jane Horinek looked like she should still be planetside in a secondary school. Horinek's gaze met Bolan's through the five semi-transparent screens that surrounded her couch. He gave her a slight nod and smile of appreciation before turning back to his duties.

*Discipline problem or not, this is actually turning out to be one of the best and **gutsiest** jumps I've ever seen.* Bolan pressed a stud on his command chair, bringing the sensor information up on the forward viewscreen. The display immediately passed from a standard damage control schematic to a detailed, three-dimensional map of the Solomon system. The pirate vessels initially appeared as triangular vector symbols, then swiftly resolved into three-dimensional outlines, one larger than its two companions. Boyles assigned letters to each of these icons, with the larger being designated Contact Alpha, the two smaller as Contacts Bravo and Charlie.

"Contacts are getting underway," Boyles reported.

"All batteries prepared for action," Commander Newton Sinclair, the *Constitution*'s gunnery officer added. He sat to Bolan's starboard front, his own console another group of touch screens that displayed the *Constitution*'s offensive weapons array. Average height, with broad shoulders, Sinclair was allegedly one of the best "gunners" in the fleet. So far, Bolan hadn't seen anything to doubt the man's reputation.

"Standard hail, Mr. Herrod."

"Aye aye, Captain," Lieutenant Charles Herrod, the ship's communications officer, reported. The tall, lanky officer pressed a couple of buttons on his station's console, then turned to Bolan. "Your position, Sir."

Bolan pressed the transmit button on his right arm rest.

"Unidentified vessels, this is the C.S.S. *Constitution*. Heave to and prepare to be…"

"Weapons lock on!" Boyles interrupted, her report causing Bolan to let off of the button. "Contacts Bravo and Charlie are preparing to fire!"

"Evasive pattern November, Mr. Sakai," Bolan barked. He felt the *Constitution's* angle shift as Sakai put the massive battlecruiser into a corkscrew pattern designed to throw off solution computers.

Well now that formalities have been observed...

"Weapons lock, both contacts," Sinclair barked.

...let's get to work.

"Mains on Contact Bravo, secondaries Contact Charlie," Bolan ordered. "Sensors, what's..."

"Alpha is accelerating out of system, Captain," Boyles interrupted.

Well she's got some good engines on her, Bolan thought as he watched the vessel's vector line extend rapidly. *But so do we...*

"Engaging enemy contacts!" Sinclair reported tersely.

The *Constitution*'s main battery consisted of twelve Category One (C1) railguns in four triple turrets arranged with a pair mounted on her ventral and dorsal sides. Each triplet was aimed by the vessel's main computer and used electromagnetic energy to accelerate a 4,000-kilogram solid slug of depleted uranium down their 180-meter length. Exiting at several thousand kilometers a second in a bright flash and plume of plasma, the slugs hurtled downrange in a spread that was designed to intersect with their target's expected position. Simultaneously with the battlecruiser's expulsion of heavy metals, her secondary battery stabbed microwave energy towards Contact Charlie.

The energy needed to power the combined assault caused the *Constitution*'s bridge lights to perceptibly dim. Its effects were far worse on the vessel's targets. Represented as a series of bright lines joining the *Constitution*'s icons with Contact C, the masers' firing and impact were almost simultaneous. Contact C's icon briefly flickered, signifying shield activation, attempting to keep the terrible energy from the hull. In sheer seconds the *Constitution*'s second volley arrived, dissipating the last of Contact C's energy barriers before flaying against the vessel's hull.

Before the twelve dual-gun secondaries could fire again, the battlecruiser's initial main battery salvo intersected with Bravo. Flashing in the reflected light from right before impact, the railgun penetrators slammed into the vessel amidships with devastating force. The vessel was simply there one moment, then gone the next as its fusion power plant lost containment. The bright flash of radiation, particles, and disintegrating matter was portrayed as a red globe on the *Constitution's* main screen, an area double the diameter temporarily going black as the electromagnetic pulse blinded the battlecruiser's sensors.

Death's Halo indeed, Bolan thought, the common naval slang term for the phenomenon's nickname coming unbidden to his mind. Its origins came not just from the likelihood that none of Bravo's crew had survived the explosion, vessel disintegration, or sudden introduction to vacuum. The term also aptly described how the spreading sensor blackout made it as if the Angel of Death was at work, his black halo preventing observers from seeing the flash of his harvesting scythe.

"Contact Charlie no longer has weapons lock," Boyles reported drily. "Enemy vessel appears to be disabled."

"Rail guns to Alpha, continue to engage Contact Charlie with secondaries and generate a solution for missiles," Bolan barked. There was a slight sound from Sinclair's station as if the man was getting ready to protest, then silence.

"Sir, Warhawk One is requesting permission to launch."

Sakai's simple intonation made Bolan suddenly kick himself for forgetting about the *Constitution's* air wing.

"Denied," Bolan replied tersely, thinking of the gyrations necessary to launch fighters from the *Constitution's* bays. "All ahead full after Alpha."

"Aye aye, all ahead full," Sakai echoed. Bolan felt himself pushed back into his seat as the *Constitution* broke from her evasive pattern and began accelerating after the fleeing unidentified vessel. The lights dimmed once more when the masers discharged again at Contact C.

"Power fluctuations in…" Sakai began.

The helmsman never got to finish his sentence, as without warning the *Constitution's* bridge suddenly went completely dark. That, however, was the least of the crew's worries as the bridge door sealed with an evil *hiss* followed by his suit's seals audibly shutting.

Life support just went offline! Bolan thought. *As suspected, the engineers underestimated just how much power the masers would take.* Whether *Constitution's* planned power outputs would actually match reality had been a long and bitter argument between Bolan, the Fleet's acceptance team, and Bath Shipyards, Inc.

Gee, sometimes being right isn't all it's cracked up to be, Bolan thought bitterly.

"Damage report!" he barked, his voice echoing inside the helmet.

"Reactors 3, 4, and 5 engaged in a safety shut down," Sakai said, his voice several octaves higher than normal. "We still have helm, weapons, and sensors at degraded levels."

"Sensors to my position," Bolan replied, his eyes starting to adjust to the gloom. The *Constitution's* main plot appeared as a semi-transparent image on the front screen of his face shield. With a start, he realized Alpha had reversed course.

"Why is he closing?" Bolan muttered to himself.

"Missile launches detected!" Boyles reported, her tone just short of panic.

Oh, that's why.

Alpha's icon seemingly blossomed like a dandelion in a stiff breeze, a cloud of red dots surrounding it. The twenty-four smaller icons swiftly grew a gradually lengthening vector behind each of them, the elongating lines starting to lengthen and orient towards *Constitution's* stationary icon.

"Secondaries and point-defense offline."

"Try to get them up, Mr. Sinclair. Helm?"

"Shields at twenty-seven percent," Sakai replied, despondent. "Sir, I need more power from the guns!"

"Hostile missile impact in thirty seconds," Boyles interrupted, a scarlet 29 appearing in the upper left hand corner of Bolan's helmet faceplate.

The downside of accelerating towards the enemy is it makes his missiles close faster than your outgoing ordnance, Bolan thought, annoyed.

"Negative to power shift," Bolan replied in clipped voice. "Guns, continue to engage Contact Alpha! Sound collision!"

The warbling sound of the impact warning echoed three times across his helmet speakers.

"Sir, I..." Sinclair started to protest, turning towards him.

"I say again, continue to engage!" Bolan snapped, the timer passing "25."

The *Constitution* vibrated again, Bolan's visor display representing the outgoing slugs as twelve glowing dots. Two of the dots winked out along with six of the incoming missiles, the vagaries of space combat causing a fatal merger out in space. Three of the remaining slugs impacted with the target, Alpha's last moment turn having taken the target out of the *Constitution's* gunnery solution.

13

Was counting on that finishing him, Bolan thought with disgust. While the missiles likely had internal sensor systems, they guided far better with a constant update from the launch vessel.

"Secondaries back online!"

"Engage enemy missiles, barrage fire!" Bolan replied, the timer passing "19." "Starboard thirty, down four hundred kilometers dorsal!" He felt the restraints tighten on his chair as Sakai heeled the massive vessel over into a starboard turn while concurrently employing her dorsal thrusters in order to "drop" four hundred kilometers relative to the ecliptic. The pinwheeling effect compelled Bolan to swallow hard to avoid spewing his breakfast all over the inside of his helmet. A strangled cry over the bridge internals told him that someone else had failed to do so.

For the love of God, I hope that wasn't Sinclair, he thought, imagining how a helmet full of vomit might harm the gunnery process. Bolan's fears were dispelled when, after another precious tick of the timer to "10", the gunnery officer directed the secondaries to expend their charges in a series of smaller, more rapid bursts. The effect was to transform the masers into an anti-missile system, filling the space between *Constitution* and the incoming ordnance with microwave energy. Bolan watched as the missiles began winking out, one by one. With a start he realized that some of them were changing vector to avoid the standard barrage pattern.

Should have let Sinclair divert power to the masers, he thought as the three red icons merged with the *Constitution*'s at the center of his helmet's display. With a roaring in his ears, his command screen went blank along with every console on the bridge. Exhaling, Bolan waited for the inevitable.

"Sir, the *Camelot* is hailing us," Herrod reported, referring to the training observer / controller ship that was sitting motionless 500,000 kilometers from *Constitution*'s stern.

"Mr. Herrod, my station," Bolan said. "Mr. Sakai, divert all power from weapons to life support until engineering can get all the reactors back online. Division chiefs are to conduct internal after action reviews (AARs) and report their findings to me."

Those after action review comments should be very interesting, Bolan thought with a wince. *How many variants of 'the captain is an idiot' will I get to read?*

14

Hangar Deck Alpha
Constitution
0715 SST

The *Basilisk* space fighter's canopy opened with a harsh, sibilant sound. Standing up, the pilot's bright silver battle armor reflecting the hangar's lights, the cockpit's occupant snatched his helmet off and let out a thunderous expletive as he almost flung it to the deck before catching his temper. With his high cheekbones, light brown complexion, broad face and sky blue eyes, Commander Jason Owderkirk looked like the outcome of a science experiment that threw multiple ethnicities in a genetic blender. This effect would have been even greater if he had let his hair grow rather than leaving his head completely shaven, as his natural blonde dreadlocks were many shades lighter than the dark brown, barely regulation Fu Manchu mustache.

"Thanks Chief Wilson," the *Constitution*'s commander air group (CAG) shouted over the sound of the hangar deck's giant blowers forcing air into the compartment. Jason's rage returned full force as he stepped out of the cockpit and onto the boarding ladder. Reaching the ground, he turned to look down the long row of identical *Basilisks* sitting in front of *Constitution*'s port launch tubes. Belonging to the VF(S)-41, a.k.a. the "Black Aces," the eighteen fighters' distinctive coke-bottle shape, needle-point noses, stubby wings, bulging tri-thrusters indicated their role as space interceptors.

Arranged in two identical rows of eighteen behind them were No. 803 ("Raging Bulls") Squadron's thirty-six *Thunderchief II* strike fighters. The *Thunderchief II*s, due to their need to occasionally operate in atmosphere, were blessed with large variable geometry wings, a broad trapezoidal fuselage, angled twin tails, and canards mounted on their noses.

An entire carrier air wing, and how many do we launch? Absolutely freakin' zero! Jason thought, watching as his subordinates disembarked.

*Yes, this has been a great set of vacations. Too bad I was lead to believe we'd be on **trials***, Jason thought.

"Well, glad to see that our good captain continues to demonstrate why they should have put a bloody carrier man in charge of this monstrosity," Lieutenant Commander Charles "Flash" Gordon muttered as he walked up beside Jason. The Australasian officer's broad face was set in a scowl, a rare display of emotion for the usually taciturn Bulls leader.

Jason glanced around, ensuring no one else was in ear shot to overhear Gordon's comments.

"Wait until we're in the ready room," Jason replied lowly. "Keep officer business among officers."

"I see Chuck is making his usual efforts to charm and influence others," Lieutenant Commander Jacquelyn "Catnip" Tice observed from Jason's right side. Jason turned, surprised at not having heard the woman walk up beside him.

I hate it when she does that, Jason thought. In addition to being naturally light on her feet, the short, voluptuous redhead possessed a voice most women would have killed to call their own and looks that could make most heterosexual males contemplate homicide to gain her attention. If one did not know her reputation, it would be easy to dismiss the Black Aces' commander as a pretty face who may or may not have used her charms to propel a meteoric rise through the ranks. He watched as Gordon gave her an appraising look.

Yep, she still gets 90% of the people who meet her distracted by her looks, then kicks their ass during King of the Hill, Jason thought, referring to the required one versus one mock combat every air wing conducted as part of its trials. *I guess I'm immune.*

"Flash isn't stating anything that I'm not intending to mention in the after action report. He just needs to do it when it's just us folks around," Jason replied. Tice heard the subtle rebuke in Jason's response and nodded her understanding.

"Speaking of which, release your flight leaders—no need to make them sit through the XO's pontification on how he thinks an air group should be operating," Jason continued.

The two squadron commanders looked at him in surprise.

"Uh, boss, do you think that's wise?" Gordon asked. Jason turned and gave him a hard look, the intensity of which made Gordon almost take a step back.

"You let me worry about whether or not the XO's upset," Jason replied. "We're to meet him in the ready room in fifteen minutes. The uniform is flight suits."

That got him a strange look from both of the squadron leaders as well as Lieutenant Colonel Isoroku Nishizawa, a.k.a. "Kaiju One." A tall, almost gaunt man with almond eyes, Nishizawa hailed from the Eurasian Partition and was in charge of the *Constitution's mecha* detachment. Previously the stuff of science fiction, *mecha* had recently

16

been developed for the Eurasian Compact's Self Defense Force. Due to EC's senior senator, Tomiko Kimura, ascending to head of the Confederation's War Committee, the Confederation Space Marine Corps (CSMC) had been forced to field the machines. Able to transform from bipedal, humanoid combat vehicles to rather large strike fighters, the fifty-four *Kaiju Mk. I*'s were allegedly the future of warfare to their supporters, but wasteful oddities to their detractors.

As evidenced by his black battle armor, complete with a yellow *Kaiju Class Mecha* patch on one side and the *Consitution*'s ship crest on the other, Nishizawa was a marine and thus nominally did not work for Jason. Technically by date of rank the two men were precise peers, having worn the silver oak leaf for a little over a year. Practically, the two had rapidly come to the agreement that the *Constitution* blurred enough lines that adding additional friction would not help, especially with Nishizawa doubling as the battlecruiser's senior Marine. A consummate professional, Nishizawa had impressed Jason with his knowledge of space fighter and battle group tactics.

There are days I think he knows my job better than I do, Jason thought. *Even if he does drive a funny ride.*

"Commander Owderkirk, begging your pardon, but Commander Alexander was quite clear in his guidance on when and where we could wear our flight suits," Nishizawa said carefully, his Asian features expressionless.

"I am aware of Commander Alexander's policies," Jason said evenly. "And I quote from his welcome briefing to the air group: 'If we're expending live ordnance, these rules are, of course, relaxed,'" Jason replied with an evil grin. "Well, last time I checked this vessel just expended live ordnance, even if we didn't."

The three other officers shared a pained look. It was quite obvious to everyone aboard the *Constitution* that its executive officer, Commander Tristan Alexander, and Jason had a minor friction problem. So "minor" indeed that the *Constitution*'s wardroom had an unofficial pool on when and where the two men would come to blows. Jason looked at his watch.

"See you all in thirteen minutes," he said.

An Unproven Concept

"That is quite possibly the stupidest idea I have heard in over forty years of spacefaring," Captain Abraham Herrod said, his voice flat. Steepling his hands under his gray beard, Abraham regarded the man at the opposite side of the small conference room's table with a withering glare. With broad shoulders, long arms and a lined face that showed every one of his seventy-five years, Abraham looked like a man who should be enjoying his grandchildren's antics on his front porch, not sitting at the head of a gleaming table within the executive suite of the Confederation of Man's newest starliner. Despite his appearance, there was no mistaking the steel in his voice.

There was a sharp intake of breath from two of the other three men in the room. It was the kind of collective gasp that most often came from people who had just witnessed a scene of unexpected violence and were anticipating some horrible response. One of the three men wore identical navy blue, double-breasted Czarina Lines uniform with the company's trademark salmon shirts and gold ties. The other two wore gunmetal gray morning coats with the same shirts but bowties in place of the uniform's longer fare.

"I beg your pardon?" Ivan Federov, Vice President of Czarina Lines asked, cocking his head to one side as if he was a predatory bird that could not believe its prey really was that stupid. His voice was calm, and the lack of facial expression gave the appearance that Abraham's comment had not really registered. While not as tall as Captain Herrod, Federov was hardly a small man. Standing over one hundred fifty centimeters from the deck to the full shock of brown hair atop his skull, Federov's frame reflected his constant weightlifting.

"I said..." Abraham started, only to be interrupted by the second suited gentlemen.

"I think we all heard you, Captain," Mark Speyney, Czarina Lines' Chief Solicitor, said quickly. "Perhaps if you explained your reasoning, we'd understand the vehemence behind your statement," he continued, his tone indicating a clear intent to spread some rhetorical oil on the room's stormy seas. A heavyset man with black balding hair and a fleshy face, Speyney was renowned for his silver tongue and ability to make anyone believe they were getting the best of a deal even if the attached contract would result in them selling off their firstborn child into slavery.

18

"Section 195 of the Spacefarer's Code for starters," Abraham spat. "Or did you and the solicitor forget about that little bit of legislation when you came up with this harebrained scheme?"

Abraham felt his skin crawl as Federov leaned forward in his chair, the man's green eyes meeting his with an intensity that would have caused one of the Gorgon sisters to piss herself.

"We are well aware of that particular law, *Captain*," Federov replied. "Indeed, it is not coincidence that our passenger rolls include almost every senator which voted against it and only two that were for it."

What in the hell... Abraham started to wonder.

"I'm sure you're wondering why I would do something like this, no?" Federov continued with a slight smile.

"That thought did just cross my mind," Abraham said, grudgingly.

"The rewrite of Section 195 was the one thing that Czarina Lines and all of our competitors could all agree on was bad for business. Half the thrill of booking a star cruise was, I don't know, that people got to see actually *stars* that most other people hadn't."

Abraham exhaled loudly.

"I see you do not agree with me," Federov continued, baring his teeth in a facial gesture that was a smile in name only.

"There were reasons for Admiral Malinverni's concern," Abraham replied, speaking of the head of the Confederation Fleet. His statement drew a snort from both Federov and Speyney.

"Some ancient ruins and a bunch of dead scientists is not a good reason to restrict interstellar commerce," Federov sneered. "Malinverni is more concerned with the Confederation Fleet's budget than with people's lives."

It is easy to see neither of you have either had to take part in an interstellar rescue. Or had to clean up from a starwreck, Abraham thought bitterly. *Nightmares of frozen bodies just might change your opinion.*

"Pardon me if I'm a bit less cavalier about a law with a possible death penalty for the offending vessel's captain and all his senior officers," Abraham replied. "While I've never experienced it first hand, I'm told death via vacuum is rather unpleasant."

Out of the corner of his eye, Abraham saw Marcus Martin, his head of security, stiffen.

Well that was a rather large foot in my mouth, Abraham thought grimly. He did not know the particulars, but there were rumors

19

that Martin had been the sole survivor of a boarding action gone wrong back in '40.

"The Confederation Fleet has not summarily executed anyone besides pirates in over three hundred years! For that matter, with the exception of those barbaric Spartans and the Pannies," Speyney said, referring to the Spartan Diaspora Republic and Pan Islamic Caliphate respectively, "no one in the Confederation kills people for anything other than rape or murder. Malinverni had that clause inserted in there just to scare weak sisters and rattle his saber."

"Have you ever met Admiral Malinverni?"

Martin's question caught all of them by surprise. Just above average height, with olive skin, dark hair and green eyes that were several shades darker than Federov's, Martin did not have the sheer physical presence of Czarina's Vice President or Captain Herrod. What he did have was an aura, build and demeanor that reminded Abraham of a Noveau Croatia Baskerville Hound.

Lovely guard dogs. All business, those creatures, right up until it comes time to rip throats out, Abraham thought, repressing a shudder. *Then you suddenly realize just how much muscle the Maker crammed into that package.*

"No, I have not," Federov replied, raising an eyebrow.

"The man is not a bluffer," Martin said quietly. "At all."

"Even so, we're a Confederation of laws, not despotism," Speyney snorted. "I hardly think that man is going to toss anyone here out of an airlock just because they catch us in an unnamed system. To be quite blunt, we've evolved past that."

Martin looked like he was about to say something more, but was cut off by his captain.

"No, but there are other things to worry about besides the Confederation Fleet," Abraham said, his tone exasperated. "Pirates, navigational hazards…"

"Mr. Martin, how many security personnel do you have on board?" Federov asked calmly.

"Two hundred full security, another one hundred auxiliaries if you count all the security details," Martin replied.

"In your estimation, how many pirates would it take to overcome your three hundred personnel?"

"If they don't just put several torps into *Titanic* and turn her into a hulk?" Martin asked, disdain dripping from every word. "At least five hundred."

"Remind me again how close someone would have to get to 'just put several torps into' us?" Federov replied.

"Roughly ten thousand kilometers," Martin said, his tone clipped.

"Or, if I am not mistaken, fifty thousand kilometers within the effective range of our rail guns?" Federov said, leaning backwards with a smug grin.

"Yes, Sir," Martin replied through gritted teeth.

Okay, that's enough of this bullshit, Abraham thought angrily before speaking. "Is there a point to asking questions you already know the answer to, Mr. Federov? Because I'm sure Mr. Martin has other things that he could be doing than sitting here answering pointless queries."

"My *points* are that this liner has plating and shields equivalent to a light cruiser, C3 rail guns, electronic countermeasures, maximum intersystem speed that approaches a courier vessel's, and enough security personnel to hold off a small army," Federov said, ticking off each item on his carefully manicured fingers. "All of these things, by the way, that Chairman Fisk paid for with the understanding he would be getting a return on his investment."

"Well taking us out to where this ship will be destroyed would certainly be one way to do that," Abraham said flatly. "Although I seem to recall insurance not being paid on a ship operating in an unsafe manner."

"Captain Herrod, have you ever considered the implications of the Herbert Drive on your profession?" Federov asked.

"I don't think I understand what you're asking?" Abraham replied slowly. *Or its relevance*, he added silently.

"Well we already have the ability, albeit expensively, to send small message buoys instantly across distances that previously took couriers ships days, if not weeks, to cross," Federov said. "Tell me, how long do you think it will be before we can do this with, say, ships?"

"No one cares if a messenger buoy ends up in the center of an asteroid," Abraham observed. "I understand the Fleet had a bit of a problem with a ship that did the same."

"Oh, there are numerous problems," Federov said with a slight smile, causing Speyney to shift uncomfortably. "Or so I've heard."

I guess that truly confirms that bastard has contacts everywhere, Abraham thought. Trading in secrets was technically a major offense in the Confederation Fleet. Unfortunately, with a few exceptions, secrecy regulations appeared to be more honored in the

21.

breach than in the observance. Although allegedly Malinverni had changed that law as well.

"Soon, however, some Fleet boffin is going to figure out those problems," Federov said. The man stood, stretching as he walked to the holographic painting on the room's bulkhead. The work was entitled *A Lady Taken Before Her Time*, and was a representation of the original *Titanic* steaming into the sunset on April 11th, 1912.

"A few years after that, depending on how much the damn merchants scream and shout, that technology will be available to shipbuilders. At which point, gentlemen, liners will no longer be about getting from Point A to Point B in the most comfort possible," Federov said with a snort.

"After all, what will be the point of comfort in a metal tube for two months with a few thousand of your closest friends when going from Earth to Strata Nechty can be accomplished in a matter of hours?"

He turned to regard the painting again.

"Consider that Earth's original ocean liners survived two bloody world wars, numerous disasters and companies going out of business," Federov said, his back to the other men. "Beautiful ships, grand accommodations, doting staffs and all for naught because people see no reason to take one moment longer to get somewhere than they have to."

To his surprise, Abraham suddenly felt a bit of sympathy for Federov. The man had been in the star lines his entire life. Whereas Abraham could, if worse came to worst, simply become captain of an ore hauler in some backwater of the Confederation, Federov was truly a man looking into the abyss of his life's work.

"Well gentlemen, I for one do not intend to have someone add starship liner crew to buggy whip manufacturer, tablet chiseler and rotary phone repairmen as jobs that were once critical to society yet became useless overnight. This vessel will give our passengers something so grand they will tell their grandchildren about it," Federov said, turning back to face the men with his face set in grim determination. "I am told that the Zed-815 system has the most beautiful gas giant in the entire Confederation, a planet that has already been dubbed 'Sapphire.' That, my friends, is why I suggested it."

"Sir, I don't…" Abraham began.

"Captain Herrod, I am no longer asking, I am telling. Make best speed for Zed-815."

There was a poignant silence in the small room.

22

"Mr. Martin," Abraham began, fighting to keep his voice calm and level. "Begin whatever preparations you see fit. You have two hours before we will depart this system for Zed-815."

Federov whirled from the painting, his eyes flashing. He opened his mouth to speak, Abraham cut him off.

"You can *tell* all you want," Abraham said lowly. "I am still the master of this ship, and I am not going to jump into an alphanumeric system without making some preparations. If *you* have a problem with that, you can order me to the brig right now."

Martin stiffened beside Abraham.

Although if you order me, you just might find yourself actually going in my stead, Titanic's master thought with a slight smirk.

"So be it," Federov bit out. "Two hours. No more. Until that time, not a word of our destination goes beyond anyone in this room."

"How do you expect me to make…" Martin started, only to be cut off.

"Figure it out," Federov snapped. "I hear you're good at keeping secrets…now."

Thirty-five minutes later, Federov's comment continued to eat at Marcus Martin as he sat by himself in the crew's mess.

The Black Prince. Mr. Obsidian. Shadowheart. Now I guess I know why the bastard has so many nicknames, Marcus thought as he looked at his personal tablet. The device was projecting a three dimensional representation of *Titanic* roughly twelve inches above the tabletop. Rectangular in shape, the vessel was exactly one thousand, nine hundred and twelve meters in length, four hundred and one meters across in beam, and six hundred meters in height from the base of her ventral side to the "sky bridge" lookout station that protruded from her dorsal skin. Her three maneuvering / engineering pods extended in bulbous projections from her port, dorsal, and starboard quarter. With multiple subdivisions from her twelve horizontal decks and eighty vertical frames, *Titanic* was a cathedral to the art of modern shipbuilding and a pain in the ass to defend.

Okay Mr. Federov, you've given me a shitty mission. Let me see if there's a way I can do it without getting every single member of my squads killed.

"If you grip that table any harder mate, you're going to owe the line some back pay," a familiar, female Australasian contralto stated, interrupting his thoughts. Marcus turned around with a smile that went nowhere near his eyes.

23

"Sweet mercy, Marcus, you've obviously shit on the liver," Anjelica Barton, *Titanic*'s purser, noted as she took an involuntary step back into her companion. Heavyset, with dark honey skin, black hair and brown eyes, Anjelica had been the purser on the *Majestic*, Marcus' first security assignment when he had joined Czarina Lines. Then in her mid-forties, Anjelica had taken the younger man on as the child she had always been too busy securing money to settle down and have.

"Ow!" Sarah Jones, *Titanic*'s Head of Hospitality, exclaimed in pain and shock as Anjelica's high heel came down on her foot. Both women were dressed in reasonable facsimiles of early Edwardian women's fashion, with Sarah wearing a cream-colored, empire-waist formal gown that accentuated her tall frame and Anjelica in a light blue, full-necked dress with white trim that contrasted well with her skin.

"Sorry dear," Anjelica responded. "A certain security officer was giving me that look he usually saves for when he's about to disembowel someone."

"So I see," Sarah said, her blue eyes narrowing as she bestowed Marcus with an uncharacteristic glare. With her blonde hair up in a classic chignon bun, the look made her resemble a cross between an angry schoolmarm and Norse goddess. Hailing from the planet Ostfjord, Sarah's family could trace their lineage all the way back to the initial explorers that had taken humanity's first chaotic steps out of Sol's home system. Given this, it was unsurprising that she was one of the strongest willed women that Marcus had ever met, nor that she was Czarina Lines' youngest department head.

I still don't know how I got so lucky, Marcus thought to himself.

"Sorry," he muttered, forcing himself to let go of the table and take a deep breath.

"Now that you've apologized to the table," Sarah said, her voice cooler than her homeworld's epic blizzards, "how about you explain what has you ready to go full berserker in the middle of the crew mess?"

"I can't tell you," Marcus responded flatly.

"Oh here we go with the 'Marcus's Incredible Secrets,'" Anjelica said, rolling her eyes. While not as derisive, Marcus could tell Sarah was similarly unimpressed.

"I'm serious," Marcus said, holding up his hands as if to ward off both women's anger.

"No one has any doubts about that," Sarah replied. "You're very serious about your secrets."

Okay, someone's not in a good mood, Marcus thought, seeing Anjelica wince out of the corner of his eye.

24

"It's something I learned the hard way, once," he replied evenly, trying to defuse the situation.

"Sarah! There you are!" Hagop Al-Madur, *Titanic*'s First Mate, exclaimed from behind Marcus. Hailing from the Pan Islamic Caliphate, Al-Madur was a man who personified "average" in almost all areas of his appearance with the exception of his smile. His broad grin shone like a white spotlight from his caramel complexion as he hustled across the crew's mess, his suit tails almost horizontal due to his rapid gate.

"Mr. Federov told me to schedule a meeting with all the ship's tour guides in an hour," Al-Madur said lowly once he was closer. "To include people who are off shift."

"Uh, okay," Sarah said, looking at her watch. "I've only got a handful of folks who have probably gone to sleep anyway. Do you know what this is about?"

"No idea," Al-Madur replied with a shrug. "Marcus, do you know what's going on?"

"None at all," Marcus said without missing a beat. "But I'm glad I saw you—I was wondering if you'd gotten my e-mail about switching the crew's footgear out?"

Al-Madur's grin faded.

"Yes, and I found it rather odd. Why would we switch to those godawful magnetic shoes?"

"Spoken like a man who doesn't have to wear Edwardian woman's fashions," Anjelica interjected *sotto voce*. Al-Madur looked back and forth between Marcus and her.

"Our passengers," Al-Madur began, "signed up for a specific experience. We're trying to be as historically accurate in our presentation as we possibly can."

"Minus the iceberg and hypothermia, I hope," Anjelica replied sarcastically.

"Which means that I will not let someone's paranoia," he said, looking pointedly at Marcus, "or *discomfort* detract from what Czarina Lines has promised."

Marcus could tell that Anjelica was less than pleased with the air quote gesture Al-Madur made around discomfort. Sarah had complained mightily about how it had taken several days to get used to the various shoes ("They were torture devices, more likely…") that the female crew members had been forced to learn how to wear.

"It is not paranoia…" Marcus began, only to be cut off.

An Unproven Concept

"I'm sorry, Marcus, I'm not debating this with you," Al-Madur said abruptly, his smile completely vanishing. "Sarah, if you could make sure your folks are available for Mr. Federov," the man said as he turned to walk away. The trio watched him go.

"Well, Marcus, it appears as if you're making all sorts of friends today," Sarah observed. "Guess I better go wake some people up." With that the blonde turned and left the mess, pulling her datapad from her oversized purse as she went. Marcus watched her go, a bad feeling in the pit of his stomach.

"She's not throwing in the towel, if that's what you're worried about," Anjelica observed quietly. "I'm sorry, by the way. I think I'm the reason you're catching it in the daks from her."

"Okay, so what did you do?" Marcus asked archly.

"I was talking about how you came over from the Corps as such a hard charger," Anjelica replied apologetically. "She asked me if I knew what you did back then and I told her no, no one really did."

Marcus grimaced.

"You know, she's a keeper," Anjelica observed. "I mean, I'll admit you've pulled some real derros since I've known you, but Sarah's totally shipshape. Which I guess is why you've gotten her that little number in your left pocket."

"What are you talking about…" Marcus started, reaching into his suit trousers. His fingertips brushed against a ring box and he looked up at Anjelica with a shocked expression.

"How did…" he started to ask.

"Shhh, not so loud," Anjelica admonished as a couple of crew walked by. "The jeweler got the ring done earlier than he predicted."

Gee, wonder if he had any help in doing that?

"So, as I was saying, she's the best catch I've ever seen you haul in," Anjelica continued. "But mate, you really need to stop being Mr. Mysterio about your life. Lots of crazy shit happened when the Spartans were joining the Confederation. I don't know what you did or why you left the Corps and ran almost as far away from that chaos pit as you could. But I'm pretty sure Sarah will love you no matter what…but only if you tell her why you wake up screaming in the middle of the night."

Marcus pursed his lips.

"I hope you didn't bring that up to her," Marcus replied. "Because no woman, no matter how broad minded, likes to hear about her current fling's sleeping habits from another one."

Anjelica snorted.

26

"Oh yeah, like she doesn't know that I'd be more likely to seduce her than you," Anjelica replied. "Besides, while I'm not *quite* old enough to be your mother, I'm closer than I like to admit."

Marcus laughed at that comment.

"Yes, well, that's more true than you realize," he replied, a hint of sadness in his voice.

"See, and that's what I mean about you being secretive. I've known you for almost a decade and I can count the number of times you've talked about your parents on one hand. Yet I know you go home to Baginis at least once every two years. Usually after someone dumps you because she's sick of feeling like she really can't connect with you," Anjelica said bluntly. "And now you look like you bit down on a lemon."

"No, just wondering which one of us is the security freak," Marcus replied evenly, then looked at his watch. "Speaking of which, I really need to figure something out, so I'm not going to be much of a conversationalist for the next thirty minutes."

Anjelica gave him a wan look.

"Down come the blast doors," she said quietly, then stood up. "Remember what I said, Marcus. Even if she says yes, it won't stick unless you start talking." With that, Anjelica walked off, leaving Marcus to continue staring at *Titanic*'s outline.

Battle Station Malta
1100 SST

"You know, you no longer work for the guy," Commander Anna Fletcher said, making her contralto voice even lower. "It's not illegal to ask him out."

Leslie fixed her friend's dark brown eyes with her own. The two women were sitting in the *Malta*'s shuttle waiting room killing time until the next station-to-ship ferry was ready for boarding. Besides them the cavernous room was completely empty, a status that signified *Malta*'s position at the edges of the Confederation of Man's occupied space. Neither woman minded, as it gave them impromptu privacy.

The thought of being rejected has never crossed Anna's mind, Leslie thought grimly. *Probably because it has never happened.* "Some of us," she said aloud, "don't immediately attract the eye of every heterosexual male in the room when we walk in."

Anna gave a bemused shake of her head. With her coffee-colored skin, dancer's frame and black hair, Anna could have been the

27

poster child for 'exotic.' In contrast, Leslie's skin was pale where it wasn't densely freckled, with her dark auburn hair the only thing that truly distinguished her. While she was far from ugly, she was under no illusions that men fell at her feet. Anna, on the other hand, had a beauty that even the Confederation Navy's dark blue utilitarian space suits could not hide.

"Yes, well, I think that you and I both know that's a waste of their time," Anna said with a smile.

"Speaking of which, how is Jessica?"

"Tired," Anna replied. "The twins are kicking her ass with teething."

"Guess this would be one of those times you're happy to be heading back to *Golan*," Leslie said with a slight laugh.

"You know an XO's work is never done," Anna replied. "But neither is a mother's, and things sure as hell don't get easier just because there are two of you. Nice change of subject, by the way."

Okay, so you're going to be a bit persistent I can see... Leslie thought unkindly.

"Look, you and I both know one Mackenzie Bolan is not going to give a second thought to an invitation out on a date from 'The Queen of Frump.'"

Anna had the good grace to look guilty.

"You know, you only bring that up when you're trying to get me to stop questioning you," Anna said with a sigh. "It's somewhat amazing how far our friendship has come since that day."

"Only because I immediately showed you just because I could stand to lose a few pounds didn't mean I couldn't kick your ass," Leslie observed.

"See and *that* is something I would trade you those so-called 'looks' men give me for," Anna replied wistfully. "You just don't screw around when you want to do something, and you've always had the brains to go get it."

"Yeah, well, the man I want no amount of brains is going to help me get," Leslie said. Anna fixed her with a skeptical look.

"Right. Tell that to someone who has not seen you two together. It's a wonder you guys didn't rip each other's clothes off the minute he cased *Vincennes'* guidon."

"*Anna!*" Leslie said, coloring. "Thank you very much, there were enough rumors of that when I was his XO as is."

"Well at least that would have been something pleasant that happened during his year in command," Anna observed grimly, then

28

held up her hands in defense when Leslie fixed her with a glare. "Hey, I'm not saying he wasn't justified in everything he did, but sheesh...."

Leslie could feel her nostrils flaring as her friend let the sentence trail off. Footsteps behind her stopped an impromptu reenactment of the first time the two women had met.

"Excuse me, Commander, but is this the shuttle to Quadrant eight zeta?" a voice asked as she turned around in her seat. The speaker stood almost a foot taller than Leslie's own 5' 6". He wore the matte black uniform of the Confederation Space Marines, with six-pointed major's stars affixed to each collar his only adornments. Like most Marines, the man looked like a walking brick building.

"You must be new to *Malta*," Anna said lightly. "Yes, this is the correct shuttle bay."

"Thank you, Ma'am," the man replied flatly. Leslie saw a brief twinkle in her friend's eye.

Uh oh.

"So just what brings you to *Malta*, Major...?" Anna continued, her voice suddenly with a slight bit of what she liked to call 'honey' added to it.

"Agenor Acheros, ma'am, and I am currently on assignment."

"I'm classmates with Lieutenant Colonel Andrews, and he didn't mention getting a new operations officer last night at dinner."

There was a pause as the man regarded Anna coolly.

I feel like I'm looking across the ice floes of Styx, Leslie thought, fighting the urge to shiver.

"I have orders for the commander of the destroyer *Shigure*," Acheros replied, his voice coldly polite. Leslie noted the man's use of the word "commander" as opposed to "captain" even as she kept her face a study in stillness.

Someone needs to brush up on his naval etiquette, she thought.

Anna gave a pitch perfect shudder.

"I'm sorry," she said lightly. "I hope *that* is not your assignment, she's a glorified garbage scow."

Leslie dug her nails into her palms as Anna delivered the last line with a slight giggle.

*Okay, I am **so** buying the twins a drum set for their first birthday*, Leslie thought. *When Jessica asks, I'll be sure to bring up this conversation.*

"No, I was en route to the Marine detachment on the *Duke of York* when I was diverted," Acheros replied. "It seems getting courier qualified when I was at Fleet Operations was a very bad plan. I was not aware that the *Shigure* had such a poor reputation."

"She's the oldest destroyer in the fleet," Anna continued, rolling her eyes. "I don't even know why they keep her in commission. Pirates would consider her a light snack—makes me glad I'm on the *Golan*. Commander's not too sharp either—sort of the reason she ended up in that job."

Acheros sighed.

"I hope that I have been diverted for something more important than telling someone there's a cleanup in aisle 5."

"You mean you haven't taken a peek?" Leslie asked, genuinely surprised. Couriers were rather notorious for getting a leg up on the latest gossip. Acheros turned towards her, a look of slight surprise on his face.

"You didn't see Fleet Message #3050-1200, Ma'am?" he asked.

"Yes, but I figured the section on couriers was the standard 'don't poke your nose where it doesn't belong' boilerplate," Leslie replied. Acheros gave a thin smile.

"Admiral Malinverni seems to be a bit more, shall we say, *strict* about fleet regulations than his predecessor," Acheros said, speaking of Confederation Navy's current commander. "There have been a few couriers who opened their documents prior to arriving at their destination, only to find out that the messages now delete without having the recipient's DNA marker inserted within five minutes."

Anna inhaled sharply at that as Acheros continued.

"In addition, the part in courier school where they mention you can be incarcerated for up to five years now means you can plan on spending one thousand eight hundred and twenty-four days on the prison planet of the Admiralty's choice. I hear Admiral Malinverni thinks that Eloko spike leeches have a way of focusing the mind."

That caused both Leslie and Anna to shudder. The planet Eloko had been named for a demon found in the lore of Terra's Africa continent in no small part because of its varied and deadly wildlife. Spike leeches were famous throughout the Confederation for all the wrong reasons.

A tone sounded from the airlock, and with a start Leslie realized the quadrant ferry had pulled up to the station. The shuttle, like most of its kind, had been built to transit from space to atmospheric operations at will. As such, the pilot had to rotate the craft's nose up 90-degrees in order to approach *Malta*'s docking lock.

Eventually the new magnetic launchers and landing bays will get retrofitted to battle stations, Leslie observed. Then no one will ever again have to stand by a transparisteel window hoping that the little ol' lady at the shuttle factory didn't mess up the autopilot. Allegedly transparisteel could absorb a low-speed merger from a shuttle, but no one who actually worked in space trusted manufacturers claims.

Something about having 100 tons of shuttle meeting three inches of, oh, just about anything makes me skeptical. With a last minute firing of its maneuver thrusters and a slight vibration the shuttle met the airlock, causing the three solid red lights above the orifice to switch to a blinking amber. A minute later, there was another series of tones and the lights above the airlock turned green just before the inner door irised open. A chief petty officer stepped through the door, his lined dark face and brown eyes quickly surveying the room. Seeing the three officers, he rendered a salute, the palm of his hand facing the three officers. Leslie, as ranking officer, returned the gesture.

"We did not have anyone heading this way, Commander Hawkins," the man said in a clear tenor. "We are ready to go when you are."

"Well, let's get this show on the road," Leslie said. She gave a slight pause, turning so she could see Acheros's face. "You've got one for *Golan* and two for *Shigure*."

Acheros's face paled as he saw the look in Leslie's eyes. He started to open his mouth.

"Save it, Major," Leslie said in a tone that could have flash frozen human flesh. "How about we get back aboard to find out just where I need to go in order to take out the trash. Chief, Major Acheros has orders for me, so perhaps you could drop us off first before you run Commander Fletcher to the *Golan*."

Anna stopped and gave Leslie a shocked look, then narrowed her eyes. The *Golan* was far closer to *Malta* than Leslie's destroyer. Leslie had just added at least an hour to Anna's transit time from the station to the battlecruiser.

"What?" Leslie said, feigning innocence as she looked at her friend. "I hear they've got a pretty good library aboard those big ol' battlecruisers—you didn't check out one of those trashy romance novels you're always reading?"

"No, Commander Hawkins, I did not," Anna said, her voice clipped. *You bitch,* her eyes transmitted in that way only a best friend's could.

31

I love you like a sister, but you're gonna pay the bill when you make fun of my ship.

"I'll have to sort through the 'garbage' when I get back aboard," Leslie replied, passing through the hatch. "I can probably send you home with something that's been 'gently used.'"

Chapter 2: Surprise Is Such An Ugly Word

Malta Ferry
1220 SST
20 June 3050

Looking out her window, Leslie allowed herself a slight smile as the shuttle's maneuver engines fired once again, this time to bring the craft in towards the *Shigure*'s stationary bow. Looking out her window Leslie allowed herself a slight smile.

Garbage scow or not, she's mine, she thought to herself. As Anna had intimated to Major Acheros, *Shigure* was the grand dame of the Confederation fleet, being just a couple months under fifty. With a length of one hundred and fifty meters and a mass of roughly 25,000 metric tons, the *Shigure* was also one of the smallest vessels. From directly ahead it was difficult to see the destroyer's orca-like outline that, like her name, signaled her construction in the Eurasian Partition. With another blast of the shuttle's jets the dark-blue destroyer dropped out of view.

"Isn't it a bit odd to be approaching head on?" Anna asked nervously. Leslie turned and realized her friend was as pale as she ever got.

"Amidships airlock is non-functional due to a problem with the seals," Leslie said with a sigh. "Found out last month that they don't make the parts anymore, so BuShips is trying to figure out if it's cost effective to have a manufacturer make a new one."

"What?! Isn't that unsafe?" Anna asked.

"To quote *Malta*'s safety inspector, 'It'll be fine as long as you never open the inner hatch,'" Leslie said with a slight shrug, her tone making it clear she was less than pleased. She noticed Acheros swallow and pale a little bit himself. Marines seldom worked on vessels without massive amounts of subdivisions. Destroyers were not known for their robust construction.

Nicknaming us tin cans is being generous, Leslie thought with some disquiet.

With a *thump*! and sharp quiver the shuttle linked with the destroyer's bow. As the airlock tone sounded, Leslie hopped to her feet.

"Shall we, Major?" Leslie asked. "Wouldn't want to keep Commander Fletcher waiting too long."

Anna mouthed something impolite at her over the Marine major's shoulder as she stepped down through the opening into the shuttle's exodus compartment. Major Acheros dropped in beside her.

"Ma'am, with all due respect, I did not know that you were the *Shigure*'s commander," Acheros said grimly.

Oh don't even think about trying to wriggle off this hook, Leslie thought.

"You also didn't ask," she said as the compartment quickly rotated through 90 degrees. With a slight *hiss* the door opened to reveal a gleaming white compartment and two personnel. The one on their right was a tall, wiry lieutenant commander with a shaved head, blue eyes, and severe features further marred by a puckered scar that ran from the tip of his left ear all the way down his bronze cheek to the end of his chin. The other individual was a short, black-haired man of Eurasian descent. Both men had a momentary look of surprise that Leslie had a Marine with her but quickly recovered.

"Major Acheros, my executive officer, Lieutenant Commander Alika Iokepa, and Command Master Chief Ryuichi Yasuhiro," Leslie said.

"Gentlemen, a pleasure to meet you," Major Acheros said with a slight nod.

"XO, the two of us are going to need the wardroom," Leslie said. "I'll also need you to be present."

"Will do, Captain," Iokepa said, his voice a gravely rasp.

"I'll do the necessary honors, Ma'am," Chief Yasuhiro said. "I take it the shuttle's hanging around until Major Acheros returns?"

"Yes, they are," Leslie replied.

"I'll see if anyone onboard wants some coffee," Chief Yasuhiro said, heading back towards the airlock. Leslie gestured for the XO to lead the way, falling in behind him as he opened the door at the rear of *Shigure*'s reception compartment. Leslie stepped through the hatch then turned around to see the look on Acheros's face as he followed her. The major's eyes widened as he stepped through, the door whispering shut behind him.

"Not bad for a garbage scow, huh?" she asked with a smile. The three officers were standing in the middle of a corridor that took up a third of the destroyer's ten meter beam and stretched the vessel's entire length. Like the reception compartment, the corridor's walls were so clean and white they almost glistened. Leslie watched as Acheros' eyes briefly narrowed with the realization he was looking at all new construction. As if to confirm his suspicions, a hatch to the Spartan major's left whispered rather than squeaked open, four junior officers spilling out of it a moment later.

"Ah, I see we broke up the afternoon chess match," Leslie said with a smile. "Major Acheros, meet the junior half of my wardroom. In no particular order, Ensign Helena Griffon, my Communications / Navigation officer from New Peoria, Transvaal."

"Sir," Ensign Griffon said with a slight bow, her long blonde hair sweeping forward with the movement. Leslie was struck once again at just how young the officer looked.

Was I that gangly and awkward once? she mused to herself.

"My Sensor / Weapons officer, Lieutenant (j.g.) Kenrick Southwell from the Spartan Diaspora," Leslie said.

"Well met, Sir," Kenrick said, extending a thick arm. Acheros extended his own, the two men grabbing each other's forearms in the Spartan fashion. Although Kenrick stood a full head shorter than Acheros, Leslie had the sense of two Kodiaks sizing each other up.

At least Kenrick doesn't shave his head, although that crew cut's not far off, Leslie thought. She had seen her W/S officer's childhood photos and knew that his hair was a naturally curly black mop.

Of course, he probably hasn't worn it that way since he was ten.

"As well, Lieutenant Southwell," Acheros said. "Where are you from in the Diaspora?"

"Aries, Sir," Southwell said. "Hopetown, to be specific."

"Oh very good," Acheros replied. "My uncle hails from Aries, can't remember where though."

"If he's lucky, not Hopetown," Southwell said wearily. "There's a reason I'm here."

Acheros gave a slight smile at that, then turned to the woman standing in a pair of simple denim overalls beside Southwell.

"My chief engineer, Lieutenant Villborg Talo," Leslie said, "from the planet Kiche, Australasian Sector. Or, as we call it, the land of the giants."

"G'Day, Sir," Lieutenant Talo said, also with a slight bow. Her freckled face split into an infectious smile that reached her blue eyes. "I'm glad to see there's finally someone else who actually took their vitamins when they were growing up." Acheros returned the smile, shaking his head at the tall strawberry blonde.

"All right you lot of misfits, enough fun for the day. I take it Ensign Doba is the officer of the deck?"

"Yes Ma'am," Southwell answered as the three senior officers stepped into the wardroom.

"Well her loss, we need to get Major Acheros back aboard that shuttle when he's done," Leslie said from the wardroom hatch. With that, she closed the hatch behind her. Turning around, she noticed Major Acheros giving an appreciative gaze around the small but well-furnished compartment. There were two wooden tables, one rectangular and the other square, that dominated the center of the room with their four chairs. Two more conformal chairs, the outline of their last occupants still fading, sat in each corner with holographic projectors in front of each.

"I must say, Ma'am, this is also a much better wardroom than I'd expect for a vessel this size," Acheros said.

"We spiders always try to keep a nice parlor," Leslie said deadpan.

Acheros gave her a puzzled look.

"Never mind, just something my mother used to say. I assume the orders came via holo?"

"Yes Ma'am," Acheros said, reaching into his pocket and pulling out a small device slightly larger than his hand. "DNA collector is on right."

Leslie nodded as she took the device. Sticking her finger onto the slight indentation on the right, she felt a quick sting as the DNA collector snatched a few dozen of her skin cells. A moment later, the initiator button glowed green signifying the device had verified her DNA sequence.

"Well, we might as well sit down and grab something to drink while we watch," Leslie said.

"I'll get us coffee, Captain," Iokepa said. "Major Acheros, what will you have?"

"Just water, please," Acheros replied.

Leslie sat the square device down in the middle of the square table. Iokepa returned with her coffee mug, and she grasped it with an appreciative nod. *Shigure*'s master then took a long sip in an attempt to try and drown the butterflies in her stomach, sat the ceramic container down, then pressed the start button. There was a moment pause as the device switched out of standby, followed by the hologram springing to life in the form of a 6-inch tall figure in the uniform of a full admiral, Confederation Navy.

"You didn't mention that the communication was from Admiral Malinverni himself," Leslie said, her eyes wide in surprise. Admiral

Malinverni's physically imposing presence, with his olive skin, massive frame, dark hair, and piercing brown eyes, seemed to carry over to holograms as well.

"You didn't ask, Ma'am," Acheros replied, deadpan. Iokepa started coughing on his coffee as Leslie gave the Marine major a healthy glare.

"Touché, Major," she said evenly, getting a slight smile in return.

"Commander Hawkins, greetings. I trust that this hologram has found you and was personally delivered by a Marine field grade officer who has Omega-Level Clearance. Please confirm at this time before proceeding," Malinverni said in his sonorous tone.

"I am cleared Omega, Ma'am," Acheros replied. Leslie allowed the hologram to continue.

"Twenty-four hours ago, the survey ship *Columbus* entered the Alpha-825 System," Malinverni said. A moment later his hologram vanished, replaced by the 3-D representation of a Class F star with 6 planets. An extraordinarily thick asteroid belt girdled the entire system
.

"When passing through the outer belt, the *Columbus* detected two energy sources on a nearby asteroid," Malinverni's voice continued, the two rocks in question highlighting in red. "Closing to investigate she sighted what appeared to be identical structures containing the energy sources in question. Following Xeno Protocol, the *Columbia* immediately reentered hyperspace."

Well shit, Leslie thought, knowing what was coming next.

"You are to take your vessel, as well as the Marine officer who delivered this message, and conduct an investigation of the two alien facilities in the Zed-816 system in order to determine whether they are still occupied. If you encounter alien vessels, you are to make every effort to avoid them. If you are pursued you are not, I say again, you are *not* to return to an occupied system until such time as you have lost pursuit. If necessary, you may request assistance, but you are to make every effort to shake your pursuers prior to doing so."

Malinverni paused after that last statement.

"My intent is to avoid provoking a general engagement with an unknown alien race, Commander. With that in mind, your rules of engagement are also not to fire first unless you feel your ship is in danger of being destroyed or captured. You are to depart as soon as practicable after receipt of this message. Godspeed Leslie."

With that, Malinverni's projection disappeared. There were a few moments of silence as Leslie digested the information.

"Well that wasn't what I was expecting to be doing when I got up this morning," Iokepa said, his voice stunned.

"You? I was expecting to be commanding a battleship's Marine detachment," Acheros replied, almost as stunned.

Glad to know what I have to look forward to when we tell the rest of the crew, Leslie thought. *Time to snap them both out of it.*

"XO, how soon can we be ready to go?"

"One hour, tops."

"No need to be crazy, let's go for correctly instead of quickly. I want an all-officers meeting here in forty-five minutes."

"Aye aye, Ma'am."

Major Acheros looked at both of them like they were mad.

"You can't seriously be getting ready to accept that mission with a blown rear hatch!" he stated. "I'm no naval expert but even I know that's against regs!"

Leslie and her XO looked at each other, then back at Acheros.

"Major, I think it's time we showed you what's behind Door #1," Leslie said with a broad grin. "But first, we need to get Commander Fletcher and the shuttle away. Follow me please," Leslie said, pushing away from the table.

"Why do I get the feeling I'm not going to be seeing the *Duke of York* anytime soon?" Acheros asked resignedly.

Five minutes later, Leslie and Major Acheros stood just outside the wardroom once more.

"Well Major, how much do you recall of fleet operations from the war college?"

"Quite frankly, Ma'am, not a whole hell of a lot," Acheros replied. "I am sort of surprised that a single destroyer, much less the oldest one in the fleet, is being sent on a possible First Contact, however."

"Hopefully you'll not be shocked after the next fifteen minutes," Leslie said. She gestured down the ship's central corridor. "Tell me, what do you see?"

Acheros looked at her like she was insane. When he realized that she was serious, he gave her a quizzical look then answered.

"A corridor."

"Right, but wrong. What you are actually looking at is a support tube of neuranium alloy, the density of which is 25% greater than that used to armor the *Duke of York*."

"Um, what? The *Duke* is less than five years old. They didn't even make neuranium when this…" Acheros began, failing to keep the incredulity out of his voice.

"Precisely. Externally the *Shigure* is a fifty year old, toothless mare that is long overdue for the glue factory," Leslie said with a slight grin. "Internally, she's been completely revamped and remodeled to the point where this vessel could probably kill a hostile light cruiser without breaking a sweat. Walk with me."

The two began moving down the corridor, dodging crewmen as they moved to and fro. Acheros suddenly got a puzzled look on his face.

"Something bothering you, major?" Leslie asked.

"Ma'am, I just realized that this ship's official complement is a little over one hundred people. You've just gone to yellow alert and I've seen only enough people moving to suggest half that many. What gives?"

Leslie cracked a smile. "I guess I shouldn't be surprised a hammerhead was counting bodies, even subconsciously. Automation has cut he original crew in half, which means *Shigure* can stay out longer."

"What about damage control or boarding parties?"

"We're not expected to fight pirates," Leslie replied. "It was believed anything encountered that we can't outrun will probably kill us."

Acheros winced at that cold logic as they came to the aft end of the corridor. There were three doors in front of them, numbered '1,' '2,' and '3,' in large block text. Underneath the '1' were slightly smaller numbers that said 'Aft Airlock.'"

"Hatch #2 goes to engineering," Leslie gently corrected with a smile. "Hatch #3 goes down to the missile flat."

"Wait—I thought destroyers don't carry missiles."

"*Most* destroyers don't carry missiles," Leslie replied. "That's because standard missiles are too large for a ship of this size. The boffins figured out something new for us—it's called the *Pufferfish*. Missile the size of a torp tube, with an implosion warhead."

The color drained from Acheros' face. "What?! I thought implosion warheads of that size were unstable. As in, 'wreck a star system if you're not careful' unstable."

Leslie gave a shrug.

"It's allegedly only unstable if you use it too close to a star," she replied. "Plus if you run fast enough you don't have to worry about the wormhole."

Acheros raised an eyebrow, then realized Leslie was being serious.

"You know the Spartan Self-Defense force experimented with implosion ordnance quite a bit," he said gravely. "You also know why they stopped. I don't care what modifications they've done to this ship, she's not outrunning a gravitational front."

Leslie gave a slight smirk.

"Would you care to make a wager on that, Major?"

"I know I don't want to bet my life!" Acheros snapped back.

"Well, why don't we see what's behind Door #1?" Leslie replied, her smile growing broader and more impish. "That is, unless you're scared of a busted airlock."

"Most sane people are, ma'am," Acheros replied archly.

"Well, I can promise you that you're not going to get to see what *Shigure* looks like from her rear end," Leslie replied, stepping up to the hatch. She raised the access panel to the opening's starboard side, placing her hand flat on a seemingly plain glass panel. There was a moment of coldness, then warmth as the security system scanned her palm and opened the door to a pitch black compartment.

Freak out in three…two…one, she thought, then stepped forward and seemingly vanished from Acheros' sight.

"What the f…" Acheros started to say.

"Easy Major, just take two steps forward," Leslie called back over her shoulder. "Be quick about it, there's a time limit on the hatch."

Major Acheros followed her direction, stepping quickly two steps through what he thought was an inky shroud to stand beside her. She watched several emotions flit over his face before she turned back forward to regard the tall, broad cylinder which stretched the entire compartment. Its sides were smooth, gleaming black metal, the top of which came to just below Leslie's nose and Acheros' chest.

"Okay, I'll bite," Major Acheros said after a moment, his voice even. "What the hell is this and why does it look like this compartment is totally blacked out from the corridor?"

"This," Leslie said, tapping the top of the cylinder, "is the first operational Herbert drive in the Confederation Navy. In other words, a fold engine."

Acheros looked thunderstruck, causing Leslie to give a slight giggle.

"Sorry, Major, but you look like you don't know whether to run screaming for the hills or if you wish there really was an open airlock hatch here."

"With all due respect Commander I know what happened to the *Aries*!" Acheros snapped. "Pardon me if I'm a bit nervous about seeing the middle of a planet."

"First off, the *Aries* jumped into the center of a plane*toid*, not a planet," Leslie replied, her voice making it clear that she did not appreciate Acheros tone. "Second, what is not common knowledge is that they got all of her data from the jump."

"What?" Acheros asked.

"Long story that's not important right now," Leslie said. "What is important is that this drive works."

Major Acheros's face went blank.

"When they analyzed *Aries'* data at Wonderland Station, they realized that all of the jump experiments had operated under a flawed assumption, i.e. that the relationship between a ship's mass and the power necessary to jump it was a constant. What they found was that the greater the vessel's length and beam, the greater a jump's inherent error."

"So basically what you're saying is that they didn't take into account the *Aries'* length?"

"No, they didn't take into account the relationship between her length, mass, beam, etc., etc.," Leslie replied. "Let me put it in simple terms—the *Shigure* is about the longest, heaviest ship that can reliably jump into a system. Even so, we can only jump accurately across a certain range. Beyond that the formula starts to fall apart."

"So even with that, why not put drives into heavy vessels that have the space? Even if you have to come in a few million kilometers outside of a system you've got a huge advantage of Lucas drives."

"When I say the formula falls apart, I mean literally: the test vessels have arrived back in norm space in pieces," Leslie replied grimly. "When the first piece arrives about six million kilometers above the ecliptic, the second twenty million below, and the third eight million miles away from the intended arrival point, all the sudden those extra four or five hours under the Lucas drive don't seem so bad, do they?"

Acheros turned away from her and looked down at the Herbert drive.

42

"In that case, no. I guess I just got carried away thinking about what a change for mankind this would be," Acheros said quietly. "I mean, to be able to go from one point to another anywhere in the galaxy…"

"Not quite," Leslie interrupted him. "So far the furthest successful jump has been four hundred light years."

"That's not a small matter!" Acheros said, his eyes widening in surprise. "Four hundred light years in the blink of an eye?!"

"It also wrecked the drive," Leslie replied. "The boys at Wonderland think one hundred light years is about reasonable. There are cool down factors and such that go with that as well."

"Cool down?"

"If you jump too many times close together it starts to do all sorts of bad things to the power supply, both for the Herbert drive and the main plant."

"I imagine by 'all sorts of bad things' you don't mean the lights flicker, do you?"

"No. Add to that the fact that you have to be darn near stationary when jumping and you can see why some folks aren't fans."

Leslie's chronometer beeped. Looking down, she took a deep breath.

"Well, guess it's time to get this show on the road," she said, looking over at Acheros.

"Ma'am, thank you," Acheros said. "I'm sorry if I took time away that you would have rather spent saying goodbye to Commander Fletcher."

Leslie shrugged.

"I'll catch her when we get back, it's not like the *Golan* is due to go out for another two weeks. I'm more apologetic that you got yanked from what quite possibly could have been a good assignment."

Acheros laughed, causing Leslie to look at him quizzically.

"This ship is about to possibly make history," Acheros explained. "If those are still active alien structures rather than just ruins like the McClusky Expedition found a few months ago, I'm possibly going to be around for First Contact. I can wait for the next BuPers shuffle."

Leslie's smile dimmed a little bit before she recovered.

There are lots of ways to make history, she thought to herself. *Sometimes one's purpose in life is to serve as an example of utter folly.*

It had not taken long for the exercise officer ab
complete the AAR.

*If I didn't know better, I would swear that the good Rear
Admiral Mategna's report was written before the exercise even began,*
Bolan thought bitterly. Especially since the last words out of Belinda
Mategna's mouth had been the directive to report to Admiral Hector
Steiner, Commander Confederation Fleet Training Command (C-CFTC)
aboard the Confederation Training Station (CTS) *Boyd* no later than
1245 that same day.

*Five and a half hours to report in an office that 65% of the fleet
could not have possibly reached in less than four,* Bolan thought
bitterly. *Especially since I had to delay our own internal AARs in order
to get the engines fixed. No, this doesn't seem like a set up at all.*

Bolan looked out the shuttle's window at the receding
battlecruiser and pondered what he could have done differently. As an
engineering officer, Mategna was not technically a member of the
Carrier or Line factions that jockeyed for power, funds and personnel
within the Confederation Fleet. However, from the zeal with which she
had laid out his mistakes prior to summarily dismissing him, Bolan had
little doubt that the woman knew who buttered the bread in her current
job.

*Outside of launching the air group as soon as I came in system,
I don't see what else I could have done differently,* he thought. *Of
course, that's probably going to be enough for Steiner.*

A tall man, Admiral Steiner gave the appearance of joviality
with his full head of white hair, blue eyes, jowls, and laugh lines.
Unfortunately, the man's personality could not have been more different
without spontaneous murder being involved. Nicknamed "The
Hatchet," Steiner had ascended to the third most powerful post in the
Confederation Fleet based primarily on his political acumen, alleged
willingness to murder his entire family, and proven ability to transform
shattered careers into a pedestal upon which he could build his own
power base. Bolan was aware that Steiner had been quite vocal in his
belief that, if the navy was determined to commission an abomination
such as *Constitution*, then said vessel should be commanded by a
Carrier-qualified commander as opposed to a Line officer. As C-CTC,
Steiner had the authority to relieve any captain who made a gross error

ᴊudgment during a vessel's trials. It was quite possible that Bolan had ᴊust given Steiner more than enough rope to hang him.

So be it, Bolan thought disgustedly.

His helmet's earphones crackled and interrupted his thoughts.

"*Boyd* control, this is *Constitution Pinnace One* with my actual. Request permission to come aboard."

Turning to look out the starboard viewports, Bolan was suddenly reminded of why he loved being in space. The Nellis primary as a Class K star named for the famous North American training center. Its orange form was on the far left of the viewports' field of view, looking like a massive roiling piece of fruit. On the far right was *Boyd* station, named for the aforementioned training center's most distinguished occupant, with the planet Creech four hundred miles "below" it. The reflected light from the ocean world caused the 200-megaton station to glitter like a teardrop as it hung in geostationary orbit over the planet's north pole. Like glittering minnows, intersystem transports buzzed back and forth between the planet, nearby freighters, and the multiple warships in various stages of conducting their shakedown cruises.

"Roger *Pinnace One*, your callsign is now Puma Seven. Follow access vector Juno your best speed."

Well, guess Steiner just can't wait to take my head off, Bolan thought grimly.

"Roger *Boyd*, Puma Seven now inbound."

Bolan felt the kick of acceleration as the pinnace's engines fired and began rapidly increasing the small craft's velocity. Muttering a small prayer towards the inertial dampener gods, *Constitution*'s master settled in to enjoy the view as *Boyd* station grew rapidly larger. As the range closed, Bolan noted three other vessels in near orbit around the training station. Two of them, the battleships *Kirishima* and *Montana*, were half-sisters that had just begun their trials. Resembling a pair of Trevidean Megalon sharks feasting on *Boyd* station's mammoth flank, the massive vessels were designed to be the Confederation's next generation of interstellar brawlers.

Located on the opposite end of *Boyd* station from the battleships, either by design or coincidence, was the carrier *Shokaku*. Unlike the bulky, cucumber-shaped battleships, *Shokaku*'s hull was built in the distinctive catamaran design that had been a hallmark of Confederation carriers for over a century. A great aid to the launching and recovery of attack craft, the double hulled configuration was seen as a waste to the Line community. As Bolan watched, the carrier began cycling for flight operations, the duranium "flattop" looking like a cookie sheet being slid out of an antique oven. As the flight deck came up to rest against its stops, the carrier's hangar deck rose with the air group already assembled in formation for their launch. Bolan sighed as he watched the eighty-six craft simultaneously fire their thrusters and vault off the deck as one unit, then turn to accelerate underneath Pinnace #1.

I'd hate to think that the carrier community was sending me a message, Bolan thought, his eyes narrowing. The whole process had taken less than five minutes. Ostensibly *Constitution* could match that rate, but a more realistic goal was to accomplish a launch in seven, with ten at the outside. When one factored in the time it would take Warhawk to assemble after launch, it was fair to say that *Shokaku* could have her strike group in action in roughly half the time.

On the other hand, she can't fight her way out of a wet paper sack if her air wing doesn't get launched, Bolan thought dismissively. *Which means the Fleet has to spend more money for escorts, to include another capital ship.*

"Sir, we're about five minutes out," the pinnace's pilot said. "Starting deceleration."

"Thank you, Ensign Powell," Bolan replied.

Six minutes later, Bolan stepped out of Pinnace #1's airlock and came to attention before Rear Admiral Fidelio Nicoletti.

"Captain Bolan, reporting as ordered."

Nicoletti's face remained impassive as he returned the salute. Admiral Steiner's Chief of Staff, Nicoletti was known as "The Chopping Block" to most of the fleet. With the exception of his time commanding the light carrier *Block Island* and the fleet carrier *Prometheus*, Nicoletti had always served as Steiner's deputy, chief of staff, or all around enforcer. Like Bolan, Nicoletti looked like a man who had missed his calling as a holovid actor. Unlike Bolan, there were often questions whether or not Nicoletti had any will or desires independent of Steiner's.

"Captain Bolan, you will follow me to Admiral Steiner's office at this time," Nicoletti said, his tone clipped.

Well so much for an open and fair trial period, Bolan thought bitterly. *Looks like off to the Board of Inquiry we go.* A captain relieved for any reason had the right to demand a Board of Inquiry consisting of five of his peers. One of the board members was chosen by the relieved captain, two by the relieving officer, and the remainder by the CINC, Confederation Fleet. Restricted to thirty days deliberation by law, the Board straddled the fine line between a gamble and a gambit for the officer in question. Should the five officers, all of whom had been vessel masters themselves, determine that the relief was justifiable and correct then the relieved officer would be immediately cashiered from the service with the rank of commander. On the other hand, should the board feel that the captain had been justified in his actions or made an honest mistake, then the relieved officer became first in line to command new construction in his respective branch.

Which means no more commanding the CINC's hermaphroditic brain child, Bolan thought bitterly.

It was a short journey to Admiral Steiner's office. Just short of the doorway, Nicoletti stopped and turned to Bolan.

"I'm going to give you a piece of advice," the man said, his voice icy. "The last man who made this walk with me did not listen very well. He is no longer holds the job he used to have. You understand?"

"Sir, permission to speak freely?" Bolan asked, his tone matching Nicoletti's in frigidity.

"Certainly, *captain*," Nicoletti replied.

"Quite frankly, if I wanted to command a carrier I would have lobotomized myself a long time ago. I look forward to my Board."

Nicoletti's fair features began to redden and he opened his mouth to speak. Catching himself, he compressed his mouth to a thin line.

"Well captain, thankfully for yourself and the fleet we both serve, you currently do not, nor will you likely ever, command a carrier. I suggest you check your attitude at the door."

"Aye aye, sir," Bolan said, saluting. Nicoletti returned the salute with nothing approximating enthusiasm, then turned and began heading back the direction they had come.

That's a little odd, Bolan thought. The Block had gotten his nickname because, as surely as a chopping block was a chicken farmer's indispensable tool, Nicoletti was Steiner's indispensable witness when the latter was meeting with a subordinate officer, especially if the meeting was a negative one. Bolan continued along the curved hallway towards Steiner's office. Making one last check of his uniform in a mirror strategically placed just for that purpose, he turned the corner...

What the hell...? Bolan thought, slowing his approach.

The last time he had visited Steiner's office, there had been the standard two Space Marines that every flag officer had stationed outside of his office. While there were still the same number of 'Hammerheads' standing outside of the office door, both of them wore the chevrons and rockers of Master Gunnery Sergeants. More importantly, they wore the scarlet piping and formal black dress uniforms of the 1st Confederation Marine Regiment rather than the standard black silk jumpsuits of line space marine units. Bolan had just enough time to be curious as to that change when the door to Steiner's office opened to reveal an extremely young Marine 2nd Lieutenant. Indeed, one so young that he was probably the most junior officer of the fleet and thus…

"Fleet Admiral Malinverni will see you now, Captain Bolan," the young man said, coming to attention and saluting.

…the aide de camp to the Confederation Fleet's Command in Chief, Fleet Admiral Henrique Ocelot Malinverni.

Oh hell, Bolan thought, returning the gesture. *There is no God.*

The first thing that Bolan noticed as he passed into the office's inner compartment was that it had undergone some rather severe renovation in the seventy-two hours since he had last called on Admiral Steiner. Gone was the massive, imposing desk that had dominated the far end of the room. Constructed of black Arborean oak, the desk gave one the impression of standing in the kill zone of a fixed fortification. Also missing was the outline of a pair of shoes, the orientation of which had been indicative of an individual standing at attention. An affectation that the Hatchet had carried over from his days of captain's and admiral's masts, the bright orange footprints had added a little more stress to those who were easily flustered. When combined with the dark blue walls, the previous compartment's décor could have been described as "Post-Modern Stygian."

In place of Steiner's massive desk was a table of roughly half its size. Adorned with a faux wood paneling, the rectangular furniture's depth and clear glass table top immediately clued Bolan in that it was a holographic AAR table. Four comfortable-looking chairs, each with what looked like a control console, were at the device's corners. As he scanned the room, Bolan saw several more chairs aligned against the room's walls and realized there was enough room for every one of his division chiefs and their deputy officer…or for an air group's squadron and flight leaders.

I can only imagine how chaotic one of those AARs could get if they aren't run by someone who knows their business.

Mentally shaking himself, Bolan came to attention as he finally found the man whom he was here to see. Regarding the eight holographic paintings and twelve three-dimensional models attached to the wall on the right side of the doorway, Fleet Admiral Malinverni looked like an old Terran rugby player who had inexplicably found himself in a museum. With his massive, broad-shouldered build and height near two meters, Malinverni would likely have been an international sensation as a prop in the scrum. Given the man's pugnacious temperament, it would likely have been a job that suited him.

"Captain Bolan reporting as ord…"

"Stop all that happy horse crap and get over here," Malinverni said in his sonorous voice. "This is as good a place as any to start recounting the many ways you screwed the pooch."

"Sir, will you be needing anything else?" the Marine 2nd Lieutenant called from behind Bolan, startling the captain.

"No, that will be all, Lieutenant Boyne," Malinverni said. Bolan noted how quickly the man's tone could change from its previous gruffness to that of a benevolent uncle talking to his nephew.

Wish I could compartmentalize anger like that, Bolan observed with a small bit of envy.

Walking over as ordered, Bolan stood next to his CINC. Regarding Malinverni briefly, Bolan felt himself in slight awe of the man. The senior officer was eighth generation Confederation Fleet and, if rumor was anywhere close to fact, the martial tradition ran even further back. Like most of humanity at this point, traditional ethnic labels were useless when describing Malinverni's features. With a complexion akin to the color of a fierce sandstorm, dark eyes that were almost black and a close-cropped salt and pepper hair, the man's bloodline could have had any number of possible origins.

"If memory serves, your major during commissioning was military history," Malinverni began, his voice slightly less perturbed. "Do you recognize any of the models or paintings?" Malinverni asked.

Bolan took a moment to scan the wall.

"That painting is the old United States warship *Enterprise* during the Second Phase of the Great Global War," he said cautiously, pointing at the portrait on the far left. "Next to it is a painting of her second namesake during the Fourth Phase of the Great Global War, right before the Reaper virus was unleashed. To its right is a model of the second English Empire carrier *Illustrious*, circa the early 1980s Falklands Conflict. To its right…"

"Impressive," Malinverni cut him off, his tone indicating that he did not choose the word lightly. "Let me cut to my larger point—what do all of them have in common?"

Is this a trick question?

"Every last one of them involves a carrier."

"Completely unsurprising, isn't it?" Malinverni replied, his tone grim. "Even less surprising would be if I told you that my office is the yin to this yang, correct?"

"I'm not totally familiar with the term, Sir. I slept through most of Religious Philosophy…"

"Where you see carriers, replace with battleships," Malinverni explained. "Where Admiral Steiner has a fetish for ships named *Enterprise*, *Ark Royal*, or *Illustrious*, I have a fascination with vessels named *Warspite*, *Washington*, and *Duke of York*."

The sadness in Malinverni's voice caught Bolan off guard.

"However, I think that if I looked in your cabin, Captain Bolan there'd be a bit of a hodgepodge, would there not?"

Actually, we wouldn't find any models, Bolan thought quietly. *Those are for children, and I have a problem with my cabin looking like some teenager's room.*

"Of paintings, Sir."

"If memory serves, a trio of them that all serve as reminders, do they not?"

Okay, should I be concerned that this man has investigated me this thoroughly?

"Yes, sir," Bolan replied cautiously. Looking at Malinverni, he could see sticking with an officer's four basic responses was not going to extricate him from the CINC's intellectual web.

"The painting of Nelson falling at Trafalgar is to remind me that even victory has a price. *Pawn Takes Castle*," he continued, referring to a rather obscure painting of the Battle of Midway, "is to remind me that sometimes Fate can turn on the smallest of matters, but that a commander must be willing to take a risk in order to move Her."

"I understand the last one was given to you by Senator Modi as a gift," Malinverni said with a slight chuckle, referring to the senior lawmaker from the Spartan Diaspora Republic. "I often wondered why you accepted it, given that you refused the numerous other items people tried to give you for 'saving the Confederation' as some senators have put it."

You would find that less amusing if you had to pay the security firm to check it for hidden explosives, poisons, or malicious medical nanobots, Bolan thought.

"The holo-painting of *Vincennes* is to remind me that it is sometimes necessary to do horrible things in order to prevent something far more terrible from occurring."

Malinverni smiled.

"Ah. I'm just not sure I could keep a painting entitled *The Butcher's Blade* if I was allegedly the butcher in question. I initially thought Senator Modi was being spiteful in shipping you that work."

"I haven't seen any evidence that would make me dispute that supposition," Bolan replied evenly, fighting to keep his voice neutral.

"Then you would be surprised to know that his glowing endorsement of you was one of the primary reasons I placed you in command of the *Constitution*?"

The magnitude of Malinverni's information defeated even Bolan's military bearing.

"I blew up an entire space station full of his constituents and had a hand in killing over five thousand more aboard several system defense ships," Bolan replied, his voice raw. "Why would he…"

"Because Senator Modi, along with most of his constituents with IQs over standard shipboard temperature, realizes just what a Spartan Secession would have wrought," Malinverni replied. "If unsuccessful, it probably would have meant the deaths of millions, if not billions, of Spartans."

If for no other reason than an example would have had to be made. We don't have the Fleet for our health.

"If successful, it likely would have meant the disintegration of the entire Confederation and, within a generation, warfare among mankind once more. How do you think that would have turned out?"

Bolan felt his stomach flip at that thought.

"A six way brawl that would have made the Cats of Kilkenny seem like mildly squabbling siblings," Bolan replied.

"I've always wondered why you seemed somewhat sympathetic to the Separatists in your report," Malinverni replied, then waved away the start of Bolan's protest. "I'm not questioning your loyalty, Captain—we wouldn't be standing here if I wondered about that. I just wondered about your tone is all."

"I don't blame the Spartans for being upset," Bolan allowed after a moment. "The pre-Confeds stuck one hundred thousand people on a bunch of tin cans with a bunch of embryos then shoved them through a wormhole pretty much against their will."

"Well that's not exactly the way they teach it at the Academy," Malinverni said with a slight laugh. "But please, continue."

"Sir, you know from my file that my father was an activist as well as a literary historian," Bolan said with a slight smile of his own. "I got more than a portmanteau name of two pulp fiction heroes from him. The Spartans got screwed by a bunch of people showing up and ordering them around almost millennia after they got to be guinea pigs."

"I think you can understand why some people believe you're sympathetic?"

"Admiral, I'm not sympathetic to batshit crazy. The Separatists thought smoking a couple of star systems with implosion missiles would have meant the rest of mankind left them alone forever."

"I take it this is an opinion you do not share?" Malinverni asked bemusedly.

"I think if someone destroyed my home star system then they might have problems finding safety in the same universe, nevermind the same galaxy," Bolan replied bluntly. "I can only imagine what the Fleet would have done if they'd succeeded. I saw a chance to decapitate them and they'd already fired the first shot. Better to take my chances than waiting to see what happened if more Spartans showed up."

"Precisely. I think Providence, God, or whatever deity you believe in would not have pulled us back from the abyss of species extinction a second time," Malinverni said.

Yes, the 21st Century was probably our last opportunity for divine intervention, dumb luck, or whatever kept humans from becoming nothing more than interesting wreckage.

"While Senator Du," Malinverni continued, referring to the Spartan Diasporan Republic's junior Senator, "would still gleefully rip out your entrails with his bare hands, that has more to do with his brother being space debris than any rational thought. Your ability to act quickly and decisively is the reason why, despite the protestations of some idiots such as Steiner, you were selected to prove a concept in addition to commanding your ship."

Bolan looked at Malinverni, his face showing his lack of comprehension.

"This comes back to the earlier conversation," Malinverni continued. "There are a myriad of problems within our fleet, but the biggest one is that we've allowed our service to ossify into two hardened camps."

Malinverni gestured once more to the wall.

"On one hand, the Carrier admirals. Convinced that their vessels are the true queens of the spaceways, able to savage an entire system in a matter of hours if allowed to launch unmolested."

Malinverni reached out to touch the model of the carrier *Vibhishana*, one of Steiner's former flagships.

"Unfortunately each of these vessels is so expensive in its own right that the Fleet is only able to build two a year, yet so fragile that each requires at least five escort ships, if not more. A chore, of course, which is everything a Line captain can hope for and then some."

Bolan gave a grimace at the last.

"They also have a stunning ability to never be around when, say, a young cruiser captain needs one because Fleet Intel was, once again, wrong about the pirates in a particular system."

Or the "pirates" are sanctioned by the Confederate that oversees the system, Bolan thought. He realized that his emotions had crossed his face again when Malinverni continued.

"Of course, I'm talking to Davies about the Black Hole when it comes to just how spread thin the Fleet is. You're a Line officer, after all."

Ain't that the truth, Bolan reflected grimly but remained silent.

"The times we're not dying of boredom we're fervently hoping that when, not *if*, the pirates come that our superior technology, training, and dumb luck will be enough," Malinverni continued as he began moving towards the holographic table. The fleet admiral pressed a button on the side of the machine, and it gave off a low hum as it powered up.

"You see, what our Carrier counterparts do not understand is that it's not a whole lot of fun surviving successive tours long enough to rise through the ranks just to ride herd on their ungrateful asses," the admiral bit out. "Then, finally, getting the brass ring of being sufficient rank to control your own battle group, only to find battleships are the sledgehammer that only allows you to kill the occasional fly that stumbles across your path or makes too much a nuisance of themselves."

Bolan was struck by how bitter Malinverni sounded. The admiral, realizing that he may have said too much, gestured for Bolan to take the chair opposite from him at the holographic table. As the junior officer did so, a holographic representation of the Solomon System appeared approximately ten inches above the table. After another couple of moments, a miniature *Constitution* winked into being just in

53

front of Bolan's eyes, heading away from him towards the center of the system. Malinverni paused the playback of sensor data at that moment.

"The preceding comments and what is about to follow needs go no further than this room, Captain Bolan," Malinverni said.

Even if I was foolish enough to repeat what he said, the tone of his voice right now makes it clear that I'd be lucky to be rent limb from limb by a Neo-Siberian Kodiak compared to what he'd do to me.

"Understood, Sir," Bolan replied.

"I have dealt with the reality that our Fleet resembles an estranged couple staying together for over thirty years just for the kids."

Bolan winced at that thought before he could catch himself. The fifth of seven children, part of the reason for his attending the Academy had been to escape the madness his parents' marriage had been descending into. In addition to making him resolve to be a bachelor his entire life, the experience had made him realize that not everything was internally the same as it may appear to outside observers.

I wonder if my parents' marriage is part of my dossier? The night my mother finally snapped and swallowed a jug of Kappa Beetle poison...

"I see that you realize what I am talking about," Malinverni went on, jerking Bolan from his thoughts.

"Yes Sir," Bolan said quietly. "I know all too well."

Malinverni considered him for a moment.

"I'm sorry if I dredged up anything unpleasant."

Bolan shrugged.

"It was life, Sir," he replied. "No different than the other two hundred billion people in the Confederation."

"Yes, and the problem with our fleet resembling such a situation is that we are unable to protect those two hundred billion people if we are fighting amongst ourselves."

Bolan's head snapped up.

"Have you been tracking the latest analysis of the McClusky Expedition's ruins?" Malinverni asked conversationally.

"No Sir, I have not," Bolan replied, scanning his superior's face for any sign of disapproval as he answered.

Playing poker with him must be horrible.

"Let's just say the archaeologists' reports, as well as something our scouts may have found, have given us pause," Malinverni continued.

So there is some truth to the rumors that have been floating around. Bolan hadn't heard anything definite, but there had been mutterings about several Exploration Corps vessels coming across interesting things in the last few weeks. Such chatter went in cycles, but there had been a little larger grain of truth in these cases. When all of the rumors seemed to have common traits, it was an indication that something was up.

"But Sir, we've found civilizations before," Bolan responded. Malinverni grimaced.

"In those cases, the civilizations were clearly ancient and had been wreckage for a few centuries if not millennia."

Bolan felt a ball of ice in his gut as Malinverni continued.

"This is not the case with the latest ruins. Some of them may have been abandoned as recently as forty or fifty years ago, and some elements of their technology still functioned."

The ball of ice spread up towards Bolan's head as the blood drained from his face.

"Did you ever wonder why I pressed so strongly for an update to the Navigation and Spacefaring Acts? Specifically Section 195?"

"A vessel whose primary purpose is the carrying of passengers will be prohibited from entering a system until it is properly named," Bolan thought, recalling that Malinverni's insistence had ruffled more than a few feathers. Rescuing people from a vessel was an extraordinary undertaking in the best of times. The aggregate success rate of interstellar rescues was only 35%. While that included events from the initial stages of FTL drives, the fact remained that two professional crews, with minimally manned vessels, still managed to end up losing all hands aboard one or both ships two-thirds of the time. Wondering whether or not an asteroid was going to come in and smack one or both vessels because its orbit was not properly mapped added an additional degree of difficulty. If one added aliens it rapidly ventured into "a captain is excused from attempting rescue if it would hazard his or her own ship"-territory.

"I seem to recall people thought that the current penalties were harsh enough," Bolan admitted cautiously.

"Seizure of the vessel for thirty years usage as a fleet auxiliary *and* a ten billion credit fine would have stopped most lines," Malinverni allowed. "But the major ones? The Confederation Fleet had been too lax for too long in enforcing it, so the amount people paid for a chance to 'oh' and 'aw' about some random planet more than counterbalanced

55

the odds of losing the odd ship. I had to change the risk analysis a little bit."

Sometimes having the same boogieman for thousands of years means that people get numb to it, Bolan thought. *Especially when those people don't usually think of ships as just one big container that probably looks suspiciously like an old-style soup can.*

"Captain?"

Bolan shook himself.

"Sorry Sir," Bolan said, then shared what had crossed his mind. Malinverni looked at Bolan as if he could see the horrible events the younger officer posited in his own mind's eye.

"In this case, Captain, there *are* monsters under the bed," Malinverni said after a moment. "Which is why I need you to prove the concept your ship represents, and quickly. Because we cannot afford to be a divided fleet any longer."

With that, Malinverni resumed the hologram. Just as the three hostile targets appeared, the CINC stopped it again.

"Oh, and one other thing that does not leave this room. Originally, this exercise was intended to force you to use your air group. I provided explicit, written orders to that effect, actually."

*Well, guess **that** didn't happen,* Bolan mentally winced.

"Contacts A & B were in the correct location," Malinverni continued on, manipulating the table to display purple wire outlines that demonstrated where the three ships *should* have been relative to their actual position. "Contact C, however, was supposed to be at a bearing of 200 relative, 50,000 kilometers away, and accelerating away from you."

An up the kilt shot that would have required orienting away from the two other bogeys in order to be pulled off, Bolan thought. *Yeah, that would've done it, as otherwise it would've been the classic "one in the hand, two in the bush" scenario.*

"Admiral Steiner apparently saw fit to ignore my directives," Malinverni stated flatly. "Which is why he should be, if my guess is correct, preparing to board the liner *Calvin & Hobbes* in low Creech orbit. From there, I suspect he'll be enjoying his retirement in the Eurasian Partition."

The calm with which Malinverni announced the destruction of Admiral Steiner's career took Bolan aback.

*Guess Steiner **won't** be succeeding Malinverni after all,* Bolan thought, mildly awestruck.

"To put your mind at ease over the next hour or so, understand that I will *always* tolerate honest mistakes," Malinverni continued, his tone growing perceptibly colder. "However, I have *zero* patience with disobedience. *Vice* Admiral Steiner will have a great deal of time to reflect on that in his dotage."

Holy crap! Losing his command and being forced into retirement was bad enough. The fact that Malinverni has apparently taken a star and, with it, 10,000 credits a year plus additional privileges meant the CINC was sending a message.

"Now, where were we?" Malinverni asked. "Ah yes, the point where you were operating like a heavy cruiser captain rather than the commander of a capital ship."

Three hours later, Bolan found himself thoroughly chastened as he made his way towards *Boyd*'s Shuttle Bay 10.

The CINC knows his stuff, he thought as he played the engagement over in his mind. The AAR had been more than a simple run through of what Bolan did right or wrong. After the first hour, Admiral Malinverni had brought in two of his staff officers and a BuShips representative to conduct a larger discussion on how best to use the *Constitution*'s capabilities. Using the holo table's simulation capabilities, the CINC and Bolan had run through several different scenarios that had exposed several strengths and, more importantly, some weaknesses in the battlecruiser's combination of systems. In addition, Bolan had quickly come to realize Malinverni was the rare type of senior officer who actually *listened*. To the point where he almost pitied the engineers at New Bath Works.

Of course, we need to get those fixes in place before tomorrow morning, he thought wearily. Admiral Malinverni had informed him that the battlecruiser would be conducting another exercise, this time with multiple opponents.

Gotta love warning orders that basically tell you where you're going, but not much else. Still—looks like someone's going to get to see more of my "freak show" than they expected, Bolan thought with grim purpose. Reaching Docking Bay #17, Bolan suddenly stopped dead in his tracks as a familiar figure stood up from the relatively uncrowded waiting lounge.

Uh oh, he thought grimly.

"Master Chief Dunn, I somehow doubt you're here because you needed to make a beer run," Bolan said.

"Sir, I wish I was just collecting some alcohol," Master Chief Bowen Dunn replied, coming to attention and saluting. Built much like the oaks that made his home planet Crawdor famous, Dunn had been in the Confederation Fleet for 27 years. With his craggy face, black hair, and blue eyes, Dunn looked exactly like what he was—a man best not trifled with who had risen to his current position through sheer determination, hard work, and attention to detail.

He's wearing his Captain's Mast face. Someone has seriously screwed the pooch.

"Let's hear it, Chief," Bolan said resignedly.

"Actually, Sir, I think you probably want to hear this inside the pinnace. Too many ears around here."

Bolan felt the pit of his stomach drop at the Chief's tone.

"Very well. Shall we?" Bolan asked, his inflection making it clear that this had better be good.

"After you, Sir," Chief Dunn replied.

Captain's Day Cabin
Titanic
1600 SST

Traditionally a day cabin was supposed to be a place where a captain can conduct ship's business in a relaxed atmosphere. As opposed to handing things that should be easily dealt with by the ship's company, like disputes between the First Mate and Security Officer.

"Sir, I cannot agree with Mr. Martin's actions!" Hagop Al-Madur snapped harshly, his tone just barely the right side of belligerence.

Captain Herrod took a deep breath as he calmed his temper.

It's not Al-Madur's fault that Federov is an asshole, Abraham thought to himself. *Do not unload on him just because you can.* Despite his internal reproach, the gaze Captain Herrod gave Al-Madur let the subordinate know that there was a rhetorical crackling sound beneath his feet.

"It is *not* your role to *agree* with Mr. Martin's actions, Hagop," Abraham said crisply. "Indeed, that would be why the Head of Security is the only department that answers directly to the ship's captain, not the First Mate."

Al-Madur stiffened and was about to open his mouth when the door chimed behind him.

58

"Enter!" Abraham barked. The hatch slid open to reveal *Titanic*'s chief engineer, Ichabod Blum. The young, brown haired crewman did not step in, but merely nodded to Captain Herrod.

"Excuse me for interrupting, Sir, but we will reenter normal space in fifteen minutes," Blum said politely. "The bridge asked me to pass the message along personally."

"Thank you, Mr. Blum," Abraham responded, noting his First Mate's look of surprise. *Yes, sometimes it pays for a Captain to have his own secrets.*

With another slight bow, Blum departed and let the door close behind him. Abraham turned and looked at the grandfather clock that was ticking behind his First Mate, letting a full minute go by before he continued.

"As I was saying, Mr. Martin was given license by me to take whatever measures he deemed prudent prior to this vessel arriving in the Zed-815 system. To be blunt, I do not give a rat's ass what effect that has on the 'authentic experience,'" Abraham snapped, making air quotes, "that you are trying to create."

"Mr. Federov…"

Abraham slammed his hand on his desk, causing the pen holder at the front to rattle. The First Mate shut his mouth so fast that his teeth made an audible sound coming together.

While it is not your fault he's an asshole, it is your fault that you're allowing him to subvert my authority, Abraham thought with a snarl. *Time to clear that up.*

"Perhaps you are confused as to who is captain of this ship," Abraham said, his voice several octaves deeper than normal. "It has been a common malady today. So let me be a bit more blunt since your mental facilities appear to be diminished from having your head so far up Mr. Federov's ass you're starting to suffer from oxygen deprivation."

With that, Abraham stood up from behind his desk, causing Al-Madur to take a step back.

"First off, if you ever attempt to implicitly or explicitly contradict a decision I make again, I will relieve you and throw you in the ship's brig for mutiny. Is that an *authentic* enough recreation of Edwardian-era writ for you?"

"Y-y-yes, yes Captain," Al-Madur said, his face as pale as his complexion would allow.

"Second, you will give Mr. Martin whatever assistance he desires or requests no matter whom it may inconvenience or upset. If the man wants to jury rig the ability to pump raw plasma into every common area of this vessel, your answer will not be to inquire why. No, instead, it will be to tell him how long it will take and to remind him that all modifications to vessel's central hull require Safety Board authorization. Are you comprehending so far?"

"Yes Captain," Al-Madur replied, his voice not much more than a whisper.

"Good. Last but not least, I am giving you a direct order that you will not have any communication other than incidental with Mr. Federov for the remainder of this voyage. I have had enough of your backstabbing and preening in the hopes of getting your own vessel a little bit earlier than you expected. Do your goddamn job rather than trying to get mine. Dismissed."

Al-Madur looked at Abraham as if he'd been struck. After a moment, he came to attention, gave a half bow, then about faced and moved quickly out of Abraham's cabin.

I wonder if E.J. Smith had the same issues with Lightoller and Murdoch? Prior to being tabbed to take command of *Titanic*, Abraham had not even heard the name. Gaining sufficient knowledge to at least be passably familiar with the subject, he had often found himself wondering what went through the late White Star captain's mind on that fateful voyage.

Then again, other than the pushy supervisor, I hope that we don't have much in common, Abraham thought. *Although if we get hit by some chunk of frozen gas, I swear they'll find my corpse with both hands firmly around Federov's neck.* Abraham smiled at that thought as he stepped out into the passageway leading to *Titanic*'s bridge. Clearing his mind of homicidal fantasies, he entered his personal entry code in the touchpad to the right of the bridge's square entryway, then waited for the retinal scan that was required for entry into all critical areas.

After a moment, the heavy hatch slid to the side with almost complete silence. Abraham stepped through the portal onto the liner's spacious bridge. Crescent shaped, the space was bi-level, with the hatchway opening onto the lower deck, a.k.a. 'the pit.' To Abraham's left stood the vessel's navigational officer, Manaba O'Connor. A tall woman, with light brown skin and a broad, plain face, O'Connor was the first to see Abraham as he entered the bustling compartment. Beyond her towards the crescent's port tip moving forward along the crescent towards the bow, stood *Titanic*'s sensor station. Abraham was shocked to see the station was unmanned and made a mental note to have a sharp word with Mr. Coors.

60

*Yes, sensors are next to useless in hyperspace. That does **not** mean that someone steps out and leaves the station unattended!*, Titanic's master fumed.

"Captain on the bridge!" the woman sang out, her thick accent causing Abraham's subdermal translators some difficulty.

Transvaals, he thought, referring to O'Connor's home of origin in the Transvaal Consortium. It was not O'Connor's fault that the translators did not function well—even nano-computers dealt poorly with Afrikaans crossed with Bantu then baked with North African Arabic. While a millennia of translation technology had nearly eliminated mankind's troubling tendency to misunderstand meaning, the fact remained that the Confederation's multitude of planets, atmospheres and ecologies had caused the word 'dialect' to be almost useless.

"At ease," Abraham said, waving everyone back to their posts. Stepping past O'Connor, he climbed the stairs onto the slightly raised platform that held his chair. While most merchant and liner bridges were similarly laid out in arrangement, most of the lines had their own particular quirks. In the case of Czarina Lines, the captain's chair was offset to the right of the entry hatch and on a slight rise. The end effect of this placement was to maintain Abraham's natural sight line at the point where he could turn to look at any station yet have the display that dominated the forward bulkhead still be in his peripheral vision.

There were only two ways to access the bridge's second level. Externally, a VIP entrance allowed access only to Abraham, security personnel, and Czarina Lines' senior officers. Internally, a single-person lifting platform that was to the command chair's right rear allowed transit to the second level from within the bridge. When in its upmost position, the lift itself formed part of a catwalk that connected the port and starboard second level. Along the port side, a small viewing area allowed distinguished guests and visitors to observe the bridge crew conducting their duties from six luxurious cushioned seats. Opposite the viewing area, two bridge stations were present for Security and Engineering representatives to use in an emergency. Normally unmanned, Abraham noted that a young, athletic blonde woman from security was standing at one of the alcoves. With a pale, almost translucent oval face, the woman calmly surveyed the bridge with cold, almost empty blue eyes under a severe bob cut. Abraham noticed that the woman wore a floor length skirt as opposed to the regulation Czarina Lines uniform .

I wonder if that was for modesty's sake or the fact she's probably carrying multiple concealed weapons? Abraham gave the woman a slight smile as their eyes met, receiving a polite but curt nod in return before she continued sweeping the bridge.

"Entering Helgoland System, Captain," O'Connor said. A moment later, *Titanic*'s jump alarm sounded three notes, the descending tones informing all aboard that the ship was leaving hyperspace.

There are days I wonder when we'll get rid of that thing, Abraham thought. Originally hyperspace alarms had been a universal way of telling people they needed to grab onto something, as entering and leaving jumps was known to be about as rough as driving over rutted roads in a ground car. While allegedly a clumsy navigator or poorly calibrated equipment could still lead to a good shaking, Abraham had yet to actually observe or even meet someone who had suffered so much as a bruise due to a rough entry.

Oh well, I guess it's like the fact that all merchantmen must maintain a visual lookout at the front of the ship, Abraham thought. *The one time someone does not sound the warning will be the instance where a person slips in a bathtub, breaks their neck, and makes numerous relatives very rich.*

"Thank you, Nav," Abraham replied. "How long do you need to confirm your fix for the message buoys?"

"Thirty minutes," O'Connor replied. "I would prefer…"

The communications panel on Abraham's right armrest chimed. Looking down at the small holoscreen, he saw the Czarina Lines Crest outlined in forest green.

Gee, I wonder what Mr. Federov wants to ask me, Abraham thought with slight mirth as he pressed the 'HOLD' button.

"You were saying, Ms. O'Connor?" Abraham asked.

"I would prefer forty-five minutes," O'Connor replied.

"Forty-five minutes it is then," Abraham said, then turned back to look at the main display where a visual representation of the Helgoland system was taking shape. Four planets conveniently arranged in a habitable band around the red supergiant primary. As would be expected, the worlds' great distance from everything had limited their development. As a result, only the planet Midnattsol was inhabited by a small settlement of roughly five million souls.

"Mr. Erdermir, keep us outside of the mandatory control limit. I don't feel like having a conversation with the system defense coordinator," Abraham said, adding a mental for obvious reasons. *Titanic*'s helmsman was seated in a recumbent chair in a recessed well three meters in front of the captain's chair, the posture allowing him to look at his own personal screen between his feet. With his black hair, golden skin, dark eyes, and goatee, Hizir Erdermir looked like an ancient Terran Pharaoh reclining on a settee rather than the man responsible for ensuring *Titanic* didn't slam into something.

"Aye aye, Captain," Erdermir replied, softly turning the control yoke in his hands. Abraham felt a soft shudder through his chair as the liner's maneuver thrusters fired. Looking at the screen set into his left armrest, Abraham watched as the *Titanic*'s orientation began to change, with the bow coming around to port even as it rose above the solar plane.

To think people on old Earth would buy tickets to ride machines that moved like this, Abraham thought bemusedly.

Again he looked over at the empty sensor position, his annoyance at Coors was starting to become outright anger. He looked up at the display once more.

Let's see if my plan works, Abraham thought, pressing the button to take Federov off hold. After a moment, the Czarina Lines Crest faded to reveal Federov standing in the corner of *Titanic*'s squash court, the exec's face clearly indicating that he had made the call mid-match.

"Captain Herrod, why are we stopping?"

"We are calibrating the emergency message buoys," Abraham replied simply, keeping his voice and expression utterly bland.

"What?!" Federov asked, the question and tone resembling a volcanic eruption in its intensity. "I will be on the bridge in twenty minutes, Captain Herrod! You can explain this delay when I get there!" The comms screen blanked out.

I can't wait to see how this goes, Abraham thought.

True to his word, Federov arrived precisely twenty minutes later. Seeing the VIP hatchway slide open out of the corner of his eye, Abraham stood and walked over to O'Connor's station. As he walked, he noted that there was still no one at the sensor station.

"Ms. O'Connor, who is supposed to be on sensor duty?" Abraham asked lowly.

The navigation officer looked uncomfortable as she drew herself erect.

"Mr. Coors, Captain," she replied crisply.

What in bloody hell?

"Do you have any idea where Mr. Coors is, Ms. O'Connor?"

"Mr. Coors was not aware that we would be stopping in the Helgoland System, Captain," O'Connor replied, unable to meet Abraham's eyes.

She's trying to keep from backstabbing the bastard.

"That is *not* what I asked," *Titanic*'s master gently replied. "Out with it."

"Mr. Coors had a bad reaction to…"

The bridge's entryway opened to reveal a red-faced, slightly out of breath Aidan Coors. Taking one look at him, Abraham actually found himself sympathetic. It was clear the man was in some sort of distress.

Still, I can't let this pass.

"Mr. Coors, glad of you to join us," Abraham observed coolly. "I was just remarking to Ms. O'Connor that I sincerely hoped she was capable of manning your post as well as hers for another twenty-five minutes."

Coors drew himself to attention and opened his mouth to speak. Abraham had never seen someone's face turn simultaneously red and green, but apparently there was a first time for everything. Making a mewling sound and covering his mouth, the *Titanic*'s sensor officer immediately reversed and ran back out the entrance. Judging from the sound that reached the bridge area just before the hatch closed, the man did not make it to the nearest head.

"Ms. O'Connor, inform the First Mate that we need a replacement at sensors," Abraham said, concerned. "When Mr. Coors returns, instruct him that he is to proceed directly to sick bay and get checked out by the surgeon."

"Aye aye, Captain," O'Connor replied, her face concerned.

"Ms. Vo?" Abraham said, calling diagonally across the bridge to the communications station.

"Yes Captain?" the young, Eurasian woman answered, her black hair just visible over her station console.

"Hold all internal communication for me until I am done with Mr. Federov," Abraham said crisply as he walked across the bridge to the lift. "Answer only official hails from Midnattsol."

"Aye aye, Sir," Vo replied as Abraham pressed the lift call button. Abraham could see the short, slight woman staring intently at her screen, her almond eyes narrowed in concentration.

I probably don't want to know what she's concentrating so hard on, he thought, then had a snap of recall as he stepped onto the lift.

Shaking his head, he realized just how labor intensive Vo's job had become.

New comms allows her to upload and download packets from the in-system buoys, Abraham thought. *She's probably sorting through everything trying to figure out what goes to which passengers, plus who paid for the highest priority.*

Stepping off the lift, Abraham made a note on his wrist tablet to ask Vo for recommendations on how to make her job easier. The simplest fix would probably be to have *Titanic*'s computer automatically sort the messages, but Abraham recalled there being problems with different communication companies' encryption files. As he walked, he looked at the ship's clock out of the corner of his eye.

Twenty more minutes, he thought. *C'mon...c'mon...*

"Captain Herrod," Federov began as soon as he stepped inside the VIP enclosure. "How nice of you to finally join me."

"Mr. Federov, I assume you are aware of my responsibilities," Abraham returned, his tone pleasant. "Specifically the one that requires me to ensure the safety of this ship should we enter into distress?"

"Cut the bullshit, Captain Herrod," Federov snapped. "Why are we stopping?"

"As I stated, Ms. O'Connor needs to recalibrate our message buoys," Abraham said simply.

"Yes, yes, I heard you. Explain!" Federov responded, his face starting to color.

"This is the last human settlement we pass before getting into uncharted space," Abraham began slowly. "You know that hyperspace travel incurs navigational error, which is why civilian vessels are restricted to entry avenues at least three AUs from the outermost planet in any given system."

Federov regarded him with an icy glare.

"So are you going to continue talking to me like I'm some hick who has never been on a space ship or are you going to get to the point?"

Abraham gave the Czarina executive a smile that would have made a Kursk Megalodon envious.

"Well, I attempted to explain things to you as I would to a fellow shipmaster, yet find myself standing on the bridge of my own vessel being snarled at."

Federov was about to retort when the door to the VIP room opened, letting in the noise from the bridge. Both men turned to find themselves staring at the young security officer whom had been watching over the bridge earlier.

"We are not to be…" Federov started, his voice rising only to be undercut by Abraham's unperturbed inquiry.

"Yes, Ms. O'Barr?"

"*Captain*," O'Barr said, stressing the word without even looking at Federov. "Ms. O'Connor reports that she is confident that she has a 100% certain navigational fix."

"Thank you, Ms. O'Barr," Abraham said, controlling his voice not to show the mix of fear, disappointment and anger that was roiling inside of him.

I feel like a man who is about to step off a bridge.

"Do you need anything else, Captain?" O'Barr said, her tone making it clear that "anything" included removing Mr. Fedorov.

"No Ms. O'Barr, that will be all," Abraham replied, noting that O'Barr's relieving officer was also staring intently at the VIP space from across the bridge. "Thank you."

Federov looked triumphantly at Abraham as the door closed.

"I trust that this will be the final stop before the planet Sapphire?" Federov asked smugly.

"Certainly, Mr. Federov," Abraham replied. Of course, you'll be glad we made this one if we do have to use our emergency buoys. Having one of those fold into a sun would rather defeat the purpose of calling for help, no?

"Well then I'll let you get back to your duties," Federov stated. With a curt nod, Abraham turned to go.

"One more thing, Captain," Federov said to his back.

"Yes, Mr. Federov?"

"I usually play squash with Hagop," Federov continued conversationally. "He informed me that he was indisposed this afternoon as something had come up, and that it would probably keep him through dinner. Is there something I should be aware of?"

Abraham turned, flashing the same predatory smile he had earlier. As the VIP area's hatch slid downwards into its recessed position, he noted that O'Barr stood attentively within earshot.

"I informed the First Mate that I needed some help with a few matters. I'm sure you understand that the change of our itinerary has led to some adjustments which required a senior officer's attentions."

"Ah, that's very unfortunate," Federov returned. If not for the tightening around his eyes, Abraham would have thought that the man was utterly unfazed. "Perhaps he will find his workload decreased once we reach Zed-815."

"Perhaps," Abraham replied. "If you'll excuse me, Mr. Federov." Not waiting for an answer, Abraham finished stepping through the door and began to make his way across the bridge, giving O'Barr a slight nod as he went. Cursing silently, he took a deep breath then released it.

Ten minutes isn't going to make much of a difference. Despite that thought, Abraham took his time in returning to his seat with Federov's baleful glare almost a visible weight on him.

"Take us to hyperspace, Mr. Erdermir," he said, settling into his chair.

"Aye aye, Captain," Erdermir replied. Again there was a slight trembling as the helmsman pointed *Titanic*'s prow one hundred and eight degrees away from the system's star. As the jump tones sounded in an ascending scale, the helmsman began gradually advancing the throttle located to the left of his chair. With a much more pronounced vibration, *Titanic* began to accelerate. Looking at the main screen, Abraham watched as *Titanic*'s icon began to grow a vector line, the symbol growing ever longer as the massive liner accelerated towards the speed of light. At maximum acceleration, the starship would have reached hyperspace in a little under ten minutes. Given the restrictions that the Spacefarer's Code placed on inertial dampeners' workload aboard starliners, Erdermir stretched the transition to a little over twenty-five. With a bright flash seen by no one, *Titanic* began her journey to Zed-815.

Roughly a billion kilometers away, on the dark side of Midnattsol, a short, slightly frumpy colonel exhaled. Seated in the System Defense command post located twenty miles away from the planet's capital city and a half mile under its crust, the middle aged officer had been awoken from a sound sleep by the officer of the deck (OOD), Lieutenant Belyayev. The young officer had been frantically talking about a 'huge contact' that just jumped into system.

I'm glad he held it together as well as he did. I think if something the size of a carrier had arrived unannounced I probably would have shit myself at his age.

"Thank the gods," she muttered, her brown eyes wide. She then continued in a louder tone with only slightly less relief, "Was that contact still showing a false code before she left?"

67

"Yes Colonel Aaltonen," Belyayev replied, the response coming in a rush as the short, stout interceptor pilot blew out a breath he hadn't realized he was holding. "She even started to access the message buoy with the right codes, but we got that locked down once we realized *Titanic* wasn't scheduled to be anywhere close to here."

"Cancel the yellow alert," Aaltonen said, standing up to walk over to the arrivals terminal. She had already checked the system's shipping arrivals three times, but decided to give it one more check to make sure.

People are going to be freaked out and rushing in here in a few minutes, she thought. *I want to be absolutely sure before I'm telling the Planetary Minister what the hell happened.*

"Well one thing's for sure, she's one of the few merchies that would give off a hyper signature that size," Aaltonen mused aloud. "Save the data, we'll upload it for the *Theodosius* when she gets here."

"Damn Fleet needs to patrol out here more often," the OOD muttered, running a hand through his crew cut. There was a brief warning tone before one of the sensor technicians cut it off. Looking at the holographic projection of the Helgoland system that dominated the center of the room, Colonel Aaltonen watched as a green icon with UNK next to it winked into life two AUs out of system.

Well it's a good sign this one came in on the same side as the planet, she thought. A moment later the icon changed colors to blue, followed by the room speaker crackling to life.

"Midnattsol Control, this is the Confederation Star Ship *Theodosius* inbound to your system. Kangaroo boxing is dangerous in the sun."

Aaltonen allowed a slight smile as she looked up the pass code and counter challenge.

Someone found a unique way to use 'boxing.'

"Roger *Theodosius*, Lady Godiva rides in the moonlight. We've got a strange contact we'd like to upload for you, please let us know when you're ready to receive."

"Copy Midnattsol, ready for transmit."

Maybe they can figure out what ship that really was, the colonel thought, looking at the three clocks across the room. *Would have been a lot easier if they arrived about ten minutes earlier.*

It'd been awhile since Aaltonen had been to staff college, but she had remembered it being a standard (and secret) policy to stop any vessel that was more than a hundred light years away from its stated itinerary. Many a pirate had found themselves on the wrong side of an airlock because they had wandered too far afield with a captured prize.

Then again, contact that big might have ate a heavy cruiser for lunch and came down to the planet for dessert.

With that discomfiting thought, Aaltonen turned back to the system schematic…and once again thanked the pantheon that there were no such thing as aliens.

Kaiju Class Mecha Platform Patch-Variant A (Young and Nagy)

Chapter 3: Adults and Engineers

C.S.S. Shigure
1630 SST
20 June 3050

"Okay, we've all watched the orders twice and had time to look at the system map," Leslie said, looking at her wardroom. "Thoughts?"

There was a slight pause as the junior officers looked at each other then back to where she, the XO, and Chief Yasushiro sat at the head of the longer table. The officers were in various state of dress—the XO had had told them to come *immediately*, preferring to have them on hand and waiting on Leslie than vice versa. Ensign Doba remained as officer of the deck on the bridge, a sequence of events that probably rendered the pixie-like engineer ready to vent raw plasma.

If we discovered that these structures are filled with a breed of intelligent, but angry, badgers whose height is roughly a meter and a half with light brown fur, Leslie thought, *then I've now got someone aboard whose name we could attach to them.*

Lieutenant (j.g.) Southwell started to speak, then closed his mouth.

"Go ahead and say what you're thinking, Guns," Leslie gently prodded.

"I was thinking that we should definitely make sure to come in a different way than *Columbus* did," Southwell replied. Seeing several of the gathered group looking at him strangely, he continued. "If that *is* an active outpost, *Columbus* probably spooked them. If they called for help, whomever showed up will probably be looking in the same direction she came in from."

"All right. Anyone else?" Leslie asked.

"Probably should come in below the ecliptic as well," Lieutenant Iokepa said after a moment. "Kick out our recon drones and let them swim up through the sun's corona into the plane, radiation will probably hide their drives."

"All right. Nav, do we have astro charts that will let us do that?"

"Yes Ma'am, I should be able to plot the jump easy enough with *Columbia*'s maps," Ensign Griffon replied. "I'd prefer to come out of hyperspace a bit far out due to the high number of asteroids in that system."

Yes, that might be a plan, Leslie thought grimly. *Don't want a stray rock ending our little adventure before we've even begun.*

"All right, we'll come out of hyperspace five hundred thousand kilometers out from the outer edge, one hundred thousand kilometers below the ecliptic. Anyone else?"

There was silence.

"Okay then, go back and inform your divisions. XO, get Major Acheros a combat suit then send him up to the bridge—we'll put him in the observer's chair."

"Aye aye, Captain," Iokepa replied. "Major Acheros, follow me." The two men walked out of the hatch.

"Nav, once you work out a time of travel let the XO know. Speed is of the essence, but I'd prefer to give everyone the opportunity to get one sleep evolution in before we go to general quarters."

"Yes Captain," Ensign Griffon replied as she pushed back from the table.

"That would include you, ma'am," Chief Yasuhiro said softly where only she could hear. Leslie gave him a slight nod to show she had heard him. She mentally ticked off whether she had possibly forgotten anything but found nothing.

"All right then, let's get on with it," she said, standing. The rest of the group followed suit, obviously starting to mull over their tasks. Chief Yasuhiro waited until they all filed out, then turned to look at his captain.

"I've already cut off all non-essential comms," he said. "Chief Pharmacist Yates will have sleep aids available."

See, and that's why it pays to have a great chief, she thought with a slight smile.

"We need to figure out where Major Acheros is bedding down," she said after a moment.

"The XO already asked me to set up a jump bunk in his quarters," Yasuhiro replied. "He figured that was a better option than hot bunking or having him set up in the junior officer's quarters. Although Lieutenant Talo probably wouldn't mind."

Leslie whipped her head around and gave the Chief a questioning look.

"The good Lieutenant should realize that walls have ears, and that maybe the bridge is not the best place to tell Ensign Dabo about the 'smashing' Marine that just came aboard."

"Do I need to say something to her?" Leslie asked.

"I already gave her a gentle chiding. The XO was a bit more direct in his own private way."

Leslie winced.

"No wonder she looked like a Flyshark had just taken her ears off."

"Well, in her defense, he *is* the first man she's seen that hasn't been in her chain of command for six months," Chief replied. "I would suggest when we get back that she finally go on that leave she keeps putting off. Sort of like another officer I know."

"Is this your way of saying I need to lead by example?"

"Captain, I would never try to tell an officer of your great capabilities and experience how to lead."

"In other words, not just yes, but *hell* yes," Leslie replied, unable to keep a smirk off her face. "Noted, Chief. Now let's get out of here before the inmates start running the asylum."

"Aye aye, Captain," Yasuhiro said.

Major Acheros was waiting for her, combat suit in hand, when she stepped off the lift to *Shigure*'s bridge.

"Either I'm moving slower or you must be easier to fit than I thought," Leslie observed.

"Lieutenant Commander Iokepa scares me," Major Acheros said.

Well that makes two of us, but glad to know he frightens people who probably don't scare easy, Leslie thought.

"Took him less than ten minutes to search fleet records, find my size, then have one of the suits from your inventory altered while we were in the middle of the planning session," Acheros said, his tone full of awe.

"There's a theory the XO is actually two clones who are both aboard ship," Leslie replied. "So far no one's got conclusive proof of this...but it hasn't been disproven either."

"Schrödinger's XO?" Acheros asked, deadpan. Leslie giggled before she caught herself, then flushed slightly.

"You never saw or heard that," she said with mock severity.

"What?"

You know, Chief is right: I do need to go on vacation, Leslie thought to herself. *Or maybe make up my mind about a certain former superior so I stop letting life pass me by.*

73

"Exactly," Leslie said, getting a slight smile from Acheros before she opened the hatch.

"Captain on the bridge!" Ensign Kaitlyn Doba sang out, standing up from the captain's chair. The petite officer's shoulders and head were barely visible above the chair's angled back, the visual effect making Ensign Doba look like a pale, dark haired jewelry store mannequin levitating just above the deck. The junior officer's hazel eyes swiveled to Acheros before coming back to meet Leslie's.

I still wonder how they found a jumpsuit that small. Well, outside of the children's section, Leslie thought.

"As you were," *Shigure*'s master replied aloud, stopping the three petty officers sitting at their stations from getting up. "Ensign Doba, this is Major Acheros, the Marine liaison that Lieutenant Talo told you about."

Doba's face remained expressionless even as she colored slightly.

"Sir," she said with a slight nod.

Keep that poker face and you'll go far, Leslie thought.

"Ensign Doba, you and your watch are relieved," Leslie said. "Go get briefed up by Lieutenant Talo while I get Major Acheros acquainted with our humble abode."

"Aye-aye, Captain," Doba said, coming to attention and giving Leslie a slight nod. "Welcome aboard, Sir."

"Thank you, Ensign," Acheros said, nodding. Doba and the three petty officers stepped past them and out the hatch they had just come in. Leslie gestured grandly at the small compartment and its three stations arranged in a semicircle around the central chair.

"There's no viewscreen?" Acheros said, his voice somewhat subdued.

"Exactly. When *Shigure* was built BuShips was still having a struggle about whether or not view screens actually served a purpose," Leslie said. "You'll also notice that the every station is looking in towards the captain's chair as opposed to facing forward."

"That's not good ergonomics," Acheros observed.

"Well, at the time it was thought that the captain would be the nexus to which all information flowed," Leslie replied. "It was a strange time."

"So why didn't they fix everything when they remodeled the ship's interior?"

"Wiring and space constraints," Leslie said with a shrug. "It took a few simulator runs to get used to it, but we've got things pretty much figured out."

"Next question—where am I sitting?" Acheros asked.

"Oh, sorry," Leslie said. "Starboard of the captain's chair is Sensor/Weapons. Port of the captain's chair is Comms/Navigation. The one in the middle is Helm/Engineering. Your chair is in a bulkhead compartment directly behind the helm."

"So we're basically going to spend this whole operation looking at one another?" Acheros asked, then realized how it had come out.

"I assure you, contrary to urban legend, the last observer didn't turn to stone, Major," Leslie observed archly as Acheros started to color.

"Ma'am, I didn't..." Acheros started, then realized that Leslie was fighting to hold in another laugh. The bridge hatch opened, interrupting the major's response and causing Leslie to immediately resume her poker face as Ensign Griffon walked in, followed by the XO.

"We can be there in a little under twenty-four hours, Captain," Ensign Griffon said. "We can jump to the Patroclus system, then hyper into Zed-816."

"Do we have jump back points established?" Leslie asked.

"Zed-720 is our first one, then Zed-815, then Zed-350."

"Those are awfully big bites for the Herbert drive," Leslie observed.

"They're also the systems with the most asteroid fields or nearby nebulae to hide behind," Iokepa rasped.

We don't have time to recalculate, she thought to herself. *Plus he's right—I'd prefer to run than to fight. The upgrades aren't that good.*

"All right, what's the timeline then?"

"I've got the galley serving dinner right now," Iokepa said. "I expected that we'd get underway in thirty minutes, hit the sensor limit in forty-five minutes, then execute Herbert jump."

It's kind of annoying having to skulk around from our own fleet, Leslie thought. *Oh well, that's how secrets stay secrets.*

"After jump, we begin transit and go to skeleton manning for the sixteen hours of hyper, with the officers having a last huddle one hour before we arrive followed by general quarters," Iokepa finished.

Leslie nodded at the XO's plan.

"Very good. Let's make it another hour past the expected sensor limit just in case someone gets under way that we don't know about," Leslie said. "I'd hate to start a Fleet Emergency by simply vanishing. Major Acheros, I assume you don't have any other plans for dinner?"

Captain's Day Cabin
Constitution
1800 SST

This is the very definition of not good, Jason thought to himself, his mouth dry. *Why do I get the feeling that this is not going to be a pleasant conversation?*

Drawing himself erect before the hatch to Captain Bolan's day cabin, the CAG pressed his palm up against the flat, amber panel to the door's right. The panel went green with the sound of four chimes, followed shortly thereafter by the hatch opening to reveal *Constitution*'s captain standing and looking at a holopainting, his back to the door. Standing at parade rest roughly three meters inside the dark blue compartment was Commander Tristan Alexander. Jason felt the blood rush to his face as he saw the short, squat executive officer.

Get a grip moron, that's why you're here in the first place, Jason thought, forcing his anger back down as he came to attention.

"Commander Owderkirk reporting as ordered, Captain," he said.

"You can stand next to Commander Alexander," Bolan said, his tone disappointed. Jason assumed the position of parade rest, fixing his eyes on the holographic painting. It appeared to be a period piece from the Second Global Conflict, a nighttime scene with myriad moving surface vessels. As he watched the scene play through its standard programming, searchlights stabbed out into the painted gloom, one of them slowly panning over the artists' point of perspective.

How much art does this man have? Jason thought mentally, recalling that Bolan's regular cabin was also adorned with three holopaintings.

"Are you gentlemen familiar with this piece?" Bolan asked conversationally. There was a pause as Owderkirk and Alexander tried to figure out who needed to speak first. Just as Jason was about to speak, Bolan continued in the same chilly, almost reptilian tone.

"It's called *A Lunga Barroom Brawl*. The artists' perspective is from that of the old Terran cruiser *Atlanta*, right before she was crippled by an enemy torpedo, then shot up by her own flagship."

Bolan turned away from the painting.

"I'm going to assume that both of you are familiar with the more recent *Atlanta*," Bolan said, walking over to the small, black wooden work desk that sat almost equidistant between the two standing officers and the painting. Still looking forward, Jason noticed that the desk was bare minus three manila folders, a picture of a redheaded woman in a shimmering green evening gown, and a simple wooden pen holder. As Jason watched, Bolan picked up the middle folder, opened it, and began reading.

"The Members of the Board have determined that the loss of the CSS *Atlanta* was due primarily to defects in material and design methodology," Bolan read, his tone clipped. "These shortcomings were exacerbated by a ruinous working climate established by a weak captain, poisoned by the presence of two rival cliques led by the cruiser's gunnery and executive officers, and populated by subordinate officers who forgot that their loyalties were to their ship's master as opposed to petty, would be tyrants."

Bolan closed the folder and placed it on his desk. His eyes met Jason's, the intensity making the CAG flinch involuntarily.

"It is the opinion of this Board," Bolan continued, his tone growing almost prosecutorial, "that future captains should treat the loss of this vessel as a cautionary tale and make every effort to ruthlessly suppress the establishment of any clique, group, or faction that undermines his or her authority."

Bolan looked back and forth between the two men.

"Given that both of you are intelligent, experienced senior officers, I trust that you reviewed my personnel file en route to this vessel and know who gave the majority of the testimony about the *Atlanta*'s inner workings. You know, due to that little matter of her being lost with all hands. "

I don't know what's more alarming: The fact that he has not raised his voice once or that if he stares at me any harder I'm certain that the fire alarm will go off?

"Captain Alois had that painting commissioned for every single plank owner in *Atlanta*'s wardroom," Bolan continued after letting his comment sink in. "She then paid the artist an extra percentage to destroy the mold. You're looking at the last copy in existence. Again, because two officers could not do their damn jobs and a captain allowed them to get away with it."

With that, Bolan opened up both folders. To his shock, Owderkirk saw matching sets of orders in both folders. The blood started to run from his face.

Oh shit, Jason thought.

"When I spoke with Admiral Malinverni earlier today, he asked me if there was anything that I needed to increase the effectiveness of this ship. He assured me that he was not asking out of politeness, but from an earnest desire to see this vessel succeed."

Bolan paused to look both men in the face, his jaw firmly set.

"At the time, I told him certainly not and truly believed it," Bolan seethed. "However, after hearing from the chief *enlisted* man on this boat that my two senior officers had nearly come to blows in one of the ready rooms, and in front of a pair of petty officers no less, I wondered if this was Providence telling me I was a bit off."

Jason watched as the captain allowed himself a slight smile and felt a shot of adrenaline at the look.

"After all, maybe this incident was giving me a chance to correct a problem before you two caused some serious damage. So, as you can see, I came back and spent two hours I could have put to a much better use salving my ego after the bruising it took from the CINC typing up transfer orders for both of you instead."

Andrea is going to kill me, Jason thought, thinking of his wife. His eyes must have involuntarily widened, as Bolan swiveled towards him like an anti-aircraft turret.

"Oh, don't worry Commander, the orders are *only* for yourself," Bolan continued conversationally. "Lieutenant Owderkirk has been doing exemplary work in Engineering, and there's no way Commander Liu will part with your wife over such a trivial manner like you trying to end up in the infirmary."

In the infirmary?! From this fat son of a bitch? Jason thought, then cursed as he realized the disbelief probably flitted across his face.

"I can see we differ on our opinion of what Commander Alexander is capable of," Bolan replied, the steel in his voice so strong it could have formed a bulkhead. "We'll just agree to disagree. Of course, I can't have an executive officer who seems to think that leadership via pugilism is a command technique no matter how insubordinate the junior officer is being."

Jason fought to regain his military bearing as Bolan both questioned his fighting ability and sharply reminded him Alexander was his senior by almost a full year with regards to date of rank.

"So, gentlemen, by all means, if you'll sign the highlighted spaces, we can solve all three of our problems. For you, Commander Owderkirk, you would solve my problems by accepting a billet aboard the brand new *Zuikaku*, due here on station in little under two weeks. According to the most recent personnel release, her CAG had an unfortunate encounter with a micro-meteor while doing combat maneuvering and will be in the hospital for eight weeks."

Bolan then turned to Alexander.

"Things would have been slightly more problematic for you XO, given your past billets, but thankfully it appears that the *Royal Oak*'s XO's eldest just got diagnosed with Garm's disease."

I wouldn't wish that on my worst enemy, Jason thought. Garm's disease was an autoimmune affliction native to several planets in the Eurasian Partition. Attacking the brain's speech centers, the recovery typically took up to a full year even with nannites and advanced medical technology.

"Unfortunately, Commander Alexander, the *Royal Oak* isn't due into this sector with her battle group anytime soon. I've checked the Tac Book," Bolan said, referring to the master file of expected warship deployments kept aboard every Confederation vessel, "and both the *Rescorla* and *Sendler* are headed in that general direction after they conduct exercises with us. I'm not sure they'll have much room for you to deadhead, but at least you'll have twelve hours to pack."

Jason felt Alexander stiffen next to him. The *Richard Rescorla* and *Irena Sendler* were both destroyers, meaning it was highly unlikely either vessel would have room for Alexander to bring much more than some changes of uniform and a few knick knacks.

I get the distinct impression Captain Bolan would have this same measured tone of voice while feeding a man his own spleen, Jason thought.

"Alternatively, you can both remain aboard this vessel," Bolan said. "At which point, I will assume that you have also decided to conduct yourselves as professionals. For in the name of whatever deity you believe in, if we *ever* have to hold this conversation again, the results will not be pleasant."

The last was delivered in an utterly plain tone, yet Jason realized the truth of it was as solid as the deck under his feet. Captain

Bolan moved his gaze between both men for several long seconds, then looked pointedly at the two folders.

"I see that both of you are taking the 'let's not be dumbasses' option. So, Commander Owderkirk, I trust that means you recognize that Commander Alexander, as the executive officer of this ship, speaks with my authority?"

Jason started to speak then found that his mouth was too dry. Swallowing, he wet his tongue.

"Yes Sir," he rasped.

"Good. I fully understand that you guys do things a bit different on the Carrier side," Bolan continued. "However, I do not expect to *ever* hear about you speaking negatively about either my command abilities or the way this ship is run. Do I make myself clear, CAG?"

Jason felt himself color.

"Yes Sir," he said.

"Good. Commander Alexander, what time do you need to see Commander Owderkirk for initial mission planning?"

"Nineteen thirty, Sir," Alexander said levelly.

"Commander Owderkirk, you will meet with Commander Alexander in Wardroom A at nineteen thirty. You probably want to grab Lieutenant Colonel Nishizawa as well. Dismissed."

Jason was slowed for a moment as he tried to process what Bolan had just said. Catching himself, he came to attention, executed a sharp about face, and started heading out of the room.

What in the hell is he talking about, "mission planning?" Jason thought as the hatch closed behind him.

Captain Bolan turned back towards his executive officer. Balding, with droopy eyes and a pale complexion, Alexander usually attempted to keep what little remained of his brown hair in an awkward comb over. When combined with his somewhat lackadaisical adherence to uniform standards and usually haggard appearance, a casual observer would be forgiven for wondering just exactly how the man remained in the Fleet, much less attained the rank of commander.

I personally think Alexander cultivates the image of being a bit of a raggedy man just so people keep underestimating him, Bolan thought.

"Pull up a chair, XO," Bolan said, gesturing to the simple wooden furniture aligned along the compartment's wall. He waited until Alexander complied, then sat down himself.

"Now, how about you tell me what the hell happened?" Bolan continued, his voice only slightly less frigid then when he had been speaking to Owderkirk.

"That son-of-a-bitch was…"

"No, actually I was meaning with the little power failure we had. I'll get to your complete loss of professionalism in a moment," Bolan snapped. "One of these items is rather problematic, especially for a fleet unit on its trials. The other I consider to be mostly cleared up given that you're not packing your gear."

Alexander stiffened slightly, then almost as quickly gathered himself mentally.

"The power conduits to the secondaries have a feedback problem when we are running with full shields and hot cats," the XO said flatly. "As Commander Liu suspected, Bath Yards failed to conduct a full test with weapons, shields, and catapults during trials."

"What?!"

"According to the builder's logs, such a test was not requested by BuShips," Alexander said. "The cats were not used because *Constitution* was classified as a Line vessel."

Bolan resisted the urge to smack his forehead at that statement.

Of course, that's not all their fault as we're the first of our kind.

"Can Liu fix it?"

"If we were in combat, yes," Alexander replied. "But given that we are on trials, regulations prohibit him taking the risk."

"So we'll have to conduct the remainder of our trials without being able to fire our full weapons if we intend to use the air group?" Bolan asked incredulously.

"Officially, yes," Alexander replied stiffly. "There is a significant chance that if we try to fire all of our armament at once we will experience the same power failure."

"Unofficially?" Bolan asked resignedly.

"I instructed Commander Liu to conduct the repairs while you were in your meeting with Fleet Admiral Malinverni" Alexander replied. "He stated that he was not comfortable carrying out such an order without your stated approval."

Bolan started to reach for the communication but stopped as Alexander continued.

"I informed him that if he wanted to be executive officer of this vessel he should put in the necessary paperwork," Alexander said. "But until such time he would begin carrying out my orders and we'd do the 'cover your ass' drill when you had the time, Sir."

Bolan sat back in his chair with a deep breath. The XO was supposed to be a vessel's hatchet man, but Alexander was sticking his neck pretty far out.

"I'm going to still give Liu a written directive," Bolan said. "CINC gave us authorization to experiment, plus if Liu's worried there's probably a reason."

Alexander grimaced.

"Or perhaps you can just tell me what the other shoe is?" Bolan said with a raised eyebrow.

"Given the repairs, there is a slight chance that the vessel could experience total and complete power failure."

Bolan suddenly saw why Liu wanted authorization. A complete power failure was one of the ways that a vessel could suffer what mariners commonly called the "Heinz Maneuver," i.e. a total failure of the inertial dampeners…usually followed by the crew becoming a ketchup like substance on the nearest bulkhead if the vessel was under acceleration.

"What in the hell is Liu doing?!"

"Sir, with all due respect, it'd take too long to explain," Alexander replied, his countenance becoming even more grim.

Some captains would be insulted by that, Bolan thought, letting the silence drag for a second. *Unfortunately, he's right—gun bunnies don't do 'arcane arts.'*

"Then tell me what's the percentage chance of that happening?" Bolan asked, his face a couple shades paler than normal.

"One percent," Alexander replied, his alacrity indicating he was expecting the question. "That number is rounded up. Considerably."

Bolan raised an eyebrow.

"You know, a one in a hundred chance of getting turned into meat paste isn't exactly low."

"Ah, but Sir," Alexander said with a slight smile, "as one of the people who would be special sauce with you, I have complete faith in Commander Liu and my judgment."

"I would be much more likely to concur with that assessment if I hadn't heard about you and the CAG nearly coming to blows," Bolan replied.

Several emotions played over Alexander's face before he regained his composure. "Commander Owderkirk and his officers were out of uniform," Alexander began levelly, matching Bolan's gaze. "He was also disrespectful towards you…"

"I hardly think having the AAR comment 'perhaps we could use the air group for something other than display purposes' is disrespectful enough to require violence, XO," Bolan replied. Alexander looked at him in shock.

"Sir, that comment was completely unprofessional in a public forum," Alexander replied.

"It was also true, and probably what every single pilot in that ready room was thinking," Bolan responded. "By the way, that same comment made, almost word for word, by Fleet Admiral Malinverni."

Bolan gave his XO a slightly bemused look after letting his rebuttal sink in.

"You will note I did not attempt to assault the CINC. That being said, I understand that there were a couple of additional comments made which may have inspired your desire to help Owderkirk with his dental work. "

Alexander opened his mouth then shut it.

"I knew that Owderkirk was a hothead with a mouth before I agreed to have him be the CAG," Bolan continued. "His constant questioning of authority had a great deal to do with him being available for this billet. As a bonus, we got his wife, who I understand is a large part of the reason Commander Liu has the time and energy to think of ways to kill us in a spectacular fashion."

With that, Bolan pushed back from his desk, waving for Alexander to remain seated. He walked over towards the drink dispenser that stood on its own table to the left of *A Lunga Barroom Brawl*.

"XO, would you like something to drink?" Bolan asked. He watched as Alexander tried to figure out what was the proper response in the situation.

Yes, I am keeping you off balance, Bolan thought with an internal chuckle.

"I've got coffee, tea, hot chocolate…" Bolan said, his tone expectant.

"Coffee, Sir, please," Alexander responded. Bolan could still see some confusion, then realized what it was as he prepared the first cup.

"I'm not a big fan of being waited on by a steward when we're not underway," Bolan said. "The Confederation's not paying to have someone make my coffee when he can be twice as useful helping the wardroom staff with all the officers."

Finishing both cups, Bolan brought the mugs over on a small silver tray. Setting Alexander's down first, the captain continued.

"As much as he pushes the envelope, Owderkirk pushed our air group through the best trials cruise in sixty years, to include both strike squadrons being rated an 'E' in anti-vessel warfare," Bolan continued. "If I had remembered to launch them, they probably would have had their contact destroyed before it even made it one thousand kilometers."

Bolan saw Alexander's eyes narrow at that last statement, but chose to ignore it.

"Now in the real world, we both know there's never a carrier around when you actually need one," Bolan continued, his voice even. "The fact remains, this ship is intended to be fought as a mix of both line vessel and carrier and, despite his character flaws, Owderkirk gives us a pretty good chance of doing that."

Bolan paused to take a sip from his coffee mug.

"On the other hand, XO, just how much do you think your little display helped with regards to getting us towards that goal?"

"Not at all, Sir," Alexander choked out.

"So if there are future problems, XO, which of you do you think I will find at fault? Owderkirk, who is apparently the officer good little pilots strive to be when they grow up? Or an officer who allows the fact that his wife ran off with an aviator color his professional conduct?"

Alexander's face went completely pale.

"Sir, with all due..." Alexander started to seethe, his fists balled.

"Answer my question, XO," Bolan interrupted. The dead calm in his voice made Alexander stop his protest dead in its tracks. Bolan could see the man was practically trembling in rage.

"Myself, Sir," Alexander choked out, his voice barely a whisper. He broke gaze with Bolan, focusing on the bulkhead behind the captain.

Yes, it was dirty pool, Bolan thought. *But we don't have time to dance around the real root of the issue.*

"Of course, such a chain of events would be very, very bad for this vessel," Bolan continued solemnly. "Before this incident, you have been the best XO I've ever had."

Alexander looked at him in shock and surprise.

84

"Yes, that includes Leslie Hawkins," Bolan continued. "Leslie's an excellent Line officer, but by her own admittance Carrier tactics confuse the hell out of her."

We'll also leave out the fact that her being my XO again would have been...complicated, Bolan thought. *But at least she recommended a more than able replacement to me.*

"Sir, you act like it's not confusing to me," Alexander said quietly.

"Well you definitely seem to be getting the hang of the maintenance piece, and I'm pretty sure the tactics will start to gel rather quickly once you stop wanting to throw the CAG out an airlock."

Alexander took a deep breath at that.

"Thank you, Sir," he said, his attitude clearly easing back towards its normal range.

"You're welcome," Bolan responded. "In that same vein, I have had zero complaints with the programs and mechanisms you have put in place with the rest of the departments. I even told Admiral Malinverni that you're the main reason we're thirty-five days ahead of schedule with our trials tasks."

Alexander looked at Bolan in shock. The expression was so comical Bolan had to fight to keep a straight face.

"Minus the little fiasco with power today and my own piss poor decision making, I'd put us up against any other vessel in the fleet right now, nevermind in thirty days."

There was a tone from the speaker mounted in the cabin's overhead.

"This is Captain Bolan. Send your traffic," Bolan said.

"Sir, we have a message packet from Boyd station," Lieutenant Herrod stated. "It is marked PRIORITY."

"Understood," Bolan replied. "Decrypt it, then provide courtesy copies to the CAG and XO."

"Aye aye, Sir," Herrod stated. Bolan glanced up at the speaker to make sure Herrod had terminated the connection before continuing.

"Tristan, you have been fighting with Commander Owderkirk since the air group came aboard. If you had a problem with aviators, and Lord knows I can understand why, you never should've taken this job."

Bolan saw Alexander's shoulders slump.

"Sir, I'm sorry," the XO said. "I screwed up."

"Hey, we all have. It's not like I'm used to having an air group, but Admiral Malinverni wasn't taking no for an answer. Told me my options were *Constitution* or a research vessel."

Alexander snickered.

"Well, maybe it's a messed up thing to say, but I'd much rather have an air group than engines that might accidentally fold me into the middle of a planet," the XO replied.

Bolan nodded at that statement.

"Especially since the only vessel available was the *Lise Meitner*."

"I'm not familiar with her, Sir," Alexander replied, his voice trailing off.

"She's the *Aries'* direct replacement," Bolan said. His statement drew an intake of breath so sharp it whistled.

"Holy shit!" Alexander said, his eyes widening.

"Exactly," Bolan said. "While I hear saving the data can get a destroyer named after you, I'd much prefer to be living than memorialized." There was a chirp from his desk. He pulled back the central drawer to reveal that it actually housed an electronic terminal. Looking at the screen, he smiled.

"Well, looks like you've got some reading to do. You and the CAG better get to it. I'll have my initial guidance to you in about thirty minutes."

Alexander looked slightly puzzled.

Yes, I know, most captains believe in trying to figure everything out themselves. We tried that approach earlier today, Bolan thought to himself. *Didn't end well.*

"What? You're expecting me to do all the planning? That's what I have you two bright young lights for."

Alexander recognized a dismissal when he heard one. Standing, the XO came to attention and gave a slight neck bow.

"Thank you for giving me a second chance," Alexander said, his voice sincere.

"Don't fuck it up," Bolan replied simply. "That's all the thanks I'll need."

Owderkirk Quarters
Constitution
1845 SST

"Then I get told that I've got to meet with that son-of-a-bitch at nineteen thirty and by the way, get out," Jason seethed.

As the third ranking officer aboard *Constitution*, Jason rated a double compartment. Which was a way of the Fleet saying he had moved from a breath mints container to a shoebox. Given that their quarters were shaped like a rectangle roughly five meters on the short side, eight meters on the long, the mental comparison was particularly apt. Looking over at where Lieutenant Andrea Owderkirk sat in front of the quarter's vanity after having just stepped out of the shower, he allowed himself a small smile.

At least I like my roommate, he thought with a slight smile.

"Honey, have you ever considered, maybe for a moment, that it would be better for the ship if the CAG and XO got along?" Andrea said, stopping mid stroke where she was brushing out her hair. With her pale complexion, dark blue eyes, delicate features, and jet black hair, Andrea had more than earned her Fleet Academy nickname of "Snow White."

"One of us needs to go," Jason grunted, the smile disappearing off his face.

"Well golly gee, maybe you should have totally screwed your career and our marriage by signing on to the *Zuikaku*," Andrea snapped, resuming brushing her hair.

Uh oh, Jason barely had time to think before his wife continued.

"I mean, do you *ever* check the depth of a pool diving in head first? The reason Captain Bolan told you that you were about to get a one way ticket to sick bay is pretty apparent if you've read Commander Alexander's bio."

Jason give his wife a blank look, resulting in an exasperated sigh.

"I wish I could be a Line or Carrier officer so I could go through life confident in my ability to overcome whatever's in my path," Andrea continued snarkily. "Unfortunately, I'm an Engineer, which means I can't just piss all over someone with the confidence that I can avoid them the rest of my career. *That* is why I look over every officer's personnel jacket when I get assigned someplace."

Jason shrugged.

"I just trust in my ability," Jason replied with a rakish grin. "It's worked so far."

"Yes, just like when we first met on Ostfjord and you had an utter fail with your first pick up line," Andrea muttered, shaking her head then impersonating Jason's voice. "'Well maybe I can show you the slopes sometimes' the fighter pilot said to the Tri-Systems downhill champion."

"Look, we don't have time nor desire to fly from planet to planet for silly games over in the Anglo-Saxons," Jason returned as he colored slightly. "We're a little more spread out than you guys are over in the Eurasian sector."

"Or alternatively if you get too many of you crazies in one place you start arguing over who needs to be in charge," Andrea replied snidely, sticking several bobby pins in her mouth than reaching up to start tying her hair in a bun.

Now that's just not fair.

"One would think after two assignments with Commander Tice the mere presence of breasts wouldn't render you speechless," Andrea said around the mouthful of metal.

"I'm afraid that the view isn't nearly as spectacular with Commander Tice," Jason said without thinking.

Oh shit. Whomever said the truth will set you free had obviously never put his foot in his mouth.

"Been mentally comparing, have you?" Andrea responded with a partial grin. "Anyway, try getting enough of your blood back to your brain to listen up."

"You know, some day you're going to complain about me not looking at you like I used to," Jason growled.

"Yes, that will probably be because you're dead and I'm not into necrophilia," Andrea responded. She reached over and grabbed a singlet that was hanging off the corner of the mirror. "Better?"

"No."

"Pervert."

"Tease."

"Jason! We don't have the time for you to be a smartass, especially if you're about to go meet Commander Alexander."

Jason let out an exasperated sigh.

"Okay, so enlighten me how I was being stupid."

"The Tri-System Games, like the old Terran Olympics, have a summer and winter version," Andrea said. "They're usually held on Europa because it's got enough space for everyone."

"Wait, how many people come to this thing?" Jason asked as his wife finished her hair, slipped the singlet back off, and walked over to her footlocker.

"Well you remember how I said 'Tri-System' is a misnomer from when they first started?" Andrea said, crouching down to enter the combination into the lock at the front of the container.

"Yes, when I finally got over the sheer terror of nearly dying while following you down that Level 5 trail in the dark," Jason replied, leering at her. "I still think it's worth it, by the way."

Andrea rolled her eyes even as she smiled at him.

"Yes, well, the only reason you got dinner that night is because 'nearly' is involved in that sentence," Andrea said. "I figured you were going to do me the courtesy of breaking your leg five minutes in…then I got pissed off after you wasted another ten minutes of my time."

Jason looked at her in shock.

"Wait, so you were *trying* to get me hurt?"

"Do you really think you were the first arrogant fighter jock on his dirtside leave to hit on me?" Andrea asked. "Why do you think that pair of ski patrol guys were trying to tell you that maybe you should just leave me alone with my book? I had a reputation to uphold."

As Jason stood there shocked, Andrea pulled out a one-piece garment that looked like it belonged underwater, not in space. Jet black and covered in several crystalline particles that gave it a slight sheen, the uniform looked like a wetsuit designed by the Terran artist Liberace. Unzipping it, Andrea began sliding into the skintight garment while continuing to talk.

I remember reading once they used to call the engine room crew 'The Black Gang' because they were always covered in coal dust, Jason thought. *No matter how many times I see it, I'll never get used to the fact Engineering apparently get to go to work naked. Of course, the crystals turn cherry red when exposed to high amounts of radiation and the nudity is so it's easier to decontaminate if something goes wrong, but still…*

"Anyway, the summer game crowds make those at the winter games seem like a charity concert audience. So imagine about 150,000 screaming people in a confined dome."

Jason looked at his watch.

"Shit hon, you need to speed this up," he said.

"Fine. In 3032, Commander Alexander competed in freestyle martial arts as the representative from the planet Kerensky."

"Freestyle martial arts?" Jason asked blankly.

"Anything goes, octagon, four go in, one comes out?" Andrea responded, trying to jog her husband's memory. Jason shrugged, and she continued.

"Well, Commander Alexander made it to the finals. Two of his opponents were the last two champions, the other one was some farm kid who'd just gotten lucky everyone annihilated each other in his bracket. Place is going wild, so loud that they actually had people get physically ill."

"Can I just say you Eurasian folks are a bit weird?"

"Look, no one's forced into an event," Andrea said, shaking her head. "You go into the Octagon of Doom, you know the risks. Anyway, not only did Commander Alexander win, he killed the champ from 3030."

"What?!!"

"Yeah, you ought to look up the video sometime when we're back on a planet. It's scary," Andrea said. "It's standard chaos until Commander Alexander breaks the farm kid's collarbone and actually stops to make sure he hadn't killed him."

"Wait, I thought you said…"

"Oh, the 3030 winner thought that was a good time to jump him from behind. When they interviewed him after the fight, Commander Alexander said that he didn't remember what happened next," Andrea said with a grim look. "Well, I can tell you anyone who has seen that video remembers and that place went from thunderous to church in about ten seconds. Seeing a man get his spleen ruptured and bleed to death will do that."

"Sweet Mercy!"

"Yeah, the problem with the old Octagon is they didn't stop until someone won. Which is why the poor bastard died as Commander Alexander proceeded to cripple the 3031 champ for life."

Jason looked at his wife with wide eyes, a look of utter horror on his face.

"Are you sure you people aren't Spartans?!"

Andrea shrugged.

"They made changes in the rules after that," she replied simply. "But at that time? Prize money of a couple million credits, corporate sponsorships, and several other awards—it's not tiddlywinks," Andrea said, then leaned up and kissed him.

"You gotta go, I'm heading to dinner. Glad you can still talk," she said, then gently groped him, "and have the use of everything below your waist."

"Thanks for that," Jason said. "Now I'm going to have to think of something utterly unsexy in the next thirty seconds."

"Just making sure you still want me after a year," she said with a smile.

Well here's to hoping you're feeling this way in twelve hours, Jason thought.

"You're lucky I have a meeting or you'd be going to your shift hungry."

"Promises, promises," Andrea replied with a giggle, then opened the hatch.

Ballroom A
Titanic
2000 SST

Gee, is it too obvious that I'm expecting trouble? Marcus thought as he leaned on the balcony railing while looking at several of his security personnel working below.

Looking around the room, Marcus fought the urge to reconsider his planning. *Titanic*'s Ballroom A, located on the liner's port side, was seventy meters in length and twenty in height. Rather than the standard high traffic carpet foam, the compartment's floor was overlain with highly polished teak. The room's sole entrance consisted of a single 6 x 10 meter opening along the internal bulkhead, with the orifice's hatch descending into a seamless groove when not closed. When upright, as it currently was, there was a smaller scuttle in its center that could be opened only by crewmembers, thus allowing individuals to enter and leave without going through the hassle of messing with the main hatch.

While the ornate wood paneling, gold-laced transparent balcony that stretched along the inner wall bulkhead and massive chandeliers gave the room a resplendent, Edwardian air none of these compared to the chamber's crowning feature: its space window. Constructed of polarized transparisteel and stretching from deck to overhead, the observation port gave the appearance of being a completely seamless opening to the stars. Although Marcus knew that it was actually interwoven with various materials that strengthened it while maintaining the transparency, he still had a distinct feeling of dread every time he entered the room.

Transparisteel and a bunch of polymers I can't pronounce are nice, he thought, *but I still have visions of something making it past the navigation shields and coming right through that thing right in the*

91

middle of a ball. The viewport's opacity was currently set to jet black, a provision that kept everyone inside from having to deal with the constant glare that arose from traveling through hyperspace.

A pair of slender arms slid around him from behind, squeezing him tightly as a familiar chin placed itself on his shoulder.

"You're thinking about that window again, aren't you?" Sarah asked softly as Marcus turned around, shocked. Before he could answer, she kissed him lightly on the lips.

"I'm sorry for earlier," she said, putting a finger to his lips before he could protest they were still on duty. "There aren't any passengers to see and the XO's busy hobnobbing with the hoity toity."

"Uh, shouldn't *you* be hobnobbing with them?" Marcus asked, surprised.

"Oh, I'm going there," Sarah replied. "But I just wanted to tell the man I love I'm sorry for being a complete bitch earlier."

Marcus raised an eyebrow, drawing a smile from Sarah.

"No, I didn't just come from leaving an ice viper in your room," she continued.

"I always figured you more for a booby trap kind of gal anyway," Marcus retorted, drawing an exasperated sigh from Sarah.

"Why can't you just accept my apology?" she asked.

"Well let's see," Marcus started, then couldn't maintain his straight face when Sarah started to glare at him.

"You're not funny, Marcus," Sarah said.

"No, I'm just a man whose girlfriend ripped his face off for not disobeying a direct order," Marcus responded evenly. "Who, in turn, is having some fun at her expense because she thinks a hug and two words makes up for several hours of mental anguish."

"Oh yes, you were *sooooo* anguished," Sarah responded, starting to smile herself.

"I was," Marcus replied, making his tone sound labored. "It was torture every moment I thought you were angry with me and I just could not function."

"That's why Corridor C," she said, referring to the crew only thoroughfare that ran the length of the ship, "looks like an obstacle course and I've seen multiple groups of your security gang wandering around as if they were marking out places they intended to make stands against a boarding party."

Okay, I obviously need to have a word with the squad leaders, Marcus thought. *Because if Sarah saw it, that means the passengers saw it. Which means Al-Madur is going to have a case of the ass.*

Sarah's smile broadened as she looked at him, and Marcus had the distinct feeling his concerns had been rather obvious.

"Don't worry, rumor has it the First Mate has found many new and interesting ways to explain away the precautions."

"Get out of my head."

"I love you," Sarah said with a giggle. "It's so funny when I can read your mind and annoy you."

Marcus shook his head.

"I just know that's got Al-Madur fit to be tied," Marcus said with a sigh. "I don't want him taking it out on you."

Sarah shrugged.

"He takes it out on me, he starts getting the newbies down on 'Red Deck,'" Sarah replied simply.

Marcus looked at her in shock, eliciting a giggle.

"I thought..." he sputtered.

"What, that his 'religious beliefs' would keep him out of a brothel? Ha! He might make it a point to mention he bows down with Senators Champeau and Falak, but let's just say that man's employee discount definitely gets a workout."

Sarah looked around to double check no one was in ear shot.

"Besides, if you were worried about him retaliating against me then maybe you shouldn't have gone over his head to Captain Herrod," she continued, her tone still teasing.

Marcus put his left hand against his chest.

"I'm sorry, are you accusing me of doing what I thought was necessary to protect this ship?"

Sarah rolled her eyes.

"I sometimes think you'd merrily toss me out an airlock to 'protect this ship,'" she said, mockingly curling her fingers to simulate quotes around the last phrase. Something in her tone made Marcus wonder if she was still joking, but they were interrupted before he could clarify.

"Hey lovebirds!" a gruff shout came from below, causing both of them to snap their heads around. Marcus exhaled in annoyance as he met the speaker's gaze. Quentin Thendaron was a short, squat man whose Czarina Line uniform looked like it struggled to contain his muscular frame. The leader of Roving Squad #1, Thendaron looked every inch of the former Gunnery Sergeant he'd been just three years before. That is, if the viewer discounted the full black beard and mustache which would not have been out of place on a 20th Century biker.

"Yes Quentin?" Marcus asked.

"We're done down here boss," Quentin replied back with a smile. Looking around the room, Marcus nodded.

"Looks good to me," Marcus replied. "You guys are off until tomorrow."

"Roger, boss," Quentin replied. "You guys heard the man, and I'm buying down at *Rose's*."

*Someday I will understand why there's a bar named **Rose's Floating Wood** down in the crew section*, Marcus thought.

Sarah stood and looked out over the ballroom as the security team left, pushing their light hover crane in front of them. She exhaled in a slight sigh as the main hatch *thunked* shut.

"Marcus, I love you, but don't ever go into interior decorating," she said with a shake of her head. "You just basically cut the dance floor into thirds with the tables and planters. That's going to make the charity ball tomorrow...*interesting*."

"Slalom dancing?" Marcus asked with an innocent look on his face. "Or the three rows mean you can have a tournament for best dancer? You know, three tiers?"

"Or more correctly it means some Senator's wife is going to be upset that everyone in the room can't see her in all her magnificence," Sarah said archly as they descended the balcony stairs.

"Suddenly remembering why I like Security over Hospitality."

Sarah looked sideways at him.

"Even though you have to worry about things like pirates?"

"Yes. Because I can shoot pirates," Marcus said, opening the secondary hatch to let them out. "You don't have that option with passengers' wives."

"Yes, most of us tend to frown upon our spouses getting shot," a baritone voice interrupted, startling both of them. "Judging from how many security preparations I've seen, it is probably a good thing that Geertje did not make this trip with me."

Marcus finished stepping through the hatch and turned to face his speaker as the tall, slender man with Asian features continued.

"I have to say, travel on Czarina Lines is far different than what I expected when I undertook this passage," Senator Geirmund Du continued, his tone clipped and dark eyes colder than a flechette gun barrel. "In Spartan space, captains and line officers generally make themselves available upon request for concerned passengers' questions. Then again, we tend to encourage *observance of the law*."

Marcus drew himself up to his full height, forcing a smile.

94

"Well Senator, Czarina personnel do try and honor the customs of the *entire* Confederation," Marcus replied with impeccable politeness. *The Confederation you did not want to join, you treasonous asshole*, while silent, was obvious to both men. Marcus felt Sarah place her hand on his back in the guise of steadying herself as she stepped out of the hatch.

Yes, I know I need to tone it down a little, he thought uncharitably.

"Senator, we have completed our…" a short, wiry man started to say as he came around the corner, then stopped upon seeing Marcus and Sarah. Two others, one male, one female joined the man. All four wore scarlet outfits, with the men in slacks and tailored blazers that Marcus was certain concealed various weapons. The woman, on the other hand, wore a crimson blouse and blood red pencil skirt that hugged her dancer's figure so tightly that to the untrained eye it would have been questionable whether she was wearing undergarments, nevermind weapons. To the trained eye, from the way she moved to her choice of footwear and the three long hairpins that held her light brown tresses up, it was clear that she was a hand to hand combat expert.

Never trust a Spartan with a pretty face, Marcus thought bitterly.

Of the three men, the two most recent arrivals looked as if they could have been brothers, their features suggesting that their ancestors had hailed from Indonesia or Malaysia. The third man looked as if he shared a bloodline with Senator Du despite the fact his first name made him sound Japanese. The woman, on the other hand, had blue eyes that made even Sarah's seem ordinary and proud, beautiful facial features that would have harkened to Eastern Europe on ancient Terra. It was not the woman's beauty, however, that made Marcus's breath catch, the pulse start rising in his ears, and his hand start to drift towards his pistol before he stopped himself.

"Thank you, Tsubasa," Senator Du said, speaking to the first man while looking at Marcus with open curiosity. "Mr. Martin, you look as if you've seen a ghost."

Before Marcus could respond, the woman stepped closer with a half -smile.

"That's because Mr. Martin's eyes are telling him he has," she said, her voice soft and flirtatious even as her gaze blazed sheer, undiluted hatred as she moved slowly towards Marcus. "Or perhaps he is instead having a pleasant memory."

95

Exactly what kind of memory she had in mind was clear, causing Sarah to inhale sharply behind him. Marcus ignored his girlfriend's shock, never taking his eye off the woman's defiant gaze as he met it with one of his own.

"I don't believe in ghosts," Marcus snarled.

The woman grinned broadly, wisely stopping her advance towards Marcus.

"I imagine that is for the best. It would probably be hard to sleep with a Lancer reunion every night," she said.

Marcus blew out a deep breath at hearing his old platoon callsign.

Okay bitch, it's on.

"That is enough, Aimi!" Du barked. The senator's tone caused the woman to stop as if he'd hit her with a length of steel pipe, her head snapping around in shock. Seeing he had her attention, Du continued. "I would appreciate it if you did not embarrass me."

"I am sorry Senator," Aimi said diffidently, with a look that made Marcus almost believe her.

"Leave us. Now," Du snapped. "Return to my presence when you can control your emotions."

Aimi stiffened at the rebuke, her face becoming impassive. Bowing to the Senator without comment, she turned and began walking off.

"Wira, Dian, escort her back to her cabin," Du continued. "Make sure she understands that no dishonor has been done."

"Yes, Senator," the two men said simultaneously.

Why do I think 'no dishonor has been done' is code for 'don't let her slit her belly open'? Marcus thought. The Spartan Diaspora Republic had some social and moral codes that would have made most of Earth's ancient warriors seem like carefree libertines.

*When you actually have a **planet** named Bushido…*

"I apologize for Aimi's behavior, Mr. Martin," Senator Du replied. "Although I was not aware that Aimi and you had met before."

"Well that makes several of us, it seems," Sarah replied brightly. Marcus hoped he was the only one who heard the daggers behind her cheerful façade.

"I do not know her," Marcus replied thickly, his mouth suddenly dry as his mind meandered back to several memories. "But I have to ask, is she a twin?"

Du's face became emotionless.

"Not exactly," he replied, and Marcus had a flash of cognition.

She's a genie, he thought. *Oh my God.*

One of the...*sticking points* between the Spartans and their fellow Confederates had been the former's full on, ursine embrace of genetic engineering, cloning, and artificial birthing. Given that the said technology and any research in that vein had been so illegal in the pre-Spartan Confederation that any convicted practitioners had been internally exiled to barely inhabitable planets, both sides had been forced to conduct give and take. Or, more correctly, figure out what would piss off only 49.99% of their respective populations. Genies took their lives in their hands on almost any non-Spartan planet.

As they say in some parts of the Caliphate, 'Terra is a long way from here, while the Prophet's justice is only a breath away,' Marcus thought.

"I was not aware that you and she had any sort of connection," Du continued. "Or I would not have brought her aboard."

Marcus let out a short, bitter laugh. Again he felt Sarah's hand on his back, and he realized that a lot more hurt must have bled out than he realized.

"Not many people do," Marcus replied. "But that's not what you wanted to ask me about, Senator."

Du nodded, his face becoming grave.

"In addition to seeing your men crawling all over the ship, members of my team have brought it to my attention that Helgoland was not on our itinerary," Du said. "Given the information they've obtained from Senator Falak's detail, I have to wonder if this vessel is about to conduct a Section 195 violation."

Thank you, Islamic Caliphate, for developing a portable Qibla device, Marcus thought with a sense of resignation.

"You'd have to take that up with Captain Herrod or Mr. Federov, Senator Du," Marcus said simply.

Du snorted.

"Do you really expect me to believe that the Security Officer does not know where we are going?!"

Marcus shook his head emphatically.

"No, Senator, but I think that you are well aware as to how a ship's hierarchy is arranged. I will be happy to assist you or answer any questions with regard to security, but I cannot speak to legal matters or navigation."

Du opened his mouth, then shut it when he realized that Marcus was meeting him halfway without blatantly stating so.

"That will do, then," Du replied. "How soon do you anticipate before we arrive at our next destination, wherever that may be?"

Marcus looked at his watch.

"A little under four hours until we're in system, another three before we are in orbit," Marcus replied.

Du pursed his lips.

"*If* I am correct, you are aware that is a long way from help," Du replied, then continued before Marcus had a chance to answer. "I will have Tsubasa provide you with our team's particulars if you do not have them already. In addition, while I understand there are likely professional and *personal* reasons you may not want to share your plans with us, I would appreciate a general idea of what we can do to at least get out of your way."

Well that's a shocker, Marcus thought. *Something has him very spooked.*

"Thank you, Senator," Marcus replied out loud. "I will be happy to provide some generalities to Mr..."

"Ugaki," Du's security chief answered, extending his hand. Marcus shook it, noting the man's firm grip. "Is 0800 tomorrow a good time?"

"Probably be a better idea to make it 1000," Marcus replied. "It's been a long day, and I don't anticipate things getting any easier."

Ugaki nodded at that.

"I completely understand. I will see you tomorrow morning then," the man said, his tone pleasant.

Senator Du favored Sarah with a smile.

"I apologize, Ms. Jones. I'm sure you had other things to worry about than listening to us discuss security matters."

Sarah gave a resigned grin.

"Comes with the territory when you're around Marcus," she replied without rancor.

"We'll take no more of your time then. Good evening to you both," Du said. With a slight nod, Ugaki and he both turned and went the other direction, leaving Marcus and Sarah standing in the corridor. Once they were out of sight, Sarah turned to Marcus, her face full of concern.

"Are you okay?" she asked.

"No," Marcus said, his mouth suddenly dry. "I am not okay at all." He took a deep, shuddering breath, his hands clammy. "Let's get the hell out of this hallway before something else from my past shows up."

The two of them had barely taken four steps before Sarah's pager went off. Pulling out the flat device, she quickly scanned the information then cursed several times.

"That good?" Marcus asked tiredly, getting a weary shake.

"No," Sarah replied. "Not good at all when there's a problem down in the casinos." Stowing the flat device back into the concealed cutout on her dress, she leaned in and gave Marcus a quick kiss.

"Anything I need to worry about?" Marcus asked.

"No, Lorraine specifically told me to tell you that she's got it handled," Sarah replied. "It's almost like she knows you or something."

"Remind me to have a discussion with Ms. O'Barr about which one of us is in charge," Marcus replied.

"She said to tell you, and I quote, 'He is, but I also know he hasn't been to sleep since 0300 this morning due to someone's insatiable appetites,'" Sarah said, coloring slightly despite the triumph in her voice.

"I am so glad that you two get along like gangbusters," Marcus replied, his tone making it clear that he was anything but pleased.

"As well as she's gotten to know you in just a few months?" Sarah inquired. "If we weren't good friends, I'd have to toss her out an airlock just to be sure. Sort of what I'd like to do with Miss Old Flame back there."

Marcus's felt his face tighten, then calmed himself.

"I am sure there is a story about that," Sarah said, her own face scowling.

"She's not an old flame," Marcus snapped curtly.

Okay, maybe I said that a little more forcefully than I intended.

"No, she just apparently looks enough like one that your ever impeccable self-control fell apart. Oh, and you wanted to shoot her. Which appeared mutual."

"I'll walk with you towards the casinos," Marcus said, holding up his hand as Sarah started to protest. "I promise, I'll let Lorraine handle whatever's wrong. I'm probably not in the best shape to be making decisions right now anyway."

Sarah looked at him in genuine shock.

"I think that's the first time I've ever heard you admit something like that," she said, nodding to a group of passengers as they passed.

"Let's get out of this passageway and I'll start to explain why," Marcus said, gesturing for Sarah to lead. Ten minutes later, they found a connecting passageway that led to Corridor C. The darkened corridor began to light as they opened the hatch.

"How familiar are you with Spartan society?" Marcus asked once they were alone. "How most of them live in kibbutzim?"

"All I remember is that they have a hard on for everything martial, are almost invariably batshit crazy, and think King Dracon is a deity?" Sarah remarked sarcastically. "It says something that the overwhelming majority of them that are on this ship came with Senator Du."

Marcus gave her a wry glance.

"For shame, Ms. Jones," he said, mocking Senator Du's voice.

"That man scares me," Sarah said with a shudder that drew a look from her boyfriend. "No, no, nothing he's *done*, much less to me. Just looking at him, I always have the feeling that he's trying to figure out how to kill everyone in a given compartment."

He scares me too, and I've been sure he's up to something since he booked his ticket.

"Not usually," Marcus replied bitterly aloud. "Spartans pretty much figure that out in the first thirty seconds after they meet people, then have as much fun as a lion can have lulling the gazelles before gutting them."

Sarah turned her head to look at Marcus, then gasped in shock.

"Marcus," she whispered. "You're crying."

Surprised, Marcus reached up and realized that tears were indeed starting to run down his face. Much like the pain from a stab wound only seemed to be felt when one looked at it, the wave of grief, anger, and depression slammed into him without warning. With a sob, Marcus sagged against the nearest bulkhead, shaking uncontrollably.

"Marcus!" Sarah nearly screamed, stepping towards him.

"I'm...I'm okay," Marcus stuttered as she gathered him into her arms.

"*What happened?*" Sarah asked fiercely.

Well, here goes nothing. Best get this over with now.

"I killed Katina," Marcus said simply. He felt Sarah stiffen.

"What? Who?" she asked, trepidation in her voice.

I don't know if she doesn't understand...or doesn't want to.

"Katina. Aimi's...hell, I don't know what you call someone who comes from the same genetic map you do," Marcus said in a rush. "I shot her in the face with a flechette gun."

If Sarah had felt stiff before, her body posture suddenly became that of a person who had surprised Medusa in the shower.

100

"I understand if…"

"Just tell me why," Sarah said softly, cutting him off.

"She killed my men by blowing open a merchie's side," Marcus replied, then hurried in a rush before Sarah could interrupt again. "Then she laughed at me about it. Called me a pitiful excuse for a leader because I didn't die with them, told me I didn't have the stones to shoot her, and then tried to activate a warning beacon."

Marcus felt Sarah shift, opening her arms.

Well that was…

His thought was interrupted by her hand gently cupping his chin, pulling him around to look at her.

"If you're a poor excuse for a leader, I don't want to see what she considered a good one," Sarah said, her voice quavering with emotion. Before Marcus could react, she kissed him, wrapping her arms around him as she did so.

"Everyone has a past, Marcus," Sarah continued, her breath on his face. "All that's important to me is the man you are now, not the person you were then."

Marcus felt as if a massive weight had been lifted from his shoulders. Before he could speak, there was a diplomatic clearing of the throat a few meters behind them.

"I know that we're in a restricted passageway," Anjelica said, her tone slightly disapproving as she walked up to the duo. "But don't you think you two lovebirds should maybe get a room?"

Sarah was about to give a snarky reply when Anjelica belatedly noticed Marcus' puffy eyes.

"I'm sorry," Anjelica said. "Marcus, hon, are you okay?"

"Yes," Marcus said, mildly amused at Anjelica's protective tone. "I…"

Sarah's pager buzzed again, eliciting a string of curses.

"Okay, I have to go," she said, shaking her head. Looking left and right to ensure no one else was making an appearance, she kissed Marcus again.

"I love you," she said. "I'll see you for breakfast tomorrow. Go get some sleep."

"So what happened?" Anjelica asked after Sarah was out of earshot.

"Nothing," Marcus said.

"You know, I would think that we'd been friends long enough for you to not insult my intelligence," Anjelica replied.

"We ran into someone," Marcus said. "I'll tell you about it over tea at my place."

"Oh great, one of *those* stories," Anjelica said, rolling her eyes.

Shokaku Enters System (Holland)

Chapter 4: Bolan's Dine and Dash

The warm body slipping into the bed and the cold hand worming into his boxers brought Jason out of what had been a fitful sleep.

"Would it have killed you to warm up…mmmph," he started to say, the protest cut off by Andrea kissing him.

Okay, someone has obviously been simmering since earlier, he thought bemusedly.

"No time for whining," his wife said throatily when they came up for air. She didn't give him time to argue, kissing him as she slid over on top of him. "I hear we've got general quarters in a few and someone here spent too much time talking earlier."

"I spent too much time talking, Ice Hands?" Jason asked in mock indignation, then gasped a second later as Andrea slipped him inside of her.

"I assume," Andrea said, her voice coming out as a mixture between a moan and giggle, "the temperature now meets with your approval?"

Two hours later, the blaring alarm clock woke Jason up in a far less pleasant manner. He shut it off and yawned as Andrea stirred.

"I hate that thing," she said groggily, her head on his chest. "Explain to me again why we're getting up an hour before General Quarters?"

"Because I'd rather shamble to the Hangar Deck than get run over by a bunch of over enthusiastic ratings on their first assignment?" Jason observed.

"You have such a high opinion of the crew," Andrea replied, still under the covers.

"No, I actually remember when I was a young twenty-one year old pilot who was so happy to be underway that I would have run merrily through that bulkhead," he said, gesturing behind him, "if it meant I got to get out and fly."

Andrea gave him a wry look.

"Wait, are you trying to say that this is different from what you'd do now? Because I'm pretty sure…"

"I would use the door the designers were kind enough to put there for us," Jason said, getting undressed. Andrea rolled over in bed and gave him a predatory look.

"I figured you could start the coffee," he said with a smile, "as I'm pretty sure there will be shenanigans that we don't have time for if we try to take a shower together," Jason added with a smile.

"You don't love me," Andrea said, blushing slightly as she put her face into a mock pout.

Dammit she does that shit on purpose, Jason thought, feeling the first stirrings of arousal. *I must get ready before General Quarters. I must get ready before General Quarters.*

"Yeah, yeah, yeah," Jason said, forcing himself to step into the latrine. When he walked out five minutes later, Andrea was waiting with his cup of coffee after having finished hers.

"So what's the scoop?" Andrea asked, handing him his cup then going into the latrine. "Because all Commander Liu could tell us last night was that we would be going to General Quarters at 0300, jumping out at 0400 with an arrival time of 0800."

Jason took a sip of the coffee, grimaced at its strength, then reached for the cream and sugar.

That coffee will put some hair on your chest, he thought. *Not that I blame her—it's going to be a long day.*

"We're going back to the Solomon System," Jason said. "I'm pretty sure this time I'll actually get to see what it looks like."

Andrea stuck her head out of the latrine door.

"I really hope that didn't come out in your meeting!" she said.

"Well after being informed that my last comment put me one step away from a wheelchair for eternity, I did manage to keep that particular thought to myself," Jason observed wrily.

"Good," Andrea replied, drying her hair with a towel as she stepped back out into their main room.

Yes ladies and gentlemen, she's hot, smart, and takes showers in under five minutes. I just might keep her.

"Intel says it's going to be a carrier and three, possibly four escorts. Largest vessel should be a heavy cruiser, so looks like the Bulls and Aces are both going to get some work."

"Um, isn't that a bit much for one ship to take on?" Andrea said, her face puzzled.

"We've only got to kill or disable the carrier," Jason replied.

"So rather than me repeating my question, how about you tell me how that changes anything."

"Oh look, the Engineer doesn't know…*ow!*" Jason yelped as Andrea kicked him under the table.

"I think out of the two of us, it's far more likely that *I* stayed awake in Tactics class rather than just charming someone out of their notes," Andrea replied pointedly.

"Okay, so then you remember the problem with carriers?" Jason queried.

"You're using the singular because..?" Andrea replied, a mock look of puzzlement on her face.

"Ha ha, very funny," Jason replied. "Fine, the *particular* problem I am referring to is the load limitation on the flight deck machinery?"

Andrea nodded as she poured herself another cup of coffee.

"For planning purposes the inertia dampened limit is five times the force of gravity during launch operations," she responded. "Although I remember modern carriers being able to take as much as 8gs of acceleration or maneuvering while retracting or extending the flight deck."

"So that means you either kill your velocity or make darn sure there's nothing in front of you when you start to open the can of whupass," Jason said. "Either way, you're a big, fat target until the birds get away and the deck gets retracted."

"Still don't see why they don't cut holes in the flight deck like they used to with the original carriers," Andrea said, causing Jason to snort.

"They've tried that every few decades. Always came back to the problem of having to either thin out the deck too much or put in almost just as much machinery to move the elevators, not to mention the build time from cutting the armor patches."

Finishing the last of his coffee, Jason looked at his watch.

"Speaking of time, we have to get dressed," he said, standing up to go grab his flight suit. Stepping into it, he pondered how to truncate his explanation.

I think I got it.

"The difference between *Constitution* and a normal carrier is the launch tubes and axial hangar bay, we can recover regardless of how much acceleration she's under," Jason said. "That's *huge*, and I don't think either the XO or Captain got that until yesterday."

Andrea gave him a blank look, causing him to smile again.
"Well not such a know it all now, are you?"

"Bastard," she replied, zipping up her suit.

"In theory, we can do something that no other ship can," Jason
continued. "I call it the 'dine and dash,' the XO calls it the 'smash and
run.' Regardless of name, the effect is the same: every offensive
weapon plus the air group hits something along the same vector, then
we recover at full acceleration while heading out of system."

"Um, isn't that slightly *dangerous*," Andrea asked, her eyes
wide. "I mean, I haven't sat down with my feet dangling off the stern
lately, but I thought the thrust exhaust plumes were a little, um, *huge*
when we're at full acceleration."

Feigning hurt, Jason gave her a smile.

"You don't trust my ability to fly in between some exhaust
plumes while the ship is accelerating at almost a dozen g and
maneuvering in all three axes?" Jason replied mockingly.

"You crazy son-of-a-bitch! You're going to…"

"Tractor beams, honey," Jason said, holding up her hands.
"Remember we land via tractor beams. We got used to them on the
Argus, might as well see if the new technology works under operational
conditions."

The look on Andrea's face could have been placed next to the
phrase 'sheer terror' in a slang dictionary.

"You are still *out of your fucking mind*!" she said. "I don't care
if you land using arcane magic that requires pixie dust and human
sacrifices, those thrusters will *vaporize you* if you're just a little off!"

Jason looked at her, his face resigned.

"Well then you'll save money on the funeral costs," he replied.
His watch beeped before she could respond.

"Shit. We're late."

"What?! We are so not ending this conversation like this!"

"Well if I'm going to die, you might want to kiss me goodbye
before I leave," Jason said, turning for the hatch door.

"You *bastard*!" Andrea snapped, but came across the
compartment before he reached the hatch. Jason took two steps to meet
her part of the way, and the two kissed fiercely.

I should tell her I might die more often, he thought as they
parted.

"I love you, you lunatic," she seethed. "I am so going to beat
you when we get back here this afternoon."

107

"Ohh, I like it when you play rough," Jason said, then opened the hatch before she could respond. The two of them stepped out into the empty hallway.

"I love you too," he said lowly, touching her hand quickly before turning to head to the hangar deck.

Starview Restaurant
Titanic
0430 SST

"Marcus!" Sarah said, her voice full of shock as she looked at the two fresh, made to order omelets in front of them. Even if she hadn't seen the two cooks prepare the food right at their table, it would have been obvious from the meals' texture that they were *not* from a food replicator. "What are we doing here?"

I love it when you're surprised. Even if it means I've got to wear this monkey suit. He adjusted his tie as he leaned back into the plush leather chair, smiling mischievously as he did so. Sarah had known something was up when he'd shown up at her quarters wearing the olive green suit, khaki shirt, and black and silver tie. They'd established a tradition of eating breakfast together while underway early on in their relationship, as planning anything later never seemed to go well.

We clean up well for Oh Goddess Thirty in the morning, he thought happily as he met her eyes over the table. She had let her hair down straight, the long locks dropping halfway down the back of her blue-green formal dress. As was her usual when off duty, she'd forsaken makeup. Contrary to what most people believed, Marcus thought that made her all the more achingly beautiful.

"Whatever do you mean, Sarah?" he asked, wide-eyed.

"Either Security Officers get paid a lot better than I was led to believe, or you are out of your ever loving mind!"

The Starview Restaurant was, as its name implied, an eatery whose roof was on *Titanic*'s ventral side roughly two thirds down the liner's length from the bow. As with most Czarina Lines ships, the passenger cuisine was provided by independent sub-contractors as opposed to the company's own cooks. Getting one of the twelve private rooms was a miracle akin to surviving an hour in vacuum wearing nothing but a bathrobe for a suit and cooking pot for a helmet.

"Sometimes good deeds get rewarded rather than punished," Marcus said with a slight smile. "Or alternatively having a former Marine as the restaurant owner means you get first dibs on cancellations. Besides, aren't you glad you get to wear normal formal clothes for a change?"

"I think there have to be lots of former Marines on this ship," she said lowly. "I think there's a lot more to this story than you're telling."

"Okay, fine. Klaus *is* a former Hammerhead, but Anjelica also called in a favor," Marcus said.

"I sometimes wonder if that woman has yakuza connections," Sarah replied incredulously. "I mean, if I asked her for a unicorn she'd probably have one standing outside my cabin within a couple of days."

Marcus was about to respond when they were both interrupted by a long, low rumble that caused the water in their glasses to start vibrating. Looking up at the ceiling, they watched as the star field began to rotate above their heads.

"Starting pre-orbit burn," Marcus said, looking at his watch. *Which means we've got about an hour together before the fun and adventure starts.* He looked up to see Sarah staring captivated at the passing star field, a look of wonder on her face.

If ever I needed confirmation this was the right thing to do, he thought as he gazed at her. Resting his head on his hands, he continued to gaze at her as she giddily smiled. *I love this woman so much.*

Feeling Marcus's eyes on her, Sarah looked down with a start. Giggling, she started to blush.

"I'm sorry," she said. "I…"

"I want to spend the rest of my life with you," Marcus burst out, cutting her off.

Here goes nothing, Marcus thought, sliding out his seat and down to one knee. His heart thudded in this ears as he fished out the ring with shaking hands. Sarah gasped as she saw the box, her eyes wide.

"Oh shit!" she said, then blushed.

"Sarah Renee Jones, will you marry me?"

Sarah appeared ready to faint as she looked at the open box. Closing her eyes and clasping her hands, she gathered herself.

"Y-y-yes!" she squeaked, nodding vigorously. Marcus fought the urge to jump for joy as he gently took Sarah's shaking hand and slid the ring onto it.

"I love you Sarah," he said. Rather than responding, Sarah grabbed his face in both hands and kissed him, hard. After a moment's shock, Marcus kissed her back, wrapping his arms around her and started to pull her out of her chair. Pressing her hand to his chest, Sarah laughed throatily.

"We are not making out on this table, Marcus Martin," she said softly. "Especially not as expensive as these omelets probably were." With that, she kissed him softly one last time.

"I love you too," she said, her eyes glistening. "Now hurry up and eat."

Fifteen minutes later, after settling up the tab, the two of them walked swiftly through the crew berthing spaces hand in hand. Marcus looked at Sarah out of the corner of his eye and started to smile.

"Stop it," Sarah whispered. "Anyone seeing us is going to know what we're up to," she said as they came around the corner towards her cabin...to find Lorraine O'Barr and Aimi standing outside of her hatch. The former wore the pants version of her Czarina Lines uniform, while the latter was dressed in a simple crimson pantsuit over a plain white blouse, her hair again pinned back by two large hair spikes. More curiously than the Spartan's outfit, however, was the shoe box she was carrying.

What is she doing in crew quarters?! Marcus thought with alarm. He felt Sarah tense as well, his fiancé releasing his right hand without having to be asked.

"Senator Du insisted," Lorraine said by way of explanation. "The First Mate said it would reflect poorly on the line to refuse."

Remind me to find the First Mate a ladder to fall down, Marcus thought grimly. Aimi refused to meet his gaze, looking stone faced at the box in her hands. Meeting Lorraine's eyes, Marcus saw his subordinate nod slightly.

Lorraine made her go through the scanners, he thought, relaxing somewhat. While the security sensors weren't perfect, a trip through them at least meant that the shoebox didn't contain enough explosives to blow all four of them to kingdom come. Before the blonde woman could say anything further, Du's guard began to speak.

"Ms. Jones, I apologize for my behavior the other evening," Aimi said in a tone that made even Marcus begin to believe she was sincere. "As a token of my sincere sorrow, please accept this gift from Senator Du and myself."

How in the hell did he know already? Marcus thought, fighting to keep his face calm even as Lorraine looked at him, then Sarah's hand, then back to him with smile starting to form before she resumed her blank face. *I feel like Du's having me followed.*

"Thank you," Sarah said graciously, taking the shoe box. Not giving anyone a chance to say anything, Sarah opened it to find a pair of shoes exactly like those she wore. Before she could ask about them, Aimi began to explain.

"The shoes have been fitted with a Spartan magnetic system," the woman continued. "They will have the same effect as the safety shoes worn by Mr. Martin's security officers."

Holy shit! Marcus thought, his eyes widening. When it had come time to fit out *Titanic*'s crew, he had priced shoes with the less cumbersome Spartan technology. The cost had been prohibitive. As in, the security crew would have had to go to work naked, unarmed, and in a state of indentured servitude for several years.

To get those made by our cobbler, nevermind in less than twenty-four hours? I hope that was worth it to someone, Marcus thought.

"I see," Sarah said, her tone confused. "Thank you again."

"You are very welcome," Aimi said, then bowed. She looked like she was about to say something more, but the group was interrupted by another loud rumble and steady vibration.

"If you'll excuse us, we have to get changed," Sarah said.

"Oh, of course," Aimi replied.

"Right this way, Miss Eguchi," Lorraine said. As she and the shorter Spartan turned away, Lorraine looked at Sarah's finger, smiled, and flashed Marcus a discrete thumbs up. Marcus gave her a smile in return, then watched as the two moved off around the passageway's corner.

"I hope you understand that the mood is totally broken," Sarah said, a slight tremble in her voice. She turned towards her cabin, then realized her hands were full. Marcus reached over and grabbed the shoe box, allowing her to run her hand print on the door reader. Holding it there for an extra moment to signal she had company, Sarah stepped through the hatch before it was fully open.

Marcus followed close behind her, stepping into the moderately-sized common room at the front of the compartment. The area was dominated by a square glass table surrounded by four mahogany chairs. Combined with the surrounding red walls, the chairs gave the room a sense of warmth. A small settee was against the far bulkhead, the entryway to the bedroom just to that furniture's right.

"So last night you asked me how much I knew about Spartan culture," Sarah said, starting to unzip her dress. "Was there something in Czarina Lines' handouts about beware of Spartans bearing insanely expensive gifts? Or that they were mind readers?"

Marcus could tell Sarah was well and truly shaken.

I wonder if that was Du's intent? Shaking his head, Marcus went over to the cabin's small kitchenette and started fixing Sarah a hot chocolate.

"As far as I know, the Spartans aren't telepaths," Marcus said. "I bet if I asked Anjelica, she could tell me how he found out about me popping the question."

"Okay, that doesn't explain the one hundred thousand credit shoes," Sarah said in a rush. "Or that he sent the woman who wants to cut out your liver and feed it to you to deliver them. Which, I get that you killed someone in her family or whatever, but that bitch is a little crazy."

Marcus thought carefully how to respond to the last bit.

"She's not crazy," he said slowly, a comment that stopped Sarah in the middle of buttoning up her dress. She gave him a look of shock, shaking her head at him.

"I looked up her passenger information," Marcus began to explain. "Not only was Katina apparently from the same genetic batch, they're from the same kibbutz."

Failing to see how this explains the crazy, Marcus!" Sarah replied, drawing a slight smile from him. Seeing her face starting to color even more, he quickly continued before she actually began shouting at him. If there was one thing he'd learned in their relationship, it was that once Sarah started raising her voice things usually went downhill from there.

"Spartan society is steeped heavily in honor and revolves around their kibbutzim," Marcus said. "Your kibkin, regardless of actual bloodlines, are closer than most family on other worlds. The kibbutz elders decide who gets plots, when you get selected for planetary service, punishment, etc., etc. In return, each individual owes their first fealty to the kibbutz, their second to the planet, then the next after that to the Diaspora itself."

"So basically she's out to kill you because her kibbutz says so?! That's almost the *very definition of crazy*, Marcus!"

"Okay, you'd lay down your life for your brother and sisters," Marcus said. "How is this any less crazy?"

"Because my brother and sisters aren't pirates or whatever that *woman* was," Sarah snapped.

"You only say that because we've been raised to put the Confederation first, planet second, family next, then maybe, somewhere back there, our communities," Marcus said evenly. "You've also only heard my side of events."

"I haven't even really heard that much," Sarah observed bitterly, picking her hot chocolate up from the table. "Tell me, are there any other bodies in your past I should know about?!"

Marcus felt his stomach drop out.

"If you're reconsidering your answer earlier," he managed to choke out, his mouth dry.

Sarah turned to glare at him, then stopped. Closing her eyes, she took a deep breath and softened her features.

"Marcus, don't be an idiot," Sarah replied. "I can't think of anything in the world that would make me change my answer. I'm not just saying that, either. I'm just a little…*frightened* I guess. I've never seen a person so filled with hatred but able to control themselves with everyone else."

If you knew half the precautions I've taken or the reasons I did so, Marcus thought.

"She owes her fealty to Senator Du," Marcus replied simply. "If she embarrasses him or herself, it will bring incredible disgrace against her and her kibbutz. Given how important Du is in Spartan space, at best she would be allowed to commit suicide. At worst, she would be explicitly forbidden from seeking solace in death, shunned from all communication with her kibbutz, and exiled from her planet."

"I just love how none of this shocks you!" Sarah replied, her tone and face aghast.

"I spent three years in the Spartan sector," Marcus said. "You get used to the nuttiness. Every sector has its eccentric behavior. This one just happens to involve blood feuds, dueling, and cloning. But in return there's no megacities, you can walk the streets in total safety, and they don't just pay lip service to equality."

"Yeah, well, I think that dueling is insanely savage," Sarah muttered. "So does this mean that you can't ever go to Spartan space again?"

"There is only one man who is less likely to show up on a Spartan planet than I am," Marcus observed contemptuously.

An Unproven Concept

"Sir, the *Constitution*'s weapons are properly secured," Captain Bolan reported. "I am prepared to conduct simulated operations at this time."

"Very well, Captain Bolan," Fleet Admiral Malinverni replied with a nod. The two men stood on an observation platform overlooking a massive open compartment. Employing magnetic repulsors, the circular stand hovered roughly five meters off the deck. Beneath them, hanging in place almost like a dense fog, was a holographic projection of the Solomon System. Wide enough for eight individuals to stand comfortably and with a transparent floor, the platform currently held only Bolan, Malinverni and Rear Admiral Mategna. Beneath them, Bolan watched the *"Constitution"* swim through the projected miasma, small craft periodically ejecting from her side like hatchlings from their mother fish.

"I see that you've taken our earlier discussion to heart," Admiral Malinverni observed wryly.

"Well last time I was standing on one of these platforms, I was being loudly informed of my idiocy and incompetence for forgetting to do so," Bolan observed wryly. "I assure you the combined guidance made an impression."

"Good," Admiral Malinverni replied pleasantly. "I'm sure Rear Admiral Metagna will bring that keen insight to her next assignment in the Caliphate."

Bolan saw Metagna stiffen, her face briefly frowning before she caught herself.

Female admiral dealing with the Caliphate? That's a special corner of hell.

"I will say you have an interesting deployment plan," Malinverni continued. "Rather aggressive given the numbers, don't you think?"

"Intelligence report stated one carrier, four escorts," Bolan replied simply. "If it's two carriers, we run. If it's a carrier and more than two capital escorts, I play it by ear…"

"No need to cover contingencies," Malinverni interrupted him. "Just an observation provided with the hope you're not overcompensating for earlier sins."

"I specifically gave guidance and let my senior officers hash it out for that reason," Bolan said with a smile. "I wanted to avoid overcorrecting to negative stimuli."

"Well there shouldn't be any of that," Malinverni said pointedly, glancing at Metagna. Reaching into his pocket, he pulled out a small remote. Pressing a button, he set their platform into motion towards the hatch located two hundred meters away. Moving just fast enough to generate a steady breeze, the trio of officers passed over the *Constitution*'s holographic doppelganger once more.

"I have an assignment for you concurrent to your speed trials," Malinverni stated. "It appears that there's a problem in the Helgoland System."

"Sir?" Bolan asked, surprised. While it was not unheard of for a vessel to head to inhabited systems as part of their trials, said journeys were usually *inward*, not towards the outer planets.

"System defense picked up an unknown vessel yesterday," Malinverni continued. "Merchant ID said she was the new liner *Titanic* and she tried to access a message buoy as such, but unless Czarina Lines has given her military drives without authorization there's no way she could make it to her next plotted destination from that location."

Bolan pursed his lips.

"Do you think we have a code violation on our hands, Sir?" Bolan asked.

Malinverni gave him a pained look.

"Either that or there's a very large pirate vessel that has Czarina codes," Malinverni replied. "System Governor's nearly shit his pants though, as his sensors confirmed that the size was right for *Titanic* even if the codes are stolen."

"Isn't she one of the..." Bolan began.

"Not one of, *the* largest liner at the moment," Malinverni replied. "Although Duchess Lines are allegedly going to have a larger one in service next year."

Bolan furrowed his brow in thought.

"Sorry, I should have waited until after this exercise to spring this one on you," Malinverni said, genuinely concerned.

"Sir, what other ships are in system?"

"The heavy cruiser *Theodosius*," Malinverni replied, the platform making a quiet *clunk* as they reached the entry hatch to the holobank. "Captain Gadhavi is her master."

"I don't think I've met him," Bolan spoke cautiously.

"He came up as an engineer. Most of his time was spent in the Australasian Sector."

"Well I don't blame him asking for help," Bolan said. "*Theodosius* is a little long in tooth."

Malinverni smiled as Bolan stepped off the platform and into the hallway.

Yeah, I just basically told the Fleet CINC that water was wet, Bolan thought, cursing himself. Admiral Malinverni let him stew for a couple of seconds before breaking the awkward silence.

"Good luck, Captain Bolan," the CINC said with obvious sincerity.

"Thank you, Sir," Bolan replied, coming to attention and saluting. Malinverni returned the salute, the holobay hatch closing with both men facing each other.

Warhawk One
Constitution
0810 SST

Jason took a deep breath and attempted to calm his jitters.

Yes, my name is Jason, and launch tubes give me almost incapacitating claustrophobia, he thought, fighting the urge to shift nervously in the seat.

Don't want to start causing unnecessary wear, he thought grimly. While the fighter's cockpit had been built to fit a pilot wearing his flight armor, the accommodation's edges and armor's curves sometimes rubbed against each other in unforgiving ways. Jason settled for flexing the fingers on each hand, starting with the left where it rested on the bestudded throttle, then the right on his control stick. The motion caused a soft rattling, as the metal gauntlets that usually covered his hands rattled in their storage sheathes on his greaves.

Feel like I should be riding a charger and gripping a lance, he thought with a smile. There was a push among some pilots to go towards lighter armor for flight suits, with proponents arguing the current uniform was a last remaining vestige from the days before small craft had their own navigational shields. Any meteor or asteroid chunk strong enough to slash though a navigational shield, the thinking ran, was probably going to keep right on trucking through the transparisteel, battle armor, and pilot.

116

Oh Sweet Maker, don't let us have a malfunction, he thought, suddenly keenly aware of his bladder. The gleaming white exterior hatch beckoned to him from one hundred meters away as his fighter finished sliding into launch position. With a loud crash, he heard the interior hatch close behind him followed by the dual, sharp hissing as his flight suit and cockpit simultaneously sealed.

"Helm, Warhawk One requesting permission to launch."

"Warhawk One, Helm, you are cleared for launch," Lieutenant Commander Sakai's voice sounded in his ear.

"Roger Helm, Warhawk One has a hot cat," he said, looking at the large green light on the tube roof. Theoretically the symbol meant that his landing gear was firmly mated with the electromagnetic shuttle that was about to hurl him into the void.

Of course, if it's wrong then there's going to be a 40-ton pinball going down this tube, he thought.

"Launching," Sakai replied. Jason had just enough time to register the exterior door descending and brace himself before a dragon dropkicked him in the chest. The gleaming white of the launch tube blurred by as the starfield beyond grew larger, then he was slung away from the *Constitution*'s port side.

Holy shit I'm still getting used to this, he thought, taking a shuddering breath as he automatically put his stick over to the left. *I might put up a good front with everyone, but I keep thinking that someday that door's not going to open before the catapult fires*.

"Warhawk One, Warhawk Two is cleared and at your five o'clock," his wingman, Lieutenant Luljeta "Slush" Baris, said. Turning and looking back over his shoulder, Jason saw Baris's *Basilisk* sliding into position five kilometers abreast and three behind him to starboard.

"Warhawk One, *Constitution* One on your push."

Well there's a surprise, Jason thought, swinging his head back around forward.

"Roger *Constitution* One, Warhawk One," Jason replied, looking at his sensor display.

"I'm inbound to *Constitution*," Bolan said, the green icon that represented Pinnace One blinking a split second later. "Status report."

"I'm inbound to my hide position now," Jason replied. "All other birds are in position, Kaiju One is set."

"Asteroid field bearing zero zero zero, range one hundred kilometers," his computer interrupted loudly, its feminine voice followed by his HUD being outlined in bright red. "Initiating auto avoidance in ten seconds."

"Override," Jason barked, grabbing his stick.

"Warhawk One, did you copy my last?" Bolan asked.

No, I'm a little busy flying my bird right now, Sir, Jason thought uncharitably.

"Negative *Constitution* One," Jason replied. "Entering Beta belt."

"Roger, good hunting, data packet inbound." Bolan replied. "*Constitution* One out."

I hope I didn't sound as annoyed as I felt, Jason thought, shaking his head. *Probably hear about it later if I did.*

"Asteroid field in fifty kilometers. Please proceed with caution."

No shit, really Betty?

Solomon Beta belt was much larger than its Alpha sibling, the former a dense field of rock that stretched as far as Jason could see. Kicking both rudder pedals and yanking the stick straight backwards, he watched stars whirl by as he flipped the *Basilisk* end over end. Once the maneuver thrusters ceased firing, he advanced his throttle to full power, the three main engines roaring in unison as he brought his relative velocity down. Satisfied with the number, he repeated the maneuver and started searching for corridors between the slowly whirling planetary fragments in front of him.

Cosmic dodgeball at its finest, he thought, seeing the navigational shields spark as he began entering the belt's outer edges. Checking on Baris, he saw the junior officer's *Basilisk* surrounded by the same arcing globe that girdled his own fighter.

Never was I so happy for an automated cockpit canopy that dims that light show inside the fighter, Jason thought. *Otherwise this would be like flying an aircar through a switchback mountain pass in the middle of a blizzard. With Sisyphus' clones flinging their boulders at you.*

"Position Echo in five minutes."

Grunting, Jason whipped his fighter around a rock the size of a hovertruck. While the navigational computer did most of the work, there were limits to what even the best processor could do at his current speed.

To think they tried to have computers take over flying back in the twenty-first century, he thought, grunting again as he maneuvered around another rock. *Yeah, the meat sack in the seat does limit some things, but no one's figured out a computer that can adapt quite as fast as ye olde hairless monkey.*

"Warhawk One, Kaiju One, I have you on tally," Lieutenant Colonel Nishizawa radioed, indicating that he had visually spotted Jason's fighter.

"Roger," Jason replied, smiling slightly as he dodged another rock.

Probably not hard to spot us at a distance, Jason thought. *Only thing giving off more light than us would be a comet.*

A little under five minutes later, Jason was firing maneuver thrusters to land on the surface of an innocuous, rotating planetoid. A little over a hundred meters away, two humanoid figures bearing a massive cylindrical container over each of their broad shoulders stood crouched on the asteroid's gray, dusty surface.

*I will never get used to seeing the **Kaiju** in "golem" mode,* Jason thought. *It just looks unnatural.*

"Welcome to Point Echo," Lieutenant Colonel Nishizawa said, using his *mecha*'s direct laser communication rather than its higher signature gravity counterpart.

"Like what you've done with the place, Kaiju One," Jason replied. "I mean, the décor, the view...why, if you added a little atmosphere this would be a great resort."

Nishizawa gave a slight chuckle.

"Oh yes, an out of the way rock that is being bombarded with more radiation than a million X-rays. That's just where I want to spend my vacation."

"Every asteroid a paradise, every space flight a carnival, and every meal a delicacy," Jason snickered. "Plus would you rather be here or in a shut down floating barrel?"

Constitution
0915 SST

'Shut down' would have been a slight exaggeration when used to describe the *Constitution*'s current condition. A vessel that truly shut down in space transitioned very quickly from marvel of technology to floating coffin. Instead, the battlecruiser's situation was much more analogous to a Terran submarine that had rigged for silent running. Hovering at the "upper" limit of the Beta belt, the battlecruiser was moving at a rate that kept her tucked into geosynchronous orbit with a thirty by fifty kilometer planetoid.

119

An Unproven Concept

This is the part they always forget to mention in the holovideos, Bolan thought, looking at his helmet's internal chronometer. *I guess the interminable periods of waiting probably don't sell as well.*

The bridge was almost completely dark, the only glow the lights from each officer's internal helmets. With her drives dialed down to the bare minimum to maintain life support, every erg of energy put out by the battlecruiser's fusion bottles was more precious than gold. Which meant things like the main display were somewhere down on the priority list right next to hot food.

"I'd just like to apologize to everyone," Commander Alexander said over the battlecruiser's senior officer channel. The XO yawned before continuing. "Being bored to death was not part of our original scheme."

"Shhhh, XO, I'm about to reach the next level in *Zombocalypse Now*," someone muttered lowly, purposefully disguising their voice.

Bolan shook his head, smiling slightly.

"Since you all obviously have read the packet I sent you, thoughts on Helgoland?" he interrupted.

There was a prolonged moment of silence.

"Sir, Guns," Commander Sinclair interjected. "Do we have any better sensor data on the bogey? The thought has occurred to me she may be something much smaller and is enhancing her signature."

Bolan nearly smacked his helmet face.

Of course, he thought. *That's one solution to how someone could have built a 400,000-ton hull in secret.*

"Unless they've got military grade decoys, that's a bit of a stretch," the XO replied.

"Roger XO, but what is more likely? Someone built a backyard battlecruiser, or that they snuck a 100-ton decoy network out of the factory?"

"Actually, I'm inclined to lean towards the rogue hull," Commander Lin interjected. "Sensor decoys are controlled items. Even worse, in addition to being signed for at every stage of the supply process, they are matched to the gaining vessel."

I forgot Lin worked in acquisitions, Bolan thought appreciatively. *Glad to have an expert aboard.*

"There are lots of controlled items that end up in smugglers hands," Sinclair replied, obviously unconvinced. Lin responded before Bolan could intervene.

"I'm not saying it's impossible. I'm just saying if I had a choice between paying a two million dollar fine for failing to register a hull or doing a hard twenty-five on a prison planet for trafficking in military hardware, I think I'm going with the former."

"We'll assume full-sized hull for the moment," Bolan stated, cutting off the debate. "Guns, what would you hang on a hull that size?"

There was a short chuckle from Sinclair.

"Given her dimensions, I can put just about anything I want up to and including Class A energy batteries," Sinclair replied, drawing a snort of disbelief from Lin. "However, as Commander Lin is probably about to point out, the question would be getting the appropriate paraphernalia to support that. So we're talking rail guns, and probably broadside mounted to save weight."

"Broadside?"

"Well it's what they did with *Titanic* and the savings in weight and complexity would still be the same factors. It's not like I'm planning on fighting warships, so why worry about turrets?"

Bolan was about to respond when Lieutenant Boyles interrupted the conversation.

"Hyperspace footprint! Bearing oh one zero, range one zero astronomical units!"

Showtime, Bolan thought, pressing the buttons on the side of his screen to bring up a schematic of the entire Solomon system. Viewed in two dimensions, Solomon' twin belts served as handy dividing lines for the star's six planets, with two planets inside each belt and the last duo almost equidistant outside of Beta. Currently *Constitution* had the fourth planet at bearing two two zero, the fifth planet at bearing zero three zero, and the outermost sixth planet at two oh oh.

Clear path to run, but nothing to hide behind if we take damage, Bolan thought as he watched all three planets moving clockwise relative to *Constitution*'s current heading along their orbital paths.

"Looks like you guessed right on which side of the system the battle group would come in, XO," Bolan observed. "Let's hope you and Warhawk One keep that streak going."

"Thank you, Sir," Commander Alexander replied.

"Okay Sensors, let's cue up the brass section for this particular orchestra," Bolan said. "Aye aye, Sir," Boyles replied, pressing the necessary buttons on her console.

Now we wait, he thought. *Again.*

An Unproven Concept

Warhawk One
0945 SST

"Apparently the mirror balls still work," Jason muttered to himself. Remote sensors, often called mirror balls for their resemblance to a certain twentieth century artifact, were self-contained sensor arrays. Relatively cheap, they were considered expendable items whose miniature fusion reactors allowed them to function for up to a full decade. Thankfully the ones the Explorer Corps had scattered throughout the Solomon System were nowhere near that old, meaning that with a little bit of hacking the *Constitution* was able to use them to generate a tactical picture without activating her own sensors. Still, Jason definitely noted the lag between their activation and the update of his tactical screens.

Eight contacts?! he thought with some alarm. *That's not what the threat briefing said.*

"Kaiju One, you getting...*holy shit!*" Jason said, the updating tactical screens belatedly providing the composition of the incoming task force.

Two capital class signatures, two cruisers, and a passel of tin cans?! Jason thought.

"Roger Warhawk, I am seeing the update," Nishizawa said in a voice that was far too calm.

"Looks like we're going to be getting out of system," Jason replied. "The plan called for the heaviest thing we fight being a cruiser."

"*Constitution* has not sent the recall signal yet," Nishizawa replied. "We might not be running."

Oh, we're running. There's no way we're fighting two capital ships.

"Contacts identified," his computer intoned. Pressing a button on his control, Jason changed his display...and became even more convinced staying would be insanity.

"I'm reading one *Shokaku*, one *Stalingrad*, an *Exeter*, an *Atlanta*, and five tin cans," Nishizawa said. "Does your computer say the same?"

Jason shook his head at the *mecha* commander's steadfastness.

"Mine's showing the *Exeter*-class as a second *Atlanta* but, yes, the analysis still comes out as 'let's get the fuck out of here.'"

122

"Oh ye of little faith," Nishizawa said, and Jason suddenly realized the Marine was looking forward to the upcoming fight.
The man is mad.

In actuality, Jason's computer was the more accurate. *Shokaku*, nameship of her class, had entered into the system in the center of a wedge formation. Forming the wedge's tip from port to starboard were the destroyers *Anu Nayyar*, *Marie Rossie*, and *Harpy*. Roughly eight thousand kilometers behind the three destroyers were five more vessels in line abreast, with the destroyers *Joseph Galloway* and *Samuel B. Roberts* on the flanks, the heavy cruisers *Paris* and *Sarajevo* inboard of them, then *Shokaku* and the battlecruiser *Asculum*. While lacking the sheer ability to trade punches with a line of battle, the strike group possessed an almost optimal combination of speed and firepower. Almost as one, the nine vessels rotated their prows one hundred and eighty degrees, then engaged maximum thrust to begin killing their velocity into the system.

"Okay, looks like we've got two *Rescorla* and one *Harpy*-class in the lead, a pair of *Batras* behind them, with two *Atlantas* to go with the *Stalingrad* and *Shokaku*," Jason said, attempting to confirm the class types his computer was now displaying after processing the new sensor data.
Nothing like a deceleration bloom to clear out the confusion. Pretty sure everyone on this side of the primary saw those engine blasts, Jason thought, referring to each Confederation ship class' unique engine signatures. Not that I blame them for decelerating. It was either kill speed or get four thousand klicks over the ecliptic to get away from this belt.
"*Batras* are going to be a bit of a problem," Nishizawa observed, causing Jason to laugh sharply.
"Yeah, that's an understatement," he replied. "I was there when they did the concept test for that design. Nothing but flak railguns and short-range missiles. Won't matter if someone doesn't get the other escorts away from…"
"Multiple contacts detected," his computer interrupted. Jason looked at the screen to see multiple yellow symbols spring into life around the battlecruiser and two heavies. After a moment each icon grew a line symbolizing their speed and vector.

123

Drone launch, he thought. Counting quickly, he noted that there were twenty of the drones moving out in crescent-shaped patter ahead of the task group.

"Looks like someone out there doesn't like being painted by sensors while being stuck in the dark," Nishizawa observed dryly.

"Guess we know that Lieutenant Boyles is just as good at encryption as she is at hacking mirrorballs," Jason replied. Left alone the mirrorballs' data would have been accessible to all Confederation vessels. Boyles had rigged the signals to appear distorted on any computer that did not enter the correct alpha-numerical sequence when trying to access the arrays' data. Like all codes, the encryption could be broken with enough time and effort, but Boyles had been reasonably certain doing so would take a couple hours at least.

If we're still here in a couple of hours, it will mean things went really, really bad, Jason thought, glancing at his watch. Looking over at his comms board, he checked once more to see if the *Constitution* had sent the recall order. With his communications screen blank, Jason turned back to his tactical overlay.

Trust the plan...trust the plan..., he reminded himself mentally.

"Okay Kaiju One, we'll be back," Jason said. "Slush, let's go earn our pay."

Pulling back on the stick and firing his maneuvering thrusters, Jason sprung up from the asteroid in a cloud of dust. Once he had gained a hundred meters in relative altitude, he turned to make sure Warhawk Two had also separated cleanly from the spinning rock. Seeing that Slush was tucked into her proper spot, he began gradually shoving his throttle forward, the acceleration pressing him firmly back into his seat.

"Designate drone contacts, alpha numerical format, letter code November," Jason said calmly. After a couple heartbeats, the accelerating drone contacts were numbered 1N to 20N from left to right on Jason's screen.

"Push designation on tactical net, full power," Jason said. "Activate sensors, full power."

"Requested operation will violate EMCON," the computer stated, referring to the 'emissions control' profile the Warhawks had been operating under.

"Override," Jason replied, kicking himself for not having changed profiles before lifting off.

Sure it's the equivalent of running through a dark room with pants aflame and a whooping siren on my head, but that's the whole point, Jason thought. *Although just to be on the safe side…*

"Evasive pattern Sierra, four g limit, followed by pattern Lima after two minutes," Jason ordered. Theoretically he was well out of weapons range from the onrushing task group, but rail slugs were cheap.

"Okay Slush, you've got targets 11 and 12 November," Jason ordered, using the phonetic code for the letter 'N.' "I've got 9 and 10 November. Let's get our sticks out."

"Warhawk One, Aces Five, we're after 1 through 8," his comms crackled, informing him that VF(S)-41's second flight was also going after the drones.

This is going to piss some folks off, Jason thought with a grunt as his fighter suddenly jinked downward, then to starboard, then added additional thrust. As he watched, the drones acceleration lines began to decrease, indicating that their operators were trying to reduce the closing speed.

Burn that maneuvering fuel, boys, Jason thought. *Not going to make a wit of difference with the lag time.*

"Targeting lock detected," the computer intoned, followed by 9 November starting to flash a faded crimson.

"Heads up folks, they've snuck a couple of rams in with the sheep," Jason warned over the comm. With his thumb he flicked his weapons selector switch from the *Basilisk*'s laser cannon to missiles. There was a slight rumble behind him as the fighter's weapon magazine moved from standby to active, then checked the eight *Asp* missiles within its confines.

Come on, come on, Jason thought, looking towards the main task group. *You've got at least six fighters out here about to cut your drones in half and you're not launching yet?* On one hand Jason could see why the *Shokaku* was hesitating to unload her brood. It was far easier for the carrier to change her vector and velocity towards a new threat then have her fighters burn precious thruster fuel doing so.

*I mean, it's obvious we're nothing but **Basilisks** out here thanks to our acceleration*, Jason thought, *but still—we're about to **stab you in the eye with a pencil**.*

As if on cue, his earphones began echoing with a low, pulsing tone that indicated he had reached maximum *Asp* range. Checking the probable hit numbers, he gave a slight chuckle that was cut off by another evasive maneuver.

Well, maybe not quite stabbing yet, he thought. *Not at this range.*

"Aces Five, Fox One."

Although apparently some of us are willing to take ten percent odds as good enough, Jason thought wryly.

Panning the tactical display over, Jason watched as Aces Five's four missiles headed towards their intended prey, the vector lines seemingly trebling in an instant. Contacts 1N and 2N seemed to tremble slightly as their operators engaged the onboard electronic countermeasures (ECM). As the *Asp*s closed, both drones' headings and velocity radically changed, their courses finally settling roughly ninety degrees to starboard of their original path.

That's a pretty weak evasive maneuv...whoops, too soon. The drone operator had been being cagey, forcing the oncoming missiles to burn some of their own maneuver fuel do to their much higher closing velocity. As the *Asp*'s had reoriented on their new collision course, 1N and 2N had suddenly begun performing like hooked marlins on a line, going through radical gyrations. In the case of 1N the tactics worked, the pair of *Asp* that were locked onto it exhausting their ability to change course, hurtling past their prey, then self-destructing. 2N was not so fortunate, its participation in the exercise terminating in a flash of simulated brilliance.

So you just burned half your ordnance on a pair of drones, Jason thought angrily. *The AAR is not going to be your best life experience.* Looking at his display, he watched as 9N began accelerating towards him again while 10N pointed its nose 90 degrees "down" from the ecliptic and began accelerating once more.

*Why yes, if I were dumb enough to chase the **unarmed** drone, this would perhaps end poorly*, Jason thought, once again shoving his throttle forward. *But now I'm about to demonstrate drone killing 101.* Gaining velocity, he brought his throttle back to neutral and punched off a decoy each to his starboard and port.

One thousand...two thousand...go. Pushing the stick forward, he rotated the *Basilisk* into a tumble, maximizing his shields. As he had guessed, the next couple of seconds confirmed that 9N was armed with energy weapons, as the port decoy was converted to simulated slag and his dorsal shields took a blow that dropped them to ten percent.

Oh wow, they just burned a crapload of that thing's energy reservoir firing at full charge, Jason marveled, as the weapons tone in his ear grew into a screaming siren song. *Not going to be much use for recon even if I mess this up, plus that's at least five seconds before they can fire again without melting the cannons.*

Continuing his rotation to bring his undamaged forward shields towards the drone, Jason punched off a single *Asp* as 9N's weapons cooled. Feeling the vibration as his missile magazine rotated, Jason checked to make sure the weapon separated and ignited before barrel rolling his fighter. The gambit was not a minute too soon, the starboard decoy "vanishing" in a hail of energy bolts that passed through where his fighter had been.

Never get into a head on run with a drone, Jason thought. *The computer's got nothing to lose.*

The lag between the drone's sensors perceiving something, relaying it back, and the drone operator initiating maneuvers meant that the *Asp* had covered half of the range to impact before 9N changed its velocity or heading. Although the drone's subsequent evasion was valiant, it was no match for its opponent despite cutting a corner that would have turned any human pilot to a strawberry-tinged paste. The bright, brief flash on his canopy plus the disappearing contact told Jason that *Camelot*'s computers had adjudicated 9N's destruction.

"Warhawk One, splash 9N," Jason transmitted, pushing the stick forward to stand the *Basilisk* on its nose. "Going after 10N." He looked at his display and was shocked to see 11N and 12N still active and headed back towards the task group, Slush in hot pursuit.

"Slush what's your status?" he asked, bringing the *Basilisk*'s nose around to track 10N.

"11N was a missile drone," Slush replied angrily. "I am Winchester decoys, have only my port cannon, no further damage."

Oh damn, that sounds like it was all bad, Jason thought. 'Winchester' meant that Slush was completely empty on decoys, plus burning out a cannon shooting at a missile meant she'd been lucky to survive the encounter.

"New contacts detected."

Looking at his screen, Jason fought back the urge to curse.

"Break contact *now*, Warhawk Two," he ordered. "Company's coming, and they're not bringing wine."

Constitution
1005 SST

"*Shokaku* is launching," Boyles reported. "I count eighteen contacts at maximum acceleration towards Warhawk One and Aces Five."

"Roger," Bolan said, sitting more erect in his chair. "Prepare to swim decoys at Points Golf and Baker on my mark."

Looking at his projected helmet screen, Bolan started to chew his lip.

Point Golf is at bearing oh seven five relative from that carrier and just about 300,000 kilometers away, he mused, mentally doing the tactical geometry. *Baker is about two nine zero and 400,000 kilometers away. If I was an escort commander and had two large contacts appear on both my flanks...*

"Sensors, did you get a profile reading when she started launch operations?" Commander Sinclair asked, startling Bolan out of his reverie. Boyles looked at the other officer for a moment as if she didn't understand the question, then turned back to her screen.

"Okay Guns, even I'm at a loss," Bolan said, turning towards Sinclair.

"Sir, we know where we are thanks to the navigational fixes," Sinclair said. "If we have a solid sensor picture of what that carrier looks like when she launches, we'll have a really good idea where she'll be going for about five minutes."

"With the lag time off the mirrorballs, we might be swinging at empty space by the time the slugs get there," Commander Alexander interjected. "Better to wait for her to try and pass over the belt as planned."

"Except if we hit and cripple her, we can focus on the screen with the main *and* secondaries and simultaneously finish the carrier with missiles."

"Sir, I don't think it's a good idea to change the plan with Warhawk about to engage," the XO replied, concern in his voice.

No plan survives first contact, and Sinclair's got a huge point, Bolan thought.

"Sensors, do we have the data?"

"Aye Sir, we do," Boyles replied, having completely missed the debate occurring on the senior officer's channel.

"Prepare to radiate on my mark," Bolan stated. "Guns, set the velocity to allow you three salvoes, maximum spread on the railguns' current charge. Thin as the *Shokaku*'s hull is we don't need to drive nails through ironbark."

"Aye aye, Captain," Sinclair said, touching his screen.

"Engineering, I'm going to need all the juice you've got once we start this dance," Bolan stated. "Helm, I don't want to make the same mistake we're pretty sure that carrier's about to make. Once we're clear of the rocks, I don't want us holding the same course for more than twenty seconds. It'd be rather embarrassing to have a *Stalingrad* outshoot us."

"Aye aye, Sir," Sakai and Liu replied in unison.

"Comms, once we go active you need to open a channel to Warhawk One so the XO can inform him of the changes," Bolan stated, knowing Alexander would pick up on the implied task in his statement. He quickly zoomed in on Warhawk One's position, noting the swarm of fighters that seemed to be concentrating towards Warhawk One's icon.

"That is, assuming Warhawk One isn't knocked out at that point," he said lowly.

Warhawk One
1010 SST

Jason would have been less than happy about Bolan's doubt if he'd known about it. Despite the eight *Basilisk*s hot on Slush and his tail, he was confident that the situation was well in hand.

"My aft shields are at ten percent!" Slush said, her voice several octaves higher than normal.

Well no one told you to go charging an entire task group, Jason thought bitterly.

"Swing your nose around again," Jason replied out loud. He followed his own advice, quickly kicking the fighter's orientation around while moving four thousand meters down ecliptic. His prudence was rewarded as numerous energy bolts passed overhead, leading to him initiating a fifty kilometer sideslip that allowed him to evade another group of blasts while looking at Slush's fighter. Several bright flashes along her shields told him that his wingman was not nearly as instinctive in her maneuvers.

129

An Unproven Concept

We are going to have a nice, detailed discussion about tactics for the next few weeks, Jason thought. Since every time the pair rotated they lost relative velocity, the constant game of having to reorient meant their eight pursuers were closing rapidly into missile range.

"Two minutes to safety hazard line," his computer intoned. "Reduce velocity to move hazard line intersect point."

Gotta love those exercise rules, Jason thought. While ten percent real world casualties were considered acceptable for starfighter versus starfighter combat, maneuvering around asteroids meant some artificial rules were put into place to prevent massive chaos.

Because there's no way a bunch of fighter pilots would let their egos lead them into doing things like going into an asteroid belt at unsafe speeds, Jason thought. *Or having a dogfight through the rocks.*

"Kaiju One, ol' Slush is getting pummeled and I'm two minutes out," Jason said. "I guess this as good as it gets."

"Yes, seeing as Warhawk Two dodges about as well as I sing," Nishizawa replied back teasingly. "I've got telemetry handshake, ready on your mark."

"In ten ... nine ... eight ... seven ... six ... five ... four ... three ... two ... mark!"

Unknown to Jason, his antagonists were from VF(S)-75, the "Dire Guards." Having seen the destruction of 9 and 10N, Dire One had realized that the opposing *Basilisk* was obviously flown by someone who knew what the hell they were doing. Now, as she watched the two fighters running for the asteroid belt, Dire One let a slight smile cross her thin, avian face.

"Powers to your shields, gents. You know what happens when you've got a pair of rats corn...*what the fuck?!*"

What had inspired Dire One's cursing was the fact particularly large asteroid bearing two nine oh relative had seemingly exploded. Then, after the computer had a moment to go through its protocols, it realized that the "fragments" were actually missiles. The entire swarm of which had started accelerating at a rate that, when combined with her closing speed, meant she had exactly thirty seconds to figure out how to avoid flinging herself into their deadly cloud. Stamping on her rudder pedals and hauling the stick around, Dire One's vision constricted to a single pinpoint of light, the computer's warning about over-g slipping to a distant caterwaul as she barely maintained consciousness.

Jason's face was set in a feral grin as he mirrored Dire One's maneuver, albeit at a much lower g. He fired his thrusters to kill his velocity, stopping fifteen seconds short of where *Camelot*'s computer would have forced him to turn.

Bet you didn't see that coming, did you? he thought, giggling maniacally.

The cylinders on the pair of *Kaiju*s were part of their modular weapons suite, meaning they could mount anything from indirect fire rockets to line of sight guided weapons. In this case, the choice had been *Gungnir* ground-to-space missiles. Named for Odin's legendary spear, the *Gungnir*'s initial stage was intended to get it clear of both atmosphere and gravity. In the vacuum of space, this translated to a truly horrific initial acceleration, while the extensive onboard ECM suite convinced Dire One's sensors that she faced sixty-four warheads rather than sixteen.

I almost feel sorry for those poor bastards. Almost. Looking at the enemy fighter, Jason saw repeated gravitational signals. One didn't have to be telepathic to imagine that the majority of them were panicked reports of what had just transpired.

"Kaiju One at your seven o'clock," Jason's headphones crackled. Turning, he saw the two rapidly accelerating *mecha* firing their thrusters to join up in formation with Slush and him. In their fighter mode, the *Kaiju*'s platypus noses, canards, shoulder mounted railguns, curved fuselage, and canted twin tails made them look like an aerospace genetic experiment gone wrong.

"Roger Kaiju," Jason said. "Hope you didn't sign a hand receipt for those things, as I don't think anyone's going to find that particular rock without a long search."

"In combat those are single use," Nishizawa replied easily. "In training, they have a locator beacon that will activate when the exercise is over."

On his tactical screen, the *Gungnir* had finally closed to a range that forced their eight targets to react. Looking like a starburst, the gaggle of *Basilisk*'s went into various directions, deploying decoys as they evaded. To Jason's morbid fascination, only two of the *Gungnir*s took the bait.

This is why you don't go dirtside without jammer support, he thought grimly. *Those big ass missiles pack a shitload of electronics.*

"Kaiju One, Fox One," Nishizawa said, the call being echoed a moment later by his wingman.

Forty-five thousand kilometers in front of them, the deadly ballot played out to its conclusion. The Direguard *Basilisk*s proceeded to open fire with their laser cannon, the energy weapons strobing azure lines on Jason's tactical display. This method worked slightly better, leaving only eight of the missiles to impact their targets. With the inevitable double targeting, three *Basilisk*'s survived the *Gungnir* onslaught…only to be subjected to a storm of *Asps* as Kaiju One and Two's missiles arrived. Caught flatfooted, the three fighters quickly blinked out.

Jason exhaled a breath he didn't realize he was holding.

That worked like a charm, he thought, closing his eyes for a moment.

"Warhawk One, destroyers inbound!" Slush stated, a moment before his own sensors warned him he was being painted by shipboard fire control. Both *Rescorla*-class destroyers and a single *Batra* had left the formation and were starting to accelerate towards Point Echo.

*They think the **Gungnirs** came from a ship*, Jason thought, bringing the nose around yet again. The *Basilisk* and *Kaiju* could all outrun the destroyers, but the margin was not as great as Jason would have liked.

*Be great if the **Constitution** joined this party*, he thought, suddenly feeling every minute of the fight in his aching muscles.

Constitution
1015 SST

"All enemy vessels have gone active sensors at full power," Boyles observed crisply.

Well that was probably a most unpleasant shock, Bolan thought as he gave Boyles a nod of acknowledgment. *Almost feel like we should be broadcasting 'Crecy! Crecy! Crecy!' on all channels.*

Shaking his head at the mental tangent, Bolan continued to look at the fight's geometry as it was projected onto his small screen.

"How long until we have sensor IDs?" he asked Boyles.

"Two minutes or less, Sir."

"Thank you, Sensors," Bolan replied.

The incoming task group had engaged in another massive velocity kill, approaching the Beta belt far more cautiously after the Direguards' decimation. Having detached the three destroyers, the main body had changed their formation into a loose circle around the *Shokaku*, with one heavy cruiser and the remaining tin cans forming one side, the *Stalingrad*-class vessel and the other cruiser the other. It was a very conservative deployment, and Bolan did not blame whomever was commanding that task group one bit.

Let's encourage some more of that trepidation, Bolan thought.

"Swim the decoy at Point Golf, hold the one at Baker," Bolan ordered.

"Aye aye," Boyles said, touching her console.

With their sensors going active, the residual noise should cover the burst transmissions.

"Swimming" was shorthand for a slow, minimal acceleration of a decoy or other countermeasure. In this case, the intent was for Boyles to briefly expose one of the *Constitution*'s decoys from where it currently lurked in the shadow of Solomon 4. Coated in highly reflective material, studded with signal amplifiers, and equipped with an array of computers that were capable of ensuring its maneuvers matched those of the parent ship, the one hundred meter long device was extremely convincing at long range or in a degraded sensor environment.

"Warhawk One and Aces Five are continuing towards Solomon 4," Lieutenant Herrod stated. "The Bulls are joining."

Selling the decoy, Bolan thought with a slight smile. To hostile sensors, it would likely appear that the group of fighters were beating a retreat towards a carrier to refuel and rearm.

"Well *that* wasn't part of the plan," Commander Alexander observed drily.

"Just wait, XO…just wait."

"Enemy battlecruiser coming about," Boyles said breathlessly. "Computer has positive ID as the *Asculum*, enemy cruisers are the *Paris* and *Sarajevo*, and destroyers are the *Nayyar*, *Rossie*, *Harpy*, *Galloway*, and *Roberts*."

Bolan took a moment to go through his mental rolodex and figure out if he knew any of the opposing captains. While there was a slight thread of possible cognition with regards to the *Asculum*, he could not fully grasp it.

Not important right now anyway, he thought.

"Not sure I'd send a battlecruiser after a carrier," Alexander observed.

"I'd send one to try and flush said carrier before I committed the air group," Bolan replied. "Especially if the *Galloway* peels off to give her some extra anti-fighter support."

As if on cue, Boyles interrupted their discussion.

"Destroyers are breaking off from approaching Point Echo."

Looking at the velocity lines, Bolan could see that his Sensors officer's analysis appeared quite sound. The three tin cans' icons were moving off to the *Constitution*'s port bow, paralleling the forward edge of the Beta belt in a path that would lead to their gradually intersecting with the *Asculum*'s current course. The distance between the four vessels and the *Shokaku*, already at a little over one hundred thousand kilometers, was starting to rapidly increase as the vessels accelerated.

"Three dimensional view, main screen," Bolan ordered, the fight beginning to get so complicated he couldn't follow it on his helmet screen anymore. After a moment, the main display snapped to life, confirming that the *Asculum* and her three accompanying destroyers were "climbing" to gain sufficient distance above the ecliptic plane to allow their clearance of the Beta belt. This maneuver would simultaneously allow them to peer "behind" Solomon 4 while putting them in position to accelerate at maximum power without fear of an asteroid collision.

That's the bad thing about hiding behind a planet on a three dimensional chess board. While it was entirely possible to turn and flee "down" ecliptic, the acceleration curve was usually much harsher unless a ship was running towards the system primary. There were many, many reasons why accelerating to hyperspace towards a star was a bad idea.

"Sensors, let's show them what they hope to see with that decoy," Bolan said. "Don't run too fast, we still want them to think it's a carrier."

"Aye aye, Captain," Boyles said, her tone conveying some annoyance at being told how to suck eggs.

"Why isn't that carrier launching?" Bolan asked on the command net.

"CAG mentioned something about a carrier possibly switching ordnance around if she loses too many fighters," Alexander replied. "While the *Thunderchief* isn't great at space combat, it beats a whole lot of jack and shit."

"How long will it take them to switch ordnance?"

"Best guess Commander Owderkirk had was five to ten minutes depending on what the ship was doing. That massive deceleration probably added another five minutes at least."

Yes, screwing around with two thousand kilogram ordnance at eight g is a recipe to have someone turned into Mrs. Newton's Ol' Time Spaghetti Sauce, Bolan thought.

"Point Baker decoy, three quarters acceleration," Bolan ordered. "Tell Warhawk One to attack the destroyers."

Warhawk One
1020 SST

"You've got to be shitting me. You have absolutely got to be shitting me," Jason muttered darkly, looking as the burst transmission scrolled a second time across his helmet.

"Acknowledge receipt," he bit out. "Start a thirty second timer."

I'll be damned if I'm going to hurry up and commit suicide, he thought. With the twenty-four *Thunderchiefs*, ten *Basilisks*, and eight *Kaiju* currently trailing his craft he technically had enough firepower to see off all three destroyers. Of course, there would be heavy casualties among his air group, and that was even before one factored in the battlecruiser charging forward with the proverbial bone in her teeth.

His communicator buzzed again, this time with a single word: EXPEDITE.

"Oh fuck you! Fuck you, Captain Bolan!" he seethed. Reaching down, he toggled his push to talk.

"Okay Warhawks, looks like we get to play kick the tin cans. Aces One, Bulls One, I'm going to need you to bring your folks all around Solomon 4."

"Warhawk One, Bulls One, you came in broken. Did you just state we're going to attack that *Batra* head on?"

Easy Flash, don't make me rip your head off over the command net, Jason thought.

"Well as long as you blokes don't drop your bundle, I'm not seeing the problem," Commander Tice chimed in. "Aces and Kaiju have already drawn blood, can't imagine the Moo Cows are scared of a teensy, weensy destroyer. We'll even hold your hands."

Thank you, Catnip, Jason thought with a grim smile.

"Right then, let's get on with it," Gordon spat out. "Wouldn't want Aces One to get the impression they have done some work today."

"Pushing the ID relay from *Constitution*," Jason said, sending the information as he began designating targets for the air group's attack. "Priority target is the *Galloway*, the other two tin cans should be cake once we get her taken down."

"This is Bulls, roger," Gordon replied, his voice still surly.

135

"Aces roger."

"Warhawk One, Kaiju One. Do you want us to form up with Aces for flak suppression or…"

"Holy shit, look at that bastard!" someone cut off Nishizawa. Jason saw what had caused the consternation, as the *Asculum* suddenly leapt forward. He closed his eyes and muttered a curse.

"Okay, she's selling out to catch up with the destroyers," Jason said, referring to the transferring of almost all power to the battlecruiser's thrusters. It was an incredibly dangerous gambit, as it meant that the warship had dumped her shields.

Not a bad call when you're only facing starfighters, Jason thought. *Means it's going to be a bit hard to get turned back around when fucking Bolan decides to attack.*

"Bulls are all formed up," Gordon stated.

"I've still got a couple of stragglers, but we can get some flak beat down with what Kaiju has at hand."

"Okay, let's use the belt to our advantage. Follow me," Jason said, leading the assembled group into a hard port turn.

Constitution
1025 SST

"*Paris* and *Sarajevo* are accelerating towards Point Baker," Boyles said.

"Rather messed up sending a pair of heavy cruisers to take on a capital…" Commander Alexander started to observe before Boyles cut him off.

"Launch profile!" she sang out. "Going active!"

"Target bearing oh three zero! Range 150,000 kilometers!" Sinclair said.

Oh wow, this is so far outside of effective range it's not even funny, Bolan thought.

"Open fire," Bolan barked. "Up four zero degrees, port two zero degrees, all ahead flank!"

From the *Shokaku*'s perspective, it was as if the Beta belt had suddenly sprouted an angry, spitting warship from almost dead ahead. In the midst of a launch, the carrier's captain could only watch as the new contact accelerated towards his vessel, three salvoes rippling from her in quick succession. With less than two minutes until impact and four minutes until the vessel completed her launch cycle, the carrier captain found himself hung on the horns of an awful dilemma.

This issue was nothing compared to that facing the members of *Shokaku's* screen. The *Paris* and *Sarajevo* were confronted with two capital ship contacts. While the one currently charging down the *Shokaku's* throat was apparently the greater threat due to its opening fire, the one coming in from the task group's port bow was both closer and accelerating. Indeed, if left unmolested the vessel would pass "beneath" the carrier well within weapons range. It was possible to slow the port contact while leaving the starboard to the carrier's *Thunderchiefs*, but only if the two cruisers committed immediately.

Bolan watched as the two cruisers made their choice, the *Constitution's* acceleration pressing him deep into his chair. The bridge's normal lighting had still not been restored, Liu and Sakai shunting every bit of energy into charging the battlecruiser's shields and her engines.

"Thirty seconds until impact," Sinclair said, his voice trembling with excitement. Bolan watched as the flock of simulated slugs arced towards the *Shokaku*. The carrier was in a gentle turn, red icons beginning to spill from her hull and accelerate towards the *Constitution*.

Those are about to be some very angry stick monkeys, Bolan thought, watching as the timer ran through the last ten seconds.

The first twelve slugs missed completely, the *Camelot's* computers having estimated that Sinclair had failed to account for the *Shokaku's* change in orientation. This was more than made up for by the next salvo, which the exercise computers judged to have put over half of the depleted uranium penetrators into the carrier's wide open flight deck. If it had been actual combat rather than electrons, the resultant impact would have torn the extended flight deck from the carrier's hulls, destroyed her bridge, wrecked half her engines, and ignited the thruster fuel she maintained for her air group. Rather than a raging, space going cauldron, the exercise computers quickly rendered the carrier a derelict, disabling almost all of her non-essential systems. In the same instance, half of the *Thunderchiefs* that were still accelerating away from her hull were adjudicated to have been destroyed by spraying spall and debris.

"Enemy carrier is crippled," Boyles stated simply as the *Shokaku*'s icon became a deep amber just as the third salvo missed ahead.

Bolan felt a giddy sense of exuberance that he forced back into himself.

Bitch ain't dead yet, he thought.

"Guns, secondaries on the *Harpy* and *Roberts*," Bolan said, seeing the two tin cans starting to accelerate towards the battlecruiser. "Mains on the *Paris* and *Sarajevo*."

"Aye aye, Sir," Sinclair said. The two heavy cruisers had reversed their orientation and were also attempting to close the range while avoiding providing Sinclair with another easy solution. The resultant evasive maneuvers negatively affected their ability to close the range, and Bolan watched as their predicted vector lines slid slowly down *Constitution*'s starboard side, finally settling at a point that indicated their pursuit would eventually become a stern chase.

*Of course, they're **Atlantas**,* Bolan thought grimly. *We're going to beat them to the carrier, might even beat them to hyperspace, but it's going to be close.*

"Commander Liu, energy status?" Bolan grunted as Sakai put the *Constitution* through her own quick series of course changes. The prudence in doing so became apparent a moment later, as the *Asculum* fired her own salvo from just over 250,000 kilometers.

"I'm not diverting any power to the catapults, so I am not sure how well our fix would work if we still had to launch fighters," Liu said. "But so far it's working very well, almost to the point that I'd codify it as an emergency fix going forward."

Bolan felt some satisfaction at the engineer's report.

"Well then you and the XO can get cracking on that once we're out of here," Bolan replied.

"Engaging enemy destroyers," Sinclair reported.

A moment later, energy discharges stabbed out from the *Constitution* at the charging *Harpy* and *Roberts*. The former's design had been geared towards eliminating hostile counterparts in a hypothetical fleet engagement. As such, she possessed an extensive energy battery of her own but few of the unguided torpedoes that were a destroyer's best weapon against heavy ships. Thus, even as her own gunnery officer opened fire at the onrushing *Constitution*, it was more out of desperation rather than any real expected effects. In any event, *Harpy*'s shielding was quickly ravished by Sinclair's initial burst of microwave energy, with her captain's rapid attempt to rotate an undamaged shield being undone by Sinclair's shrewd staggering. Hit full on, the *Camelot*'s computers adjudicated that while the vessel herself had not been destroyed, the entire crew in her forward compartments would have been cooked like some ancient Terran delicacy.

"Missiles inbound!" Boyles warned, her voice steady. Bolan took his focus from the *Harpy* to where the *Paris* and *Sarajevo* had just sprouted twenty-four red dots apiece. Boyles displayed the impact countdown before he even got a chance to ask. The glowing 8:00 signifying eight minutes caused him to shake his head.

Maximum range launch, ballistic profile, he thought. *Just trying to make us burn energy and hope they get lucky.* He turned back just in time to see Sinclair hammer the *Harpy* with another blast, the gunnery officer ignoring the rapidly approaching *Roberts*.

"Guns, she's a hulk," he said gently. "I don't want to get everything topside flayed by that flak can."

"Aye aye," Sinclair said sheepishly. If they'd not had their helmets on, Bolan was pretty sure the man would have blushed slightly at the mild rebuke.

*Yes, one of the knocks against the **Batra** class is their utter uselessness in situations like this, but I also don't want that little shit ripping our missiles to shreds*, Bolan thought.

"Hit on the *Paris*!" Boyles said excitedly. Bolan waved to indicate he had heard her, looking at the fight's larger geometry. The *Asculum* was still approaching from port, but at 220,000 kilometers was not going to reach a firing position in time to prevent the *Constitution*'s missile launch. The three destroyers that had accompanied the battlecruiser were losing ground due to the Warhawks' dogged pursuit.

Warhawk One is just harrying them, Bolan noted. *Which works, as it looks like he's doing it without losses. The air group's done enough for the day.*

"Lieutenant Herrod, send 'Buford' to Warhawk One," Bolan ordered, watching as another flock of twelve slugs reached out towards the *Paris*. Sinclair was alternating between the two heavy cruisers, and it appeared that the *Sarajevo* had been slowed by at least one of her hits.

Another two minutes and they'll be at maximum effective range, Bolan thought. *That could get unpleasant.*

"The *Roberts* is breaking up," Boyles reported. Turning back to the screen, Bolan saw that the secondaries had obviously hit something critical aboard the oncoming destroyer. He had just enough time to process the fragments splitting from the onrushing icon before the tin can's fusion bottles lost containment. The screen flickered as the Death's Halo blinded the *Constitution*'s active sensors, forcing the battlecruiser to rely on the mirrorballs' relay.

These exercises are almost too realistic at times, Bolan thought, feeling a damp sweat start to form inside of his suit.

"Engaging enemy missiles with secondaries," Sinclair said, switching to the incoming missile salvo from the two heavy cruisers.

"Cease fire main batteries, transfer energy to helm," Bolan ordered.

"Aye aye, Captain," Sinclair replied, his hands moving over his console.

"Helm, ventral two hundred kilometers, ten degrees to port," Bolan said. "Guns, cease fire with the mains, give Lieutenant Commander Sakai all the power he needs."

"Aye aye!"

Bolan felt himself try to lift out of his chair as Sakai pushed the battlecruiser further below the ecliptic. As he watched, the secondaries began engaging the missiles that were inbound. Lacking the fuel to make radical changes in course due to the extended range at which they were launched, the missiles were a textbook gunnery problem that the *Constitution*'s computer easily solved.

"If we're ever tasked to attack a system, might I suggest the first thing we take down is anything that's radiating a sensor paint?" Commander Alexander remarked. "That Death's Halo would have truly screwed our targeting."

"Better that she charged us than stood by the *Shokaku*," Commander Sinclair remarked, watching as the secondaries continued to reap the incoming missiles. "Her defensive fire would have made it a hell of a lot harder to kill the *Shokaku*."

Bolan looked at the countdown timer as the last inbound missile was destroyed, the 1:45 blinking twice before going dark.

"Warhawk One acknowledges Buford," Herrod reported.

The mention of *Constitution*'s air group caused Bolan to suddenly remember one of Boyles' reports.

"Where did the *Thunderchiefs* the *Shokaku* get off go to?" Bolan asked, looking at the screen.

"They are remaining close to the carrier, Sir," Boyles replied. "I cleared them from the main board to reduce clutter."

"Thank you," Bolan said with a note of approval.

She's good. Doesn't have to have her hand held and was an ace with the encryption. Might have to recommend Boyles go back into the

140

school house to teach other offices sooner rather than later. Her talents, while appreciated, are being wasted here.

With the incoming missiles dealt with, Sinclair turned back to the task that had brought them to the Solomon System: killing the *Shokaku*. With the range to the drifting carrier at just under 105,000 kilometers, the carrier was in the heart of the battlecruiser's missile envelope.

"*Mako*s away," Sinclair said. There was a long, shuddering vibration as the *Constitution*'s magazine simulated the operations necessary to shift the next volley of missiles to the eight-cell vertical launcher behind the bridge. At one hundred and fifty tons apiece, the twenty-eight meter missiles bore more than a passing resemblance to their namesakes. Within two minutes of the first octuple being flung into space, Sinclair had forty-eight of the deadly weapons accelerating at top speed towards their target.

Normally I'd say that was a bit of overkill, Bolan thought as he watched half of his missile magazine in flight, *but the **Shokaku** was allegedly built with some of the best point defenses in the fleet.*

"Enemy cruisers engaging," Boyles reported. Bolan pursed his lips as he watched the *Paris*'s salvo begin crossing the 85,000 kilometers between the two ships.

"Mr. Sinclair, let's remind our friends that while we are at the edge of their maximum range, they are well within ours."

"Aye aye, Captain," Sinclair replied. "Reengaging with main batteries."

"*Shokaku* is engaging with point defense weapons," Boyles stated.

Unlike the dual-purpose secondaries found on many capital ships, Confederation carriers were equipped with a massive array of point defense weapons. A mixture of energy, rail, and missile platforms, the sole purpose of the arrays was to prevent missiles and torpedoes from reaching lethal range. As the *Constitution*'s missiles crossed the 30,000 kilometer barrier, those point defense (PD) batteries that had survived the rail gun carnage began spewing destruction towards the inbound *Mako*s. For their part, the missiles began performing a chaotic ballet of heading, velocity and orientation changes, all with the intent of gaining sufficient proximity to detonate their twenty megaton warheads.

The entire process occurred almost too fast for the human mind to register. While the handful of *Thunderchief* fighters tucked in closely to their carrier attempted to cover the gaps caused by the earlier devastation, it was truly a case of far too little, too late. Unlike torpedoes, missiles did not have to actually impact the hostile hull to detonate. In the end, the *Shokaku*'s severe damage and inability to maneuver meant three missiles passed through the typhoon of point defense to detonate within lethal range. Once more, the *Camelot*'s computer applied clinical analysis to a situation that would have involved flying debris, explosive decompression, and charred crew ejected like so much detritus from the catamaran. It took roughly a millisecond for the computer to determine multiple reasons that the hits would have been fatal.

"*Shokaku* is *breaking up*," Boyles said, the last part delivered almost as a joyful cheer.

"Yes, and now her escorts are closing with blood in their eyes," Bolan remarked grimly, throwing a bucket of cold water on the incipient cheer. As if to prove his point, the *Paris*'s latest salvo passed perilously close to the *Constitution*'s icon. The heavy cruiser's triumph was short-lived, however, as Sinclair finally managed to land multiple slugs on the maneuvering vessel. While not fatal, the heavy cruiser's icon went from a pale amber to dark gold, indicating one or more significant systems were believed to have been injured. More tellingly, the icon began to change direction and rotate, indicating that the heavy cruiser had suffered damage to her helm.

I really hope that's just simulated on our screen and not aboard the vessel itself, Bolan thought, feeling his stomach go queasy just looking at the spin. Before he ruminate on things further, suddenly every speaker aboard the *Constitution* crackled to life.

"All vessels, all vessels, this is the *Camelot*," a disembodied voice stated. "ENDEX, I say again, end exercise."

Okay, that is truly freaky, Bolan thought. I will not miss having that software and hardware operational.

"Okay Helm, take the pedal off the metal," Bolan said with a slight smile, his exuberance definitely reserved compared to the broad grins he knew were on everyone else's face.

"Aye aye, Sir," Sakai replied.

"Sir, incoming message from the *Camelot*," Herrod said. "Stand by for Kraken Actual."

142

Bolan sighed as he motioned for the transmission to be linked to his station. A moment later, Admiral Malinverni's voice was coming across to his ear.

"Captain Bolan, that was a combination of the luckiest shooting and most piss poor escort execution I've ever seen," Admiral Malinverni said. Bolan could almost feel the man's grim amusement over the comms, and he genuinely felt for the entire *Shokaku* task group.

"I somehow doubt we were what they were expecting, Sir," Bolan replied.

"Oh, don't try to save anyone's ass, Captain," Malinverni said. "I'll take into account the fact that your ship is one of a kind when I'm conducting the AAR. Speaking of which, as we discussed you have your next destination. I ended the exercise early so you had time to upload your log and combat files then get them over here."

"Aye aye, Sir," Bolan replied, suddenly exhausted.

"I figured that was better than spending another thirty minutes seeing if you could recover your air group without incinerating anyone while dodging the *Sarajevo* and *Asculum*'s fire," Malinverni continued. "Although I think I may have screwed up some wagering here on *Camelot*."

Bolan choked back a laugh.

"My apologies to Rear Admiral Metagna for costing her some credits," Bolan replied easily, drawing puzzled looks from several of the bridge crew.

"Oh, I'm sure she'll consider it a small price to pay for the education she just got to observe," Malinverni said, humor in his voice.

Well I wasn't sure it will be that helpful in the Caliphate…

"At any rate, I will have to get your side of matters once I get something out to Helgoland to relieve you," Malinverni said. "Is there anything you need me to expedite?"

"We're going to need to replace our decoys, Sir," Bolan said. "It would take me another six hours to recover and refit them at this point."

"I wouldn't worry on that account," Malinverni replied. "I've already got the *Kula Gulf* and *Malvinas* plus escorts en route to that sector—they should be relieving you within a week. You can keep yourself out of trouble that long, I assume?"

Two battlecruisers plus escorts? Should I be more worried than I am?, Bolan thought.

"Sir, I think we can pull that off," Bolan said. "Should I be restricting liberty call?"

An Unproven Concept

"I leave that up to you," Malinverni replied solemnly. "Don't want to appear to be overreacting to a single ghost echo."

But again…nevermind.

"Aye aye, Admiral. We'll see what Captain Gadhavi has scared up when we get there."

"Godspeed, Captain Bolan. Kraken Actual, Out."

Kaiju class Mecha--Golem Mode (Sanders)

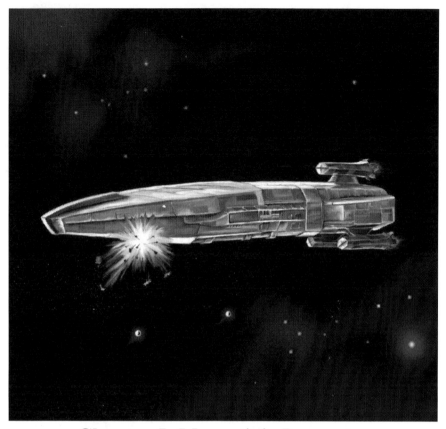

Chapter 5: Mercutio's Lament

Shigure
1615 SST
21 June 3050

I hate suits, Leslie thought to herself as she passed her hand over the subatomic fasteners that sealed her into her own. *Namely the false sensation of needing to take a piss I always get right after I connect to my seat.*

"Mommy, I have to go to the bathroom..." Major Acheros said. Leslie looked up across the bridge and shook her head.

"That joke was old a century ago," she replied after making sure she had the proper comm channel.

Can't let the bridge crew hear us making nervous comments, she thought to herself. *Of course, why should I be nervous? Every moment in space is a gift.*

"You know, you never did explain why you joined the Marines last night when we were at dinner," Leslie said after affixing her suit's tube to her chair's output. With a press of the button she switched from the internal tank to the ship's air, closing her eyes as stray dust particles briefly circulated around her helmet.

There was a pause, and she could see Acheros considering how to answer.

"My uncle was a merchant marine officer," Acheros replied, his voice grim. "His vessel was the *Summoner*. Have you ever heard of her?"

"No, can't say that I have," Leslie said. "You know, you don't have to answer…"

"Enh, it's no big deal. Her inertial dampeners failed because the jackass captain was basically skimming the maintenance money off the top," Acheros continued.

Leslie winced.

"I believe you Anglo-Sax call it the 'Heinz Maneuver.' We Spartans call it Blood Pudding. Coincidence of coincidence my father's other brother was the master of the armed cutter that found her."

Leslie felt her stomach turn.

"I'm so sorry, Major Acheros," she said.

Acheros shrugged.

"Glad that it was Uncle Bart, actually," Acheros said. "That way I knew that it wasn't just a pretty lie when the owners said Uncle Marty died in his sleep because he was off watch."

Leslie fought the urge to shiver. An inertial dampener failure definitely fell into a spacer's worst fears.

One second you're moving along at thousands of kilometers per hour, the next you're a red stain on an unforgiving bulkhead, Leslie thought.

"Captain, we will be coming into system in twenty minutes," Ensign Griffon said, startling Leslie. Looking over at her nav officer, Leslie nodded.

"Thank you, Ensign Griffon."

"I think you forgot to switch channels," Major Acheros said. Leslie looked down and cursed.

"Well that would have been bad in about five minutes," Leslie said. "Good catch."

"No problem."

"Thanks for telling me, as well," Leslie said.

"You're welcome."

"Captain, I just thought of something," Lieutenant Southwell said.

Uh oh, Leslie thought, then made sure she had the correct microphone activated.

"Yes, Guns?"

"We should probably load normal warheads on missiles nine and ten," Southwell replied. "If we come in and have a target right in our face we're not going to want to hit it with an implosion warhead."

Shit. How could we not have wargamed that?!

"How long to switch?"

"Ten minutes."

"What? It's been awhile, but I know that you don't just throw a couple of bolts to switch warheads, Lieutenant."

Southwell looked briefly nonplussed, then cleared his expression.

"Captain, the torpedo flat is already depressurized, so we don't have to wait the fifteen minutes or so to take care of that," he replied evenly. "Plus the *Pufferfish* was designed with a modular warhead for just this eventuality."

Leslie considered her next steps for a moment.

"Have them take their time, but go ahead."

"Aye-aye, Captain."

Why did I just have the mental image of a beagle being let off the leash in a field full of fat vermin? Leslie thought with slight affection.

"Ten minutes."

Leslie reached down and touched several studs on the side of her seat. With a barely discernible whine her suit visor went opaque then, as the screen recalled her settings and schematics appeared along both sides. Squinting at one in particular, Leslie called up a semi-transparent representation of *Shigure's* current damage control, weapons, engineering, and shields status.

While I still prefer command chairs, they've come a long way with visor technology, she thought. *Guess we can thank the Airedales for that.*

"I must say the Navy has apparently been holding out on us Marines," Acheros said, his tone genuinely appreciative. Leslie switched back to their private channel.

"There are downsides. Screw up and suddenly you'll have so much stuff on your visor you can't even see the bridge."

There was a pause.

"Okay, I can see what you mean," Acheros replied. "How do you close…"

"Five minutes."

"Focus on the red x projected at the top of your visor screen," Leslie said, then switched channels and looked at Lieutenant Talo.

"Load evasive plans Theta and Omni," Leslie said.

"Aye aye, Captain," Talo replied. Leslie noticed the young officer's pallor.

"I trust your driving, Lieutenant Talo," Leslie said. "But if someone starts shooting at us as soon as we come through the door I want you monitoring shield power and getting the Herbert Drive ready for a jump instead of dodging."

Talo nodded as she input the necessary commands.

"Exiting hyperspace in ten …nine … eight … seven … six… five …four …three…"

There was a slight shudder as the *Shigure* reentered normal space. Leslie switched her view to the star system's schematic, the asteroid belt and planets' dimness reflecting their uncertain position.

"Drones away, Captain. Sensors…contacts! Multiple contacts!" Southwell barked, his voice rising in octaves as four yellow icons sprang into life on Leslie's screen. Three of them were to *Shigure*'s frontal arc and over one million kilometers away, while the one aft was just over 185,000 kilometers distant. A moment later, the three contacts to their front were designated A, B, and C from port to starboard, with that behind them designated D.

So this is what the mouse feels like, Leslie thought grimly.

"Looks like it was a good call not to come in along Columbus's vector," Acheros observed, getting a quick nod from Leslie.

"Ninety degrees to starboard, all ahead flank," Leslie ordered coolly. "Get us in the nearest asteroid belt."

A moment later it felt as if a giant was pressing her back into her chair as *Shigure*'s engines kicked into full thrust.

"Contact Delta is radiating active sensors," Southwell grunted.

"Launch two more sensor drones," Leslie replied, her breath sounding as if she were running a marathon.

"Not to be rude, but why aren't we jumping out?" Acheros gasped.

"All contacts accelerating," Southwell grunted again.

148

"Recon drones need time to get good paints," Leslie replied as the destroyer's acceleration tapered off. "I want definite proof that our sensors weren't just spoofing off some abnormal asteroids or reflecting radio waves."

As she spoke, Leslie watched Contact D slowly drift back behind them. The other three contacts were rapidly closing, albeit not at the optimal interception angle.

It's almost like they know something we don't know... Leslie began thinking.

"Energy signature increasing from Contact D!"

"Evasives, now!" Leslie barked. Talo stabbed a button on her console while she simultaneously released the control joystick that extended from its bottom. Leslie had just enough time to inhale before she felt the bridge's bottom drop out, followed by a monstrous kick sideways as *Shigure*'s maneuver thrusters fired.

Thank goodness for restraining belts, Leslie thought. *Still, going to be sore in the...HOLY SHIT!*

Contact D had sprouted an azure line that was initially brilliant than began fading on her viewscreen. The far end of the line terminated in a gaggle of multiple gold dots, the Confederation symbol for recently detected navigational hazards.

"Did that son of a bitch just fuck up an asteroid?" Southwell asked, his voice shocked.

Well, glad that we didn't try to jump right out, Leslie thought, a wave of nausea rolling over her. *We would have been still hanging stationary when that bastard fired whatever the hell that was! That's more powerful than a planetary defense laser!*

"Nav, start plotting an escape axis out of here," Leslie said grimly.

"Aye aye, Captain, computer inputting astral data...oh dear," Ensign Griffon said, her voice panicked. "Captain, the sensors cannot get a navigational reading with that debris cloud!"

"Engage jammers, eject decoys. Helm, Bravo, Lima, and Sigma for the next maneuvers."

"Aye aye captain!"

Looking at her screen, Leslie watched as the icon representing *Shigure* split into five blips. After matching the destroyer's speed for ten seconds, the decoys executed radical maneuvers to random bearings.

We've only got four more of those, Leslie thought.

"Energy fluctuations!"

The bright line repeated itself, and one of the decoys winked out.

"Sensors, figure out what that thing's cyclic rate is," Leslie snapped, the first tendrils of true fear starting to knot in her stomach. "Helm, start putting us on a constant evasive pattern, time now."

Think Leslie! Think! She felt panic's fingers starting to tighten in her head.

"Ma'am, I'm pretty sure that's a spinal weapon," the XO's voice rasped in her ear.

"What?!" Lisa snapped.

"A laser that powerful would probably run the whole length of the ship," Iokepa repeated patiently, then laughed. "Or else we're really screwed."

That's right, he worked on Weapons Development, Leslie thought as she felt the calmness in Iokepa's voice wash over her like cool water. *Wait, wasn't one of the drawbacks of a spinal mount an inability to effectively track a smaller target?*

"Which means it's got a limited arc," Leslie said thoughtfully, then louder, "Helm, down two thousand kilometers, starboard one hundred eighty, then all ahead flank!"

"The shots were roughly two hundred seconds apart," Southwell reported.

A scarlet '140' appeared in the upper right hand corner of Leslie's display as Talo shoved her control stick forward then right. Looking at Acheros, Leslie saw the marine as a red-tinged outline gripping his seat while *Shigure* figuratively 'dropped' like a rock. Then her vision dimmed as the destroyer's engines engaged, pushing back against the vessel's momentum to accelerate back towards Contact D.

"Contact D is slowing, aspect changing," Southwell grunted, his voice sounding far away as Leslie fought to keep consciousness. She noted the flashing '00' at the edge of her tunneling vision.

I hope I'm right or we're all dead, Leslie thought. *He can't turn fast enough o keep a bead on us, and we'll be giving him something else to think about in a second.*

"He's tracking a decoy!" Southwell said, just as the scarlet numbers wound down to zero. The bright line speared from Contact D, just missed the radically maneuvering decoy, and smashed into the asteroid belt behind.

"Nav…" Leslie grunted.

"Approximately ten minutes, Captain!" Griffon replied, her voice strained as well.

"We don't have ten minutes, Nav," the XO replied from Battle Two.

Looks like running isn't an option, which leaves blasting our way past him, Leslie thought grimly. *Time to see if those **Pufferfish** work.*

"Sensors, do we have a reliable paint on Contact D yet?" Leslie asked.

"He's capital ship size, computer estimates 350,000 tons, length over 800 meters."

"Thirty degrees down angle on the helm, maintain course. Stand by *Pufferfish*."

Leslie quickly ran over the geometry in her head.

"Contact D is reorienting!" Southwell said. "Contact slowing!"

Imagine so, tracking us at this closure rate can't be fun, Leslie thought. *Even with inertial dampeners, mass is still mass…and that bastard has a lot of it.*

"In range!"

"Fire tubes one through eight!"

The crew felt a long, sustained rumble as *Shigure*'s torpedo tubes irised open at the bottom of her bow. A moment later the ship shuddered as electromagnetic launchers ejected eight of the *Pufferfish* at just over eight hundred kilometers an hour. Roughly ten meters in length, each missile contained its own pulse fusion drive that ignited once a safe distance had been achieved.

"Eight missiles successful launch!"

"Down fifty degrees, pattern Zeta!" Leslie barked. Once more the world went red, then gray as *Shigure* corkscrewed to starboard. Bracing her muscles to try and keep blood in her head, Leslie watched the countdown until impact as the eight green icons sped towards Contact D. Suddenly her screen blossomed as Contact D became the center of an azure spider web followed by six of the missiles winking out. Less than a second later, the final two missiles reached their one thousand kilometer proximity range…and the *Shigure* shuddered like a hovercar as the collision alarm started to scream.

"Gravitational distortion!" Southwell shouted, as a sickly green-black icon sprang into life where Contact D had been. The center of the icon began whirling, signifying a black hole.

*We're dea…*Leslie had enough time to think just before the icon winked out just as quickly as it had appeared.

"Disregard gravitational distortion! Contact D is breaking up!" Southwell reported, relief and joy in his voice.

151

An Unproven Concept

Well having two black holes open right on top of your ship will do that for you, Leslie thought. She suddenly felt hollow as what they had just done sunk in. *A Confederation ship that size would have about two thousand aboard...*

"I am become Death, the destroyer of worlds," Acheros softly murmured. She looked up to see the major's face completely ashen, his eyes wide. She started to say something to the man, then stopped.

We can talk later, she thought.

"Sensors, range to closest contact?"

"Contact A is at nine hundred thousand kilometers and closing at a rate of one thousand kilometers a minute."

"If we stop to enter hyper how quick will he be here?"

Southwell entered data into the tactical computer.

"Twenty minutes assuming that all three hostile contacts are already moving at maximum acceleration."

You know what they say about assumptions...but no real other choice.

"Nav, start the Herbert calculations for Zed-720. Helm, full stop."

"Aye aye," Griffon and Talo said almost as one, the latter reaching forward pressing two buttons on her keyboard. There was a dull roar as *Shigure*'s maneuver thrusters fired at full power to immediately flip the destroyer end over end, then her entire crew felt the deceleration as her engines went to maximum output to kill her relative velocity.

"Sensors?"

"No change to contacts' rate of acceleration...they're refining their intercept angle, however."

"Thank you," Leslie said, hoping that her voice didn't show just how deep her relief was. "Make sure all of our data is being backed up to the message buoys. We'll launch one as soon as we hit Zed-720."

"Aye aye," Southwell said.

"Herbert countdown started, Captain," Griffon said.

"Good job, Nav," Leslie said, seeing that Griffon had halved the jump time to five minutes instead of the expected ten. "I probably don't want to know what you did."

Griffon blushed slightly at the praise.

"Thank you, Captain," she said.

"This is the longest five minutes of my life," Acheros muttered on the internal channel. "Next time they ask me to be a courier I'm going to throw myself down a flight of stairs."

Leslie looked up at the Marine and raised an eyebrow.

"I thought Marines never admitted they were scared?" she said with a slight smirk.

"We also usually end up being able to literally see our opponents," Acheros replied, his voice grim. "This waiting to die in a tin can is for the birds."

"Enemy contacts are *slowing*," Southwell said.

"What in the hell..?" Leslie asked.

"They better not be able to hit us with something at this range..." Iokepa growled.

If they can, maybe it's better that we don't make it back, Leslie thought, then angrily fought that thought away.

"I'm not going to tempt fate by saying they couldn't hit an Taurian Rhino at this distance, but I think that would give whole new meaning to 'Golden laser', XO," Leslie replied. Looking at the countdown timer, she grinned. "And they'd better figure it out, because in thirty second we're not going to be here anymore."

"Stand by for Herbert jump. All hands stand by for Herbert jump," Talo intoned. Leslie took a deep breath as the counter reached zero and her world went white...

...then just as quickly returned to color and focus.

"Zed Seven Two Oh system, Captain," Ensign Griffon said, her voice distant and faint.

She sounds like she's at the end of a great hall filled with cotton, Leslie thought. I think jumping that far is going to take some getting used to.

"Get a message buoy ready then send it," Leslie choked out. "Status report, all divisions." Her stomach lurched as *Shigure*'s sections all reported normal operations. Zed-720's single red giant and four planets were briefly projected onto her command visor, with *Shigure*'s icon appearing ten thousand kilometers above the ecliptic. The five asteroid belts ringing the central star appeared as dashed rings, the nearest of which was twenty-five thousand kilometers away off the vessel's port side.

"Are...jumps...always...like that?" Acheros gasped.

"We've only had five and, yes, so far," Leslie replied. "It passes in a few minutes..."

"Contacts! Multiple contacts!" Southwell reported, the last syllable coming out as a liquid gurgle. "Bearings two eight zero, one seven oh, and one three zero!"

Leslie's nausea dissipated as her adrenaline came back full force.

"Range?!"

"Four hundred thousand, three hundred thousand, six hundred thousand kilometers. Contacts accelerating…energy signatures match previous hostile contacts. Contacts are radiating sensors."

Looking at her command visor told the tale of just how well the three alien craft had boxed *Shigure* in. In order to make the asteroid belt to port, the destroyer would have to basically run in front of the contact at 280 degrees, while the other two were preventing her from moving towards the nebula roughly three million kilometers distant.

How did they track us?! Leslie thought fearfully.

"They're accelerating very slowly, Captain," Iokepa said. "Like they don't know exactly where we are."

Glad to see the stealth does work when we're drifting, Leslie thought. *Now to see if we can sneak past…*

The *Shigure* shuddered.

"Message buoy away, Captain!" Ensign Griffon said.

*Blazes! That's not going to…*Leslie started to think.

There was a brief flash on Leslie's sensor relay as the message buoy engaged its Herbert Drive.

Well there goes remaining hidden!

"Immediate jump, Zed-815 system," Leslie barked.

"Contacts accelerating and closing!"

"Aye aye, Captain!" Talo said, her voice resigned.

"Sorry Captain," Griffon said, her voice sounding like she was about to cry.

"My fault for not belaying that when they jumped in," Leslie replied wearily. "Hold further message buoys until we jump…"

Griffon did not have time to respond before their world flashed white.

This time the jump sickness hit her even harder than it had the last time, to the point where she thought she was hallucinating when her brain unscrambled.

"What did you say, Guns?!" she slurred.

"Ma'am, I say again, unidentified Confederation ship bearing oh five oh relative!" Lieutenant Southwell said anxiously.

154

"Class?!" Leslie asked, her voice rising in pitch.

Please let this be some cavalry that Admiral Malinverni stashed in system without telling me, she thought.

"Still reading…the S.S. *Titanic*. Passenger vessel, Czarina Lines," Southwell said, his voice stunned.

What the hell is a passenger vessel doing in an unnamed system?! she thought grimly. *There's a law against idiocy like this for a reason!*

"Do you want me to open a hail, Commander?" Ensign Griffon asked. Leslie resisted the urge to turn and snap at the young officer as she watched the ensign start to reach up towards her helmet then stop.

"Sort of defeats the purpose of the stealth outfit if we announce ourselves," Leslie replied gently. "Ken, did we lose our…"

The warning tone in her helmet and three flashing red icons that appeared on her command visor answered the question before she finished it.

"Well at least they had the decency to show up on the other side of the planet," Leslie muttered. "Too bad the damn *Titanic* is now between us and them." Blowing her breath up her face where it stirred her auburn bangs, Leslie wished strongly and fervently she was somewhere else. Looking around the bridge's narrow confines she felt the crushing weight of command on her shoulders.

That ship is screwed, they just don't know it yet, she thought as the three crimson triangles began growing vector lines. *It's probably wrong that part of me doesn't feel any sympathy for the dumbasses who decided it was a good idea to break Spacefarer's Code.*

"Keep us adrift, let's see if she makes it away," Leslie said grimly. "Nav, start plotting our next jump. If her captain's a big enough boy to walk down dark alleys, let's hope he's at least got the common sense to have a good watch on his sensors."

Titanic
1645 SST

Marcus resisted the urge to check his sidearm again as he walked towards Ballroom A.

Paranoid much? he mentally chided himself. While the odds were incredibly slim that Aimi would try anything for all the reasons he'd explained to Sarah, he was a bit more worried than he had let on.

"About time you woke up, sleepyhead."

Speak of the love of my life, he thought, turning around and grinning. Sarah returned his grin with a smile of her own, shaking her head as she did so. In that moment of not wearing her "Hospitality" face, Marcus realized just how long a day she must have had to that point.

"You know, perhaps you should try that sleep thing yourself," Marcus said quietly.

"Do I look that rough?" Sarah asked, taking a deep breath.

Marcus stepped aside as a knot of passengers passed them, Sarah and he both returning quick greetings.

"Loaded question," he replied with a smirk. "I just know I feel a helluva lot better after taking a short nap."

"Yes, well, I can rest when I'm dead," Sarah replied, looking at her watch. "Senator Du's charity ball is kicking off in a few minutes, so I want to make sure that's taken care of before I hit the rack."

"Funny, I was planning on stopping in to see if I could steal a couple of dances with someone."

"Well I think it'd be a huge test of Aimi's self-control to be that close to you without resorting to stabbing," Sarah said sarcastically. "But you know I don't care how you get your thrills as long as you do all your buying at the company store."

Marcus snorted.

"You are wrong on so many levels," he said, shaking his head in amazement. "Besides, I intended to make a very large purchase at the company store earlier but said individual interrupted us. Speaking of which, I see you're trying out the new shoes."

"I have to say, for a Spartan male Senator Du sure can pick out a good gift," Sarah replied, straight faced. "I suddenly have a newfound envy for his wife."

Marcus raised an eyebrow as the two of them stopped just outside of Ballroom A's hatchway.

"You know, he might be from one of the systems that allow polygamy. Or Mei Du might gut you for even having that thought," Marcus replied musingly.

"I'm glad you have so much faith in my fighting ability," Sarah retorted with mocking hurt. "I mean, my Daddy made sure I knew my way around a rifle."

"Which is why she'd probably choose claymores," Marcus said. "That woman is about forty centimeters shorter than you, but you're still giving her five kilograms and not much of hers is pudgy."

"Did you just call me a lard bucket, Marcus?" Sarah started indignantly.

"Yes, because of all the ways I could have meant that, I totally was going for telling a woman who could probably run farther than me that she's fat," Marcus replied sarcastically. "I just don't want your last sensation on this earth to be utter shock at how cleanly your left and right side separated."

Sarah shook her head at him.

"You have a vivid imagination, Marcus," she said, a smile coming to her face despite her best efforts to sound severe.

"Now I will clove you in half with a sword as big as your leg, you rampant hussy," Marcus said in mock Spartan accent, causing Sarah's last reserves to break as she started to giggle.

"While I will not even begin to ask why you're doing voice impressions," First Mate Al-Madur observed in a clipped voice, "I am certain that it's probably a good thing you did not pursue a career in acting."

"Fortunately I found a niche," Marcus replied with a smile, knowing it would irk Al-Madur to no end.

"Yes, how lucky for us all. I am told that you are the architect behind the slalom course dance floor," Al-Madur replied. "It's receiving *rave* reviews."

Okay asshole, Marcus thought, feeling his anger rising.

"Well thankfully the only critic that matters blessed off on my plan," Marcus said. "But I think you heard that first hand. Now if you'll excuse us."

Al-Madur visibly bristled, clenching his fists at Marcus's dismissal.

"I had some Hospitality—" Al-Madur began.

"Matters that can wait until we're done with a couple of dances? I'll make sure Sarah doesn't forget," Marcus said. With that, he led Sarah into the ballroom and onto the dance floor.

"You know, I think one or both of us are going to pay for that later," Sarah said as Marcus took her into his arms for the ongoing waltz.

"I don't think we will," Marcus replied with a smile as he watched the First Mate storm off. "Captain Herrod was apparently very clear in explaining just what will happen if I so much as imply the First Mate's overstepping his bounds again."

Sarah shook her head as they moved around one of the potted plants.

"Yes, but Captain Herrod will not always be the Master of the vessel you're serving on," Sarah replied with a pained smile. "Al-Madur, on the other hand, *will* likely be a captain within five years."

"Well by that time maybe I'll be settled down dirtside with a couple of kids," he replied, tickling Sarah discreetly.

"Maybe," she replied, laying her head on his shoulder as the band played on. Looking over Sarah's head, Marcus saw Senator and Mei Du whirling effortlessly around the arranged flower pots. Mei was wearing a crimson dress with almost sheer black side panels and side slits that showed off her toned thighs. Unlike the usual severe Spartan style, Mrs. Du's black hair was halfway down her back in ringlets, the heavy locks moving in rhythm as she waltzed with her husband.

Sorry Sarah, but she'd kill you in about thirty seconds, Marcus thought grimly. *With fifteen of those being spent informing you of the error of your ways.*

"It's such a beautiful view, isn't it?" Sarah asked him, causing him to jerk in surprise. "I mean the planet, not whatever woman you're staring at."

"I was actually looking at Senator and Mrs. Du. They're amazing dancers," Marcus said, turning Sarah so she could see the couple. Sarah chuckled as she looked, the Senator dipping his wife as the band finished the song. There was a smattering of applause as the couple moved towards their table.

"Well hopefully after we've been together forty years we'll be that good together," Sarah observed. Marcus embraced her from behind.

"We can only hope," he replied. "Now we better both be social before the First Mate makes me cold cock him."

"Gee, you seem *so* happy about having to talk to passengers," Sarah said wryly.

"Hey, I'm just glad I'm not on the bridge. Lorraine told me Federov's been camped out there since we got into orbit. Makes things a bit...*tense*."

Saying things were a bit...*tense* on *Titanic*'s bridge was a marked understatement.

Just because nothing's gone wrong doesn't mean we were paranoid, Abraham thought as he felt Federov's eyes boring into him from the VIP section of the bridge. Ignoring the man's gaze, Abraham looked up from the novel he was reading to the main display. The current screen was a sensor representation of the area around Sapphire, with the massive gas giant at its center instead of *Titanic*'s icon. *Titanic*'s icon was in a slow counterclockwise orbit around the sphere, with the planet's four moons at various points of their paths 250-750,000 kilometers away. Satisfied that all was well, Abraham returned to his reading.

Ancient Terrans were certainly fascinated with the end of civilization, he thought with a slight shake of his head. *Strange that its arrival seemed to have caught everyone by surprise. I wonder if this Pat Frank was caught up in the chaos...*

"Captain Herrod, a word if you please?" Federov called down from the second level.

I see we've finally had enough of me ignoring your petulance? Abraham thought. *Well get ready to wait a few minutes more.*

"Mr. Coors, status?" Abraham asked, pointedly ignoring Federov.

"Screens free and clear, Captain," Coors reported. The man looked slightly worse for wear, making Abraham feel a moment's sympathy for him. "I've finally managed to gain connectivity with all the mirrorballs on this side of the system."

"Very good, keep me informed," Abraham said, coming to his feet. He had just stepped onto the lift when Coors interrupted him.

"Sir, possible contact bearing oh two zero," Coors said, an icon appearing briefly on *Titanic*'s screen then vanishing almost as quickly.

What in the hell..? Abraham thought to himself. *That was...odd.* Before he had a chance to say anything, Coors' next sentence caused his adrenaline to surge as if a Harborean Sand Tiger had appeared on the bridge.

"*Contacts! Three contacts, bearing two four zero!*" the man nearly screamed, his face losing all color.

Oh shit, Abraham thought, feeling a moment of dizziness.

"Is it one contact or three?" Federov shouted from the VIP ledge.

"Range," Abraham asked, forcing his voice to be unruffled.

"One hundred fifty thousand klicks," Coors replied, his voice much calmer.

"Captain, I asked a question!" Federov shouted, his voice rising.

"Mr. Federov, if you interfere with the operation of this ship again I will throw you in the brig," Abraham snapped. *The answer's right in front of you, idiot,* he thought a moment later.

159

"Helm, break orbit, come to course oh five zero, up thirty degrees, and all ahead one third. Let's not have our guests pin us against the planet."

"Aye aye, Captain," Erdermir responded tersely. Abraham noted the helmsman was gripping the ship's controls with white knuckles.

*Why yes, this could be career ending for **all** of us*, he thought.

"Sir, should we begin to charge the rail guns?" O'Barr asked from the security station, startling Abraham.

"You haven't done that already?!" Federov nearly screamed, drawing a glare from Abraham.

"No, Ms. O'Barr," Abraham replied, continuing to look right at Federov. "If pirates have Herbert drive technology, I imagine that they wouldn't use it waiting for some *idiot* to order a star liner right into their web. "

The clear insult was lost on no one standing on the bridge. Federov looked ready to open his mouth until Abraham turned away from him.

"Ms. Vo, open a hailing…"

"Contacts are accelerating, Captain!" Coors interrupted. Abraham turned to see his sensors officer was dead on, the three contacts moving into a triangular formation as they rounded the gas giant's equator.

Well, that whole move slowly away to avoid attracting the predator's attention plan didn't work very well, Abraham thought, exhaling heavily. *Must be light cruisers to have that kind of acceleration.*

"They're not answering hails, Captain," Vo said.

"Well if they're not going to respond, I'm not going to slow down. All ahead full, Mr. Erdermir."

"Aye aye, Captain," Erdermir said, advancing his throttle. *Titanic* shuddered as her thrusters rapidly opened to their full capacity. The liner began to sluggishly gain velocity, the incoming contacts' acceleration vectors making it clear it was a relatively fruitless exercise.

"Mr. Coors, any idea what size those vessels are?" Abraham asked.

"Sensors indicate they're only slightly smaller than us," Coors responded.

Those have to be new vessels, Abraham thought to himself. *Whatever, that acceleration means they're clearly…*

160

"Objects inbound!" Coors shouted, as six icons split from the lead unidentified vessel.

"Hard to starboard!" Abraham barked.

Erdermir had just enough time to throw his control hard to his right before the six objects leapt across the 65,000 kilometers between the two vessels. Flickering like out of control Christmas lights, the weapons merged with *Titanic*'s icon.

The reason *Titanic*'s sensors had become confused by the inbound ordnance was the latter existed only as a theory to humanity. The Confederation Fleet's weapons boffins had long envisioned a weapon that married the high terminal energy and speed of lasers with the relatively low power requirements and rapid firing rate of rail guns. One line of thought had been so-called plasma weapons, i.e. ordnance that somehow contained an unstable field of plasma energy within an easily deployed ferrous shell. Unfortunately, the Confederation Fleet had been unable to wrangle the funds to continue plasma research out of a tight-fisted Senate. That several of those same tight-fisted senators were aboard *Titanic* the very moment the unknown contacts fired was cosmic justice at its best.

Despite the presentation on *Titanic*'s bridge, the incoming ordnance had left the hostile cruiser in a horizontally, vertically, and chronologically staggered spread. Thus the first two weapons missed, with one passing so close to Ballroom A's observation window that the compartments occupants observed it as a bright, shimmering sphere with dazzling reflective light. There was only enough time for the quicker witted to begin forming the *thought* of expletives before the next four weapons crashed into the starliner with terrible force.

The first one slammed into the ventral bow, causing the forward third of the ship to ring like a bell struck by some celestial clapper. Ripping a hole a hundred meters across and almost that far in depth, the explosion vented atmosphere, debris, and over two hundred passengers whose screams were summarily cut off by the remorseless vacuum.

The vessel was still in full vibration when the next two spheres impacted amidships, rupturing a quarter of the vessel's fusion bottles. In every case the reactors' safety features functioned as advertised, preventing the liner from being instantaneously rent apart.

The safety locks working was hardly a mercy for Fireroom #1's crew, as those not killed by spall from the initial detonation had a brief moment to feel their cells being ripped apart by the tremendous radiation shortly before vacuum ended their lives. With a quarter of the available power disappearing, the *Titanic*'s central and secondary computers made immediate and ruthless decisions on what systems were vital to the vessel's survival in the blink of an eye. The chaos that resulted from artificial gravity, internal communications, lighting, inertial dampening and, in some extreme cases, life support being summarily reduced in certain compartments was subsumed to the cold calculus that a ship unable to maneuver, have sensors, or maintain navigational shield was fundamentally a coffin anyway.

The final plasma sphere hit *Titanic*'s dorsal thruster pod in the midst of the power reallocation. Striking just above the articulatory junction point, the explosion partially severed the massive structure just as the helm's turn input was starting to take effect. Applying full maneuvering thrust at a ninety degree angle finished the amputation, the pod careened off to the vessel's port in a spray of thruster fuel and debris. Designed to be maneuvered with three thrusters, *Titanic* began to go into a horizontal oscillation that resembled a spinning roulette wheel's. Although the central computer quickly compensated, for a brief instant the remaining crew and passengers were subjected to wholly unexpected centrifugal forces.

With the loss of the dorsal pod's fusion bottles, the computer's previous ruthlessness became even more pronounced. Much like the unfortunate pod's engineering watch, many of the vessel's passengers and crew did not even have time to realize their peril before being hurled against the nearest hard, unyielding object like water balloons against a brick wall. Hard hit, devoid of half her power, the *Titanic* was suddenly an out of control piece of space junk hurtling in a decaying orbit around Sapphire.

It was the screams that shook Marcus out of his stupor. The event definitely fell under the heading of "blessing in disguise," as his back and left side screamed at him to *not...do...that...again*. Taking a deep breath, he was relieved to find that the damage seemed to be soft tissue as opposed to cracked ribs or vertebrae. After taking a couple more shuddering breaths to make sure the initial assessment, he began looking around in the half gloom cast by the ballroom's emergency lighting. Rather than holding a person rigid so that their knees, ankles or both gave under the torque imparted from being immobilized, magnetic shoes were designed to bring their wearer to a gradual rest. Marcus had fetched up against one of the planters, and he muttered a short prayer of thanks that the decorative pots came with their own magnetic rests.

162

Eight hundred pound bowling balls are one thing we do not need. With that pleasant thought, Marcus stood up from his instinctive combat crouch…and almost immediately regretted it as a screaming, flailing woman in a silver and red striped microdress attempted to grab him as she circled past his head. Ducking the redhead's grasp, Marcus looked out the observation port as Sapphire flashed by, followed by the starfield, then Sapphire again.

"Marcus!" Sarah screamed from his right. He turned to look and saw his fiancé, Senator Du, and Mei Du all gathered around the planter to his right. Marcus started a slow shuffle towards the trio, his magnetic shoes keeping him secured against the continued rotation. As his mind cleared, Marcus realized that Mei was grievously wounded, a steel segment having gone through her pelvis from left to right. Senator Du, for his part, had blood streaming down his left arm from a nasty looking gash on his side even as he crouched to help hold his spouse to the deck.

Where is Du's security detail? Marcus thought, looking around. He saw two Spartans struggling to extricate themselves from under a table as the furniture continued to slide along the room's bow bulkhead. Movement to his right caused him to reflexively turn just in time to see Aimi scuttling across the floor on three limbs, her gait and motion resembling that of a primate. Her right hand held an energy pistol, the weapon clearly having come from a thigh holster.

"Why haven't the Dutchman protocols kicked in?" the Spartan shouted to Marcus in passing, her eyes scanning the entire room.

As if summoned by the woman's voice, Marcus felt the liner's deck rumble in an intense vibration. Called "Dutchman" after the mythical *Flying Dutchman*, the automated routines were designed to stabilize an out of control vessel then bring her to a gradual, low inertia stop. Unfortunately for everyone in the ballroom, it added yet another Newtonian input to an already hectic situation. The change in motion started to send him sliding towards Senator Du, the friction brakes on his shoes gouging into the wooden ballroom floor in a shower of splinters. Even as furniture, glasses and, in at least a couple of shrieking cases, people began slamming against the port bulkhead, Aimi slid to a stop in a whirl of flashing limbs and flying splinters. As the last sickening thuds, cut off screams, and a final crash of loose objects signaled that the *Titanic* had stopped spinning, Aimi began ripping at the hem of her skirt to make improvised bandages. As Marcus belatedly arrived at the planter, he heard Mei chuckling at the security guard's actions.

163

"Aimi, you are ruining a five thousand credit dress…" the woman gasped, unable to finish her thought. For a brief moment her hazel eyes met his, and Marcus could see the immense pain Mei was in.

"Please, *Laoban*, don't try to…" Aimi replied, her voice a near sob.

"Hush child," Mei replied, her voice somewhat stronger. "It is not so deep as a well, nor wide as a church door, but it will most definitely serve."

Marcus looked over at Senator Du and saw the man's face tighten. The older Spartan grabbed his spouse's hand, his eyes glistening slightly.

"Someone shall pay for this," Du seethed. Mei reached up and brushed his face, her own visage sad.

"Even now, you are consumed by vengeance…" she trailed off sadly, tears rolling down her cheeks. "If only…"

Mei never got to finish the sentence, a look of surprise crossing her face right before her limb dropped. Aimi exclaimed in shock, moving to attempt to resuscitate Mei before Senator Du stopped her. Marcus closed his eyes and fought back despair as Mei's last breath sighed from her body. Taking a deep breath, he reopened them to find Senator Du glowering at him, his fists clenched.

"What of your vaunted security measures now, Mr. Martin? Or was this," he sneered, gesturing at the ballroom's chaos, "part of your plan?"

"I did not want to be here, Senator," Marcus snapped in response. "Perhaps when we return to authorized space you can take it up with Mr. Federov."

"*If.*" Du snapped. "Either way, it won't bring her back."

"A plague on both your houses," Aimi said softly. "You have made wormsmeat of her."

Marcus was about to respond when someone grabbed him from behind. He whirled to find a bloodied Quentin. The man looked like he had been locked into a phone booth with a flock of Mylbaran Razorwrens, his face and upper uniform a hash of numerous superficial cuts.

"What the hell hit us?" the man asked.

"I don't know," Marcus replied. "I was talking to Lorraine when that flash went by the viewport."

"We've got no comms with anyone and the bulkheads have dropped forward. Kapena's bringing the weapon cart up from the emergency locker, but whatever hit us jammed the damn door.

Artificial gravity's shot out in the corridor," Quentin said, then took a quick glance around before leaning in towards Marcus. "First Mate and five passengers are dead out in the corridor."

"What happened?" Sarah asked, touching her throat.

"Smashed face first into a console," Quentin replied. "Shards caught me as I was coming up the corridor."

"Holy shit!" Marcus exclaimed.

"Maybe these shoes were worth wearing after all, huh?" Quentin replied, his voice bitter. Marcus fought down a grim smile as Sarah recoiled at Quentin's cavalier attitude.

"You need to get those cuts looked…" Marcus started to say.

"Oh my God!" the same redhead whom had tried to grab him earlier screamed from above his head. The heavyset woman's arm was extended towards the viewport, causing Marcus to turn and look past the floating human detritus to the stars outside. What he saw made his heart start to race faster. Roughly ten kilometers away, a large, manta-shaped object was outlined in planform against Sapphire.

"What cruiser class is that?" Aimi asked, confirming Marcus' own rough estimate of the object's size as it started to grow more defined.

"That's no cruiser," Du said, color draining from his face.

"Not a human one, anyway," Marcus echoed, feeling a strange sense of detachment. He turned to Sarah, finding his fiancée with her hand over her mouth and eyes wide in shock as she looked at the approaching spacecraft.

"You need to grab what people you can, and get out of here," he said, putting his hand on her shoulder. Her reply was lost as the screams of the wounded were joined by a rising cacophony of alarm from the dozens of others still suspended in the compartment. Marcus cupped his ear and leaned in towards Sarah. To his surprise, she grabbed him and kissed him, hard for a brief second, then moved over by his ear.

"Okay!" she shouted, fear in her voice. "I love you!"

"I love you too," Marcus replied. "Now go."

With one last hand squeeze, Sarah moved away, eyes searching the compartment for something to allow her to reach the people floating above their heads. Marcus turned back to the viewport and was startled to see the alien ship was much, much closer than he had expected.

Either her captain's a virtuoso or a fool, he thought in grim admiration. Revising his size estimate upwards, he realized the vessel was a few hundred meters shorter than *Titanic* rather than only half her

165

size as he'd originally guessed. While the alien craft's thick central frame and tapering wing-like structures made it difficult to judge tonnage, Marcus guessed that the designation "heavy" cruiser would be apt. Its outer hull was a mottled red color, with a jagged surface whose texture reminded Marcus of coral.

"Boss," Quentin shouted from beside him, causing him to jump. Marcus felt a moment of intense relief as the man handed him a *Pata* flechette gun and two magazine drums. A short, 30mm bullpup weapon with the magazine drum mounted to the rear, the *Pata* functioned by shooting a cloud of weighted darts in a standard pattern designed to help fill a corridor with metal. While the range was not the greatest at roughly one hundred meters, within that distance anything that did not possess good armor, excellent luck, or some combination thereof in large quantities was going to have a bad day.

Marcus did a quick functions check and chambered the first flechette round as he strode towards the weapons cart Quentin had brought into the room with him. Roughly chest height and three meters in length, the octagonal container held enough weapons to outfit Quentin's full squad as well as some additional materials such as grenades and extra ammunition.

Marcus belatedly realized Aimi was following him when she nearly walked into his back. As he turned to ask her what she was doing, the woman stopped and stowed her energy pistol in a flash of thighs and undergarments.

There's just no way to modestly do that, he thought wryly.

"I'd prefer a rail rifle if you don't mind," Aimi said quietly as she straightened her skirt. She could not have surprised Marcus any more than if she had proposed to him.

"What the hell? Why would I trust you with a rail rifle?!" he replied after a moment.

"Because if I was so fixated on killing you, I could have easily done so at least five times now," the Spartan snapped back exasperatedly. "But more importantly, you'll want more than the two men you have up on that balcony right now. We do not have time to argue about this."

Damn you...

"Kepa," Marcus seethed, "give Miss Eguchi the *Kanabo*."

Surprise briefly crossed Kepa's broad face before he regained control. The big Australasian shook his head, and then broke open the bottom rack. Reaching in, he pulled out a long, slender rifle that looked all the world like an elongated tuning fork attached to a trigger assembly and battery pack. As Aimi took the dark green weapon and started checking it, Marcus went to the front of the weapons cart and punched in a series of numbers, then followed that with pressing his hand onto a combination palm reader / DNA scanner. With a low tone, the compartment opened to reveal a small, gold-colored satchel. Marcus reached in and grabbed the bag, looping its small retaining strap into his belt loop.

You would think people would be hoarse by now, he thought angrily, as the noise began building to a crescendo. Once again turning back towards the viewport, the alien vessel's skin peeled open exactly enough to engulf the viewport window, the edges of the opening taking on the appearance of some giant octopod sucker. The liner shuddered as the opening attached to *Titanic*'s hull, immediately followed by some sort of opaque film covering the front of the viewport.

Great. We're about to get attacked by freakin' Kraken aliens. Please Lord, if this is a nightmare let me wake up... Marcus thought.

"You have any other weapons to spare?" Senator Du asked, startling him. The Spartan was standing with five members of his security team, the men in various states of dishevelment.

"Senator..." Marcus began, only to receive the second '*Don't be an idiot...*' glare from a Spartan in less than fifteen minutes.

"I assure you, Mr. Martin, that this is not my first boarding action," Du said crisply. "They will not say 'Senator Du died shitting himself behind some table...' when they write the history of this day."

No, instead they'll say some tentacle monster blew you away because you were a fool, Marcus thought. He gestured for Kepa to start handing out weapons. The Australasian had just started doing so when the viewport brightened considerably, cutting through some of the darkness imparted by the film. Even as he turned, Marcus knew what that meant. Looking through the viewport to see the enemy vessel's outer hatch now open just confirmed his initial suspicions.

"Grognards!" he shouted, using his nickname for the security folks. "On the deck!" Even at the top of his lungs, only a few of the security heard him. Thankfully enough had turned to see what his orders were that they followed his example.

*If I get out of this alive, I am going to **strongly** suggest that security communications be considered a vital function*, Marcus thought bitterly. *Obviously some stupid engineer prioritized...*

The explosion caught him and everyone else in the ballroom by surprise. In an instant the "film" detonated with a bright, bluish-green light and thunderous wave of sound. The latter spared Marcus and

167

everyone else who survived the blast the horrid sounds of thousands of transparisteel shards scything through the room and most of its still floating occupants. In most cases, the intersection was instantly fatal, as the sharp metal cut through cloth, bone, and organs like a butcher's cleaver. However, there was a significant number both standing on the deck and floating just above when the blast hit whom were "saved" from instant death either by intervening bodies or debris that shielded their vital organs. Marcus had a momentary image of a man, formerly in an expensive tuxedo and tails, dumbly regarding his severed arms floating just before him. The man's heart continued to pump even as he floated away from his limbs, the arterial spray floating behind him like some macabre skywriting experiment.

A storm of azure energy blasts shooting across the room like summer lightning snapped his head back to the hatch. Clearing much of what the viewport blast had left from midair, the ozone smell added to the various slaughterhouse aromas that were already filling the room. As Marcus watched, several planters took direct hits from the energy bolts yet remained more or less whole.

Okay, the cover's holding up against what…holy fuck, **lizards?!**

Indeed, the first aliens to storm through the hatch were bipedal, fast moving reptiles. Roughly two meters in height, the dark green, almost black creatures walked upright on two muscular legs with thick, spined tails erect behind them. Their faces were blunt and broad, with green eyes that swiftly and coldly swept the room looking for targets as they stepped into the ballroom. All ten clutched energy weapons in their long, four-fingered hands, the azure bolts spewing out towards anywhere they thought might hide enemy.

"Open fire!" Marcus shouted, putting word into action around the corner of the weapon's cart. With an aimpoint at the center of the former viewport, he completely missed the first group of aliens as they sprung towards the sides in a coordinated movement. The storm of flechettes did hit dead center into the next group, and Marcus saw a spray of bright green blood and scales before diving back behind the weapons cart. His move came just in time, as several energy bolts slammed where he had been, causing the cart to shift. Marcus ignored a scream and the sound of flesh sizzling close behind him as he quickly turned to find more cover.

To his shock, one of the aliens had already almost traversed the ballroom, the lizard turning to engage one of his security men from the side. Marcus fired a split second before the alien did, the darts blasting the creature in half. He turned back to the front just in time to see a lizard leap over a planter, its jaws gaping wider than he would have thought possible as it bit one of Quentin's squad members in half. The lizard's victory was short-lived, as an energy beam from one of Du's security squad cut the being in half.

Gotta move, gotta move, Marcus thought, as the cart took a couple more hits. Moving at a half crouch, he darted for a turned over table. Time seemed to slow as he dashed for the next cover, azure bolts and debris spinning past him. There was a dilated *craaaccckk!* that told him Aimi had engaged with the *Kanabo*, and he had a peripheral vision of an alien whom had been about to hurl some soccer-ball sized object falling backwards into the hatch. As he slid behind the table to find two of Du's men there, a huge blast caused the deck to shake.

Violated Boarding Rule 1, Marcus thought with savage satisfaction as he set the *Pata* down and grabbed his satchel. *You either gain fire superiority, or you keep shooting the damn ship until it's a hulk.* The aliens had done neither of these, and they had paid in blood. Literally. As he palmed the first grenade from the satchel, he turned to the two men.

"Covering fire!" Marcus shouted at the top of his lungs. Both Spartans next to him rolled out from behind the heavy table, firing the rail rifle in their hands at the maximum, battery depleting rate towards the hatchway just as the third group of aliens was starting to come forward. Marcus noted that this group had deployed with shimmering, purple-tinged shields that covered their entire front as they ran forward. Pressing the detent on the cylinder in his hand, Marcus watched as both energy and kinetic penetrators were absorbed by the devices, the second rank of aliens shielded by their comrades in front of them.

Here goes nothing, Marcus thought, throwing the grenade low and with a sidearm motion. The aliens, seeing the object rolling towards them, dropped to one knee and linked their shields together into an impromptu palisade. The grenade hit the front of the purple wall and stopped dead, dropping to the base of it. There was a moment of impromptu silence as everyone looked at the black and blue device just sitting there.

Had Marcus chosen an explosive, concussive, or even incendiary grenade the action would have been exactly correct. However, the device in question had technically been discontinued due to its unstable nature. Implosion weapons, in a loose layman's description, had an effect similar to a miniature black hole. While this was not an absolute truth—miniature black holes had a nasty habit of swallowing entire solar systems through a hole in normal space the size of the average dinner table—the effect on matter in the immediate vicinity was nearly as fatal. Unfortunately for the *Titanic*'s assailants, implosion grenades had been judged too dangerous for shipboard use due to their indiscriminate nature and chaotic effects. While 99.99% of the time they had functioned exactly as designed, in the .01% of the time they'd demonstrated a nasty propensity to devastate everything for three times the planned five meter radius. As with all declined prototype weapons, this had meant that they were available for purchase by system defense forces or similarly licensed parties…such as Czarina Lines security personnel.

With a high-pitched screech, the lead alien rank, their shields, and the connecting hatchway all ceased to exist. The second rank did not even have enough time to perceive the death of their fellows as the brief, massive energy pulse eliminated their basic atomic bonds and seared back into their vessel and into the first few meters of the ballroom. Before *Titanic*'s defenders had time to truly register the blast, all loose items began hurtling towards the suddenly open gap. Marcus watched as the satchel was briefly held horizontal by the retaining loop around his belt, the sudden gale force suction attempting to tear it away. The incident was brief, however, as with the screech of hull plating on metal the observation port's emergency door slammed upwards with disturbing rapidity, causing several objects, debris and cadavers still in motion in the zero gravity to slam against it. Ominously, Marcus heard a low, sibilant hissing that told him the liner's damage had prevented the door from shutting fully.

Thank you, builders, for making the vacuum detection sensors a vital system, Marcus thought, a sudden wave of fatigue sweeping over him as he scanned the room. The returned half light made it hard to see, but there did not appear to be any of the aliens that had survived. Even so, they had minutes, if that, to get out of the ballroom before the air was exhausted.

"Everyone out," he shouted hoarsely, moving forward to make sure none of his men still down on the deck were living. His quick check told him that while the alien weapons had a problem with ferrocrete, they were devastatingly effective against flesh and bone. Turning, Marcus had the overwhelming urge to sit down.

*So…tired…*he thought, the world starting to spin. Distantly, he heard the metal clang of the corridor shutting.

Shit. His mind tried to remember why that sound was critically important, but he kept coming up with nothing as he sank to his knees.

A slender, feminine form started to come out of the smoke, its gait familiar in a way that made his heart ache.

"Katina?" he gasped. Quicker than he could react, the woman slapped him, the blow so forceful he fell to his knees. The strike was followed up by a mask being forced onto his face, with its straps ran roughly over the back of his head.

"Next time warn us, you *idiot*," Aimi snapped as she switched on the small tank attached to the mask. Marcus took a deep, shuddering breath as oxygen burned into his lungs. His mind clearing almost instantly, he staggered to his feet as he began to feel a chill.

"Hurry up! I am not dying here because of you!" Aimi snapped, striding purposefully towards the door. Marcus followed her, surprised he almost had to break into a run to keep up. They reached the inner corridor door, with Aimi banging on it twice, then three times, then once. With a warning klaxon, the smaller access door opened, and the nimble woman dived through the gap before it even finished. Marcus was almost as quick, nearly running into the Spartan's back.

"Marcus!" Sarah screamed from his left. There was just enough time to turn before her arms were around him in a vice grip, her head buried in his chest.

"As touching as this moment is," Senator Du observed, his tone frigid, "please tell me you have a plan beyond nearly killing us all."

Marcus gave the man a hard look as he took the emergency mask off.

"Yes, actually I do," Marcus replied grimly.

Shigure
1725 SST

You know, I somehow expected **Titanic** *to put up a little bit more of a fight,* Leslie thought as she watched her sensor feed. *Barely fifteen minutes after we jump into system and those cruisers are all over her like Apex Wolves on a nursery.*

"Contact Charlie is merging with the passenger liner, Captain," Southwell reported, his tone subdued.

"I don't think she figured out those bastards were hostile before they fired on her," Iokepa said quietly in her ear.

"Get out of my head XO," she snapped, then softened her tone. "Maybe she shouldn't have been out here at all if she wasn't ready to shoot at anything not displaying a transponder."

"Well at least she occupied the cruisers so they stopped looking for us," Iokepa replied, clearly nonplussed. "Of course, as big as she is I'm not surprised they forgot about a little old destroyer."

"How soon until the recon drones are close enough to get good passive resolution?" Leslie asked.

"Another ten minutes, Captain," Southwell replied.

Leslie fought down the urge to let out an exasperated sigh.

Too much thrust and the drones show up on sensors like a torch in a dark room, Leslie thought. Too little and they end up getting sucked into the planet. We've got a good enough picture right now.

"I'll give them an 'A' for aggressiveness," Iokepa remarked conversationally on the command link. Leslie nearly snapped a retort than stopped herself. "I'm not sure I'd try and jump what appeared to be a capital ship with three heavy cruisers."

Everyone one has different ways of compartmentalizing, she thought. *We've quite possibly watched the death of 5,000 people whose sole mistake was getting on a ship captained by an idiot.*

"I might if I had whatever weapons they're packing," Leslie replied evenly. "They blew one of *Titanic*'s engine pods clean off."

"Well that's why you don't put your engines external to the hull," Iokepa said sardonically. "Obviously someone wasn't paying attention in Shipbuilding 101..."

"Some shipbuilders have started doing it because it helps with in system maneuvering," Major Acheros interrupted. "It also allows you to save weight because you don't have to burn as much mass shielding the reactor spaces. I just don't see how they got that past the Safety Board."

Leslie looked up at Acheros in shock. He shrugged in his seat.

"I come from a merchant family," Acheros said. "It's hard not to pick things up."

Well that will teach me to pigeonhole someone.

Bridge
Titanic
1740 SST

"Hull breach, Ballroom A," Coors reported from his station. Abraham was amazed at how normal the man sounded, considering he had a dead body floating lazily over his head. "Emergency door has been activated."

Strange how the most intense screwups are often the coolest under pressure, Titanic's master thought. *I wonder if it's because they're too stupid to realize the utter peril they are in?*

"Ms. O'Barr, how long until engineering can get our main drives back from the Dutchman?" Abraham asked.

"Sir, I cannot get a hold of the Chief Engineer," O'Barr replied. "My nearest security teams report that they have no contact either. There are boarders between them and the Firerooms."

Abraham closed his eyes. Other than the Firerooms, there were auxiliary Dutchman access ports that were located in the dorsal maneuvering pod…which was more than likely in a decaying orbit towards Sapphire. The next group was located at the auxiliary bridge…which no one had heard from since they had been attacked. Looking at O'Connor crumpled in the corner and Vo floating lifelessly overhead with the helmsman, Abraham did not have much hope that the auxiliary bridge would be responding anytime soon. The place was not exactly an ergonomic nightmare, but it did not take much imagination to see at least a half dozen ways all eight watch standers could have been killed.

I should have listened to Martin, Abraham thought, a wave of guilt washing over him. He shook off the effects while cursing the pain medicine's tendency to cause emotional swings.

"Any word from the First Mate?" Abraham asked.

"No, Sir," O'Barr replied from her station. As if proving Al-Madur's folly, the security guard's only visible wound was a darkening bruise that covered her entire left cheek. "I have no comms with Mr. Martin either."

Goddammit! He looked towards where Federov lay strapped down, unconscious in the VIP room. While no one had explicitly stated what the executive's malady was, O'Barr had muttered darkly about him 'talking nonsense and needing sedation."

I can only hope that he wakes up in time to die screaming for this, Abraham thought, anger rising.

"Rail gun status?" he snapped, looking back towards the shattered main viewscreen.

"Seventy percent on each broad…"

"*What*?! We don't need *both* broadsides, Ms. O'Barr! There's only one side that has a fucking cruiser trying to rape us!"

O'Barr recoiled as if he had slapped her, and Abraham immediately regretted letting his rage show.

173

An Unproven Concept

My God, the First Mate really needs to get here, thought Abraham . *I'm not sure I am of sound mind.*

"Sir, message buoy uploads complete," Vu said, the last part coming out as a whimper as the woman shifted.

"I am sorry, Ms. O'Barr,"Abraham said. "Tell me when we get to eighty percent on the port battery. Ms. Vu, prepare to eject the message buoys."

I hope someone gets our message and comes quick, Abraham thought to himself. He had been brief, the better to help the buoys transmit the message then jump to the next system. Coors had uploaded the bare minimum of sensor data to convey the seriousness of the situation for the same reason.

Of course, all that will be great evidence at our Court of Inquiry. I'm sure whomever recovers our bodies...

With a visible shake of the head, Abraham stopped himself from mentally drifting.

"Eject message buoys, Ms. Vu," he rasped.

Titanic had been designed with twenty-eight message buoys. Four of them had been destroyed in the initial barrage that had crippled her. When Vu pressed her button, four more either ejected into the side of the alien cruiser or spun out of control without their Herbert drive firing. The twenty survivors immediately winked out of existence, carrying the liner's hopes, dreams and chances for survival with them.

"Buoys away, Captain!" Vu stated.

Abraham was about to acknowledge Vu's statement when there was the sound of many running feet from the corridor. O'Barr stepped away from her station, an energy pistol appearing in her hand from just inside of her waistband. Fortunately for the passenger who came running into the room, O'Barr wasn't the shoot first, ask questions later type.

"Aliens!" the man gasped, grabbing his knees. "There are aliens! They're heading this way!"

"How many?" O'Barr barked from her station.

"At least a dozen, probably closer to twenty," the man wheezed. "Big fucking lizards."

"What?" Abraham asked as Vu and Coors both gasped.

"They're lizards. About two or two and a half meters tall. I saw them kill a man, bit his head clean off."

Holy shit, Abraham thought, pulse quickening.

"Captain, with your permission I'm going to divert power from the starboard battery to comms," O'Barr said, her tone quick and anxious. "I cannot advise you if I don't know what's going on."

"Do it," Abraham said.

"Eighty percent power on the port battery," O'Barr said quietly.

Well I'm not sitting here waiting to be a main course, Abraham thought darkly. *At least we're going to die with our boots on.*

"Fire when ready, Ms. O'Barr."

The *Titanic*'s main battery had been taken from the decommissioned battleship *Maine*. Despite being four decades old, the weapons had been remodeled and refurbished, with the chief improvement being the integration of Spartan rail gun materials into the ammunition supply. As a result, Captain Herrod's statement that O'Barr need not wait for full power was somewhat of an understatement given the range. Due to the disparity in relative size between the two vessels, five of the rail guns fired their slugs uselessly into vacuum.

The misses were to be the sole mercy experienced by the manta-shaped vessel, as the three railgun slugs that did connect more than made up for their poorly-aimed fellows. Hitting forward, amidships, and astern the three hammer blows simultaneously shattered the alien ship's bridge, secondary command post and engineering. The last was the most serious, as in a brilliant starburst of radiation and light the vessel's powerplant began to destabilize.

Only the final act of an alien engineer prevented the cruiser and *Titanic* from completely disintegrating. Instead, like suicidal lovers leaping off a cliff, the starliner and her assailant began to fall inexorably towards Sapphire.

Shigure
Titanic
1745 SST

"Holy shit! *Titanic* has just vented additional atmosphere!"

Leslie's focused on the passenger liner's icon, enlarging it in time to see the last vestiges of an amber outpouring from her icon.

175

"Looks like the boarding didn't go as planned," Acheros remarked. "Would hope not with the security team the book says she has aboard."

Leslie was about to reply when *Titanic*'s icon suddenly spewed out a stream of twenty smaller contacts. Before she could inquire as to what they were, all twenty winked out of existence in flashes of energy.

"Captain, *Titanic* has just fired her main battery on Charlie!" Southwell reported.

"What?!" Leslie asked, incredulous.

"Contact Charlie is venting atmosphere and spiking ener...sensors indicate she just shut her reactors down!"

"That's madness!" Talo exclaimed breathlessly. "They could have blown her up right on top of themselves!"

It's only madness if what's going on aboard doesn't make getting blown to pieces a better alternative, Leslie thought. Looking up, she saw Acheros was coming to the same conclusion.

"Okay, obviously someone's still alive on the bridge as well," Leslie remarked.

"Well that kills my suggestion to just toss ten implosion warheads in there and be done with it," Iokepa muttered.

"Major Acheros, how long could you hold a liner of that size with her security team?" Leslie asked after a moment's pause.

Acheros pondered for a moment as he quickly reviewed the *Titanic*'s schematics.

"Assuming I had power and some semblance of life support, four hours tops. That's assuming half my security team didn't just go on an unplanned space walk. Maybe a couple more hours if the subdivisions and damage made things dicey for the boarders."

"Nearest heavy units are at least nine hours away according to planned Fleet movements," Iokepa informed Leslie before she could ask.

Shigure's captain compressed her lips in a thin line.

A captain's first duty is to the human race. Their second is to the Confederation, next is the Fleet, and last is to their crew... she thought, reciting the Confederation Fleet Captain's oath.

"Guns, get your folks to switching to conventional warheads, with all except four weapons in the last salvo," Leslie said.

"Aye aye, Captain," Southwell replied.

"XO, secure Battle Two then execute Plan Skeleton. Grab all the provisions you can from the wardroom, then report to me when you're in the escape pods ready to launch. You have forty minutes," Leslie said over the command net, her mouth suddenly cotton.

"What?! Captain, you can't..." Iokepa began to argue.

"Do not make me repeat myself, Lieutenant Commander!" Leslie snapped, then switched to the bridge's net. She paused to look over the bridge crew.

"Ensign Griffon, secure your station and report to the XO in Battle Two," Leslie ordered. There was a moment of silence as the young officer looked at Leslie in shock.

"Captain, I'm sorry, I should not have released..." Griffon began, the last part coming out as a sob as her emotional dam burst.

"Ensign!" Leslie barked, then softened her tone, "This has nothing to do with how you have conducted your duties. You're non-essential to a fight, and if we fail the court of inquiry will need witnesses from the bridge."

There was a moment of confusion, then suddenly horrified comprehension on Griffon's face. Leslie turned from the officer and towards Southwell.

"Guns, deploy the last four decoys and start bringing them towards the planet's north pole, *slowly*. Hold them just below the horizon if they beat us into our position. Helm, bring us on a course that will put us one hundred thousand kilometers below Sapphire's south pole, all ahead slow."

"Aye aye, Captain," Talo replied, turning from where Griffon was finishing securing her station. The ensign stood up and walked over to her roommate. Both officers raised their visors, Talo cutting her audio feed so the rest of the bridge couldn't hear. After a brief exchange of words Talo turned away from Griffon to head back to her chair. Leslie saw that the the Helm officer's face was so pale it was almost ethereal before Talo dropped her helmet's visor back into place.

"Station secured, Captain," Griffon said, her voice faint.

"Thank you, Ensign Griffon. Now get going, I'm sure the XO will need you to oversee setting up the escape pod comms."

"Aye aye, Captain." With that she came to attention and saluted.

"I'm not planning a death ride, Helena," Leslie replied as she returned the gesture. "You're going to feel awfully silly when you and Lieutenant Talo are playing chess in the wardroom a week from now. Now get going."

The young officer smiled at that, then turned and left, her shoulders shaking. Leslie watched her go, then turned back to see the rest of the bridge looking at her.

"I think you all have jobs to do," she said simply. "Time's awastin'.

The Ballroom (Adams)

Chapter 6: Clarion Calls and Shattered Rains

Constitution
1745 SST
21 June

"You look like you went five rounds with an automatic meat tenderizer," Andrea observed, the worry under her sarcasm quite evident as Jason exited their latrine wearing just his T-shirt and a pair of mesh shorts. Andrea was similarly loosely attired, with her crop top and sweat pants cutoffs making her look like a young woman hanging out in her college dorm.

"I feel like it," Jason replied as he gingerly shuffled over to their kitchen area. "I'm just glad that Captain Bolan decided to hold off on AARs until we get *Shokaku* Battle Group's logs, because a two hour nap was not enough to put this old man back together."

Andrea rolled her eyes at him.

"Yes, well, maybe the *old man* should have let someone else play cheese to the mousetrap," Andrea replied.

"You know cheese doesn't work all that well, right?" Jason said, deadpan.

"There are days I could beat you," Andrea observed.

"Then you remember striking a superior officer is punishable with up to sixty days confinement with bread and water?"

"It might be worth it."

"Right. Because a woman who still cuts the crust off of the food replicator bread is going to somehow endure two months of hardtack?"

"About as well as a smart aleck is going to endure two months of a different type of hardship if he keeps talking," Andrea replied with a slight raise of her eyebrows.

"Empty threats, empty...*oof*!" Jason exhaled in surprise as a dinner roll bounced off the side of his head.

"Less talking, more lasagna," Andrea muttered. "Some of us have to go back on shift in two hours, and I want to watch a holovid before then."

"Impatience is no reason to start hurling foodstuffs," Jason replied with mock indignation as he opened the replicator and pulled the tray of lasagna out. Marveling again at technology's ability to take some protein and carbohydrate paste tubes and construct a passable pasta dish out of it, the fighter pilot maneuvered the hot plate onto the table. As was their tradition, the two of them stretched their legs out to each other's chairs as they dug into their plates.

"So what's the plan, or do you know?" she asked.

"Well, apparently Captain Bolan and the system defense folks are figuring that out as we speak," Jason said. "Right now the plan is to get us into orbit around Midnattsol so Captain Bolan can meet with the head of the System Defense. Thankfully he's taking a day to do a 'system reconnaissance' before that."

"Oh I bet the System Defense loved that one," Andrea observed with a slight smirk.

"Best to get the working relationship established right off the bat," Jason replied. "Especially since *Theodosius* was quick to park herself in orbit around Midnattsol at their request."

"Okay, not seeing the problem with that," Andrea said. "I remember reading about the *Theodosius* being the 'cutting edge of technology.' I was in the 8th grade."

"So not that long ago," Jason replied, his mouth half full.

"Flattery will get you everywhere, even if you're a blatant liar," she said with a half smile. "Seriously, that ship is one of the oldest in the fleet, and I wouldn't have blamed her captain if he'd told the System Defense folks 'Um, I'm going to go get some help...' as he ran like hell out of the system."

Jason shrugged.

"There are jobs where you get to send the shit sandwich back to the kitchen. Captain of a Fleet warship isn't one of them."

Andrea rolled her eyes.

"That's noble, but there's no point in dying just to buy some random planet another ten minutes before it gets pillaged."

Jason gave his wife a wry look.

"You're so sensitive and altruistic."

"No, that's realistic. *Theodosius* is a glorified light cruiser at this point."

Andrea's vehemence was slightly surprising to Jason, as he felt her legs tense next to his.

"Okay, is there something I'm missing here?"

Andrea closed her eyes and sighed.

"You've heard me and my family talk about my secondary classmate Xavi, right?"

"Yeah, but usually in passing."

"The reason it's in passing is because he was more than a friend," Andrea said quietly. "It's just my family, unlike some other people's, has the decency not to bring up old flames all that often."

Jason winced.

"Look, Mom thinks the sun rises and sets on you now...," Jason started.

"But she wasn't sure if I was a flavor of the month and was basically "cock blocking" you to prove a point?" Andrea finished for him with a smile.

"Okay, I wasn't going to put it quite that bluntly," Jason replied sardonically.

"Oh, I'm just putting it exactly how your mother put it on my hen's night," Andrea said, a smile briefly piercing the shadow that had fallen over her face. "I thought your sister was going to no kidding piss herself in shock."

Jason was surprised to feel his face warming, but was saved from further embarrassment by Andrea resuming her story.

"Xavi's first assignment was aboard the *Leicester*, the *Theodosius*'s sister ship," Andrea said. "Like me, he took engineering as his track, as we figured that would make it a lot easier to at least get assignments in the same task group even if we didn't get the same ships."

Andrea stopped for a moment to collect herself.

"The problem with an older ship for an engineer is you're constantly putting out fires," she said, her voice quavering. "Well, two minutes after coming on watch Xavi had to deal with a problem on the *Leicester*'s number one fusion bottle. Lieutenant Avery, the previous watch officer, offered to go deal with it, but Xavi figured that was screwing him over. So he just asked Avery to cover for him long enough to go grab a couple of ratings and the EVA gear from the storage locker."

Jason saw Andrea's lip starting to quiver and began pushing his chair back.

"No, Jason, if you come over here I'm just going to start blubbering," Andrea said, her voice almost a sob.

"I know how this ends," Jason said, springing up and coming over to embrace his love. With a sob she folded into his arms, clinging to him as if he was the last handhold between her and floating off a hull.

"The captain of the *Leicester*'s board of inquiry was my sponsor when I was in the Academy," Jason said softly as he held Andrea.

182

"They…they said there was nothing he could have done," Andrea replied, her shoulders shaking as she held back sobs. "But damned if he didn't try to go back in there and save whoever he could. When they found him, they say his suit was redder than a tomato."

Jason rubbed his hands over Andrea's back, feeling helpless as he held her.

"I'm sorry," Andrea said, her breath shuddering. "I don't mean to be such a wreck…"

"Honey, it's okay," Jason replied soothingly. "I'm sorry I picked that scab."

Andrea shrugged.

"How could you have known? It's not like I told you, and I'm sorry for that. Plus it's not like two tours on the outer rim didn't kill most of the friendships I used to have, so no one else was really around to tell you."

"Why would I need to know?" Jason asked. "You remember the deal you made with me after my mother apparently decided to test how much we really meant to each other?"

"That as long as the past stayed in the past I wasn't going to let it affect the future? Yes, but…"

"But nothing. Have I ever not been about reciprocation?" Jason asked, leaning back slightly so Andrea looked up at him. He shook his head dramatically while mouthing *"Noooo."* The movement caused her to giggle, and she started to wipe her nose with the back of her hand before catching herself.

"Yes, that's right, my name is Andrea and I'm a sex goddess," she said, starting to reach for a napkin. Before she could complete the movement, Jason kissed her, eliciting a startled sound before she began to return it.

"I love you," Jason said, "snot and all."

"I love you too," Andrea replied, wiping her nose. "We should probably finish dinner. I get the feeling we're going to be very busy this next week."

A few dozen meters forward of the Owderkirks, Captain Bolan was reaching the same conclusion as he passed the XO a bottle of brandy.

"You know that brandy is far too good to ruin on coffee, right Sir?" Commander Alexander asked after looking at the label. It bore the title *Moldavian Jaeger Schnapps* in ornate golden script scrolling across the bottle. The centerpiece of the label was a grizzled old man in a traditional Germanic hunting outfit holding a muzzle loading rifle in one hand and a metal tin cup in another. Even if he hadn't recognized the brand, the painting's detail and the fact the script looked like it contained actual gold would have told Alexander how expensive it was.

"XO, when you recover a freighter full of luxury goods from pirates some folks are more appreciative than others," Bolan replied. "Besides, I only break the bottle out for special occasions."

"Like, say, monkey stomping the *Shokaku* like a Silverback Griffon?"

"Pretty much," Bolan said with a smile as Alexander took a sip of his coffee.

"Holy shit, Sir, that's good…"

Alexander was cut off by the room suddenly tilting to its right, the brandy bottle being flung off Bolan's desk to shatter against the starboard bulkhead even as both men's coffee sloshed from their cups onto the captain's desk. Before either could start cursing the *Constitution*'s klaxons began screaming the proximity alert.

"What the fuck?!" Alexander snarled. "I'm going to kill goddamn Horinek!" It had been the Navigation officer's turn to stand OOD while the remainder of *Constitution*'s wardroom had gotten some well deserved rest.

"Nav has several qualities, but excitability isn't one of them," Bolan replied grimly. As if on cue, the overhead speaker buzzed.

"Report Nav," Bolan said tersely.

"Sir, we just had an object fold into space at five hundred kilometers," Horinek said, her voice preternaturally calm. "It's giving off the signature of a distress buoy, and Lieutenant Herrod is trying to get through the encoding now."

"Why is he having problems with the encoding?" Alexander snapped.

"It appears to be damaged, Commander," Horinek replied.

Shit, Bolan thought, a feeling of dread starting to creep into his stomach.

"Sound General Quarters," Bolan barked. "Tell Comms to stop pushing through the coding long enough to get off a burst message to Midnattsol and the *Theodosius* telling them we just had a distress buoy nearly bounce off the prow."

"Aye aye, Captain," Horinek replied.

"Speaker off," Bolan said, then turned to Alexander. "I'm betting money that's *Titanic*."

"Why am I having flashbacks to History 202 and my lieutenant days?" Alexander muttered as he followed Bolan towards the hatch. The two of them had almost reached it when the *Constitution*'s klaxon began sounding 'General Quarters.'

"Gee, because "Good Ideas…That Weren't" is always a memorable class?" Bolan replied as they stepped into the senior officer's suit room.

"Thank God there aren't any icebergs in space," Alexander stated.

"No just asteroids. Although asteroids don't usually let someone get off a scream for help," Bolan said.

"They're elegantly boring like that," Alexander replied, opening the hatch to the passageway only to be nearly ran down by a rushing Sinclair and Sakai. Both men apologized as they slipped by to open the bridge hatch, followed by Alexander.

"Captain on the bridge!" Horinek sang out as Bolan stepped through the opening.

"At ease. What do we have?"

"Still working on the identity, Sir," Herrod said. "*Theodosius* is hailing us."

"My station," Bolan said as he settled into his command chair.

"Aye aye, Sir," Herrod replied.

"Captain Gadhavi, *Constitution* actual," Bolan said.

"I got word from your OOD that you nearly hit a distress buoy," Captain Gadhavi said. "Had not gotten an update so thought it'd be a good idea to make sure everything was all right."

Listening to his tone, Bolan had the distinct impression that the man was slightly miffed that Bolan hadn't responded quicker.

The man is under the mistaken impression that he is the ranking officer here, Bolan thought. Technically Gadhavi was senior to him by a full three years, plus had eight months more captain's time due to the *Theodosius* being his second command. Unfortunately, there was the little matter of the *Constitution* being a capital ship. Given that the Confederation Fleet did not habitually hand command of battlecruisers, battleships, or carriers to village idiots, Fleet Regulations were quite explicit that Bolan was the commander of all forces in the Helgoland System at the moment. Even more explicit were the orders signed by Kraken Six.

"We are coming to General Quarters, Captain Gadhavi," Bolan observed easily. "I was giving you the opportunity to finish doing the same before I troubled you with any further…"

185

"*Oh my God!*" Herrod exclaimed, his tone one of pure horror. "*It's the* **Titanic***!*"

Bolan killed his comms and whirled in his chair with one smooth motion. He did not get a chance to speak before Commander Alexander had already closed the distance to the Comms station.

Okay, so Nav is not excitable, but apparently Comms just may have to wear diapers, Bolan thought disgustedly.

"Lieutenant Herrod, I think there was a report in there somewhere," Alexander snapped. Shaking himself, the younger officer looked up from his screen, his face paler than a sheet of paper.

"Sir, the distress buoy is from the *Titanic*," Herrod replied, his voice soft.

"Onscreen my location," Bolan barked. "Then burst that message to System Defense Command and the *Theodosius*."

"Sir, it's only audio at the moment," Herrod replied. "It will be another three minutes until I can get a visual to go with it."

"Send what you have," Bolan replied, gesturing for the Comms officer to hurry up. Thirty seconds later, the message started to play in his helmet.

Lord, I swear I will never make fun of a simple asteroid again, Bolan thought frantically, fighting to maintain his calm. *The whole bridge crew needs to see this.*

"Replay that message on the central screen," Bolan started breathlessly then, gained a firmer control of himself. "Helm, inform *Theodosius* that we are preparing to depart the system while Mr. Herrod gets that on screen."

"Aye aye," Sakai replied, pressing several buttons on his helm controls. Bolan heard him start to speak as the central screen flickered then projected a slightly distorted image.

It should be clear to everyone why Lieutenant Herrod was freaking out, Bolan thought. A man who bore a marked resemblance to the Comms officer appeared on screen. Having heard the message already, Bolan had time to pay attention to the visual details.

Captain Herrod's strapped down and there's clearly no gravity, Bolan noted as objects, some clearly organic debris, floated across the screen behind *Titanic*'s master. *That's really, really bad.*

"This is Captain Abraham Herrod of the Czarina Liner *Titanic*. We are under attack by alien vessels. I say again, we are under attack by *alien vessels*. Please assist us immediately."

Looking around the bridge, Bolan could see that the message had stunned all of his officers except one. Horinek was looking at her maps, clearly doing calculations in her head. After a moment, she turned to him and spoke.

"Sir, it is three hours to the Zed-815 system," the Nav Officer began crisply, bringing her charts up on the screen. As if galvanized by her example, the rest of the bridge crew sprang into action at their stations.

"That message is over thirty minutes old, Horinek," Bolan replied. "We don't have three hours."

Horinek turned and was about to make a sharp retort than caught herself. Taking a moment to gather her thoughts, she continued in a tone that was as respectful as her words were biting.

"Sir, with all due respect, if the *Titanic*'s captain didn't want to be an ex-Ts main course, he should have stayed in established shipping lanes."

*My God, what was she **about** to say?* Bolan thought.

Turning, he saw that Herrod was starting to unstrap himself from his chair, the blood rushing to his face.

There can be no good reason for him to do that, Bolan thought.

"At ease, Comms!" he barked, then turned to Horinek. The woman did not look contrite in the least.

"You're a Nav officer," Bolan said, his voice full of challenge. "Figure me out a course that gets us there quicker. I will accept moderate risk to this vessel. You have ten minutes."

Horinek smiled slightly, and Bolan could almost hear her voice going *"Challenge accepted"* in his head.

"Aye aye, sir," she replied. Bolan noticed her face starting to get slightly flush as she turned around.

Okay, maybe I should've given her a little more guidance than that. That woman's an adrenaline junkie. Bolan turned to speak to the XO only to find the man had already slipped out of the bridge's rear hatch.

"Get me Commander Alexander, my station," Bolan said to Herrod. The Comms officer turned away from glaring daggers at Horinek to look at his captain with surprise then disgust clearly on his face.

"Aye, Sir," Herrod gritted out.

Obviously he was expecting me to give Horinek some sort of rebuke, Bolan thought with some annoyance. She'd have one coming if she wasn't right.

"XO?" Bolan asked after a moment.

"Sir?" Alexander replied, clearly running back towards Battle Two.

"Tell Warhawk One and Kaiju One what the hell is going on," Boland ordered. "Do not tell anyone else until Boyles gets the sensor data off the drone. Did you get a chance to see the message before you left the bridge?"

"I saw the start of it, then caught the rest on my suit feed.," Alexander retorted. "Figured you needed me in Battle Two more than you needed me standing there."

"Well you missed the excitement," Bolan continued lowly. "We nearly had a brawl on the bridge between Navs and Comms." *Constitution*'s master quickly filled his XO in on what was said.

"A for truthfulness, F for tact," Alexander stated, his tone indicating he was more on Horinek's side than Herrod's. "Captain, what's our plan?"

"I'm still working that through, XO," Bolan replied grimly. "We don't know if help's coming for the bad guys yet, but we do know that our nearest help is several hours away."

"Could always be the final vessels of a dying civilization," Alexander replied hopefully.

Bolan shook his head at the lame attempt of humor, a slight smile coming to his face regardless.

"Glad to see you can maintain levity in times of stress, XO," Bolan replied.

"Sir, I've stripped the *Titanic*'s sensor information out of the pods," Boyles reported.

"Understood. Mr. Herrod, a word," Bolan said, gesturing for the Comms officer to come over. The young lieutenant stood up stiffly, his body posture that of a man about to be bullwhipped.

Best to get this out of the way before it becomes a problem.

"XO, you have the conn for two minutes," Bolan stated, then killed his microphone and raised his suit visor while gesturing for Herrod to do the same. He regarded the younger Herrod pensively before he spoke.

"Lieutenant, I cannot have any more emotional displays like the one earlier. I'm going to level with you—things do not look good for the *Titanic*, and I have no intention of putting this vessel at undue risk. Do you understand?"

Herrod nodded, visibly fighting back tears.

"I have watched loved ones die," Bolan said grimly. "I have neither the time nor the desire to go through my service history, you should know my past and my reputation. If you desire, I will put you on Pinnace One under the pretense of having you hand carry the sensor data to *Theodosius*."

Herrod stiffened, and Bolan watched a single tear roll unbidden down his cheek. Before the man could say or do anything more, Bolan continued.

"There will be no black mark on your record, and the reasoning will remain between us *should I survive*," Bolan continued, making sure Herrod realized the gravity of the situation. "Of course, if I don't, feel free to make up whatever story you see fit."

Despite himself, Herrod cracked a slight smile…which was Bolan's intent.

"Either way, you need to take a moment, then decide. If you stay, you *stay* and that means everything which may go with that."

Herrod turned and risked a glance towards Boyles. Bolan noted that the sensor officer had surreptitiously rotated her seat so she could watch the two of them out of the corner of her eye.

"Sir, I'm staying," Herrod stated.

"Lieutenant, this is not something you decide based on personal relationships," Bolan replied. "Your siblings have already lost their mother and likely their father. Think carefully."

"Navigation course plotted, Captain," Horinek said. Bolan detected a note of triumph in her voice.

"Time?" he asked while continuing to look at Herrod.

"One hour and fifteen minutes, Captain." Horinek replied, pressing buttons. "Downloading to Helm and Battle Two."

Bolan turned back to Herrod.

"Sir, my answer would be the same whether Lieutenant Boyles and I were dating or not," Herrod replied, his tone raw. "My father is doing his duty. I shall do the same."

"Very well. Take your post, Lieutenant."

"Aye aye, Sir." The young officer turned back to his seat, as Bolan turned his microphone back on.

"Okay XO, what do you have for me?"

"A captain going ape shit, Sir," Alexander said irreverently. "*Theodosius* Actual has been demanding to speak with you for the last four minutes."

"He can wait. Lieutenant Herrod, give me ship wide."

"Aye aye, Sir," Herrod said. A moment later the ship's loudspeakers gave bosun's Word to Be Passed.

An Unproven Concept

Probably should have thought about this a bit further before I started to give a speech, Bolan thought with a moment's panic.

"All hands, this is the Captain. A little over a half hour ago, the starship *Titanic* was attacked without warning by unknown vessels in the Zed-815 system. Her sensor data confirms that these are alien craft."

Bolan paused for a second to let that shock wash over the crew.

"This vessel is the closest ship to render her aid. We will do so immediately. It is my intent to close with these enemy vessels and drive them off or destroy them. Failing that, we shall prevent the *Titanic* from remaining in alien hands by all means necessary."

Bolan could see Herrod's shoulders tighten, then relax as the young lieutenant murmured urgently into his microphone.

"Trust in your division officers and chiefs, do your jobs, and we *will* be successful," Bolan stated, his voice firm. "The Confederation has given us a fast ship, and it is now time for us to take her into harm's way to wreak destruction upon its enemies. Bolan out."

"Sir, Captain Gadhavi *demands* to talk to you," Lieutenant Herrod said. "He..."

The Comms officer stopped dead in his tracks as Bolan held up his hand.

"I know you're just relaying the message and he probably wanted you to quote him on that," Bolan said quietly. "But for future reference, no fellow captain *demands* I talk to them. My position."

"Aye aye, Sir," Herrod replied, his tone completely neutral.

"Captain Bolan, I have been..." Captain Gadhavi began in what was clearly a rebuke.

"Captain Gadhavi, I do not have the time to lecture you on the finer points of Fleet seniority," Bolan snapped. He noted that Herrod, Horinek, and Boyles looked at him aghast while Sakai and Sinclair continued working. A not so subtle hand gesture from the Gunnery Officer made the three junior members of the bridge crew turn back to their duties.

There is something to be said for experience, Bolan thought as the channel remained silent. Satisfied that he had Captain Gadhavi's attention, he continued.

"My Comms officer is beaming you the *Titanic*'s sensor data, our plotted navigational course, and the decrypted message. You will dispatch intrasystem craft or your pinnace to retrieve the rescue buoy, and you will stand by with your vessel to engage any enemy craft which may return here. Do you understand your orders, Captain?"

190

"Yes," Gadhavi seethed.

"Very well. If any other Confederation vessel shows up, you will immediately dispatch it for the Thumin System with all those items. Shipping schedule says that the merchantman *Tomiyama* is inbound in two hours, the liner *Carnegie* is thirty minutes behind her. I suggest you use the liner, but I leave that up to you. Do you have any questions?"

"Yes, I do," Gadhavi said, his voice rising. "Have you ever considered that this might be an elaborate ruse?!"

"Captain, were you paying attention to my Comms officer's name rather than taking umbrage, you would understand why I have discounted that possibility," Bolan stated. "I have no more time to waste on your ego, Bolan out."

After cutting the connection, Bolan turned to Herrod.

"We're done talking to *Theodosius*," Bolan stated simply. "Helm, start taking us out of the system."

"Aye aye, Sir," Sakai replied, putting the helm over. Bolan switched his communicator to his direct channel with Battle Two, raising his monocle to his eye.

"XO, did you monitor my traffic?" Bolan asked.

"Yes Sir, I did," Commander Alexander replied.

"What's Warhawk's status?"

"Warhawk One reports he is ready for launch."

Bolan raised an eyebrow.

"He didn't release his people earlier until they'd fueled and prepped an anti-ship loadout in the magazines," Alexander explained.

There's a reason I would have kept the man over you, Bolan thought with grim satisfaction.

"Sir, data transfer to the *Theodosius* is..." Lieutenant Herrod started to say, causing Bolan to look towards him. The Comms officer was interrupted by a scream of horror from behind Commander Alexander, causing Bolan to reactivate his communications screen. He was just in time to see the XO stab the mute button and whirl towards the sound's originator all in one motion. Alexander's jaw worked furiously, the man turned just far enough away that Bolan couldn't read his lips. After a moment, however, XO stopped, then paled as he turned back towards the monocle.

"Sir, has Horinek lost her mind?! She's got us going through a freakin' asteroid field!"

"Lieutenant Horinek…" Bolan started to snap, looking towards his navigation officer. Horinek looked as if she was already expecting his comment.

"Sir, the Dardanelles system's belt is comprised primarily of small rock and loosely clumped minerals," Horinek replied quickly, running a hand through her hair. "The computer reports only 5% of the rocks are large enough to penetrate our navigational shields."

"Lieutenant, we hit an asteroid in hyperspace we will *die*," Bolan barked.

"Sir, you indicated that getting there quickly enough to do the *Titanic* some good was our primary concern," Horinek replied. "We will be taking a calculated risk."

Seems to be the theme of the day, Bolan thought wearily.

"Very well," Bolan said. He noticed Sakai's shoulders tense like he wanted to say something, then the Helm officer relaxed.

In for a penny, in for a pound. At least if we get killed by an asteroid that saves us the indignity of getting our ass kicked if my gamble is wrong.

"Helm, execute navigational path in three minutes," Bolan said, his voice betraying none of his inner turmoil. "Sound jump warning."

Sakai swallowed visibly before replying, his voice cracking as he pressed the buttons to sound the warning tone.

"Aye aye, executing navigational path."

Commander Alexander diplomatically cleared his throat. "XO?"

"Sir, my navigational officer is quite alarmed at our path," Alexander stated, his own face quite pale.

"We're executing," Bolan replied, his voice clipped. Alexander looked at the camera pick up incredulously then, after a moment, nodded.

"Aye aye, Sir. Battle Two standing by for execution."

"What? Are you people *mad?!*"

This time Bolan recognized the voice as Lieutenant (j.g.) Singh, Battle Two's Navigator.

"Belay that…" Alexander barked, turning away from the screen.

"No! That stupid bitch is going to kill us!" Singh screamed, his voice verging on madness. "We can't fly through a…"

The connection to Battle Two terminated, Commander Alexander killing his feed. Bolan snapped his monocle down back into his chair. Looking up, he saw that all of the bridge crew were tending to their tasks except for Horinek. The slight woman's head was bent over her clasped hands, lips moving quickly.

"Execution in sixty seconds," Sakai said.

I hope that phrase wasn't apt.

"We're going to have to launch our drones once we come out of hyperspace," Bolan said to Boyles. "While they're swimming out, work your magic with the mirrorballs. "

"Aye aye, Captain," Boyles replied.

IF we come out of hyperspace.

"Thirty seconds," Sakai said.

"Sir, should we not send a message buoy to let the *Titanic* know we're coming?" Commander Sinclair said suddenly. Bolan saw Herrod turn, hope starting to cross his face.

"Ten seconds," Sakai stated, sounding the vessel's jump tones.

"No," Bolan replied. "I want to try and surprise them if at all possible."

"Three...two...one. Executing!"

As the *Constitution* accelerated, Bolan found the cold fingers of doubt gripping his stomach. Mentally slapping his reservations away, he began bringing up the *Titanic*'s sensor data.

Let's see what mess you've gotten all of us into, Captain Herrod.

Further in system, another captain was questioning Captain Bolan's judgment.

"I hope that idiot..." Captain Gadhavi started to growl, then caught himself.

That's the first intelligent thing I've seen you do since you've gotten into system, Colonel Aaltonen thought quite uncharitably. Shifting in her ill-fitting space suit, she kept her face passive as she regarded *Theodosius*'s master. Fifteen years living with an abusive stepfather had taught her that small men often looked for targets to reassert themselves upon after being summarily beaten by their betters. While she was technically not Gadhavi's subordinate, being both female and an outsider made her a prime target.

Some people get confused about rank and genitalia in times of stress, she thought grimly. *Probably didn't help that the idiot had his conversation on speaker rather than taking it in his suit.*

"Colonel Aaltonen, I will need an escort for our pinnace," Gadhavi stated.

"Understood Captain," Aaltonen replied, pleasantly surprised that Gadhavi was apparently not going to be an idiot.

Gadhavi exhaled heavily as the *Constitution*'s icon winked out of existence on the sensor screen.

"I am terrified that the next thing we are about to see is a pirate vessel jumping into system," Gadhavi said grimly.

"Captain, my terrifying fear is that we won't," Colonel Aaltonen replied. "I'll have a flight of *Wyverns* ready for you within fifteen minutes."

"Thank you, Colonel," Captain Gadhavi said. Aaltonen made her way over to the *Theodosius*'s communications station.

"Sir, do you know if the *Constitution* scrubbed this data before they sent it over?" *Theodosius*'s sensor officer asked. The short, thin man had a puzzled look on his face as he watched the sensor replay on his screen.

"Explain, Ensign Petrucci," Gadhavi said.

"I moved forward to about fifteen minutes before the attack," Petrucci replied. "There's a rather significant sensor anomaly before the three aliens jump in. I don't know what it is, but it's certainly nothing I've seen before."

The longer he talked, the more Aaltonen had the urge to ask the officer for an ID. However, his words seemed to have an effect on Gadhavi.

"Main screen," Gadhavi said. "Lieutenant Moharren, take a look at this."

Theodusius's Gunnery Officer turned from where she had been checking the heavy cruiser's armament for at least the tenth time since Aaltonen had stepped on the bridge. To say the tall, olive-skinned woman was nervous was like saying a Tycho Desert Cat was angry when wet. She dutifully watched the sensor screen, gesturing for Petrucci to rewind it twice before she spoke.

"Sir, I have no idea what that anomaly is, but it is definitely there," Petrucci said, her brow furrowed. "If *Titanic* had military grade sensors I could tell you more, but it looks like something comes in then immediately disappears."

Gadhavi's forehead was wrinkled in thought, uncertainty written all over his face.

"Comms, prepare a message buoy, destination Thumin system. I know of no Confederation vessel with fold capability, and that sure as hell looks like a Herbert-type drive event followed by a cloaking device."

Aaltonen fought the urge to give a nervous laugh. From Gadhavi's face she could see the man was dead serious, and what he was implying was very, very bad.

"Sir, forgive me, I don't understand," Petrucci stated when he saw no one else was going to speak up.

"I am no longer concerned, Sensors, that Captain Bolan is biting on a pirate decoy," Gadhavi replied slowly, as if concerned what he was about to say would gain the Universe's attention and thus make it so. "I am more concerned that the *Constitution* is about to make contact with not one, but *two* alien races."

Titanic
1825 SST

As he approached yet another hatch to Corridor C, Marcus found himself thinking back to his Marine officer basic course. His drill instructor, a tall, wiry Warrant Officer nicknamed 'The Spider' had been feeling rather benevolent one day after trying his damndest to kill them all in Zero-G Initial Entry. Rather than making the twenty remaining trainees queue up once again, Spider had gathered the group for some impromptu professional development.

"You idiots don't get it," Spider had told them as they were all in the front leaning rest position, his face focused on his own faraway memory. "It's not the lack of gravity that will be what sticks with you. Oh no, all you pussies who keep puking in your helmets will eventually get used to that. No asshats, it will be the *smell* that you will never, *ever* be able to overcome."

The decisions made by *Titanic*'s central computer had had devastating consequences within the vessel's common spaces. Making their way aft, Marcus and the Ballroom A survivors had seen sights that would stick with them until they drew their last breaths. A great hound the size of a small adult whining piteously as it furiously licked its master's face, the animal's back as clearly broken as the dead human's. The woman with her three small children, their arms still inextricably linked even as they floated past the viewport of a sealed emergency hatch. The layer of offal and gore that literally floated like gelatin roughly three meters off the floor, rippling like some evil god's punch bowl with the *Titanic*'s motions in the gloom.

Yet, despite all these visuals Martin was certain the smell would yield high grade nightmare fuel when...no *if* any of them ever slept again, Spider's admonition would be proven correct. Marcus had fought on crippled vessels before, but never one with so many people or activities as *Titanic*. The stagnant air, smoldering spot fires, chemical spills, and the various liquids that were a vessel's lifeblood had combined with the sudden, violent rupture of things that were supposed to be inside bodies, not floating in midair. The result was an unremitting, soul searing *stench* that had him hovering on the knife's edge of madness.

Goddamn you, Spider, Marcus thought, his anger rising.

"Marcus..." Sarah said, her voice breathless. *"Marcus!"*

It was the desperate, out of breath cry followed by the wet gurgle as she nearly vomited from inhaling that finally pierced the fog around Marcus's brain. Turning around, he found himself confronted with his very angry fiancé.

"Dammit, Marcus, you and the fucking Spartans are about to give us all heart attacks," Sarah snapped, her chest heaving and sweat pouring down her face. "We have wounded and elderly people, and half of them are having to hang onto other passengers to even move. Where the hell are we going in such a hurry?!"

Marcus felt himself nearly scream at Sarah in rage, his expression causing her to take a step back.

She doesn't realize what's going on, he thought, fighting to contain his ire. *No one besides the security folks and maybe the Spartans do.*

"Engineering," Senator Lu interjected from behind Marcus. "The first place you secure in any boarding action is the powerplant."

Thank you, Senator, Marcus thought, slightly more in control of his emotions.

"Why not the bridge?" Sarah asked, confused.

"You can't really do much from the bridge if you have no power," Marcus bit out. Realizing he had snapped, he moderated his tone while continuing to explain. "You're basically king of a little realm that has no ability to supply its own air, heat, or light. But engineering is our second stop, I'm just trying to get us into Corridor C so we can find a working intraship communication console."

"I thought we've passed two?" Sarah said.

"No power," Aimi remarked, still scanning the darkened hallway to their front through the *Kanabo*'s scope. "Whomever

196

designed this ship's subroutines should have their legs broken then left out on the plains for predators."

"Charming," Sarah observed lowly, drawing a poisoned look from the Spartan woman. Marcus hated that he found himself agreeing with Aimi's sentiment more than Sarah's. He looked and saw that their gaggle had closed up slightly.

"People have to keep up, Sarah," Marcus said lowly. "This isn't a pleasure cruise anymore."

Sarah's lips compressed in a thin line.

"It's not a death march, either," she snapped. "These people…"

"If you two would like to have a lover's quarrel, we can waste more time," Senator Du interrupted heatedly. "While I find it quaint you can argue in the midst of this insanity, pardon me if I'm all out of patience for sentiment."

Sarah turned to look at Du, then back at Marcus.

"Well, glad to see the Union of the Carnivore is showing cross sector solidarity," she sneered. "Would you like me to just shoot Mrs. Konarski due to her broken leg, or were you taking bets to see if Mr. Schembek has a heart attack first? Oh wait, I know, you're waiting to see if Konarski has a bone shard that gives *her* a heart…"

"Are you done?" Marcus asked flatly. Sarah's mouth opened in shock, then she closed it. Giving him a glare that would have melted deuranium, she turned away without another word. Marcus watched her go, then turned back forward and started walking.

"I get the feeling you're going to deeply regret that later," Senator Du said after a moment.

"If I am at a point to be sorry, it will mean I've done my damn job," Marcus responded. "She's just trying to do hers, I get that—but I'm not going to get us all killed trying to be nice."

Marcus saw Senator Du give him a speculative look.

"You know, I think I might need to tell my staff to update their information on you, Mr. Martin."

Oh the irony of that statement given who is walking in front of us, Marcus thought as Aimi reached the next passageway hatch to Corridor C.

"Betrayal changes a person, Senator," Marcus replied coolly. "Nearly dying because some people espouse honorable principles yet betray oaths does as well."

Du gave a slight grimace.

"A lion does not make deals with lambs," Du replied.

197

"So tell me, what does a lion do when confronted with freakin'
lizards?" Marcus snapped as Aimi turned back towards them, her body
language indicating that they had finally found a hatch which did not
open into an unsafe section of Corridor C. Not waiting for the Senator
to answer, Marcus walked up to the hatch's control panel.

"Shouldn't you…" Aimi had time to say before Marcus quickly
entered his code and hit the button to open the door.

"Only the crew has access to Corridor C," Marcus said, then
stepped into the open hatch.

There were three things that saved Marcus's life. One, the din
of weapons fire that the closed hatch had concealed also served to
disguise the sound of it opening. Two, the alien standing on the other
side of the hatch had been in the process of contributing to said weapons
fire and thus was fixated on its target. Last but not least, the fact he was
holding a flechette gun, a.k.a. the ultimate point and squeeze weapons
system whether one was nearly pissing his pants in fear or not.

In a move that was pure reflex, Marcus fired from the hip while
using his toes to press down on the magnetic shoes' friction release.
The *Pata*'s recoil forced Marcus backwards while the cloud of
flechettes blasted through the lizard in front of him. The metal rods
continued on to decapitate another lizard kneeling behind an overturned
table five meters away. As the bulkhead behind him stopped his
movement, Marcus noted that both reptiles and their blood fell to the
deck beneath them.

Corridor C has gravity and air circulation, he had time to
think, right before a storm of fire came spitting through the hatch where
he had been. There were screams and exclamations to his left as he
quickly reengaged the magnetic shoes and stepped to his right. Looking
into Corridor C back towards the bow, he saw another lizard starting to
turn towards him, bringing up a weapon before the *Kabano* cracked next
to his head and negated that threat. Springing back forward in a crouch,
Marcus placed his back to the bulkhead on the hatch's right, noting that
Senator Du moved smoothly to the opposite side. The *Kabano* cracked
again, Aimi's cursing and shoulder roll forward to evade counterfire
telling Marcus she had missed.

This would be one of those times comms was helpful, he thought
angrily. There was no way he knew what was on the other side of the
hatch other than *someone* had been in a firefight with the gaggle of
aliens. Reaching into his satchel, he pulled out a small, shiny object the
size and shape of a billiards ball.

"Dazzler out!" he shouted, then tossed the sphere around the corner. It hit with a metallic clink, followed a moment later by several intense strobes of light that elicited several decidedly angry sounds and a storm of projectiles from the other side of the hatch. Unlike his silver sphere, the ones that came back through the hatch exploded on the far bulkhead in a series of bright flashes, acrid smoke and, worst of all, slivers of spall that went singing down the corridor in all direction. The Spartan beside Senator Du grunted then, looking down at his reddening chest in surprise, slumped forward, and there was a scream from down the hallway.

The storm of fire suddenly stopped as there was a rising crescendo of flechette guns, rail rifles, and energy pistols on the far side of the hatch. Going prone, Marcus leaned his upper body briefly around the hatch just in time to see a last alien decapitated by a *Kanabo* slug. There was a long silence, and after about thirty seconds of no movement, it was apparent there were no more aliens in the next compartment.

"Sidney Goodwin!" Marcus shouted from the hallway.

"Cosmo Duff!" came a shocked response. "Boss is that you?"

"It ain't Santa Claus!" Marcus shouted back, drawing a nervous laugh. "Coming in!"

Ten minutes later, the ragged band with Marcus had shuffled into what had been the Corridor C "aviary." Designed as a space to allow crewmembers to forget they were on a giant can in the middle of space, the compartment's domelike shape was intended to facilitate the holographic projection of a generic planetary scene. Completing the production was the movement and sounds of various bird species selected at random from the Confederation's numerous worlds. In its original state, the illusion had been completed by the presence of faux foliage over a couple of slight rises, picnic tables, and a small refreshment stand complete with an ice cream machine.

Much like the rest of the ship, the room's current state was a stark rendering of its previous opulence. What was left of the refreshment stand lay burning in the middle, with three corpses inside well past being unrecognizable. Divots and scorch marks made the greenery look like a scene prop from a 20th century warfare holovid, while the sound system played a staccato confusion of bird calls in a constant loop. The acrid smell of smoke, smoldering artificial turf, and the usual offal that came from violent death still managed to enter his sinuses despite the valiant efforts of the air circulation fans. As Marcus listened to the report from the deputy squad leader whose life he had just saved, he found himself almost wishing he was back in Corridor B where the power wasn't working.

"Bastards blew in the door from the starboard side," Jin-su Hwang said, his voice still raw from having been screaming the last ten minutes. A full head taller than Marcus, Hwang's build reflected the hours of Tae Kwan Do instructing he had done as a former Marine. Marcus noted that the man's hands were shaking as he gestured towards the open hatchway. Marcus noted that the explosives the aliens had used appeared to have had a cutting effect rather than a raw, uncontrolled blast.

"We were heading aft when it happened, had just enough time to turn and start fighting. There were about twenty to start with, and I'm not sure they were expecting trouble because we got several right off the bat. Then they shot something through that door..."

Hwang's voice trailed off as he looked toward the burning refreshment stand.

"Whatever it was, it wasn't just the explosion but the flash. Next thing I know, they're in the compartment, and it's all assholes and elbows after that. Marina," Hwang said, referring to the original squad leader as he gestured towards a group of alien and human bodies to their left, "died over there. They're so fast."

Marcus winced sympathetically.

"I know. We're all that's left from Ballroom A, and I don't think there'd be this many of us if not for the Spartans," Marcus replied grimly. "Have you been able to reach the bridge?"

"Haven't had a chance to try. We passed Dragnita's squad on our way up here. She had the Purser with her, they were headed towards the Nursery."

Marcus's eyes widened.

"What?!"

"There were injured at the Nursery. The Purser grabbed Lavinia, said they had to protect the children. Lavinia agreed."

Goddammit!

"Set up a perimeter. Hopefully this is the only breach they've got into Corridor C so far, or we're well and truly fucked," Marcus snapped. "Get with Quentin, cross level what ammo you've got. I'm going to try that damn communicator and see if I can get a hold of the bridge."

With that, Marcus moved off towards the console. He was almost there when Sarah caught up with him.

"What is your plan, Marcus?" she asked wearily. "We've got people who aren't..."

"Sarah, enough," Marcus seethed. *"Enough."*

Sarah recoiled as if he had struck her.

"What in the hell is your problem, Marcus?!" she shouted, causing several people to look in their direction. Marcus ignored her, reaching towards his inside suit pocket in order to fish out a comms headphone. It was only at that point that he realized the entire left side of his suit was a ruin of tears and missing cloth. Sarah, following his hand motion, gasped in shock.

"You want to know what my *problem* is, Sarah?" he asked lowly. "My problem is that apparently I'm the only person aboard this fucking ship who realizes that all these pleasantries and customs you people want to keep observing don't mean shit if the aliens blow our engine room into space."

Sounding a little too scared shitless for comfort, he admonished himself, pausing to get his emotions back in check.

"So, no, I do not care that some septuagenarian whose sole importance in life is that she happened to get knocked up by a billionaire is about to have a heart attack," Marcus continued, his tone slightly calmer. "Indeed, if I were a decent human being I'd walk back there and put two in her head myself, as that would be preferable to leaving her behind for some aliens to snack on."

Sarah's expression went from shock and dismay at his obvious near injury to outright horror.

"What about me, Marcus? Would you shoot me if I chose to stay with her? Or would you figure that was my own dumb decision and I deserved whatever happened to me?"

This would be why I wanted to plug in a headset rather than use the speakers, he thought darkly. *Because the last thing I want is to revisit this conversation after getting in touch with Lorraine.*

"Maybe you should ask yourself what you think the answer to that question is, Sarah," Marcus replied sadly. "Let me know what conclusion you come to *if* I save all of us." With that, he turned to the communications console. Pressing the buttons to bring it to life, Marcus said a little prayer that the thing still worked. As if to prove some deity in the universe at large was still accepting calls, the flat screen came on. Swiftly entering his override code, Marcus patched through to the bridge.

Bridge
Titanic
1845 SST

"Captain, I have made contact with Mr. Martin," Ms. O'Barr reported from her position.

Abraham was astounded at the woman's calm given their present situation. While there had been no sounds of combat for the last twenty minutes, no one present was under any illusions that would last.

Apparently Mr. Martin is more resourceful than I gave him credit for, Abraham thought. *That and his people are far more desperate.*

The aliens initially moving towards the bridge had been checked roughly twenty meters aft. The method of "checking" had been for one of the security squad leaders to blow a hole in the *Titanic*'s deck with what had seemed like an extraordinary amount of explosives. What the poor woman had not known was that the compartment below had been filled with vacuum, meaning that the emergency doors just outside of his day cabin had dropped unexpectedly behind her. Neither death from asphyxiation nor at the hands of twenty aliens one had just condemned to die sounded pleasant to Abraham, and he had studiously avoided asking O'Barr what had happened.

This is all my fault, *Titanic*'s master thought. *All my goddamned fault.*

"Marcus, we have no control over the comms system," O'Barr said, then stopped to listen to Marcus's retort. "Because the helm station is wrecked and we have no contact with the Secondary Bridge."

It didn't take a rocket scientist to imagine Marcus' response to O'Barr's report. The woman calmly waited for his short, profane retort to end, then responded firmly.

"Because the helmsman's head looks like it's been through a log splitter, that's why," O'Barr said. "Now, you want a situation report or you want to continue making wishes?"

Abraham was amazed at how little ire was in O'Barr's last statement. If anything, the Deputy Security Officer sounded incredibly weary, as if the weight of the world was on her shoulders.

"Bad. The only good news is that the Dutchman protocols are trying to fix our orbit, but they weren't designed to account for the deadweight bitch we've got attached," Lorraine said. She took a moment to quickly recount what had occurred with the railguns.

"Sensors report that there's, for want of a better word, chaotic energy pulses coming from the wreckage. Judging from how quickly the other cruisers moved away from us and the radiation alarms we've got in a couple of compartments portside, I think whatever we knocked loose might have been important. No matter—if someone doesn't show up with a tug in about six hours this is all going to be moot."

Shigure
1850 SST

"If it makes you feel any better, I *almost* believed what you said to Ensign Griffon," Acheros said out of the blue. Leslie looked up and met the man's eyes, seeing his face set in grim resolve.

"What are Contacts A and B doing, Guns?" Leslie asked, breaking from the Spartans' intense gaze.

"Contacts Alpha and Bravo are two thousand kilometers to *Titanic*'s port and starboard, Alpha another one thousand kilometers ventral, Bravo one thousand kilometers dorsal, oriented towards the liner's stern and bow respectively."

It's almost like they're scared to close with **Titanic** *yet don't want to leave the other cruiser to possibly fall into enemy hands*, Leslie thought.

"You think they have an equivalent to the Masada Protocol?" Acheros asked conversationally.

This man lives in other people's heads, I swear, Leslie thought.

"I don't know, Major, didn't the Spartan Defense Force before the rest of the Confederation so rudely intruded on your sector of space?" Leslie responded grimly, attempting to throw the other officer off balance.

Acheros gave her a thin smile.

"We called it the Szigeth Directive, but yes," the Spartan officer replied.

"Szigeth?" Leslie queried.

"Some ancient battle where a commander assembled his command, rigged a powder magazine to explode, then rode off to his glorious end," Acheros replied. "Ended up whacking his enemy counterpart and a few thousand other muldoons."

Leslie looked around the bridge. Talos and Southwell were both focusing intently on their duties, the former looking like a woman about to face a firing squad while the latter double checked his inputs with a grim purpose.

They're expecting to die, Leslie thought.

"Guns, Helm, you both heard what I said to Ensign Griffon," Leslie said over the bridge network. Both officers looked up at her as she continued, and she detected a glimmer of hope on Tola's face.

"I don't plan on having a destroyer named after me, and I'm pretty sure neither of you wants to end up on some memorial obelisk," Leslie continued, giving Acheros a pointed look. She brought up a schematic of Sapphire.

"Guns, on my mark you're going to bring the decoys over the north pole, full dazzlers on. Helm, at the same time we're going to come around from down ecliptic all ahead flank. If this goes as plans, both Alpha and Bravo will orient on the decoys."

Leslie gave the two officers a moment to digest what she was saying, then plunged ahead.

"We'll come up between both cruisers, launching *Pufferfish* as soon as we're clear of the planet's shadow, concentrate main batteries on B as we finish the gun run, then continue for the nebula at coordinates 20, 45, 30. Clear?"

Southwell and Talo both looked at her for a moment, then nodded.

"The plan is to cripple one of the bastards so they can't run," Leslie finished, drawing an appreciative look from Acheros. "As hesitant as they seem to be to just blast the *Titanic* and the other cruiser, I have a feeling that another cripple will lead to them maybe staying in system long enough for some heavy ships to respond to the distress buoys. Let's get this done, people, and when we're done with debrief the first round of drinks is on me."

"Aye aye, Captain," Southwell and Talos said simultaneously. Leslie reached down to the side of her command chair, pressing a series of buttons to reveal a hidden compartment.

"I've got full resolution on Contacts A and B, Captain," Southwell reported. "*Pufferfish* are also ready."

Leslie nodded as she withdrew a small black box from the side of her chair.

"Captain, all non-essential crew have reported to the escape pods," Iokepa reported. Looking at her watch, Leslie marked the time.

"Impressive as always, XO," she said. "You've got one more passenger en route, he'll be there in about two minutes."

No need for you to go down with the ship if it comes to that, Major Acheros, Leslie thought.

"Aye aye, Captain," Iokepa replied, his voice sounding somewhat mystified as Leslie lifted her visor and cut her comms feed. She gestured to Acheros, standing and disconnecting herself from her chair. The Marine followed suit, meeting her at the back of the bridge.

"This is the bridge log," she stated, handing him the small black box. "It's got the feed from all stations, as well as audio recording of the command net. I need you to hand this to Admiral Malinverni himself."

"Aye aye, Captain," Major Acheros said, struggling to keep his face impassive.

Thank you, Major, for everything," Leslie replied. "I'm not just sending you because of your clearance, by the way. Please make sure Lieutenant Commander Iokepa actually gets aboard the escape pod."

"I already plan to break his legs if he resists," Acheros replied. Leslie started to laugh, then realized she would bawl if she did so.

"If I don't bring her back, tell Admiral Malinverni the old Late Rain died carrying out her first duty."

Acheros gave a short, sharp nod at that, swallowing hard. Leslie thought she saw a faint gleam in the man's eye as he extended his arm. She clasped it in the Spartan style, not even trying to speak.

"I'm sorry I called this fine lady a garbage scow," Acheros said quietly. With that, he released her arm and left. Taking a moment to compose herself, Leslie dropped her command visor and headed back towards her seat.

No use feeling sorry for yourself, she thought bitterly. *That will guarantee that we don't make it through this.* Looking at Southwell and Talo as they worked, Leslie felt a brief moment of pride.

Either way, I've put together a good crew and fine ship, she thought as she turned her focus back to her command visor.

"We've reached the edge of Sapphire's sensor shadow, Captain," Talo said.

"Guns?" Leslie asked.

"Two more minutes for the decoys," Southwell replied. "Main battery set for maximum rate of fire."

Not that I think our railguns will necessarily do all that much damage, Leslie thought. But at point blank range at least we won't have to worry about a gunnery solution.

"Program evasive pattern Yankee Victor, activate once we're past their dorsal side," Leslie said. There was a tone in her helmet.

"Escape pods away, Captain," Talo said quietly.

205

"Captain, I suggest we cut power to charging the Herbert drive and divert to shields," a voice broke into her helmet. After a moment she recognized it.

"Ensign Doba, what are you still doing aboard?!" Leslie asked, aghast.

"Figured you would want someone down here in engineering considering Lieutenant Talo is rather busy driving the ship," Doba replied, her tone unflappable. "You can ask Chief about the coin toss he lost after we're done."

Talo shook her head, obviously angry at herself.

"She's right Captain—we can increase the shield power by about ten percent."

"Execute, quickly," Leslie replied to both engineer officers.

"Switching now, will be ready in two minutes, tops," Doba replied.

"Captain, I've been watching Contact C's power. It's dropping rather rapidly," Southwell stated worriedly. "If it keeps doing so, I'm not sure *Titanic* and it will be able to maintain orbit."

Well that would take care of so many problems, Leslie thought briefly.

"Is Contact C still venting atmosphere?"

"No captain, they've either sealed off the holes *Titanic* put in her, dropped internal bulkheads, or she's a hulk."

"Well let's hope it's not the latter or that probably means *Titanic* is as well," Leslie said.

I would really hate to find out I risked this ship for a bunch of people already sucking vacuum, she thought. *Even if a few of them deserved it.*

"Decoys in place."

"Energy diverted, Captain," Doba reported.

Well, here goes, Leslie thought, feeling her heart starting to race.

"Sensor drones active, all ahead flank," Leslie ordered. "Guns, bring up the decoys, fire as we bear, all weapons!"

Shigure leaped forward like a greyhound out the gate, her thrusters swinging her wide of Sapphire's atmosphere. All ten of her torpedo tubes irised open as she cleared the gas giant's sensor shadow, the flock of *Pufferfish* ejecting a moment later. Briefly dragged down by gravity's grasp into Sapphire's atmosphere, all ten missiles ignited with brilliant flashes as their fusion drives engaged.

"Contacts Alpha and Bravo are under way," Southwell stated.

Well that didn't go as planned, Leslie thought, watching as Contact Alpha engaged her thrusters and started to move *away* from *Titanic.* Then it struck her.

"Alpha's running for it," she said.

"I'd get the hell away from implosion warheads too," Southwell said. "Main battery engaging!"

Hadn't thought about that aspect, Leslie mused as *Shigure* gave a minor tremor.

"No hits! Ten seconds until *Pufferfish* reach range! Contact Bravo engaging missiles with energy weapons!"

"Roger!" Leslie said, watching as the alien craft began orienting towards the decoys coming over Sapphire's north pole. *Shigure* shuddered again as Bravo's icon began strobing with the pulse of her energy discharges, followed by five *Pufferfish* winking out and another spinning off obviously out of control. The other four came towards Bravo from every direction, even as five of *Shigure*'s slugs crashed into the alien cruiser's starboard "wing." There was a momentary interruption in the energy bolts flying from the enemy cruiser, the lull just long enough for all four missiles to close and detonate their warheads.

That left a mark, Leslie thought as *Shigure*'s guns fired again. Energy, atmosphere, and debris streamed from the enemy cruiser's starboard side as the destroyer closed past ten thousand kilometers. The damaged craft began to rotate her bow downward towards the onrushing *Shigure,* ignoring the two decoys passing three thousand kilometers from her. Leslie watched as all ten slugs hammered the already damaged vessel, the cruiser visibly staggering under the impact.

Enough bee stings can kill an elephant, Leslie thought triumphantly.

"Bring us up her starboard side! Execute evasive!" she barked to Talo. The helm officer complied, *Shigure*'s maneuvering thrusters roaring as the destroyer fought both momentum and Sapphire's gravity. Leslie's display showed a vector line that would bring them barely fifty kilometers from the alien's starboard side.

Almost past…

Unseen by either the sensor drones or *Shigure*'s own systems, the enemy cruiser had opened ten ports along her starboard side. Three had been rendered inoperable by the *Pufferfish,* leaving seven to bear.

Just before *Shigure* passed, each spat out a single, translucent globe roughly five meters diameter. Talos's evasive maneuver and the *Shigure*'s speed caused five to miss and one to barely graze, its fury vented into the destroyer's shields. The last, however, hit the *Shigure*'s shields directly abreast her engineering spaces. Immolated at her post Ensign, Doba never had a chance to register what had occurred. Moments later, *Shigure*'s containment shielding failed, with the "Late Rains" transforming into a brilliant flash of white light and an expanding debris globe hurtled over Sapphire's northern pole.

Bridge
Titanic
1912 SST

"No...no...*no!*" Coors screamed

"Fuck!" O'Barr cursed simultaneously.

There was a pause as both Coors and O'Barr looked at their screens in stunned silence.

"Distress beacon, Captain," Coors said, his voice utterly dejected. "*C.S.S. Shigure*...never mind. Aliens just destroyed the beacon as well."

"What happened?" Abraham asked.

"The *Shigure* attacked the two vessels," Coors said, his voice barely audible. "Looks like she damaged one. It's leaking radiation, but they're both coming back around."

"Surely there's got to be another ship?" Abraham responded. "Check your..."

"There's nothing else, Sir," Coors replied.

"Mr. Coors, destroyers don't travel this far out by themselves!" Abraham snapped.

"Well this one did, Sir," Coors snapped back. "And now she's dead."

Abraham felt his shoulders start to shake. He looked down at his hands, almost expecting to see even more blood on them.

"No, Marcus, the Fleet's not here. Not anymore," O'Barr said, speaking despondently into her comms unit. Abraham listened as she recounted what had happened to the Chief Security Officer.

"Sir, I've got a hull breach, port side, frame 65," Coors said.

"Marcus, we've got problems," O'Barr stated anxiously. "Someone's apparently blown another hole in the hull, about two hundred meters forward of the engine room."

208

There is only one reason a single destroyer would attack like that: Her captain wasn't expecting any help.

"Ms. O'Barr, patch Mr. Martin through to my station," Abraham said wearily.

"Marcus, stand by for Captain Herrod," Lorraine stated, her voice sounding empty. Abraham waited a couple moments, then realized that O'Barr was not going to give him an indication he was live.

"Mr. Martin?" he asked, his mouth suddenly dry.

"Sir, you're on speaker," Marcus warned. "I'm here."

Well that complicates things. But not much.

"Mr. Martin, I need you to head post haste to Engineering. We need to resume fusion in at least one more reactor or we're all dead."

There was a long pause, then Martin replied.

"Understood, Captain. Am I to understand we have no connection with either Engineering or the Secondary Bridge?"

"None," Abraham said.

"Understood. I'm en route to Engineering via the Central Arms Room," Marcus replied. "Martin, out."

As he heard the connection die, Abraham was shocked to see O'Barr moving away from her console.

"Ms. O'Barr, where are you going?" Abraham asked, concerned.

"Sir, I'm useless to you here," O'Barr replied simply. "I have no communication, and there's no point in pumping energy into the railguns because the Dutchman protocols just shunt it back to the main thrusters."

As if to emphasize O'Barr's point, the sounds of gunfire echoed down the corridor once more. Abraham could tell it was getting closer, and this time it was punctuated by a pair of grenade blasts followed by screams both human and alien.

"I'm more use to this ship with a rifle in my hand," O'Barr said simply.

Why do I get the feeling there's a silent 'in the time we have left' missing from that sentence? Abraham thought. *Which means she'd rather just die taking as many aliens with her as she can.*

"Very well, Ms. O'Barr," Abraham said, gesturing for her to go. Lorraine nimbly swung down from the shelf, dropping to the floor in a crouch. Striding over to Abraham's chair, she climbed up on the command chair and leaned in to talk lowly to him.

209

"If it comes to it, I'll try to make sure we blow a hole in the hull," she said solemnly. "I've disabled the emergency doors to the upper level."

Abraham looked at O'Barr in shock, but the woman continued.

"Thank you, Sir, for giving me the opportunity aboard this ship," she said. With that, O'Barr stood up and headed for the exit.

Marcus was unsurprised to find himself looking at Senator Du when he stepped back from the console.

"Did I understand correctly? That there was a Confederation destroyer out here this whole time?" the Spartan asked.

"That's not what I took from that," Marcus replied, suddenly bone tired. "What I understand is that a destroyer crew just killed themselves trying to save us."

Du pursed his lips.

"You realize there's only one reason a vessel that size would launch an attack like that, correct?"

"No, but I'm sure you're about to enlighten me," Marcus stated icily. Du's eyes narrowed as he glared at Marcus' impertinence.

"Have you considered that the destroyer's captain realized that no help is en route? Or at least, no help that will arrive in a timely manner?"

Marcus was about to open his mouth with a sarcastic response than stopped.

I hate to admit it, but Du has a point. A huge point, Marcus thought. Seeing Marcus's cognition, the Spartan Senator pushed his advantage.

"So tell me, Mr. Martin, does it not appear that our choices are to die slow or die fast?" Du continued.

"Getting crushed in a gas giant's gravity well..."

"I'm not talking about that as the slow option, Mr. Martin," Du cut him off. "While getting crushed by a gas giant is not as instantaneous as you apparently think, that's still relatively swift compared to the horrors I'm thinking of."

Du gestured to the nearest dead alien body.

"Tell me, why do you think the other enemy ships have not blasted us into debris? According to what Ms. O'Barr told you, we've turned their fellow into a radiation spewing wreck that they apparently are leery of closing with. Clearly, we're an advanced species and this is hostile territory—would you stay?"

"I sure as hell wouldn't blow my comrades into pieces!" Marcus snapped back.

"No, you wouldn't," Du replied with a smile. Before Marcus could respond, the Spartan Senator sprung his rhetorical trap. "You'd call for help. But moreover, you'd do so because you'd just found a large alien ship with literally thousands of extraterrestrials."

Du turned and looked at where Sarah was using a medical kit to replace the improvised bandage wrapped around a woman's head. The elderly woman cried out in pain as Sarah pulled the dried, sticky cloth away from the wound to slap on wound sealant.

"Tell me, Martin, how do you think the alien scientists will examine us? I mean, do you think they'll take the risk of putting Ms. Jones under their anesthesia, uncertain if its effects might kill her before their curiosity is satisfied? Will they have any concept of the agony they're putting her through when they split her abdomen open? As they examine every orifice…"

"You sick bastard," Marcus snapped, starting to walk away.

"Running away will not save her from writhing naked in agony so extreme it seems perversely like ecstasy," Du continued, his tone fierce as he followed. Marcus noted Aimi subtly move so she could bring her *Kanabo* to bear on him in a moment's notice. He let the *Pata* hang on its sling as he turned to face the Senator. Before he could speak, Du held up his hand.

"I do not put these visions in your head because it brings me any pleasure," the man said, his tone sad. "I tell you this because I, at least, know that the woman I loved had the mercy, the *dignity,* of not dying being sliced apart by some scientist."

For a brief instant, Marcus thought he heard a glimmer of sorrow in Du's usually flat voice. Meeting the man's gaze, he could see the raw emotion that lurked just below the surface of the Spartan's outwardly calm demeanor.

"You called me sick," Du said, a definite catch in his voice. "I truly had no control over what happened to Mei. You, on the other hand, have a chance to save Miss Jones from being inside this ship when the gas pressure causes the atmosphere to ignite or ending up on a cold slab praying for death."

To his horror, Marcus found himself unable to argue with Du's logic nor possessing the time to make an earnest attempt to do so.

"Hwang, pick one of your people to stay with the civilians," he barked, eliciting several cries of shock and consternation.

"Marcus?! What are you…" Sarah started to say.

"We don't have time to have an argument, Sarah," Marcus snapped. "Captain's orders, and if we're not to Engineering in about thirty minutes everyone here is dead."

"Boss, I'm not sure…" Hwang started to say, then stopped as Marcus gave him a withering gaze.

"Fine, you just chose yourself. Quentin, mix the squads, wedge formation, aft exit to this compartment. Move now!"

Sarah could not have looked any more aghast if Marcus had shed his skin and revealed that he was actually an alien sleeper agent.

"Marcus, you are condemning all of these people to die," she said, her voice trembling. "You're condemning *me* to die."

Marcus gestured towards the weapons cart.

"There are enough weapons remaining to arm every person with you. If you stick to the starboard side and move towards Anjelica's office, you should be fine."

"Fine? That's what you think is appropriate?" Sarah asked, tears starting to form in her eyes.

"Mr. Martin, if we're going, we need to go," Senator Du interjected sternly. "I can leave Mr. Tate and Mr. Blanxart, but either…"

"We're moving out now, Senator," Marcus said, meeting Sarah's eyes. "Let's go."

"I love you Marcus," Sarah said, her voice just barely audible. "Don't do this to me."

Steeling himself, Marcus turned away from her. Only Du could see the slight quavering of Marcus' lip as the security chief motioned for Quentin to move out. As his small band started off at a jog it took every fiber of his being not to stop and look back.

Spartan Diasporan Republic Flag (Karapanos)

Chapter 7: Entropy's Andante

Constitution
1922 SST

Whatever deity is taking calls, Bolan thought as he fought the
urge to grip the edges of his chair, *please do not allow me to **ever**
challenge Horinek again.* Looking around the bridge, he was fairly
certain his sentiment was echoed by just about every officer there. The
Constitution had shuddered, whipsawed, and jerked the entire fifteen
minute trip through the Dardanelles system, with each oscillation
indicating either an impact or near miss with an object in realspace.
Although it had only been for a brief moment, Bolan had seen the shield
indicator on his tactical display drop to 25% with the resultant impact.

"Entering system in five...four...three...two...one!" Sakai
counted down, his voice shaken.

The bridge's center viewscreen suddenly seemed full of planet.

"All astern full!" Bolan shouted. "Down helm, forty-five
degrees!"

Goddamit Horinek! Bolan thought angrily.

"All astern, aye!"

The *Constitution* vibrated as her engines attempted to stop her
forward momentum while simultaneously pushing her vector down to
avoid the irradiated rock that was Zed-815's third planet, Polonius. The
Constitution's collision alarm began to sound, the pulsing shriek making
Bolan's heart rise in his throat. The *Constitution's* computer, having
taken the last sensor data and extrapolated the vessel's path, obviously
believed that the battlecruiser did not have sufficient braking power to
keep from plowing into Polonius's atmosphere.

Wait a second...that rock doesn't have any atmosphere! Bolan
had time to think as the *Constitution's* flipped end for end then fired her
engines. As if the computer had belatedly had the same thought, the
piercing alarm suddenly ceased. Still feeling his pulse racing, Bolan
turned to admonish his navigational officer when Boyles started talking.

"You know, that's the last time I explain ways to block off
engine bloom," the Sensors officer said, her voice shaking.

"Sir, is Nav fucking crazy?!" Commander Alexander said on
the senior channel.

Bolan looked at Horinek as she began reorienting her charts as
if nothing had happened.

"No, I think she just bought us surprise," Bolan replied quietly. "The primary is spitting out enough radiation that it probably hid our hyper signature. The third planet should have served to hide our velocity kill."

"She could have warned us that she intended to bring us in almost right on top of the damn planet!"

"By this point I'm starting to think we should have expected it," Bolan replied with a shake of his head, then switched over to the main bridge communications. "Good job, Nav."

"Thank you, Sir," Horinek replied, her tone somewhat surprised. Bolan looked up as the display switched to the system's map. If the ecliptic had been a clock, Polonius and *Constitution* were at the ten o'clock moving clockwise. Sapphire and, presumably, *Titanic* and her assailants were at the three o'clock also moving clockwise, albeit at a much slower rate. Bolan saw an opportunity to come around Polonius and use Jotun, the next planet closest to the primary, as a further temporary shield while the *Constitution* closed with Sapphire.

First things first, best check to see if all this planning is superfluous by this point, Bolan thought.

"Sensors, remain passive and get us an uplink to the mirror balls," Bolan ordered. "Helm, bring us around the eastern hemisphere, ahead two thirds until Jotun is aligned with Sapphire. After that, all ahead flank."

"Aye aye, Sir," Boyles and Sakai answered simultaneously.

" Once you get those sensors corralled, I want one sweep of the system then everything possible focusing towards Sapphire," Bolan continued, looking up at the display. He looked at the icons indicating the *Titanic*'s last known location around Sapphire.

Hold on folks, Bolan thought. *Help's coming.*

Titanic
1935 SST

In theory, the trip to the arms room should have only taken a matter of minutes. Theory, of course, had assumed every hatchway between Marcus' squad and their destination had functioned. Or that they would not stumble into a group of four aliens aimlessly roaming around. The only silver lining from the resultant firefight was that Marcus and his accompanying Grognards had lost only one member dead and another wounded in exchange for all four lizards.

We must be getting used to their speed. Not that it's going to do Rynes any good sitting back there by himself, Marcus thought. Leaving the young Grognard with a ruined left leg, a full clip of ammo, and a grenade still left a sour taste in Marcus' mouth. Shaking himself, *Titanic*'s security chief saw Aimi getting ready to open the arms room's port access hatch. Hissing, he motioned for her to stop. The Spartan turned and looked at him questioningly as he gestured for her to move out of the way.

"Did you not learn from the last time we did this?" she asked archly.

"I know there's not an alien on the other side of this wall," Marcus responded simply. Stepping past her, he flipped open the door access panel. "Oh, and since when did you have access to crew only spaces?"

Aimi stiffened for a moment, but Marcus continued on as if he had just been calmly remarking on the weather. Entering his code then placing his hand on the door scanner, he waited for the confirmation tone followed by the door opening.

The sound of anti-gravity repulsors was followed almost instantaneously by a bright beam issuing from the darkened passageway. The beam quickly scanned left to right across Marcus' shoulders, then centered on his chest and broadened in width to about the size of a table pitcher. Before anyone could react, it centered on his heart for a couple of moments, then broadened and panned upwards to his face. Cursing, Aimi gathered herself to lunge and shove him before Marcus held up his hand.

"I *really* wouldn't do that," he said quietly.

"Good evening, Marcus," a feminine, robotic voice stated. "All work and no play makes who a dull boy?"

"The man who chases Wendy for Red Rum," Marcus responded, staring unflinchingly into the glowing beam.

"Identity confirmed," the disembodied voice said. With a snap, the passageway before them suddenly became brilliantly illuminated. The gleaming white bulkheads were in stark juxtaposition to the two squat, dark blue cylindrical shapes hovering just at the far end of the corridor. The two devices were still shedding dirt, the origin of which was obviously from the scattered ferns and large craters that had left in the silver painted planters beneath their round bases.

"Fucking *Beholder* bots?!" Aimi spat. "What in the…"

"It appears that Mr. Martin is full of surprises," Senator Du observed drily as Marcus began walking down the corridor.

216

"Yeah, would have been nice if he'd let his own security folks in on all of them," someone noted from the back.

"Maybe if you had a need to know, Ikenna," Quentin snapped. Marcus ignored both men as he continued forward past the two bots. The BH1LDR was colloquially known as the *Beholder* due to its uncanny resemblance to a certain malevolent being from 20th Century North American literature. Security robots, *Beholders* had never caught on with the military despite their awe inspiring firepower.

There's only so much battery power you can pack into a package that small, Marcus thought grimly. *That's an awful lot of dead mass to haul around once the flechettes and energy charges run out.*

"If you had *Beholders* then why didn't you put them someplace useful?" Aimi asked, her tone accusing.

"Like a ballroom full of innocent passengers?" Marcus snapped in response, looking at her as the door opened. The startled gasp from inside the room caused him to whirl his head back around, *Pata* starting to come back up before his mind processed what was in front of him. The compartment, as was to be expected of any space serving its purpose, was nearly spotless with its gleaming white walls seemingly giving it more depth than its 10 x 10 meter area would suggest. Although its contents were in a far more disheveled state than normal, the appearance was still of a clean, professional space. That is, until one looked at the bloodied squad leader standing just behind the main counter, his right arm bounded tightly to his side by an impromptu bandage. As the heavily wounded man let the energy pistol in his left hand drop back down, Marcus could detect the various first aid medications that were probably the only thing allowing the individual to stand.

Quick heal and nannite gel, plus a healthy dose of uppers. His crash is going to be something else, the detached part of Marcus' mind observed.

"Marcus," the tall, wiry man grunted in greeting. His normally blonde hair was matted to his head by sweat, blood, and some other liquid that Marcus could not place.

"Holy shit Abarca, what the hell happened to you?!" Marcus asked, standing aside as Quentin and the rest of the group pressed past him to begin scouring the already open arms lockers for ammunition and equipment.

"Running gunfight with the aliens," Ivo Abarca, Sixth Squad Leader, grunted. "Thank God for the *Beholders* outside or they would have gotten us all."

217

Marcus turned and looked worriedly at the hatch.

"Don't worry, there's nothing alive in that hallway," Abarca said darkly. "Although you could have told us what you were planning to do with all of our voice imprints."

"It's not a secret if everyone knows," Marcus replied, drawing a disgusted look from the other man and an appraising one from Aimi and Senator Du. "What happened?"

"Was heading back to engineering with more ammo when about thirty of those fuckers came in from B Corridor. I'd assume everything down the port side is alien infested now. I'm guessing they cut a hole around Frame 70 to gain another access point."

"They didn't come in through the stern gangway hatch?"

Abarca gave a short laugh.

"We counterattacked that one, which is what took most of our ammo. They're not fans of *Pyromancer* rounds."

"Not many sentient beings like thermobaric explosions," Marcus observed.

"Or implosion grenades," a feminine, Spartan-accented voice observed from back in the weapon racks.

"How many back in engineering?" Marcus asked, waving away Abarca's questioning look.

"We started out with twenty or so, but security details and passengers were showing up throughout," Abarca replied. "Fireroom #1 getting blasted open sort of cut down on the direct route for security, and there's apparently some damage amidships on the starboard side that's cut off Corridors Delta and Echo. A handful of folks came up through the maintenance scuppers on starboard, but that's a long ways to go single file with aliens possibly in there."

Marcus nodded in agreement at Abarca's assessment. He had no desire to face a bunch of lizards in a series of two meter-wide passageway.

"Had anyone seen Bokari or Ribbi's squad?" Marcus asked.

"Buhandar was headed to the dorsal pod the last I knew. Ribbi and his guys were getting ready to go off shift at *Rose's*, and the last I heard the whole Red Deck got Heinz'd when the safety interlocks were cut," Abarca said shakily.

Marcus felt as if someone had placed a lead weight in his stomach. Buhandar Bokari had been an old friend from his first Marine company. Dennis Ribbi had been his roommate in college. Both of them had agreed to come to *Titanic* because he had asked them to.

How many people have I killed today? Marcus thought, guilt almost staggering him.

"Some of the Senator's detail said half of the passenger spaces got holed by fragments—there were doors dropping everywhere as they came aft," Abarca continued, oblivious to Marcus' distraction. "I know there's fighting forward, but I haven't been able to get a connection to the bridge."

"Which Senator?" Du interjected before Marcus could ask another question.

"Senator Falak," Abarca replied, clearly annoyed at the interruption. "Although several of your Spartans showed up in engineering with them, under a Mr. Ugaki."

Before Du could reply, Marcus turned to Aimi.

"Aimi, when was your last muster date?" he asked, referring to the three months required of every Spartan to remain a voting citizen.

"What?" the woman asked, her face incredulous as if Marcus had asked her the last time she'd had sex.

Forgot that Spartans are a bit touchy about discussing anything regarding their reserves with outsiders, Marcus thought as he mentally kicked himself.

"January 15th of last year," Du replied smoothly before Aimi could work up further dudgeon. Looking at his face, Marcus saw a brief glimmer of curiosity before the Senator restored his usual laconic expression. "Same as the rest of my security team."

Marcus exhaled slowly as he looked over the gathered security folks.

I have the sinking suspicion I'm going to regret this. But I also have no choice, he thought.

"Senator, you and your security detail come with me," Marcus said. "Quentin, get everyone rearmed. We'll be right back."

"Okay..." Quentin said, raising an eyebrow.

"Isn't this how the slasher holos always go?" Abarca observed grimly. "With someone splitting up the party?"

Marcus ignored the man as he strode toward the arms rooms' primary hatch.

"I wouldn't open that if I were..." Abarca started, his voice rising. Before he could finish, Marcus pressed the button...and was subjected to what could best be described as an olfactory mugging. The vileness that slammed into his nose made the previous stenches encountered seem like a mild whiff of distant skunk. Burned flesh, fresh blood, the ozone stench of energy weapons fire in a concentrated space, and the dank, dense smoke spewing from a downed *Beholder* bot's half-melted frame all wafted towards the arms compartment.

Even worse than the assault on his nostrils was the visual tableau before him. In the flickering half light, Marcus could see that where the walls weren't covered with various shades of organic matter, they were pitted and scorched. The sources of the organic debris were scattered in front of him, and his mind's eye played out the scene as if he'd seen it first-hand. The scattered human defenders lay slumped at various points in the first five meters from the arms room to the jammed passageway hatch. All ten of the men and women had died facing the now jammed opening. The two dozen or so aliens that had made it through the hatchway were clumped in a hard to differentiate green mass at the far end, with many of their bodies jammed up against the hatch. The second *Beholder* remained hovering above its planter, scorch marks and divots marring its frame.

"Oh my God, close that hatch!" someone screamed, gagging. Marcus numbly complied, feeling a strange hollowness in his soul as he turned around.

"I tried to warn you," Abarca gasped, struggling to stand back upright from where he had vomited. Unlike in the hatchway, the arms compartments fans managed to whisk much of the smell away, thus preventing most, but not all, of the others from seeing their lunches again. With a rumble of hard rubber, a maintenance bot whirred forward to begin disposing of the pools of vomit.

"You were mentioning us going somewhere?" Senator Du said, his voice thick with saliva.

"Yes," Marcus said. "Come with me." Heading back deeper into the arms room, Marcus came to a rack on the bulkhead furthest from the entry hatches. Pressing a button, he caused the rack to come free from its floor mountings as its magnetic repulsors kicked in. Lifting it carefully, he moved it in front of its empty companion to the left, then shoved backwards to lock the two racks together. His actions revealed a plain hatch stamped EVA-03.

"Wait. You're not seriously talking about us going through a fried engine room in unarmored EVA suits, are you?" Aimi asked incredulously. "Who knows what the hell is floating around in there?"

Marcus didn't say a word as he lifted the small access panel to the left of the EVA hatch. Blocking Du and Aimi's view with his body, he quickly provided the necessary bona fides and stood back as the door hissed open. The lights in the darkened compartment immediately snapped on. What they illuminated caused the individuals gathered with Marcus to utter various degrees of surprise.

"*Battle armor?*" Du asked, his face starting to lose color as he looked at the ten *Hoplite* combat suits lining the bulkheads in the opened compartment. Roughly two and a half meters tall, each *Hoplite* was basically a humanoid exoskeleton that gave its user superhuman speed, strength, and targeting abilities. Unlike heavier battle armor, the *Hoplite* did not carry its own internal weapons. Despite this and it being a full generation removed from the Confederation Fleet's current models, the *Hoplite* was still considered top of the line for system defense units and light years ahead of what most private entities could afford. Marcus had secured two red command suits then painted the remainder in Czarina colors, just like the *Titanic*'s outer skin.

"Yeah, little surprise I had in case anyone wanted to do something stupid like use this vessel as an example of how poorly the Confederation enforced its laws," Marcus replied quietly. Du whipped his head around and Marcus felt more than saw the rest of the Spartans tense in the hatchway behind him.

"Easy everyone," Marcus said, making sure none of his Grognards were in earshot. "Be a crying shame for you to be trapped in this compartment by those two fully functional *Beholder*s outside the secondary access hatch."

Du exhaled slowly, his face looking as if he'd just bit down on something rancid.

Marcus smiled.

"So now that I have your attention, was all that horse shit you fed me back in the park reality or do we have some form of Spartan cavalry coming over the hill?"

Du shook his head, his eyes burning into Marcus'.

"The intent was to make a copy of the vessel's navigational logs via a backdoor virus, then cripple her drive and signal for a 'pirate' vessel to attack her once we left Eurasian space for the Transvaal sector," Du said. "There were to be no survivors. To include my group allegedly."

"Senator, are you *mad*?" Aimi hissed. "Why are you telling..."

Du gave Aimi a glare that stopped the woman's imminent tirade in her tracks. Casting her eyes downward, Aimi bowed her head.

"Forgive me, Senator," the Spartan said lowly, her chest heaving as if she was expecting to be struck.

"Someday child, you will understand that there is a time to tell the entire truth," Du snapped.

221

"So why fake your death, Senator?" Marcus asked quietly as he stepped into the room. Selecting one of the two red command suits present, he placed his weapon in the scabbard to the suit's right and began stripping out of his clothes.

"Because I have grown disgusted with the politics of your so-called Confederation," Du replied haughtily, holstering his own weapon at the suit next to Marcus'. "The pettiness, the backbiting, the corruption..."

"I do not understand how you thought killing almost five thousand people was going to somehow stop all that?" Marcus snapped.

"It wasn't. But you're familiar with our code, our ethics. How would it look that a *Senator*, the former Vice President of the Republic no less, was killed because the Confederation wouldn't enforce its own laws?" Du asked, his eyes as flat as a snake's even as his tone was mocking.

"You were hoping to force a referendum?" Marcus replied, the light dawning. "You do realize there is almost *zero* chance of the other partitions honoring that little provision you guys shoehorned into the Charter of Unification, right?"

Du smiled, and it was a look that made Marcus' inner monkey run skittering and screaming around his mind.

"If there's one thing the last ten years has cured me of, it's any fear of the rest of the Confederation," Du growled contemptuously.

"Well that could be why your plans keep getting foiled," Marcus responded, his voice dripping with venom as he reached for the pull up bar hanging over the exoskeleton's bottom half. "But since you're about to get your wish anyway, let's hurry the hell up."

With that, Marcus grabbed the bar, brought his legs up to his body, and then swung backwards to slip his legs into the suit's bottom half. Sensing weight and pressure, the *Hoplite*'s storage mount swung the top half of the suit upwards from where it had been folded behind the legs. Once the system had locked the suit into place, Marcus swung his outstretched arms back into the opened top half's limbs and settled his body into the chest carapace. Taking a moment to sense his dimensions, the suit gave a warning tone. Two seconds later, in a storm of whirring metal it closed around his upper body while simultaneously joining with the bottom half. Once the subatomic links below were complete, the helmet irised up and over his head, then quickly shifted its dimensions to bring the yellow-tinged viewport over his face.

Here comes the part I hate, Marcus thought grimly, right before the suit exuded a thin, cold gel over his entire body. He'd barely had

222

time to gasp from the cold before a sharp tingling sensation briefly coursed through his body, signifying the battlearmor's neural connectors had activated. With a sigh, he fought back the overwhelming desire to urinate as the helmet rings sealed. The *Hoplite*'s HUD then activated, and he manipulated the fingertip controls to select the *Pata* as his primary weapon. Turning, he grabbed the hilt sticking out from the scabbard just beside his left leg.

While I'm not sure this will be any use, at this point I want as many weapons as I can lay my hands on, he thought, pulling the vibrocutlass out of its home. Like its Terran namesake, the broad bladed weapon had a curved edge and heavy frame. Unlike its ancient antecedent, the weapon's alloys and ultrasonic vibrating keen edge meant it could slash through most untreated armor it caught straight on.

Not as good as a Spartan vibrokatana, but I don't think I'll be needing a 'hundred body sword' anytime soon, Marcus thought as he slipped the weapon into the standard edged weapon slot on the back of his suit.

"What in the hell?" Quentin's stunned voice came from the hatchway. Marcus turned to look at him, knowing the man could not see his face through the clouded visor.

"Guess you didn't have a need to know," someone muttered bitterly from behind Quentin. The speaker's outline glowed briefly on Marcus's HUD, but he let the comment slide.

I would never have heard Ikenna without the voice amplification, and Quentin's probably thinking it even if he's too much of a pro to say it, Marcus thought.

"Quentin, take the other command suit and everyone else you've got. Go through the sewage scuppers. We're going for a walk outside," Marcus said flippantly.

"Are there any other surprises you've got, Boss?" Quentin asked grimly. "Like maybe a few Marines in cryogenic storage or a pocket nuke?"

"No," Marcus replied. "Bokari and Ribbi were supposed to be our aces in the hole if we got pirates onboard. I kept the *Hoplite*'s close hold until now because I needed to be sure about what we were facing."

Quentin gave a meaningful glance at the other activated suits, then nodded.

"I'll leave two folks here," he replied. "Good luck, Boss," Quentin said.

223

An Unproven Concept

"It was the strangest thing," O'Barr said, her voice still full of wonderment. "They all just broke off the attacks and started heading aft."

The security officer stood just to Abraham's right, her face covered in soot, grime and caked blood. As she finished her report, she took a long pull of water from the canteen that was attached to the bandolier cinched across her chest. With a start, Abraham realized the bandolier was completely empty, meaning her last clip of ammunition was inserted into the battle rifle she held.

"Why didn't you pursue them?" an arch voice asked from beside Abraham.

Sweet Jesus I wish someone had just overdosed him, Abraham thought as O'Barr turned to fix Mr. Federov with an icy glare. The Czarina Lines executive was floating just beside Abraham's chair, having lashed himself to its back with his suit jacket and belt.

"I can point you in the direction they went," O'Barr replied.

The lack of a "Sir" or "Mr. Federov" probably wasn't an accident, Abraham thought. *Just like my not correcting her is completely on purpose.*

Federov waited a couple of moments as if he was waiting on Abraham to say something, then continued in a near snarl.

"Well that's fine, I'm sure they're not going to break anything critical wherever they're going," Federov replied. "I mean, there's only engines, life support and, oh wait, *passengers* aft of us."

"Mr. Fedorov, I think even *you* can understand that Ms. O'Barr can't necessarily chase an enemy who outnumbers her when she's got wounded," Abraham snapped.

"All I see is a pair of people who forget what they're paid to do," Federov snapped in response.

"Captain, I'm getting a strange sensor reading..." Coors interrupted, his brow furrowed.

"Strange?! Is that idiot for—" Federov started to say. His imminent diatribe was stopped cold by O'Barr producing a knife.

"I believe the Captain understood Mr. Coors," the security deputy said simply.

Looking at O'Barr's face as she uttered the words, Abraham realized that Federov's life was literally at a knife's edge. Lacking the desire to try and talk O'Barr down, Abraham turned to doing his job.

Wow, apparently Federov does have a survival sense, he thought as the executive kept his silence.

"What do you have, Mr. Coors?" Abraham asked.

"The sensor arrays around the system have suddenly started pulsating in a rhythm. I can't quite figure out what it says, but it keeps repeating," the sensor officer replied, his brow furrowed.

"Loudspeaker," Abraham stated. A moment later, Coors' computer had converted the incoming sensor signals into a mixture of deeper and higher tones.

"It's Hanoverian Morse," *Titanic*'s captain said after a moment, referring to his homeworld. "We teach it to all of our Rangers and Guides." After listening for a few moments, Abraham's eyes grew wide in shock.

"Help is coming, Dad. Hang on," *Titanic*'s captain said, tears beginning to well in his eyes. "My God, it's the Fleet. They're in system."

Constitution
1955 SST

"Sensors, a word," Bolan said, doing his level best to keep his tone neutral.

Bolan could tell from Boyles' posture that the Sensors Officer realized she'd been caught out. He watched as she secured her station, then quickly came back towards the Captain's chair.

"Did it ever occur to you that an advanced, starfaring race might suddenly notice a change in the mirror balls' radiation patterns?" Bolan asked quietly.

"Sir, I thought the odds were sli…" Boyles started.

"Lieutenant, would *you* have noticed something like that?" Bolan asked flatly.

Boyles stood mute for a moment, uncertainty flitting across her face.

"This isn't a trick question, Sensors," Bolan said more gently. "Honestly, would something like that get your attention?"

Boyles thought for a moment, then squared her shoulders and replied.

225

"Not at first, but probably after a few minutes, Sir," Boyles replied. Bolan could see her bracing herself for his onslaught.

"Thankfully Lieutenant, I was trying to think of a way to let the *Titanic* know we are coming," Bolan said. "In the future, do not *ever* do something like that without clearing it with me first. Understood?"

"Yes, Sir," Boyles replied quietly. Before Bolan could continue, Lieutenant Herrod interrupted their conversation.

"Captain, we are receiving Confederation code!" the Comms officer said, his voice troubled. "It's coming from one of the mirror balls via direct laser."

"What?" Boyles asked, her voice rising as she turned to regard Herrod. "That's impossible, I put them into encrypted mode when I took them over."

"Sensors, back to your station. Comms, Nav, plot those coordinates in relation to our current course and anticipated path."

"On screen, Captain," Horinek said a moment later. "Coordinates are in Sapphire's retrograde orbit."

Bolan looked at the main screen, his forehead furrowed. After several heartbeats, the mirror balls' relayed active sensors indicated a small cluster of green icons at the designated point. As Horinek had reported, whatever the craft were, they were "behind" Sapphire but still in its orbital path.

"Sensors, mark the location then stop painting those objects with active sensors," Bolan said. "Those alien ships are closer to them than we are, even if they're on the other side of Sapphire."

"Aye aye," Boyles said, entering commands into her console.

"Those can't be escape pods," Commander Alexander said, the man's voice nearly causing Bolan to jump. "Not from *Titanic*."

"I would certainly hope not, given the Confederation Code," Bolan noted, the comment eliciting a rueful chuckle from the XO.

Whoever or whatever left them there placed them just outside of the gravity well it looks like, Bolan thought. *Almost as if...*

"Guns, double check the tac book, make sure we didn't miss something," Bolan said, his heart rising in his throat. "Helm, alter our course to intercept. Tell the flight deck to stand by to recover...whatever the hell those things are with tractor beams. Get Warhawk One to meet them and get the senior person to his fighter as soon as possible so I can get a backbrief."

"Aye aye, Captain," Sakai replied, giving the helm a gentle input to starboard.

"Sir, should we have the Surgeon standing by?" Commander Sinclair asked.

"Good call, Guns," Bolan replied. "XO?"

"I'll make it happen, Sir," Alexander replied.

Bolan watched as the group of dots grew closer. Sakai manipulated the ship's wheel to begin bringing her stern around, then applied one half power to slow the *Constitution*'s speed.

Mirror balls have the enemy ships in Sapphire's sensor shadow... Bolan thought, looking at the screen. *Which means they can't see us around that planet.*

"Go ahead and go three quarters, Mr. Sakai," Bolan ordered, watching the screen. "If those are escape pods, I don't want to leave anyone behind. They've probably been through enough."

"Aye aye, Sir," Sakai said, advancing the throttle further. The *Constitution* finished her reorientation maneuver, continuing towards Sapphire stern first. The battlecruiser's landing bay was now oriented towards the escape pods, and Bolan watched as Sakai began to power up the tractor beam.

There should be enough time to recover those pods and then divert the energy back to where it can be more useful, Bolan thought. *I hope Liu's patchwork quilt continues to hold.*

"Eight minutes to intercept, Captain," Sakai reported.

"Thank you, Mr. Sakai," Bolan replied, exhaling slowly.

I hope whomever's in those pods has some insight on the enemy we're facing, Bolan thought. *I could use every advantage we can get.*

Constitution On the Prowl (Mechmaster)

Chapter 8: Chaos's Allegro

Titanic
2010 SST

With a deep, heartfelt sigh of relief Marcus entered into *Titanic*'s #3 escape pod flat. A long, narrow tunnel that was accessed from Echo Corridor, the structure's primary feature and reason for existence were the sixteen evenly spaced hatches that ran its one hundred and fifty meter length. There were no extraneous furnishings or plush carpeting here, and the bulkheads were left in their original, shiny metallic finish.

Paint burns, metal doesn't, Marcus thought, recalling the reasoning given to him the first time he'd seen a starliner's escape facilities. It still felt odd to be standing in such an austere setting just a few feet away from what had been luxurious surroundings.

"It just occurred to me—could you not contact the bridge from one of the escape pods communications arrays?" Senator Du said, startling Marcus from his reverie.

Shit. No time to be day dreaming, he thought to himself. Marcus briefly considered injecting himself with one of the *Hoplite*'s three shots of simulated adrenaline. Reminding himself that one of the side effects of the drug was a truly epic "crash," he held off.

"We've got the latest model of escape pods," Marcus replied, using hand gestures to station the two *Beholder* bots he'd brought with them by the door. Neither Quentin nor Albaca had been happy with him taking the security robot, but Marcus had pointedly observed the arms room didn't seem to be an alien objective unless they were led to it. The engine room, on the other hand, seemed to be drawing the lizards like flies to refuse.

"There was a rash of pirates using pods' radios to coordinate their attacks or have some sleeper agent surreptitiously radio information on the ship's next destination," Marcus continued as he moved forward inside the flat. "These don't work until they've been ejected from their cradles."

"So instead the pod designers give Murphy one more chance to interfere with a ship that's already got problems?"

"I didn't say I thought it was a good idea," Marcus replied to the Senator as he began checking to see if any of the pods had been used. He was genuinely shocked when he returned to the structure's aft end and found all sixteen pods still in their cradles.

On one hand, it's a blessing given how close we are to Sapphire. No one with any sense is going to try and abandon ship in a gas giant's gravity well, he thought. *On the other hand, getting whacked by atmospheric pressures would probably be preferable to the other available options.*

"Might as well take a few meters off our walk," Marcus said, heading to the aftmost pod. "Engage console interface function," he ordered his suit. He was rewarded by a soft tingle over both hands followed by a sharp prick as his suit quickly scanned his palm prints then took his DNA. Rather than touching the escape pod's access panel, Marcus held his left gauntlet a few inches from its face. After a couple of seconds, his HUD displayed the launch protocols for the escape pod, signifying that the control panel had recognized him as a *Titanic* crewmember authorized to initiate abandoning ship protocols.

Then again, given the situation and activation of the Dutchman protocols, Marcus thought, *I'm sure access has been granted to everyone from the bellhops to the Red Deck companions.*

Again mentally shaking himself, Marcus moved his HUD cursor over to the button marked LAUNCH and pressed it. This initiated a hooting klaxon in the flat that caught the Spartans by surprise, causing all five of them to jump and then gaze nervously at the entrance.

"A little warning would have been nice," Aimi snapped.

Marcus pointed to the etching in the plate above the pod's hatch. A pictogram depicting an alarm going off if the pod was activated was plainly visible. Aimi's eyes narrowed as she glared at him, and Marcus felt a pang of unwelcome memory.

I'd almost have preferred her zombiefied corpse returning as opposed to a psychotic doppelganger, Marcus mused with a shudder. Looking through the viewport on the inner hatch, he saw the egg-shaped pod had engaged its magnetic repulsors and ejected from *Titanic*'s hull. As an indication how deep into the gravity well the starliner had sank, the pod barely cleared one hundred meters before it began curving out of sight. Its automated computer immediately tried to struggle against Sapphire's grasp, firing the pod's maneuvering thrusters to align its blunt nose away from *Titanic* before igniting its drive. The massive single nozzle flared bright enough to briefly illuminate the far side of *Titanic*'s hull before the entire pod fell away out of sight.

230

"Hope these suits' hull grippers work," Senator Du observed. "Looks like it's a one way trip if we get knocked off."

"It's not the hull grippers you need to be worried about," Marcus replied. "I just hope we don't walk over a spot that has no external inertial dampening. We'll either come off the hull like a hyperactive toddler off a trampoline or end up with our entire body in the helmet."

"Thank you for that positive thinking, Mr. Martin," Du said dryly. "Incidentally, I'm sure drawing attention to our position had some purpose?"

Marcus looked at his HUD.

"In about another two minutes the chamber will repressurize and we can use it as an airlock," he replied.

"What?!" Du asked.

"Compressed air tanks mounted along the overhead. Good for two cycles of the airlock. It's not exactly thick air either time, but it's good enough to get people through to a rescue shuttle."

Du shook his head.

"That had to be rather expensive," the Senator said after a moment.

"The designers thought they'd better prepare for any likely catastrophe," Marcus retorted with a slight shrug. "Who knew *Titanic* actually translated to 'she who serves as an example to others' in the ancient Terran?"

Du raised an eyebrow at Marcus' bitterness, but was unable to comment before a 'ready' flashed briefly across Marcus' HUD. Saying a prayer that the sensors hadn't been damaged by the alien attack, Marcus pressed the button to open the door. There was a slight hiss as the hatch snapped back into its recess, but as Marcus had indicated the difference between air pressure on either side of the hatch was negligible.

"Senator, we've got company," one of the Spartans by the entry hatch said quietly, stepping backwards into the pod flat.

Finnegan. His name is Finnegan, and his little Eurasian looking partner is Rhee, Marcus thought as he quickly changed his HUD input screen from the airlock controls to the *Beholder*'s command screen. Looking into the airlock's corner, he clicked his targeting reticle in order to create a waypoint for the robot, then pivoted to look back towards the flat's main hatch. As the *Beholder* swerved around the retreating Spartans, he reached into his canvas sack and pulled out another implosion grenade.

231

"Are you *mad*?" Du asked fiercely as he stepped into the airlock, Aimi right behind him.

"No," Marcus said. "Hurry the fuck up, people," he said, gesturing for the two Spartans to get into the airlock.

"How many did you see?" Du asked the two men.

"Looked like twelve of them, moving from the bow in a wedge formation," Finnegan responded. Marcus nodded, then gripped the implosion grenade's arming mechanism. As the accompanying Spartans all drew in their breaths, Marcus silently counted to five, rotated the grenade's arming switch ninety degrees, then softly rolled the device into the escape flat.

"It's a proximity fuse, not the impact. Activate hull grippers!" Marcus snapped, following his own advice while simultaneously reaching back and snapping a retaining line on the *Beholder*.

"What the hell..." Aimi started to ask. She never got a chance to finish as the outer hatch opened behind them in an explosive rush of air. The *Beholder* flew backwards until it was stopped by a combination of its own countermeasures kicking in and the fibrous retaining line snapping taut. Marcus heard and felt the vents allowing external air into the *Hoplite* shut, followed shortly by the air recycling unit located at the small of his back kick in. A green 3:00:00 appeared in the left corners of his HUD, and he fought the urge to giggle at the suit's ignorant optimism.

"Out! Now!" Marcus barked, turning and leading the way through the open external hatch. The Spartans did not question him, following his red suit out the hatch. He was pleased to see that the group automatically adopted the Confederation Marines standard star formation on *Titanic*'s hull, with the open airlock serving as the focal point. As the first man out, Marcus swiveled back from the point of the start to cover the others as they spilled out to orient towards the bow and stern. As a result, he saw the silent, bright blue flash of the implosion grenade as it detonated, the brief moment of dark emptiness that followed, then the torrent of debris as the escape pod's exit hatch vomited metal, air, debris and alien corpses in a torrent of explosive decompression.

Explosive decompression is a great force equalizer, Marcus thought grimly.

"You realize if that grenade ruptured both hatches you just cut off the entire corridor for two or three decks, don't you?" Du asked as a living alien came writhing out into the vacuum, its weapon flying out of its hand.

Marcus gave a snort.

"Well it's a crying shame to make it harder to move around a ship that we're intending to blow up as quickly as possible," Marcus replied defensively. "I think the blast radius was far enough…"

As if on cue, a huge section of interior wood paneling tumbled out of the hatch. It was followed by a handful of floundering individuals, two of them in Czarina Lines' uniforms. The reflected light from Sapphire gave the group's faces a ghostly pallor, their mouths working in silent screams as they hit vacuum. Marcus could swear one of the Lines' employees, a tall brunette woman, was reaching towards him before he forced himself to look away.

Guess that answers the question on whether the escape flat's main hatch held, Marcus thought, sickened.

"Let's go," he rasped, squaring his shoulders as he looked 'up' towards *Titanic*'s dorsal side. Looking to his left and right as they climbed, Marcus saw the two other alien cruisers lurking off the *Titanic*'s bow and stern, Zed-815's primary reflecting off their hulls. He fought the sensation of feeling like a bug on a dinner plate as they ascended, the starliner's hull vibrating as her thrusters fired again.

"Why aren't those other two ships coming in to help?" Finnegan asked. "Not that I'm complaining, but still."

Good thing these suits employ laser net comms, Marcus thought with a flash of anger. *Or chatty Kathy back there might have just gotten us all killed.*

"We have apparently crippled their friend and are clearly spinning out of control towards a gas giant," Du said drily, his voice indicating he shared Marcus' annoyance. "I can't imagine why they wouldn't want to get closer. Why don't you call out to them and draw even more attention to this section of the hull?"

Finnegan wisely chose not to reply as the five of them stopped just beneath the *Titanic*'s dorsal side. Marcus considered their options as the other four moved into a line abreast formation, Finnegan / Aimi to his left, Senator Du / Rhee to his right. Looking up, he could see the alien cruiser's hull starkly outlined against Sapphire behind it. The dark blue planet was ominously large in size, and Marcus found himself wondering just how close they were to being drawn into its atmosphere. Striking that thought from his mind, he made his choice.

"We bound over," Marcus said. "Aimi, me and the *Beholder*."

Du, Finnegan and Rhee signaled their understanding, and Marcus readied himself to run "up" and over the lip of the hull. Mentally he tried to recall whether there were any obstructions on

233

Titanic's dorsal side, but was unable to think of anything other than the observatory that was towards the bow. Setting the *Beholder* to engage only if fired upon or if he fired, he held up three fingers, then two, then one and surged forward.

The view that confronted them was stunning in its beauty. Sapphire served as the backdrop, its dark blue form dominating almost their entire field of view. Marcus had to remind himself that at almost ten times the size of Banginis, itself one and a half times Terra's diameter. Even so, the planet's vastly increased size made the starkly outlined alien cruiser far less threatening. From his new perspective, Marcus could see that his original estimate of the craft's size had been almost spot on, and he found himself wondering just how many hostiles were inside the manta-shaped hull. The cruiser threw a slight shadow on the *Titanic*, with the interplay of direct light between Zed-815's primary and Sapphire's reflected illumination combining to make the craft an off color gray. To Marcus' left and right, the starfield shifted as the starliner and her companion continued their decaying orbit. The reasons for that decaying orbit were abundantly clear between the missing dorsal pod, the divots it had gouged out of the *Titanic*'s hull, and the jagged, gaping tear two hundred meters aft of his position that was still weeping debris every time the thrusters fired. Finally, Zed-815's orange primary served as a distant backdrop behind them, with its angle making Marcus glad for the anti-glint treatments on his helmet's faceshield.

Not seeing any immediate threats, Marcus turned to motion for the remainder of the group to join them. He had not even finished moving his hand when the *Beholder* flashed an alert icon on his HUD accompanied with a low, urgent tone. A moment later Aimi hissed a warning of her own, slowly drawing the *Kabano* from its perch on her back. Moving slowly himself so as not to draw attention, Marcus went to a crouch and looked towards where both the bot and Spartan indicated motion.

What are people doing outside on the hull? he thought for a moment before his brain fully caught up to what his visually augmented HUD was telling him. The half dozen shapes that had seemingly just magically appeared two hundred meters astern were indeed wearing EVA suits and walking on two legs. However, whether it was their strange movements, the large cylinder that was too rotund to have fit out of any of the *Titanic*'s airlocks, or the suit material a fabric he'd never seen before, Marcus immediately knew that the beings in front of him were aliens. Staying stock still, he watched as they continued aft towards the hole rent over the *Titanic*'s Fire Room #1.

Constitution
2015 SST

Jason paced impatiently as he watched the last of the escape pods float slowly into the *Constitution*'s landing bay. As he watched the landing signal officer's (LSO's) carefully manipulate her controls, *Constitution*'s CAG fought the urge to erupt in a string of profanity.

Lieutenant Kelso is only doing her job, he thought angrily. *With a degree of caution that utterly disregards the urgency of the situation, but doing her job nonetheless.*

The stocky brunette, a full head shorter than Jason, had elected to err on the side of safety in bringing the five escape pods aboard one by one. While it was true that each of the small craft were half again larger than the *Constitution*'s pinnace and thus at the upper limit of the tractor beam's capabilities, it also meant that the landing bay door could not be closed until the last one was aboard. By regulation this also meant Jason could not set foot onto the landing bay deck nor could any of the survivors exit until landing operations were complete.

I know regulations are written in blood, but for fuck's sake! It did not help that Kelso was not shy in communicating her displeasure at having Jason taking up room in the already cramped compartment where she and her five ratings oversaw the controlled chaos that was the *Constitution*'s recovery deck.

"Warhawk One, Captain Bolan is requesting a status report," Lieutenant Herrod's voice sounded in his ear.

"LSO's making sure all the eggs fit neatly in the basket," Jason snapped, drawing a look of daggers from Kelso. "I suspect it will be another couple of minutes while the landing bay pressurizes."

"This is Captain Bolan. Negative, as soon as that last pod is down you go out there and figure out what in the hell is going on," Captain Bolan interjected. "I don't give a damn what the regulations say."

Jason gave Kelso a triumphant grin.

"Aye aye, Captain," he replied, already heading for the hatch out of the LSO's flat.

"Good fucking riddance," someone muttered just loudly enough for Jason to hear but too quiet for him to place the voice. Giving Kelso a look that promised the matter would be dealt with later, Jason stepped into the rotating entryway. Sealing behind him, the airlock rotated 180 degrees then hissed open after there was a warning tone. His gauntlets snapped out of their storage greaves as his suit detected the thinness of the landing bay's air. He held his fingers straight out, allowing the thicker armor to slide back and mate with his suit.

It's not vacuum, but better to be safe than sorry, Jason thought as he watched the battlecruiser's flight crews rushing out from their ready rooms. As he approached the resting escape pods, he saw that their outer skin was starting to shift in order to match the flat gray of *Constitution*'s inner deck.

What idiot puts chameleon skin on an escape pod?! he thought incredulously as the closest pod's hatch popped open then slid upwards to reveal a massive Marine officer standing with his feet spread and a flechette gun cradled loosely in his arms. The man's piercing blue eyes met Jason's even as his frame blocked the entire hatch.

Mental note: Next time I let Nishizawa form the welcoming committee, Jason thought to himself. *Because I'm sitting here armed with nothing but quick wit after we just brought a gaggle of unidentified pods into the landing bay. Lucky it was a human that opened that damn door.*

"Pardon me, Commander, but you wouldn't happen to have seen a gray kangaroo hopping by with a handbag, would you?" the bald Marine asked conversationally.

Oh shit, I'm about to die because I forgot to check the sign and countersign of the day, Jason thought, fighting back the urge to start laughing crazily.

"Don't be silly, Major, kangaroos always drive in limousines," Nishizawa answered easily as he stepped from around the other side of the pod.

I have never been so happy to see a man in my life, Jason thought.

The lieutenant colonel was flanked by two of *Constitution*'s own Marines. Although Nishizawa was wearing the flat black version of the Marines' flight armor, Jason noted with grim satisfaction that the two other Hammerheads were encased in *Hill Giant* assault armor. The two bookends made Nishizawa look like a reed in between them, while the vibro-cutlass and grenade launcher each clutched in their hands indicated they were just as prepared for trouble as the *Constitution*'s new guest. The newcomer officer visibly relaxed, relief washing over his face like a brief, violent wave before he regained his composure.

That would be the equivalent of us mere mortals sobbing in relief and running into someone's arms, Jason thought with slight annoyance as the man slung the flechette gun and stepped on the *Constitution*'s deck. The next man out of the pod was tall and far thinner than the Space Marine. Jason could see the man had a face that looked like it was in a permanent scowl, with his blue eyes boring into the CAG's own.

"I am Lieutenant Commander Alika Iokepa, senior officer of the *Shigure*," the man said quickly, his voice sounding like something which would come from a sentient rock pile. "I need to speak to Captain Bolan *immediately*."

"Wait, what?" Jason asked, taking a step backwards, his eyes narrowing. "How do you know who is the captain…"

"Sir, with all due respect, there's not that many battlecruisers with a landing bay running around the Confederation Fleet," Iokepa replied. Jason couldn't figure out if it was the man's natural voice or incredulity that made him sound on the verge of belligerency, but he chose to let it pass.

"Well funny, he'd like to see you too. Lieutenant Colonel Nishizawa, he'll probably want you to be there as well."

Acheros looked nonplussed at Jason's comment.

"Is there a problem, Major?" Jason asked, raising an eyebrow.

"No, Sir, just a brief thought about clearances," Acheros said. "But if you're here in this system, I'm sure you know what the hell is going on."

"Actually no, Major, we were hoping you guys would be able to tell us," Jason replied, his tone somber.

Bridge
Constitution
2025 SST

It was one thing to know an emotional hammer strike to the solar plexus was coming in theory. It was quite another to receive it in person.

"Sir, I regret to report the destruction of the *Shigure*, most likely with all remaining aboard, at approximately 1915 SST," Commander Iokepa said, standing at rigid attention before Bolan's chair. "As the senior surviving officer, I am prepared to give testimony to her demise."

237

The utter silence on the *Constitution*'s bridge was deafening in Bolan's ears as Iokepa finished what Confederation Fleet regulations, protocol, and tradition demanded. Feeling as if his heart was being crushed in his chest, Bolan came to his feet and returned the salute.

"May the *Shigure*'s dead find peace among the stars and her enemies face the Fleet's wrath," *Constitution*'s master replied with their service's traditional litany, hoping his voice did not betray the tears he felt welling in his eyes. "At ease, Lieutenant Commander, and what the hell happened?"

"Sir, with all due respect, I would prefer to do this through a command channel link," Iokepa said, gesturing to the bridge crew. Bolan gestured for the man to plug his suit into his chair, then pointed to Sinclair and Horinek's positions for Major Acheros, Commander Owderkirk, and Lieutenant Colonel Nishizawa to plug into. As the men were arranging themselves, Bolan took the extra time to wrestle with the guilt, anger, and grief warring in his mind.

Damn it Leslie, you should've waited, he seethed, fighting the urge to grip his hands in rage. He took a deep, pained breath and closed his eyes, then reopened them as he felt a pair of tears roll down his face. His helmet's algorithms quickly kicked in, a slight vacuum drawing the remaining tears quickly off his eyeball. The air movement caused Bolan to blink rapidly, leading to a slight shake of the head.

Get yourself together, captain, and fight your goddamn ship.

"Proceed Lieutenant Commander," Bolan said on the command channel.

"The *Shigure* received extensive modifications during her last refit," Iokepa said. "In addition to being armed with new missiles and getting her hull strengthened, we received the first operational Herbert drive."

Someone, perhaps Sinclair, muttered an expletive. Iokepa ignored it and continued his recounting. It took him twelve terse minutes of Bolan's emotional agony to finish his report.

"Starliner captain didn't have the sense the Maker gave a common garden slug," Iokepa concluded. "Or else he assumed they were Confederation vessels and was doing an obligatory run for the hills until they told him to formally come about. Either way, he got blasted, and all we know is that someone aboard got off message buoys. Which is why we didn't Masada the whole lot of them."

"Funny you should mention that thought," Alexander interjected. "It's still a possibility."

"Sounds like a damn fine plan to me," Acheros seethed.

Horinek, able to hear the whole conversation due to her station being used as a relay, snapped her head up at Acheros's fury. Bolan fixed the Marine with a hard gaze.

"Major Acheros, if you cannot get control of your emotions, you'd best report back to the landing bay and sit this one out in an escape pod," Bolan growled.

"Sorry Sir," Acheros said, his tone genuinely apologetic. "Just seems to be such a damn waste."

"Commander Hawkins was an utter professional. Her death," Bolan said, the words tasting like ashes in his mouth, "would pretty much be in vain if we just rained this vessel's entire missile magazine on the *Titanic* as soon as we got in range. I'm not going to throw good money after bad, but we're at least going to see what the house odds are before I kill a few thousand people and basically throw away Commander Hawkins' decision."

"Aye aye, Sir," Acheros replied. Bolan saw Horinek stand up and tap on the Major's shoulder. Out of the corner of his eye, he watched as his Navigation Officer raised his helmet face shield and gestured for Acheros to do the same. The Marine officer wisely turned off his microphone but indicated he was still listening to Iokepa.

"Sir, Commander Hawkins had the sensor relay going to the pods as she started her attack run. One of those contacts is damaged, and as soon as we can hook the sensor's storage disk and the bridge log up to an authorized station we can tell you more."

Bolan looked at Iokepa.

"Effective immediately, you will treat everyone on this bridge as Omega cleared," Bolan said simply. "More help's not coming for awhile, and we are spending people's lives as we speak."

Iokepa didn't even flinch.

"Aye aye, Captain," he replied, reaching into the storage bag that had been slung over his shoulder.

Titanic
2030 SST

Marcus had spent the last twenty minutes kicking himself for his stupidity.

I forgot about the communications array, he thought fiercely while running down the starliners starboard side, Du, Finnegan and

Rhee behind him in single file. The various antennas and attendant paraphernalia that allowed the *Titanic* to conduct intra-system communications were housed in a four meter high bulge that ran approximately fifty meters down her port side. Set almost dead center in the starliner's beam, the structure had allowed the aliens to cross over from their cruiser outside of his initial line of sight. Thankfully the six aliens seemed to have been in a hurry to get above Fire Room #1 and had not looked forward.

"Waypoint reached," his suit intoned, and Marcus stopped, then rotated ninety degrees so he was facing back toward the *Titanic*'s dorsal side. He took a moment to catch his breath, focusing on the small square projected on the corner of his helmet's face plate. After a couple of seconds, the projection instantly expanded to take up his entire HUD, the image slightly transparent so he could continue seeing forward.

*If I ever meet the **Beholder** design team, I'm going to buy them all dinner*, he thought with utter sincerity. Remotely accessing the bot's sensors was a terrible risk due to the emissions concerns, but there was no way that Marcus was getting into a long range shoot out with the numbers in the aliens' favor. Instead he was going to do things a little...differently.

What in the hell are they doing? he asked as he watched the screen. The aliens had placed the large cylinder on the *Titanic*'s skin and were messing with various attachments along its skin. Marcus watched as the beings allowed the smaller pieces to float away as they conducted their disassembly, and he had a mental image of poorly trained space construction workers.

It's all fun and games until a nut goes through a planetary shuttle's window, Marcus thought grimly, then shook his head at the banality of his thoughts. Worried, he minimized the feed to check his air mixture.

Okay, just fatigue, not hypoxia. Flicking his finger, he reexpanded the video screen just in time to see the aliens lift off the lid and reveal the cylinders shimmering, silver contents. Squinting his eyes, he tried to remember why the object seemed familiar...then felt bile rise in his throat as four of the aliens lifted the bottom half of the cylinder.

"Go! Now!" he screamed, running over the edge of the deck. He had barely set his foot on the ventral deck before one of the unencumbered aliens' head exploded from the impact of a *Kabano* slug. Marcus caught the other one before it could bring up the pistol in its hand, the swathe of his flechette charge almost blowing it in half in a spray of suit, air, and dark blue blood.

Even as his mind registered that the spray of gore looked different than the lizards' inside the hull, he saw the other four aliens releasing their load and trying to spring away. Two of them barely made it one step, Senator Du killing one while Finnegan and Rhee both shot the other. The third actually managed to bring up a sidearm before another *Kanabo* strike passed under the still levitating crate and through both its thighs.

Marcus didn't have time to see anything else as the fourth creature, faster and wiser than its companions, slammed into him at full speed. His hull grippers slid with the impact as he found himself faceshield to faceshield with an alien that looked like a teddy bear birthed from some psychopath's nightmare.

What the fuck?! Marcus had enough time to think before he instinctively swung his arm up to stop a strike from the creature's left arm. The blow staggered Marcus even as the creature's limb snapped, its visage split into a silent scream of agony that showed the full array of its canine like teeth. Marcus didn't give it time to recover, dancing backwards and firing the *Pata* one handed. The blast shattered the creature's skull and helmet in a radial out spray of gore. The bear-like creature dropped like a puppet with its strings cut, its heart pulsing out three final blasts of blood in a spray of liquid that stained *Titanic*'s dorsal deck.

Marcus struggled to slow his breathing down as the *Hoplite*'s cleaning routines swept the gore off the front of his face shield with a quiet hum. If he'd been outside of the armor, there was no doubt in his mind that the alien's blow would have shattered his arm and gone right through his torso. Looking down at the armor, he could see that the blow had managed to slightly dent its frame.

"We need to get this...*weapon* off the hull, Marcus," Senator Du said, snapping him out of his stupor. "Aimi, cover us."

"Yes Senator," Aimi replied. "Perhaps our fearless guide would like to turn on the *Beholder* so it can do more than observe?"

"I'm sorry, did you suddenly become an expert in alien weapons? Because I don't want to find out if this thing detonates when hit by an energy blast," Marcus snapped, looking around the deck before slinging his *Pata*. The security officer gestured towards the third alien, dead on its feet with its hands clenched to its legs and a cloud of its bluish blood around the holes in its suit.

241

"These aren't those damn lizards," he muttered, stepping up to grab one of the handles on the cylinder. The opening felt odd, like it wasn't correctly shaped for his hand.

"If you hadn't recognized the weapon, I'd have wondered if we were facing another race," Du replied.

"On three," Marcus said. "One…two…*three.*"

The four men all heaved upwards. After a moment's resistance, the cylinder raised off the *Titanic*'s hull with a surprising rapidity. The resultant momentum attempted to lift all four of them off, and with almost simultaneous cries of surprise the humans all let go. As they drifted slowly back down to the deck, Marcus watched the cylinder moving away from *Titanic*'s hull.

Any second now… he thought, waiting for the object to move roughly one to two hundred meters away.

The shock of the thrusters firing caught them by surprise. Marcus had just enough time to throw himself to the deck and try to hold on before he was sent tumbling towards the open maw of Fireroom #1. The liner's oscillations accelerated the security officer's bumping, flapping slide towards the darkened hole, and he only had time to tuck himself into a ball before he tumbled into the abyss.

Kaiju Class Mecha Platform Patch Variant B (Young / Nagy)

Chapter 9: Death's Allegrisimo

Constitution Bridge
2035 SST
21 June

"All ahead flank, Mr. Sakai," Bolan said. "Bring us around Sapphire's western hemisphere, maximize the time we're in the sensor shadow."

"Aye aye, Captain," Sakai replied, pushing the yoke forward to bring the battlecruiser's bow down ecliptic then shoving the engine telegraph through to the stops. As he felt the battlecruiser accelerate, Bolan once again made a mental run through of the plan the command group had quickly hashed out after watching the *Shigure*'s demise.

Have to stay away from their broadside, he thought. *Preferably by pinning one or both cruisers against the planet where they won't be able to maneuver as easily.*

"Sir, Contact B is shifting position towards *Titanic*," Boyles stated. Looking at the sensors, Bolan could see the enemy cruiser, plasma streaming from its starboard "wing," moving from its position astern of *Titanic*.

While I'm glad the mirrorballs give us the ability to see around the planet, there are some drawbacks, Bolan thought, gripping the arm rest. *Like this terrible fear they're going to smash both ships then fold out.* The enemy's ability to leave the star system almost instantaneously gave his opponents advantages that Bolan didn't care to think about.

At least it doesn't appear they can jump very well within system, Bolan thought. *Or else **Shigure** never would have gotten away the first time.* As Bolan watched on the screen, the cruiser icon's passed that of the *Titanic*'s without a storm of weapons flying from her port side. Releasing a breath he didn't know he was holding, Captain Bolan looked at the chronometer in the corner.

*We will be at the planet in a little over fifteen minute*s he thought.

"Comms, nearest vessel according to the tacbook?" he asked, fully aware that the projected fleet movements had been proven glaringly wrong at least twice.

"Closest expected vessel, based on previous movements, would be the heavy cruiser *Mumbai*. Heaviest battle group is the carrier *Java Sea* at six hours, Captain," Herrod replied.

"Enemy vessels are now moving adjacent to one another and coming to a halt, Captain," Boyles said, puzzlement in her voice.

Damage control assistance? Bolan wondered. *Either way, should make this plan much easier.*

Bolan turned and looked to the three "jump" seats located at the rear of the bridge. Lieutenant Commander Iokepa sat in the middle of the trio, his face studying the main screen. Figuring out what to do with the *Shigure*'s survivors, especially Iokepa and Acheros, had been a bit problematic. On one hand, as the *Shigure*'s senior survivors, the two men were almost certainly going to be absolutely critical to the Board of Inquiry that was certain to follow this operation. On the other hand, short of placing both men and every other *Shigure* survivor back in the escape pods or fleeing the scene immediately, there was no truly "safe" place aboard the *Constitution*. Moreover, he was fairly certain he'd have had to throw Acheros in the brig to avoid having the Spartan accompany the *Constitution*'s boarding party. Indeed, Nishizawa had been quite adamant that such an action would have been proper given Acheros' seniority.

I might have to rethink my prohibition against having any Spartan on board my vessels, Bolan thought. *Although I may never command anything again if Acheros gets himself killed.*

"Enemy cruisers will be out of sensor shadow in five minutes, Sir," Boyles reported.

"Okay Mr. Sakai, let's get Warhawk out the chute," Bolan said, wanting to give the air group as much initial velocity as possible before decelerating. "Ms. Boyles, let's swim the decoys."

Warhawk One
2030 SST

I hope this goes as well as the last time I was in this seat, Jason thought grimly. After checking that the catapult was ready and he had a green light, Jason keyed his microphone.

"Warhawk One, ready to launch!"

"Roger Warhawk One, launching," Sakai's voice came back. Jason once more felt the giant's drop kick. He was barely clear of *Constitution*'s hull before he was manipulating his thrusters to flip around and watch the rest of the group launch. As the last *Thunderchief* cleared the battlecruiser's hull, he looked at his chronometer.

Well in advance of the standard, he thought with a smile. If this is an utter clusterfuck they'll at least note we charged to our doom in style.

"This is Aces One, squadron formed," Lieutenant Commander Tice reported. "Request permission to engage enemy craft."

Jason smiled and shook his head at Catnip's impatience.

Yes, you can get there first, but how about we try to divvy up their flak, Jason thought, looking at his tactical display

"Negative Aces, stand by," he replied tersely. "So far I've got no alien small craft, no reason to let you go in ahead."

There was a pause, during which Jason could almost see Tice biting her tongue.

"Roger, will wait on the rest of the air group," Tice replied.

"Warhawks, Warhawks One. Arrowhead formation, Aces in the van, Bulls in the middle, Kaiju bringing up the rear," Jason ordered as the fighter craft began to accelerate away towards Sapphire.

"Warhawk One, *Constitution* Actual," his headset crackled with Captain Bolan's voice. "The cruisers have shifted their position relative the *Titanic*, please advise which one you think you can get to."

Tearing his eyes from assembling the air group, Jason turned to look at his display.

My pride says we want the undamaged cruiser, but in reality there's no difference, Jason thought.

"Dealer's choice, *Constitution*," he said aloud. "We can take the nicked up bastard, should keep him from running or interfering with the Marines."

"Very good, Contact Bravo is yours. We're killing velocity, but should be in their sensor envelope and engaging in fifteen minutes from my mark...Mark!"

For a man who just had to repeatedly watch the death of someone he apparently was in love with, the Old Man's handling things quite well, Jason thought grimly. *I'd be a wreck if I saw Andrea die.*

"Roger, understand one five mikes to show time," Jason replied, starting a timer on the upper left hand side of his HUD.

Warhawk Fly By (Mechmaster)

An Unproven Concept

As the Warhawks were preparing to enter the dance, Marcus Martin found himself in a far different predicament. As a dead engineering rating floated by for the second time, the *Titanic*'s thrusters fired again and forced him into an impromptu crouch. Marcus uttered a small prayer of thanks that the unburnt side of the corpse's face had rotated to face him on this second trip by, as it simply looked like the man had been startled by an unexpected noise, not simultaneously torched and shredded.

At least he died damn near instantaneously, Marcus thought, turning away before the corpse floated out of the shadows hiding its ruined bottom half. He took a deep breath that made his ribs ache. *Unlike the rest of us poor bastards.*

It had been a minor miracle that Marcus survived his entry into the engine room. Thankfully the residual inertial dampening from the still whole Fireroom #2 slowed him after he'd ricocheted off two of the damaged reactor bottles. As several of the other cadavers bouncing around the engine room could apparently attest, it was only the *Hoplite* that limited his damage to deep contusions after bouncing the thirty meters or so to the deck. Despite the *Hoplite* injecting him with anti-inflammatory pain killers after landing, Marcus was only able to take deep breaths with difficulty.

Of course, that might not be a problem soon, Marcus thought grimly. Something had skittered across the deck while he was barreling into the room like an armor-clad meteor, and Marcus was reasonably certain it was not friendly. Gathering himself, he sprang off the bulkhead behind him, aiming for the engine room's control compartment roughly ten meters away and a full two stories above his head. By some quirk of fate, the large, rectangular structure had retained its transparisteel windows, even as the side facing Marcus had been thoroughly perforated by shards of the *Titanic*'s hull and the engine compartment's contents. Mounted on the stern side of Fireroom #1, as Marcus grew closer he could see that the loss of inertial dampening had been less abrupt inside the four walls.

Goddamn containment fields, Marcus thought, looking again at his comms to put off having to see the ruin inside. The interference from the shattered fusion bottles magnetic components greatly reduced the *Hoplite*'s ability to transmit or receive information or use its onboard sensors. Thus, Marcus was forced to conduct his search for his lost *Pata* the old-fashioned way. After his perusal with ye olde Mark I Eyeball had produced nothing, he'd eventually given up and taken the vibrocutlass out of its sheath.

So here I am flying with a freakin' sword in my hand, Marcus thought angrily. *Oh if only Spider were here…*

"Hey Peter Pan, you realize that half the engine room can see you up there?" his radio crackled, the speaker's voice so distorted only the sarcasm told him it was Finnegan.

Turning to look for Senator Du's bodyguard was probably the only thing that saved his life. The two silver spheres that went right where his head had been detonated against the control room's hatch in bright, intense splotches of soundless light, with a resultant storm of debris that smashed off Marcus's face shield. Whipping himself around, he engaged his hull grippers to add impetus to his motion, speeding up in a manner that completely threw off his opponents' reengagement from his left side. Marcus was already running as his feet hit the front of the control panel, moving perpendicularly down the transparisteel windows away from the fire.

"…aliens…you! Turn…*Beholder*…ing idiot!" Aimi's voice screamed in his ears.

I'm guessing if I can hear my own bitching angel of death, the robot must be in here as well, he thought, reaching the far side hatch and swinging himself into the compartment. The silent eruption of the windows, impact of transparisteel fragments on his armor, and shaking of the compartment told Marcus that the aliens were still firing, and he added yet another peon of thanks and longevity to the shipbuilders' growing account in his head.

Here goes nothing, he thought, bringing up the *Beholder*'s routines and activating the robot's offensive weapons.

There was a bright, quick flash that lit up the compartment, leading to an immediate cessation of the fire impacting the control room. Closing the command menu, he rolled over on his side and found himself looking at a pair of legs and a pelvis. Fighting the urge to vomit, Marcus crawled to the opposite hatch. The heavy door had been knocked askew by some impact, and he looked through the resultant gap upon a scene of utter butchery.

Well that was money well spent, he thought shakily. It appeared that he had initially been engaged by seven or eight aliens. Seeing the two species' corpses in the same general vicinity, Marcus could identify two of the ursanoid beings approximately ten meters apart, each surrounded by three or four of their reptilian companions. From the scorch and floating ichor, it appeared the *Beholder* opened the dance with a pair of fragmentary grenades that exploded at waist height. Amazingly, it looked like one or two of the lizards still turned to return fire despite being practically disemboweled. They'd paid for their perfidy by receiving precise energy bolts through the face shields of their elongated helmets.

"...want...to...protocols?" Du asked. For a brief instant Marcus saw an icon indicating the Senator's position from where the man was crouched near the base of a fusion bottle. Calling up the *Hoplite*'s laser communications suite, Marcus entered a quick text message:

AS LONG AS YOU DON'T SHOOT ME, IT SHOULD NOT SHOOT YOU. MIGHT WANT TO PASS THAT ALONG TO AIMI.

Maybe that's a little childish, but she's made it pretty clear only the untimely interruption of our alien friends is preventing her from trying to cut my throat in my sleep, Marcus thought.

Glancing, Marcus could see where the Beholder was continuing to buzz about like a malevolent bumblebee on speed as it searched the compartment for more alien targets. Satisfied that there weren't any hostiles within the immediate vicinity, Marcus finished pushing the hatch open then stepped out and dropped to the compartment's floor. As he landed in a cloud of dust, Senator Du and Aimi stepped close enough for their icons to register on his HUD.

"Where's Finnegan and Rhee?" Marcus asked, furrowing his brow. At that moment Finnegan's icon also appeared to his front, stepping out from behind a pile of debris.

"Rhee's dead," Aimi snapped.

"We came into the engine room," Finnegan explained. "Rhee hit the lip of the hole. Face first."

Marcus winced, not needing any more explanation.

Hope he was at least knocked out by the impact, Marcus thought as he led the battered band towards the rear of the fire room. The foursome stopped just before a heavy, semi-circular hatch that led to Fireroom #2. Marcus again accessed the requisite control panel from inside his suit, opening the hatch to reveal a 6 x 4 meter compartment with a matching portal on the far end. The quartet stepped in, and Marcus turned to close the hatch behind them, causing a yellow bulb to illuminate over what was now their exit. There was whirring sound as the ceiling mounted scanner spun around, its beams adding a strobe effect to the now pitch black cubicle.

"What about the *Beholder*?" Senator Du asked.

God he sounds tired, Marcus thought.

"In about five minutes it will finish searching the engine room," Marcus replied evenly. "At that point, the bot will find the place that gives it the best sensor coverage, probably near the main hatch. If any more aliens drop into that room, they're going to have a bad day."

The hatch closed behind them, causing a slight vibration in the deck beneath their feet.

"Radiation detected," a disembodied voice sounded in all their headphones. "Decontamination sub-routines initiated."

The simple sentence was all the warning they received as hot foam was forced into the confined space. Marcus' suit screeched an alarm at him, his HUD indicating the surface temperature reached 300°.

"What in the hell is going on?" Aimi asked, and for the first time Marcus actually heard panic in her voice.

"Decontamination foam," Marcus replied, feeling amused at the Spartans' collective discomfiture.

"So if you come through the hatch after being contaminated they boil you alive?!" Finnegan asked, his voice annoyed.

"There are three different protocols," Marcus said just as the foam reached over their heads. "The compartment has sensors to detect vacuum, at which point the designers assumed everyone would be in some sort of suit."

"Well glad that none of us have leaks," Finnegan snapped, just as the grating at their feet opened to whisk most of the foam away in a roar of vacuum. The grates closed once more to allow superheated water to play over their exteriors, followed by compressed air being forced into the enclosed space. Once the sensors were satisfied the air pressure was equalized, the door swung open to Fireroom #2...and revealed Quentin facing the hatch, his assault rifle pointed right at the center of Marcus' chest.

"Took you fucking long enough," the man said, dropping the rifle with relief evident on his face. Marcus could see the man's suit was charred across its left arm, with human blood covering one of his legs.

"We got delayed," Marcus said, stepping into the engine room. As he relayed what had happened to them, he glanced around the massive space. With the bright lights glowing from the overhead and sidewalls, it was easy to see the fireroom's entire oval. Running one hundred meters in length from the Fireroom #1 airlock to the aft bulkhead and forty meters at its widest, Fireroom #2 was bracketed by Corridors A and E just as its forward twin had been. The five fusion bottles that served as the compartment's reason for existence rose in ten stories of purple grandeur from the deck to the overhead in the middle of the compartment.

Outside of the bottles' largely pristine exteriors, the only thing that kept Marcus from mentally comparing Fireroom #2 to Hell was what he'd just left on the other side of the airlock. Dead bodies, both alien and human, lay slumped around the space in various stages of dismemberment. A fire flickered in the control compartment's shattered windows, with the gray smoke wafting upwards to the air scrubbers in the overhead.

This is going to smell great when my suit opens back up, Marcus thought. As if on cue, the *Hoplite*'s seals opened, allowing the stench of the Fireroom to waft into his helmet. Ignoring the smell, he focused on what Quentin was telling him about the room's status.

"The 2-A entry is vacuum sealed, probably due to the hit to Fireroom #1," Quentin said, gesturing towards the hatchway in question.

Well that would make sense that there's spall damage on Deck 2, Corridor A given the direction of impact, Marcus thought. The set of stairs and landing to that led up to the hatch had been blown into warped ruin, with two dead men hanging from the wreckage. Glancing at the bodies, Marcus felt a moment of relief that they were not wearing Czarina uniforms.

Passengers are not supposed to die defending the ship, he thought, the brief euphoria replaced by crushing guilt.

"I'm not so sure I wouldn't put it past the alien bastards to try and blow a hole in the hatch," Senator Du observed drily. "They don't seem to be too concerned with letting vacuum in."

There's no way to open that damn hatch to make sure that's not exactly what's happening, Marcus thought. Takes a dockyard code to break a vacuum seal.

"I wouldn't put it past them either," Marcus sighed. "Not a damn thing we can do about it though. When was the last attack?"

"About fifteen minutes before you came through that hatch," Quentin said wearily. "We've gotten all the spare ammo handed out and a defense set up, with people rotating off the line."

"Holy shit, Quentin, how'd you guys get here so much quicker than us?" Marcus asked, looking at his chronometer.

"Sewage and maintenance scuppers were completely clear," Quentin replied with a shrug. "Only hold up was the methane is starting to accumulate, as the air circulation pumps went offline while we were down there."

Marcus wrinkled his nose in a pained expression at that report.

"Anyway, the bastards had been coming up 10-C," Quentin said, pointing to where a broad ramp rose up between Fusion Bottles #2 and #3. The man then rotated and indicated the hatch located almost diagonally to 2-A on the engine room's bottom level. Marcus noted the hatch in question was only partially closed.

"The last rush they got smart and came in 8-E at the same time," Quentin said. "I was down in 9-C dealing with that fight when I heard the weapons fire and screaming. Came back to find the damn hatch jammed open and about eight of those lizards left standing."

"How many do you have down at the bottom of that ramp?" Marcus asked.

"Twenty-five there, six at the hatch we jammed at frame 70 in Corridor E. Lost two suits, Haggard and Eustis, plus eight crew getting that done."

"Dammit!" Marcus said, shocked. "I thought the hit on the fireroom would have opened up the corridor."

"Seal doors on the deck seven stairwells," Quentin said. Marcus shook his head.

I'm too damned tired, he thought. I'm forgetting simple shit.

"Why'd you counterattack?" Marcus asked, then held up his hand as Quentin started to color. "I just need to know the situation, I'm not second guessing you at all, Quentin."

"Only way we could keep this place," Quentin replied simply. "Not enough people to hold both exits if the aliens got more reinforcements, so I had Haggard and Eustis go to find the next hatch that worked." He turned to Senator Du. "Sir, your security detail can fight with me anytime, anyplace. When I asked for volunteers, they all went."

Oh you'd be singing a different tune if you knew what Senator Du had originally planned for all of us, Marcus thought as the Spartan Senator nodded in return, his face showing a trace of pride.

"Where's Mr. Blum?" Marcus asked.

Quentin gave a short, barking laugh and gestured, his face grim, towards the still burning control compartment.

"Blum was up there with one of the Spartans. Ugaki, I believe. Guess the aliens decided that man killing three of them as soon as they got through 8-E was some bullshit that could not stand."

Du's face flushed at Quentin's flippant tone.

"Ugaki was a great…"

"Senator, Mr. Ugaki saved half this engine room's life with his shooting," Quentin said, his voice slightly choked. "Mr. Blum was one of my best friends on this ship."

Du regained his poker face and nodded his understanding.

All of us have our ways of coping with horror, Marcus thought. *Quentin's has always been gallows humor.* Marcus saw that Aimi was deliberately looking away from all of them. The Security Chief would have sworn the woman's shoulders were slightly quaking.

So, even the Queen Bitch of the Universe has a heart, he thought uncharitably.

"Mr. Martin, we need to put that fire out," Du said, interrupting him.

Quentin shook his head.

"If you're trying to get into the computer, don't bother," he said simply. "The only people who had the ability to override the Dutchman codes are the Captain, the First Mate, Blum, and his three chiefs. Two of the chiefs were off duty. Judging from the damage control schematic I got to see before the controls went up, they won't be showing up any time soon."

Marcus raised an eyebrow, waiting for Quentin to explain himself.

"Crew quarters are more fucked than we thought," Quentin said. "Blum kept saying something about 'the computer went all HAL 9000 on our asses,' whatever the hell that means."

"Where was the third?" Marcus asked.

"In the dorsal pod," Quentin replied simply. "Which…"

"…is gone. As in completely gone," Du said, his voice trembling. "So there is no one on this vessel who can affect the engines in any way?"

"Not anyone who is on the helpful side of a shitload of aliens or a vacuum door," Marcus said. Du clenched his jaw as he glared at the security man.

"Then what is the fucking point of us being here?" the Senator seethed, causing Quentin to look between the two of them.

"I would dare say that 'the point' of being here is so the aliens don't kill the engines, Senator," Marcus snapped. "Or is dying by implosion not Gotterdammerung enough for your Spartan pride?"

Du looked at Marcus, his eyes wide enough to show the whites as he clenched his fists. The man was about to speak when Quentin interrupted him.

"If it's any consolation, Senator, the engineers say the burn rate on the forward thrusters is increasing, and there's only forty-five minutes worth of fuel left," Quentin said snidely. "At which point, thanks to that big bitch attached to us somehow, we're probably going to hit the atmosphere at an angle which may make implosion seem like a positive outcome. So, don't fret, you may get your Viking funeral after all."

Du looked as if he wanted to snatch his vibrocutlass out and attack both men. He was stopped by Ikenna's voice over the com.

"Boss, I think you need to get down here!" the man said, slightly panicked. Marcus and Quentin shared a glance, then quickly began moving towards the 10-C ramp.

Less than thirty seconds later the duo were stepping into Fireroom #2's antechamber. Designed to allow access from Corridor C if Fireroom #1 were holed, the compartment was at the bottom of a corridor that was an offshoot from where Corridor C divided into a "Y" for access to each Fireroom. Rather than add additional subdivision where the corridor now passed below Fireroom #1, the designers had simply left an open space whose dimensions roughly coincided with the compartment above it.

I need to ask Quentin about what he saw down in the sewage scuppers, Marcus thought to himself. *I'd hate to have aliens firing up through the deck beneath us.* Although the thirty meters between Deck 10 and the ventral keel were a rabbit warren of sewage, maintenance, storage and various other functional areas, the fact remained that the aliens were probably desperate enough to find a way to make things work.

"The methane is so thick down there you could float on it," Quinn said, startling Marcus. "We had to cover the last half of the trip by giving guys shots of oxygen from the *Hoplites'* rescue hoses."

Marcus turned and looked at the shorter man in surprise.

"You keep looking at the deck like you're expecting something to jump up and eat you," Quentin said simply. Marcus felt a sudden onset of guilt.

"I'm sorry I didn't tell you about the battle armor," Marcus said, using the command only link. "Or that we were basically coming on a suicide mission."

Quentin gave a chuckle.

"Right. We're hours from the nearest help and have three alien ships all over us. I think the only person who didn't realize we were all dead back in the ballroom was Sarah," Quentin said derisively.

Marcus mentally recoiled from the cynical response, biting his bottom lip.

I want to defend her, but he's unfortunately right, Marcus thought.

"Sorry boss, that was…" Quentin said after the moment's pause.

"No, I deserved that," Marcus interjected. Catching motion out of the corner of his eye, he saw that the Spartans had caught up with them.

"Most people sprint when someone calls for them in panic," Aimi observed sarcastically, walking just behind the two of them.

I have had enough of you, Marcus seethed.

"Well, glad to see you're over your cry," Marcus snapped back.

"There is no shame in mourning the dead," Aimi replied simply.

"I promise that when this is over you two can either fight or fuck, but until it's done could you please stop?" Finnegan asked, exasperated. Aimi and Marcus both stumbled, drawing a laugh from Senator Du and Quentin. The sound died an unnatural death as they reached Deck 10 and looked out down Corridor C across the impromptu barricade that the *Titanic*'s defenders had assembled.

Oh my God! Marcus thought as he slid to a crouch below the gathered crates, metal containers, and fusion bottle parts.

Across the antechamber and the numerous dead alien bodies filling it, a growing knot of humans stood clumped together. In various stages of undress, cleanliness, and wounding, the group continued to look back behind them in an almost universal visage of fear. The group murmured among themselves, some now alternating looking behind them with glancing towards the barricade. After a few moments, Marcus' aural sensor isolated a child's voice

"What are they going to do with us, Mama?"

"I don't know honey," an unidentified woman replied. "The men down there will help us."

256

No...no...no, Marcus screamed mentally, even as he felt a cold calm fall over him.

"Quentin?" Martina said quietly, his suit having to amplify his speech over the noise echoing down the corridor.

"Yeah boss?" Quentin responded, his voice puzzled.

"*Pyromancer* grenade," Marcus said flatly.

Everyone in a suit turned and looked at Marcus, horror on their faces. Seeing their comrades turn, the others at the barricade did so as well.

"Marcus...oh my god, no," Quentin said, his face pale.

"You going to do it?" Marcus asked simply. "I'm not asking anyone else to."

"What are you talking about?! We don't have to throw a *Pyromancer* warhead at them!" Ikenna screamed at him, purposefully putting the conversation on his external speakers. Marcus looked at him even as there were murmurs of assent.

So that's the way you want to play it? Marcus thought with disgust.

"Really? So how many rounds do you have in your rifle?" Marcus asked simply. "How many do you think you can get off with, what, fifty people forced to run down a hallway towards you with aliens behind? How many of them are going to hit an alien?"

As Marcus watched, he heard several cries of consternation and fear as there was a movement among the gathered group of people. Focusing, he saw a green form moving at just below shoulder height among the gathered people.

"There's a lizard in there!" Aimi said, unlimbering her *Kanabo*.

"Mama! Mama!" Marcus heard the child cry again.

"Leave him..." an unidentified man started to cry before he was off by a wet sound and resultant *thump*! Marcus didn't need the resultant crowd screams and panicked shifting away from the dead body that briefly exposed the alien. The green alien moved before Aimi could get off a shot, the Spartan woman distracted by the small child shoved through the legs of the adults around him. The small, black-haired boy in a blue child's suit stumbled with the force, landing on his rear end in front of the gathered group in a tumble of limbs. Marcus felt bile rise up from his belly as the child sat there and screamed, looking back in shock and pain.

"You fuckers!" one of the men behind the barricade screamed. He started to stand, only to be grabbed by two of his friends and hauled back down. As the group watched in helpless anger, several other children were shoved through the large throng.

"Kill us!" a man screamed. "They're using us as shields!"

The man's words started a panic, several adults trampling the children in front and starting to run down the hallway. Like the first spooked beast in a group of prey animals, the movement triggered a stampede. Through his aural sensors Marcus heard several alien roars and sibilant hisses, then saw a flashes of movement and purple shields just beyond the running people.

Shit, he thought, suddenly realizing he hadn't grabbed a weapon. His hand jerked as someone grabbed it and shoved an object into it. Looking down, he saw the bright red of the *Pyromancer* grenade resting in his gauntlet.

I will never wash this off my soul, he thought, arming the grenade even as alien fire began slamming into the front of the barricade. Out of the corner of his eye he saw a man's upper torso evaporate as he hurled the orb, aiming for a point over the top of the running crowd for maximum effect.

"Pyro out!" he screamed for the benefit of everyone not in armor as he dropped back down, several shimmering spheres hitting all around him.

Thermobaric weapons had been conceived in the 20th century with fossil fuels as their primary source. Initially large, bulky weapons that required the use of a vehicle or large delivery device, the succeeding millennia had seen weaponeers leverage advances in power technology to put hellfire in a small, portable container. When the average hovercar carried more kilojoules in its fuel tank than an entire ancient Terran refinery had produced in a year, it was absurdly easy to put a small truck bomb in a beverage can.

Marcus actually misaimed his throw and bounced the can off the overhead. Sensing the impact and descent, the can burst its cargo of fuel pellets and flaked alloys in a gray vapor. There was just enough time for some of the unfortunate individuals in the blast radius to inhale the irritants before the burster charge ignited. Before human and alien synapses could register the irritant and initiate the cough response, the gray fog had become a swirling, incandescent festival of incineration and blast wave that swept through the antechamber at just over chest height. Those in its twenty-five meter epicenter barely felt white hot searing pain before dying, their bodies charred and savaged. The more unfortunate who were outside of the twenty-five meters, to include two men who had not heard Marcus's warning, were savagely extinguished by some combination of fire, shock, blast effect, or the resultant rarefaction bursting their respiratory organs. At the outer extremities, the wave of fire merely seared all that it touched, leaving those unlucky souls mere meters away from the barricade writhing in agony on the deck.

The silence that followed the blast was almost total for a brief moment, then the moaning and screams began. Marcus quickly poked his head above the barricade to take stock, even as the unarmored men began to take stock and try and collect themselves. There were several spot fires on the crates, with scorch marks across the top of the metal. He could see the blackened, smoking shapes of the mortally just in front of the barricade, several of their mouths working in silent agony due to their seared lungs.

"Ikessa, Senator Du, Aimi, cover us. The rest of you get those damn fires out!" Quentin shouted, grabbing a nearby fire extinguisher and shoving it into a stunned individual's arms. Marcus could see the brown-haired, older man had soiled himself, but managed to rise and begin spraying foam when shocked out of his stupor.

Quentin drew his vibrocutlass and turned back to Marcus.

"We can't let those people suffer," the other man said over the command channel, gesturing to where some passengers were writhing in pain barely five meters from the barricades' safety. Grimly, Marcus reached up and grabbed his own blade from its sheath.

Kaiju Mecha--Fighter Mode (Sanders)

Chapter 10: Thanksgiving and Reciprocity

Warhawk One
2050 SST
21 June

"For what we are about to receive, may the Lord make us truly thankful," Jason muttered as he came around Sapphire's eastern hemisphere. Looking at his display, he could see the *Constitution*'s icon swinging wide of the planet's western side, her vector extending as the battlecruiser began to accelerate.

Showtime, he thought.

"Kaiju, Bulls, wait just below the horizon to see what we shake loose," Jason barked. "Aces, strafing pattern Zeta, engage."

"Aces One, roger," Tice replied, her voice slightly perturbed.

"Kaiju, roger."

"Bulls, roger."

Yes, I know you wanted to lead the charge Catnip, but I need to see what in the hell is going on first hand, Jason thought as he shoved the throttles to the stop. Clearing the planet's horizon, he was suddenly presented with the sterns of both enemy cruisers as they had begun orienting towards *Constitution*. Unsurprisingly, Contact Bravo was lagging behind her sister, the stream of radiation pouring from her starboard side intensifying as she added power to her engines.

Someone's about to learn why you don't go anywhere without fighter cover, Jason thought fiercely. Arming the *Basilisk*'s lasers as he pivoted his fighter to the enemy's dorsal side, he began closing through two hundred thousand kilometers range. To his surprise, Contact Bravo stopped accelerating. As he watched, the vessel's hull became outlined in red, indicating some sort of energy pulse.

Is that a shield? No matter, we're committed now, Jason thought, deploying his decoys.

"Warhawk One, guns!" he barked, mindful of his cyclic rate when firing at full power. The red outline was confirmed as a shield as the fourteen Basilisk's simultaneously engaged. Shimmering, the shield withstood the assault as the fighters closed past fifty thousand kilometers range. Jason was just about to pull up when the cruiser icon suddenly changed to indicate it was radiating sensor energy.

Oh shit, that's a fire control suite, he thought, immediately triggering evasive maneuvers while simultaneously pushing the communications microphone.

"Pull up, Aces, she's..."

Jason never got to finish his sentence. Unseen to his naked eye, the cruiser's skin seemingly mottled, then opened to present dozens of energy projectors that began firing bolts of energy back at the *Basilisks*. To the startled Bulls and Kaiju it seemed as if the cruiser simply vomited energy bolts in a standard barrage, filling the space around her with a concentrated volley of lethality worse than anything they'd ever seen.

To the *Basilisk*'s, it was literally like walking into an Asgard / Olympus grudge match moments after Odin and Zeus had gotten serious. While evasive maneuvers had some benefit, the five fighters that survived the journey back out of lethal range did so mainly through sheer dumb luck. Aces One was among them, Lieutenant Commander Tice screaming inside her cockpit in helpless rage as she watched her entire command flight explode, disintegrate, or tumble out of control towards Sapphire. Jason had just enough time to register several bright flashes and Slush's death scream before his own *Basilisk* was jerked out of control by impacts to his port and upper engines. His computer attempted to auto correct, the thrusters roaring in his ears as Sapphire tumbled before him.

Dammi...

The world went black.

Bridge
Constitution
2052 SST

"*Makos* away!" Sinclair reported tersely, the deck vibration making the report almost superfluous.

"Sir, Warhawk One is hit!" Boyles broke in.

"Port forty-five more degrees, ventral three hundred kilometers, Mr. Sakai!" Bolan barked, watching as Contact Alpha continued to accelerate towards them. "Sensors, what do you mean by hit?!"

"Still trying to determine, Sir! He didn't wink out like the others, but I'm only getting intermittent transponder information!"

"Herrod..."

"Sir, Warhawk's net is a mess, I can't determine what's going on," Herrod replied, exasperated.

"Targeting solution complete, range one hundred thousand kilometers!" Sinclair reported.

If he was any happier he'd be baring fangs, Bolan thought.

"Fire!" he said aloud. Watching on the screen, he watched as the first salvo streaked out towards the enemy cruiser, followed ten seconds later by the next.

Unlike his decisions with the hapless *Shokaku*, Commander Sinclair had decided to err on the side of penetration when engaging Contact Alpha. However, to still give himself flexibility, he had opted to shunt all power from the secondaries to the main gun, then fire in half-salvos until the *Constitution*'s computer had definitively achieved the range. The end result was to present the enemy cruiser's captain with a hail of *Mako*s and rail gun slugs, the former maneuvering to present targets approaching across the cruiser's forward two hundred seventy degree arc, the latter humming in on a straight bearing from their firing point.

In the end, Contact Alpha was partially damned by her own sensors. Having detected the *Mako*s and wanting to close into the maximum effective range for her own weapons, the vessel's master had made the critical decision to maintain a straight course rather than maneuver. Thus, even as the standard barrage flashed out towards the wildly dodging *Mako*s, Contact Alpha maintained a straight path. Like a madman armed with a shotgun charging an assassin with a sniper rifle, the aliens determined there was no benefit to attempting to evade.

It was of little consolation that all twenty-four *Mako*s from *Constitution*'s opening barrage were destroyed by the resultant energy barrage or that the cruiser reached her most effective weapons envelope. Only Sinclair's spacing out his main guns as a hedge against last second maneuvers precluded Contact Alpha from catching more than three rail gun slugs. Hitting near enough simultaneously as to make no difference, the trio passed completely through the cruiser's port wing with utter devastation. Half of the cruiser's power supply disappeared in a brilliant spray of atmosphere, debris, plasma and unfortunate crewmembers. Shaking from stem to stern, Contact Alpha retaliated with her forward weapons even as the alien helmsman attempted to bring the bow around to unmask her starboard broadside.

263

Bolan felt the world shrink to a gray tunnel as Sakai, anticipating return fire, initiated evasive pattern Foxtrot. He dimly saw six flashing red icons flitted through the space around *Constitution*, with two of them finding one of the vessel's decoys.

Well it appears that returning gifts is a universal custom. I'm hoping I don't regret exchanging the secondaries for more helm energy, Bolan thought.

"All ahead flank, Mr. Sakai! Down ecliptic five hundred kilometers, port thirty degrees!" Bolan grunted. "Keep us at range from Contact Alpha!"

"Aye aye, Sir!" Sakai said, his voice breathless from the g's. Bolan watched as Contact Alpha's relative bearing moved from oh eight zero to one hundred degrees, with Contact Bravo similarly sliding around the relative bearing to almost due astern.

Keep chasing us boys…

"Energy fluctuation from Contact Bravo!" Boyles grunted.

Oh that can't be good, he thought.

"Switch to evasive pattern X-ray! Down ecliptic—"

Bolan didn't get a chance to complete his order before the first salvo closed the seventy thousand kilometers between the two vessels. The first two spheres missed forward, the second so close that light reflected from its exterior lit *Constitution*'s hull like a malfunctioning disco ball. It was the third globe that impacted the battlecruiser's hull aft and below the bridge. Detonating with a silver flash abreast the thickest part of *Constitution*'s armor, the weapon expended most of its energy into the shielding and duranium there. That which passed through, however, wrought havoc.

Bolan slammed hard against his restraints, his breath forced from his lungs as his head cracked down into his chest. A halo of electricity arced across the bridge and hurled Commander Sinclair from his station in a haze of smoke, sparks, and burnt flesh. The gunnery officer just barely missed Iokepa as he impacted the bridge's aft bulkhead with a sound like green wood snapping, his suit smoldering.

Bolan had just enough time to register his gunnery officer's flight before the next sphere impacted. Hammering the *Constitution* one hundred meters aft of the first hit, the sphere easily punched through what was left of the battlecruiser's energy shield and vented almost the majority of its power into the engineering spaces. In a wave of crackling energy, lethal spall, and incandescent radiation, two of *Constitution*'s reactors lost their containment even as air rushed out the breach.

On the good side, the two powerplants' safety features functioned as advertised, preventing an immediate vaporization of the vessel's midsection. Unfortunately for the engineering crew, said safety features unleashed a cascading energy surge through Commander Liu's jury rigged power arrangements. Liu was among the first to fall, charred at his post in the forward fire room along with a quarter of his subordinates. Power surges radiated outwards both internally and externally, jumping fused circuits and bypassed safety measures to electrocute crewmembers where they stood throughout the ship.

Despite the spectacular visuals from the rampant energy charges, Fate demonstrated she had not abandoned the battlecruiser. Even as Liu's body was transformed into a charred mummy and dozens of the *Constitution*'s crew rode the lightning, the *Constitution*'s evasive maneuvers took her through Contact Alpha's weapons pattern without further impacts. Furthermore, the unfortunately named "dead man's circuits" that Liu had emplaced to block current from frying the central computer, main guns, or propulsion conduits all held.

Contact Alpha was not so fortunate, as Sinclair's final salvo put four railgun slugs into the main hull. The resultant structural damage, loss of atmosphere, and polyphoric effects had confronted the alien crew with the twin hells of a raging propellant blaze in some sections and the complete loss of crew in others. His maneuverability options greatly hindered due to the weakening of the vessel's frame, Contact Alpha's captain turned away in an attempt to gain time for conducting repairs.

If he'd had to compare the two impacts, Bolan would have said the second was slightly less painful. Which was to say it felt like someone took a baseball bat rather than rebar to his entire body.

"Damage report," Bolan croaked out, coughing on the smoke that was wafting around his chair like a fog bank. The command net was a cacophony of screaming, and he pressed the override kill switch to cut all currently broadcasting microphones. He reflexively glanced towards the main screen, only to see the display was rent into several pieces, each of which was adding to the smoke and fumes permeating the bridge.

"Damage report!" he grunted. "Now!"

An Unproven Concept

The lights suddenly flickered, then went out. After a very long two seconds, emergency lighting kicked in.

"Helm is not responding, Captain!" Sakai said.

"Navigation computer is down!" Horinek called from somewhere behind him. Turning, Bolan saw that she was helping Iokepa in attempting to contain the blaze raging through the gunnery station's wreckage.

"Guns?! Guns?!" Bolan called, forcing himself to ignore his throbbing headache. He was about to call again when he suddenly remembered why it smelled like a pork barbecue. Turning further in his chair, he saw Boyles looking at Sinclair's broken body in numb shock.

"Sensors, you have control of the guns! Status!" he gritted out. Boyles looked up at him, her face blank.

"Naomi!" Bolan shouted, the pain lancing through his skull nauseating him. Shaking her head, Boyles came out of her stupor.

"Sir, I now have helm control but not enough power to thrusters!" Sakai called out, then began coughing.

That fire's got to get put out or we're useless, Bolan thought. Fire, long Earthbound sailor's worst foe, had maintained its implacable nature when man went to the stars. The fire that was spreading from Sinclair's station, if left unchecked, would soon get into the electrical wiring, oxygen vents, and other conduits into the rest of the ship. Taking one look at the size and ferocity of the blaze, as well as the smoke filling the compartment, Bolan made a quick decision.

"Horinek, get back to your station! Helm, prepare to vent!"

Horinek turned and looked at Bolan in horror for a moment, then dropped the fire extinguisher and dashed back to her chair. To Bolan's surprise, Iokepa followed her. With a start, he remembered that the jump seats the man had been sitting on lacked an independent oxygen outlet.

Because who would be enough of an idiot to place passengers on his bridge when going into combat? Bolan thought bitterly. Oh wait, the same idiot who didn't arm the secondaries because he was planning on staying out of range.

Pressing the button on the inside of his chair, *Constitution's* captain sealed his suit and initiated the oxygen supply in his chair base.

"Battle Two, Bridge," Bolan said.

"Bridge, Battle Two!" Alexander's strained voice replied. "Bridge is venting at this time! You have the conn!"

266

"Roger, Battle Two has the con!" Alexander replied. Bolan could hear shouted reports in the background before the XO killed the connection.

"Helm, vent the bridge!"

"Aye, aye!" Sakai replied. Bolan could see the man releasing the helm and opening the emergency panel located underneath the engine telegraph. Fighting the urge to hold his breath in anticipation of what he knew was coming, Bolan watched Sakai punch in the requisite code and then press the button at the panel's center.

The process of venting was a simple affair. After a warning tone sounded on the bridge and adjacent compartments, emergency baffles mounted in the structure's roof were forced open. Connected to conduits whose outlets terminated on the vessel's hull, the baffles allowed the vacuum of space to drag all of the oxygen out of the bridge. With a loud roar, the bridge's oxygen began to follow the path of vacuum. As Bolan was slammed against his restraints by the *Constitution* going into a turn, he saw the various flames around the bridge attempt to follow the oxygen withdrawing from the room like sinuous, blazing snakes. The display lasted only for a couple of seconds before the level of oxygen decreased past a point that would sustain flame. The process reversed itself as Bolan was again slammed against the restraints, his sphincter constricting in anticipation of more impacts.

Ten seconds and no fire or smoke, Bolan thought. *Still think I'd prefer a sprinkler system, but it works.* Like all spacefarers, Bolan didn't like giving vacuum any additional openings to try and kill him. Unfortunately the alternatives seemed to have nasty side effects like electrifying the bridge crew or flooding the compartment.

"Battle Two, status report!" Bolan said, then began coughing.

Titanic
2055 SST

As the *Constitution* engaged her two foes, a far different drama was taking place about the *Titanic*.

"It's never a good idea when the enemy starts chanting," Marcus said to Quentin.

"Not sure where that ranks in Murphy's Laws of Combat, boss. I'm guessing it's between 'If the enemy is in range, so are you...' and

267

'Shoot the funnies first...' in the eternal hierarchy," Quentin replied, his voice slightly shaken.

At first he assumed the strange, high pitched keening was coming from the last row of wounded that Quentin and he had determined were too distant to safely dispatch. It was only when it was clear those last few alien bastards had finally expired that Marcus realized the sound was coming from further up the corridor. Even worse, it was growing louder and even more unnerving.

This shit has to stop, he thought.

Titanic's thrusters fired again.

Oh, that's right, it's probably going to stop one way or the other here pretty soon, Marcus thought bitterly.

The Security Chief caught motion on the edge of his vision and turned to see Aimi jumping up onto the barricade. Before he could ask the woman what the hell she was doing, he heard the sound of her opening her external audio.

Dirt and sky...
Dirt and sky...
Ripped from Earth
For dirt and sky

Even had he not known the entire song, the rhythm and tune would have been familiar. In various forms it was common to the entire Confederation, having allegedly originated as a song of toil and torment amongst boatmen on the ancient Volga River. Aimi's voice, a stunningly clear and pitch perfect soprano, echoed across the compartment as she repeated the verse. Senator Du jumped up and joined her as she proceeded, causing Marcus to be equally surprised at the man's tenor.

Now our hearts yearn
For Sol's warmth
Now our hearts yearn
For our ancient hearth

The duet's tone became sorrowful as they continued.

You have trespassed
And are not welcome here
You have trespassed

268

As if you know not fear...
Whether ignorance or fate...
Has brought you here...
In Hell's own mouth
You shall taste your tears

As Aimi and Du held the elongated, every Spartan in the compartment began to sing the Spartan War Songs declaration. His eyes wet, Marcus found himself joining them...
Though our shields fail...
Though our hulls burn...
For your damned souls
Our blades do yearn

Even without the speakers, the assembled voices would have filled the antechamber and the corridor beyond with sound.
FOR ARIES RED SKY
AND KURSK'S GOLDEN FIELDS
FOR LOVE AND HEARTH
NONE SHALL YIELD

Aimi and Du continued singing as the remaining Spartans repeated the verse, growing ever quieter until finally the duo's voices ended the song with the somber refrain:
Our lives...for earth and sky
Our fates...for Spartans lives

As the last note rang off the steel, a brief silence returned to the corridor.

This is it... Martin thought instinctively.

Du and Aimi obviously felt the same ominous silence, both of them hopping down. It was a fortuitous decision, as the deck in front of the barricade suddenly exploded in a storm of metal.

Marcus felt a section of plating knock his legs out from under him, the sharp pain making him gasp. As he fell backwards, he saw a slab of spare fusion bottle external plating fall backwards from where it had slammed into the overhead, the red ruin on its face unidentifiable as anything that had previously been human. Quickly rolling away from the falling plate's ricocheted arc, he watched as it tore through a handful of stunned individuals.

As far as plans went, the aliens could have come up with a far worse one than detonating their warheads in the *Titanic*'s storage spaces. In a single stroke, the blast had lain low almost every man and woman who had sheltered behind the barricade without the benefit of battle armor. Unfortunately for the aliens that came rushing down the hallway firing from the hip, they had miscalculated the secondary effects, e.g. the minor matter of pushing multiple polyphoric metals through a sewage scupper full of methane.

The resultant conflagration sought the path of least resistance. Unfortunately, the amount of methane generated by literally thousands of tons of biological waste whose decay had been accelerated by various natural enzymes created a raging monster to whom metal hatches were wafer thin impediments. With the exception of the massive doors and locks emplaced to keep the liner inviolate from the relentless press of vacuum, the forces unleashed rent asunder dozens of partitions in a matter of moments. Piercing oxygen cylinders, searing vital wires, and vomiting out air vents onto unsuspecting humans and aliens alike, the methane firestorm killed as many of *Titanic*'s passengers in seconds as the three cruisers had up to that point.

As the flames swirled towards him, time seemed to slow down for Marcus. He thought of Katina...of Sarah...of his mother. Dimly he heard someone screaming, a suit icon flashing red in the corner of his HUD.

I never thought it'd end like... he started to think desperately.

Marcus didn't have time to finish before the onrushing fire storm suddenly broke upwards into a swirling column, its roar thunderous in the confined space. Shocked, he realized that the flames were being drawn upwards through several holes in the overhead...right into Fireroom #1.

Oh shit, that's not good, the Security Chief thought, the flames dancing almost as if they were in a funnel cloud from the outgoing air's velocity. *That's not good at all.*

No sooner had he had the thought than his suit's seals slammed shut, indicating that the air quality had descended far enough that the *Hoplite* believed he would not have been able to survive. Turning, he found himself unable to see anything in the gloom left by the still swirling flames and the things they had ignited. Belatedly, he felt sweat beginning to pour from his body within the *Hoplite*. As the firestorm's intensity dissipated, the sound of a man's frantic screaming filled his headphones, the battle armor indicated it was coming from behind. Turning to look, he saw a flash of green legs as a lizard ran by the ramp.

"They're in Fireroom #2!" Marcus shouted, turning to run backwards. After a moment he was joined by Aimi…and no one else.

This can't be fucking it, he thought, gripping the assault rifle with a determined air. The duo came rushing up into the Fireroom to find a scene of utter chaos, with at least three aliens in the compartment. Bringing up his assault rifle, Marcus shot a lizard that had just finished disemboweling an engineer with some sort of edged weapon. He was about to line up on a second creature when his assault rifle splintered in his hand, the second small sphere in the burst passing bare inches in front of his chest from right to left. Diving forward, he rolled and drew the vibrocutlass all in one motion, realizing the weapon was absolutely useless against an alien with a rifle.

There was a sound like ripping cloth from the Fireroom #2 hatch, and the bear like alien in question simply disintegrated. Turning towards the source of fire in shocked amazement, Marcus found himself looking at a Confederation Marine in *Hill Giant* heavy armor. The man pivoted and fired another burst from the gatling gun that extended from the battle armor's right weapon pod, and the two remaining lizard aliens both met the same fate as their ursanoid companion.

"Put your weapons down or you *will* be fired upon," the man's voice thundered from his suit's loudspeakers. Marcus didn't hesitate, letting the vibro cutlass fall to the floor as four of the man's companions sprang into the room in their own *Hill Giants*. They were followed by six more Marines in their lighter *Chasseur* armor. The men quickly spread out through the room, four of the *Hill Giants* covering them.

"Captain Mainio Juric, Confederation Marines," the first *Hill Giant* operator stated. "Identify yourself!"

I can't blame them for being a bit, shall we say, trigger happy, Marcus thought as he kept his hands up.

"Marcus Martin, Security Officer, Czarina Lines," he replied wearily.

Bridge
Constitution
2100 SST

271

Bolan had barely gotten out his request when the battlecruiser heeled over again. He cursed as he continued attempting to get his helmet's faceplate to display the vessel's sensor feed rather than a series of horizontal bars and scattered snow.

Of course the helmet's not going to work when I really need it to, Bolan thought. *How else would I know that Murphy truly loved me?*

"Contact Alpha's radiation bloom has increased!" Commander Alexander reported. "Contact Bravo is turning away to head back towards *Titanic*!"

"What?!" Bolan asked.

This is maddening! he thought.

"Kaiju One just reported the assault shuttles have reached the liner," Alexander replied. "We put a couple of salvos around Contact Bravo to slow her down and keep her from charging down our throat. When the assault shuttles docked she decided to turn around."

"Sir, Lieutenant Owderkirk is reporting Fireroom #1 is a total loss," someone in the background of Battle Two reported. "She will be able to get us more power from Fireroom #2 in approximately ten minutes!"

"Captain Bolan…" Alexander started to relay.

"I heard, XO," Bolan said grimly. With a quick shimmer, his HUD finally began displaying the sensor feed. He could see that Contact Alpha, having crossed their stern, was bearing one nine zero and attempting to open the distance. Contact Bravo had turned and was now moving past one two zero relative, heading back towards the *Titanic*.

"Sir we can come around to keep after Bravo," Alexander said.

"How many *Mako*s do we have left after that last salvo?"

"Sixteen," Alexander replied after a moment's pause.

"Let's finish off Alpha, Warhawk can get off their ass for Bravo," Bolan said, watching as the twenty-four *Mako*s that had just been launched closed with the enemy cruiser. "Bring us to port, XO, stand by to return helm control to the bridge."

The radiation plume that Boyles had observed was the continuing progressive damage caused by Sinclair's last salvo. Having lost even more power, the vessel accelerated away from the *Constitution* in an attempt to head for the fourth of Sapphire's moons. In her crippled state, the twenty-four *Mako*s that the human battlecruiser had just launched were far faster. Like a grievously wounded warrior, Contact Alpha attempts to shield herself were desperate, her drives

272

briefly winking out as the bridge crew channeled all power to their secondaries. Five *Makos* penetrated the defensive volleys, two of which bit on the phantoms of their target's electronic countermeasures. The other three, however, detonated their twenty megaton warheads within two kilometers of Contact Alpha's hull.

"Sir! Contact Alpha's radiation is increase—*she's blowing up!*" Boyles cried.

Bolan could see the Death's Halo on his helmet screen and allowed himself a slight moment of satisfaction.

"Get power to the secondaries, Mr. Sulu, then let's go kill Contact Bravo," Bolan said, looking at the plot. *Since apparently Warhawk has no intention of doing so.*

Warhawk One
2105 SST

The flash, incredibly bright even through his closed eyelids, stirred Jason into consciousness.

No! Oh God! Oh God! Jason thought desperately.

After his initial panic, Jason's fuzzy mind told him three things. First, the bright flash was not the pilot light on the furnace of hell, despite what a toxic combination of latent guilt and reform school had trigged in his imagination. Two, his breathing was echoing, indicating that he was no longer taking air from his flight suit rather than the *Basilisk's* internal supply. Third, the most likely reason for the switch to suit air was his cockpit's condition.

Well, this dump looks like it ended up on the wrong end of a flechette blast, Jason thought as several fragments of his canopy floated towards the massive gap to port of his seat. *What the hell was that flash? Wait a minute…that was a fusion drive going up!*

"Bulls One, I say again, you will bring your squadron around on my wing *right now!*" Lieutenant Commander Tice's voice sounded clearly in his right ear.

"Negative Aces One, standing by for orders from Warhawk One," Lieutenant Commander Gordon replied.

Why is he waiting for Warhawk One…wait a second, I'm Warhawk One, Jason thought groggily.

273

"Goddammit you ball-less son of a bitch, I will fucking skull drag you and slaughter your children if you do not comply!" Tice raged in response.

The sound of Aces One going ape shit spurred Jason to fight back the cotton ball haze in his head, with his five senses coming back slowly. Sight told Jason his fighter was "upside down," with Sapphire filling his field of view below. Taste told him that he'd bitten a pretty good hunk out of the side of his cheek, as he tasted lots of blood. Touch told him that he was hanging hard against his straps as gravity's remorseless grasp continued trying to snatch him out of the *Basilisk*. Smell told him that the next chance he got he needed maintenance to double check the air recyclers, as he should not be smelling his own vomit and mucus so strongly. Finally, hearing told him that there was still a fight on…and it wasn't going well.

"Contact Bravo's coming back around!" an unidentified pilot warned over the air group network.

"Bulls One, we have to go out and meet that bitch before she gets in firing range," Tice said, changing her tack from threatening to reason. "If she blows the starliner to kingdom come then it was pretty damn pointless coming out here, wasn't it?!"

"Warhawk One told us to cover the shuttles if they started to move off," Bulls One replied defensively, his voice quavering.

"Goddamit, Warhawk One is down! You will…" Tice started to scream. Her voice was cut off by Lieutenant Herrod's.

"Warhawk One, Warhawk One, *Constitution*, please respond!"

With a start, Jason realized that he was either deaf in his left ear or that speaker was malfunctioning. He reached up to touch the side of his helmet, only to find its entire left side dished in as if it'd been smacked by something moving very fast.

Well that explains the concussion. Chief's going to kill me for breaking his damn bird, Jason thought. Manipulating his fingers, Jason sprayed a small squirt of water into his mouth and immediately regretted it. Forcing himself to swallow the blood and ignore the stinging, he worked his tongue around his mouth to make sure all his teeth were present and limber the organ up.

Got to get back in the fight, he thought. Bringing his left hand back down, he found nothing but a stalk where his throttle had been.

Okay, pretty obvious I'm not going anywhere, he thought. *Hope the comms still work…*

"Aces One, Warhawk One," he said calmly. Hearing nothing in response, he transferred some of the *Basilisk*'s emergency power from

274

standby life support to the fighter's communications array. There was a shower of sparks from the busted console in front of him as he repeated his transmission, but it was readily apparent something took.

"Blimey Warhawk One!" Tice said. "You're alive!"

"Aces One, you are hereby in command of whatever's left moving up there," Jason said, his communications override cutting off Tice before she could express anymore surprise. "Bulls Five, you are hereby in command of Bulls, Bulls One is relieved."

There was shocked silence on the net as Jason gathered his thoughts.

No time for cowards out here, he thought bitterly.

"Warhawk One, Bulls Five! Good to hear…"

"We ain't got time for pleasantries," Jason snapped, his head starting to throb. "I'm bent over Sapphire, cockpit's trashed. Aces One, before we have the Bulls impale themselves, run a pattern analysis on that bastard's flak guns."

"Roger, running," Tice replied, her voice much more controlled.

"Warhawk One, Battle Two Actual your push! What the hell is going on…"

"Standby Battle Two!" Jason snapped.

"Warhawk One, I think I have a solution," Nishizawa interjected on the command channel. "We can suppress the flak."

"What?!" Jason asked. "You're only carrying boarding loadouts and self-defense missiles!"

"Trust me on this one," Nishizawa said.

"Pattern analysis done!" Tice said. "Contact Bravo's at one hundred fifty thousand kilometers and closing!"

"Send to Kaiju One," Jason said. "Kaiju One, whatever you're going to do, better do it quick before that bitch gets the shuttles in range of her secondaries!"

"Roger," Nishizawa replied. "Bulls Five, follow us once we have suppressed the flak."

The fifty-four mecha, led by Nishizawa, accelerated from where they'd been covering the Marines boarding *Titanic*. Having downloaded Tice's analysis of Contact Bravo's flak batteries, Nishizawa broke from convention and brought his entire group in from the starboard ventral side. Shunting all power towards their shields, the *Kaiju* swooped in towards their prey like a cloud of stinging wasps after a much larger beast. The alien vessel again stopped and began hurling energy at the attacking craft.

In the end, the analysis and the *Kaiju*'s superior defensive equipment sharply lowered the butcher bill. Sixteen of the *mecha* were immediately destroyed, their pilots dying in a fury of blasts even as Nishizawa rotated his nose one hundred and eighty degrees then shoved his throttle forward. Ten more *mecha* were rent asunder as the craft closed the remaining forty thousand kilometers, their icons winking out before the horrified eyes of the onrushing Bulls and Lieutenant Commander Tice. It was only in the final few seconds that everyone besides Nishizawa and his Marines knew the Kaiju commander's intent.

One hundred kilometers from Contact Bravo's hull, the *Kaiju* began simultaneously going through a transformation. If any aliens had been observing the onrushing human craft, they would have been startled to see twenty-eight bipedal war machines suddenly land on their mottled hull, suddenly too close for the guns to engage and "running" on their gravity repulsors at nearly two hundred kilometers an hour. There was no time to coordinate their fire, the individual Marines simply firing their shoulder mounted rail guns and flinging breach charges at whatever was exposed. Two more *Kaiju* had the misfortune of literally passing right in front of guns that were attempting to engage their fellows, the *mecha* crumpling damaged to the hull. As the *Kaiju* flashed off the stern, they left behind a path of devastation that had destroyed almost all of Contact B's secondary weapons on her ventral side.

The Raging Bulls, led by Bulls Five, had started their attack runs as soon as they had watched the *Kaiju*'s icons merge with the enemy contact. The alien captain barely had enough time to realize what had happened to his vessel before the *Thunderchiefs* were flinging two *Starspawn* anti-ship missiles apiece at the savaged cruiser then breaking away at maximum thrust. Despite losing six of their number as they broke off, the Bulls left seventy-two missiles streaking towards the cruiser.

In the end, it was overkill. Rapidly rotating, Contact Bravo almost managed to get her functional secondaries into the fray. Unfortunately for the aliens, "almost" in this case still meant thirty-six missiles survived to close within one hundred kilometers of the cruiser's hull. Lacking the *Makos*' computer power, twenty of the *Starspawns* were spoofed or jammed by the alien ECM. The sixteen that remained, however, all detonated their five megaton warheads within lethal range of Contact Bravo's hull. Unlike Contact Alpha, Bravo did not suffer a

276

catastrophic loss of containment. Instead, her crew was turned into frozen, suspended biological base elements as the vessel's artificial gravity, inertial dampeners, and life support were bludgeoned into inoperability.

Bridge
Constitution
2115 SST

"*Constitution*, Aces One! Scratch Contact Bravo! I say again, scratch Contact Bravo!"

Tice sounds like she's announcing a football goal, Bolan thought, fighting his own urge to grin. He was helped by his helmet display winking back out.

"XO I'm suffering helmet issues," Bolan said. "We've got no screens and intermittent power, I'm heading to your location. Bring her around towards that damn liner and let's see what we can do to help."

"Sir, we're pretty well irradiated or holed aft of your location. Unless you are planning on going EVA, I would suggest you stay put," Alexander replied. "We still have…"

"Contacts! Two hyperspace events, bearing three zero zero and two three zero relative! Multiple bogeys!" Boyles interjected.

Oh shit, it might be Masada time after all, Bolan thought. *We cannot fight anything in this condition.* He looked at the damage control screen and pursed his lips. *I'm not even sure we can really run.*

"Identification?" he asked, working to keep his voice calm.

"Computer is still working," Boyles replied, hands moving over her console. "No information yet."

"XO, get us on the other side of the planet from whoever that is coming into system," Bolan grunted. "Inform the Bulls to stand by for a Masada strike."

"Confederation identification confirmed! Computer's having trouble getting the transponder code due to some of the damage!" Boyles said. "Working the mirror…"

"*Constitution* Actual, this is Rear Admiral Moody on the *Victorious*," a clipped, feminine voice across the bridge speakers. "Do you require assistance?"

No, our midsection always radiates like that, Bolan thought with a smile.

"*Victorious*, this is *Constitution*," Alexander replied, his voice repeating through the bridge's speakers. "We do not require immediate

277

assistance at this time, but will need a vessel to immediately take *Titanic* under tow."

"Roger *Constitution*. What is *Titanic*'s status?"

"*Titanic* is still grappled with a hostile, our Marines are boarding at this time."

"Roger, *Constitution*," Admiral Moody replied. There was a pause, then Moody proceeded as if she was attempting to parse her next sentence in order to avoid giving anything away. "Have you seen any other Confederation vessels at this time?"

She's asking about the Shigure without really wanting to do so openly, Bolan thought, surprised. *This just keeps getting stranger and stranger, as no one else should have gotten here this quickly.*

Bolan was about to answer Moody when Lieutenant Commander Iokepa interrupted him from Lieutenant Herrod's station.

"Sir, the code words are Omicron Solstice," Iokepa said quietly. "Rear Admiral Moody will know what it means."

"*Victorious* Actual, a little birdie tells me I am to inform you of Omnicron Solstice. I say again, Omicron Solstice."

There was silence on the comm network.

"Roger. Please collect all additional personnel in your landing bay, I am en route. Moody out."

Bridge
Titanic
2145 SST

"Captain Herrod, I presume?"

Abraham had the terrible feeling that the Marine major in front of him was not asking the question in order to exchange pleasantries. The man's blue eyes were intense as they stared into his, his heavy black armor making him seem as if he was towering over *Titanic*'s captain even though the latter sat in his raised chair. There were large splotches of what appeared to be blood on the front of the man's breastplate, and one of his arms appeared to be scored with what looked like claw scratches.

I'm so tired, Abraham thought.

"Yes, I am, major..?"

"My name is of no importance to you," the man spat, and Abraham suddenly had the sensation he was facing a man who was still in a combat rage. "Indeed, were we in Spartan space I would be summarily executing you where you sit."

"I don't know who you think you are, *major*," Federov said, sneering. "But you will not talk to the…"

Abraham had thought O'Barr's look of repressed homicide was impressive. The Marine major made the deputy security officer's glare seem like a drunken teenager's come hither. Federov bluster died in his throat, the man holding the executive's gaze for several pensive seconds.

"I am the man who will rip your larynx from your throat, stick my finger through the resultant hole, then stir your brains as you choke to death on your own blood should you interrupt me again. But do tell, who the fuck are you?"

The statement was delivered with cold fury rather than shouted, a method that made it somehow seem far scarier. To Abraham's shock, Federov had the audacity to glower silently at the Marine.

The man truly does not understand how close he is to having an index finger spinning his pituitary gland like a top.

"Please do not make me ask you again," the Marine said quietly.

"I am Ivan Federov," Federov growled.

To Abraham's surprise, the Marine's face displayed shock.

"The Black Prince," the Marine asked.

"Yes, major," Federov sneered, taking the officer's tone as recognition he was speaking to a better. That notion was quickly dashed, as the officer smiled at him.

"Well I've never seen an executive shot before," the major replied. "But I'm pretty sure I'm about to have that changed in the next couple of days. Admiral Malinverni will be extremely happy to see *you.*"

"Major Acheros, if you speak the devil's name he shall surely appear," a tall, slender lieutenant colonel stated as he entered *Titanic*'s bridge. "I have no desire to be anywhere near Kraken Six for the next, oh, month after this so let's not use his name in vain."

"Yes Sir," Acheros replied.

That seems to be the good lieutenant colonel's way of reminding the major not to start writing checks over the C-in-C's account, Abraham noted.

"Captain Herrod, your son is safe aboard *Constitution*," the lieutenant colonel continued briskly.

What?! Abraham thought, his eyes widening. He felt his heart thunder in his chest.

I did not realize Charlie was out here! His ship was supposed to be on her trials! Abraham thought.

"I am Lieutenant Colonel Nishizawa," the man continued briskly. "I have orders from Rear Admiral Moody to take you and your primary officers under arrest as soon as *Gettysburg* finishes towing *Titanic* out of *Sapphire*'s gravity well. This process will go much quicker if you can tell me where I can find those individuals."

"Lieutenant Colonel, I must *protest* this man's actions," Federov interrupted, gesturing towards Major Acheros. "He threatened my life…"

"Mr. Federov, I have over fifty dead Marines on this ship and in the surrounding space," Nishizawa snapped, his nostrils flaring. "Major Acheros is on his second vessel of the day and got to spend some quality time dividing air supply by personnel then wondering if the number was large enough for help to eventually arrive."

Abraham looked at the major.

Maker be, the destroyer… Abraham thought.

"So, believe me when I tell you the following: Provided Major Acheros filmed it so I can include a scan in the condolence letters I'm going to have to file tonight," Nishizawa continued conversationally, "I don't care if he rips your intestines out and chokes you to death with them. Is that clear?"

"The First Mate and Chief Engineer are dead," O'Barr began, her tone clipped. "Mr. Martin, our Security Chief, was headed aft to engineering the last we heard from him."

Nishizawa nodded, furrowing his brow.

"Understood. We have already found Mr. Martin," the lieutenant colonel said. "He's lucky to be alive."

"What do you mean, he's lucky to be alive?" O'Barr asked, her eyes wide.

"When our shuttles approached you were venting flames from multiple holes in the hull from decks 7 down, Frame 10 to your stern," Nishizawa replied.

"God and Goddess," O'Barr said, holding her mouth up to her face. "The sewer scuppers."

"Both of your fire rooms are vacuum right now, and I'd hate to see what your casualties look like," Nishizawa continued conversationally.

I get the distinct impression the man is twisting the knife, Abraham thought, staggered at the cost.

"We felt vibration but assumed it was the thrusters firing again," Abraham said, his voice weary. "It'd been occurring at ever shorter intervals the closer we got to *Sapphire*."

"Well thankfully the fires started to go out as we boarded. There are a few oxygen canisters fueling the flames, but for the most part vacuum's won out," Nishizawa replied. "There was also an emergency beacon sounding from within *Sapphire*'s atmosphere, but it stopped transmitting before we got around the planet."

Abraham felt faint, his shoulders bowing as he imagined passengers taking to the escape pods in desperation only to die as they were crushed in *Sapphire*'s atmosphere.

I cannot imagine being crushed like a mouse in a beverage can, Abraham thought. *My passengers should not have had to experience that.*

"I'm surprised you didn't detect the emergency beacon yourself, Captain," Nishizawa continued.

"We determined our communications were out when we got the warning a pod had launched, but no beacon," Coors interrupted.

Abraham and Federov both whipped their heads around at that statement.

"Did it ever occur to you to mention that fact, Mr. Coors?" Abraham asked archly.

Coors gave them both a defiant look.

"In case you don't recall, *Captain*, I was somewhat busy attempting to keep Ms. O'Connor from choking to death on her own vomit," Coors snapped. "Plus you may recall we all thought we were going to die because some idiots decided sightseeing…"

"That's enough!" O'Barr snapped, stepping towards the sensor officer. "That is the captain, and you are painfully close to *mutiny*, Mr. Coors."

Coors rolled his eyes but closed his mouth with a scowl.

"Captain, Rear Admiral Moody will require a full list of your passengers and crew to begin the notification process," Nishizawa stated.

"If you give me communication to Czarina Lines we can initiate that process for you," Federov replied before Abraham could answer.

"I was speaking to the captain," Nishizawa said firmly. "Unless I somehow missed something and you are in charge of this vessel."

There was a long silence.

"No, I am not," Federov said.

Of course not, Abraham thought, clenching his fists. *That would mean you were possibly subject to the death penalty.*

"We keep a hard copy of the manifest in the purser's safe," Abraham said quietly.

Nishizawa turned towards Acheros, the younger officer's scowl deepening.

"We didn't open the safe, Sir," Acheros said. Abraham noticed the man's hands were shaking as if he was trying to suppress his emotions. "My fault, I will go get that thing open now."

"The combination is 4-12-27-9-28-22," Abraham stated as the major turned to go. Acheros nodded, pointing towards his suit then making the universal EVA sign that indicated his suit had recorded the information. Nishizawa watched him leave, then turned back to Abraham and Federov. Before he could speak, there was the sound of static and voices from his flight armor's speakers, then the *Titanic* gave a slight lurch.

"Gentlemen, the *Gettysburg* has just cast off the two lines," Nishizawa said, then came to attention. "Captain Herrod, Mr. Federov, you are both officially under arrest under Section 195 of the Spacefarer's Code…"

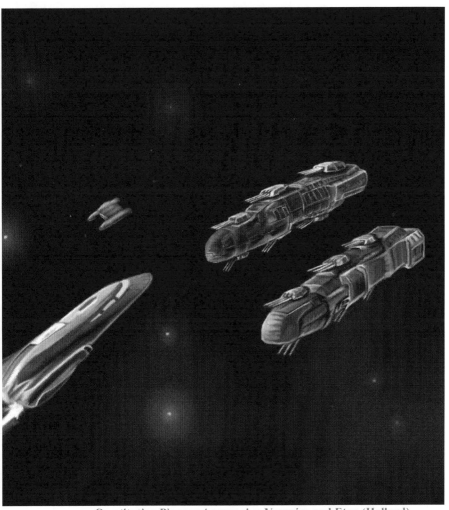

Constitution Pinnace Approaches Vesuvius and Etna (Holland)

Chapter 11: Hulks, Memories and Bad Pennies

Constitution
1245 SST
23 June

"I really like what the interior decorator has done with Officer Country," Andrea said, referring to the officers' berths all around them. She shook her gleaming bald head as she continued. "I mean, the scorched paint deco is really in on Faust this summer."

Jason looked at her worriedly, his ears telling him that his beloved was not totally recovered from her radiation sickness. The hair loss was a symptom of the decontamination regimen, and Andrea had just opted to shave it all off rather than have it come off in patches. Jason could not blame her, but it was still difficult to get used to.

I can't believe how close I came to losing her, he thought. If she hadn't stepped out of the forward fireroom to check on the power couplings aft...

"Stop looking at me like you're expecting me to drop dead any second, Jason," Andrea snarled, her voice cross. "The suit wasn't even traffic cone orange."

"I'm just worried about you pushing yourself is all," Jason replied sheepishly.

Andrea stopped and held up her middle finger.

"Gee, Commander, how about you tell me how many fingers you see?" she replied archly. "Because I think one of us doesn't have a lot of room to talk about near death experiences. I was wondering, just what does *Sapphire*'s upper atmosphere look like from the inside?"

Jason shook his head.

"I didn't actually enter the atmosphere," he replied.

"No, I think Lieutenant Colonel Nishizawa said you were just close enough to have lit one hell of a bonfire if you'd flicked a match out that giant gash in your canopy."

Jason could tell there was an edge to Andrea's joking. Thankfully they reached their destination and lost any urge for humor, gallows or otherwise.

Slush, Jason thought sadly as he reached up with gloved hand to clean off the name tag. They had never found his wingman's fighter, which meant it had either been ripped apart by secondaries or its momentum carried it into *Sapphire's* atmosphere.

An empty coffin and a box full of gear, Jason thought. *That's all her parents will get.* Entering the override code onto the front door, he stepped back as it rumbled open. He was surprised to find Commander Tice already in the room, the redhead standing next to a container identical to that in Jason's hands. Her eyes were red and puffy, and she looked up startled from the holoframe she held.

"Jason," she said throatily, then sheepishly looked as Andrea walked into the compartment. "Lieutenant Owderkirk."

"Lieutenant Commander," Andrea said coolly.

You know, someday she'll let it go, Jason thought, exasperated. *So much water and, now, blood under that bridge.*

Catnip smiled thinly at the younger woman. Jason could tell she was bemused but was good enough not to show it.

"I was collecting Ensign Landvik's stuff," she said, referring to one of her junior pilots. "I remember her telling me about her nieces and how they sent her the holos a few weeks ago."

Jason nodded, remembering the elfin, fair haired woman that doted on her nieces as well.

"We're here for Slush's gear," he replied evenly, exhaling.

"I figured," Catnip responded. "I'm about done here. Who is getting Gordon's guys?"

"Nishizawa volunteered," Jason replied evenly.

Although I did think about having you do it, seeing as how arguably you might have driven him to off himself, Jason thought. Catnip had required three men to pull her off the Raging Bulls commander after they'd all been recovered aboard the *Constitution*. Even worse had been the words she'd flung at the man, the invective all the more biting due to its veracity.

Then again, Captain Bolan telling Gordon he had two hours to get off his ship might not have helped the man's mental state, Jason thought. *Whatever the reason, suck starting his energy pistol was a bit excessive.*

Catnip looked as if she was reading his thoughts.

"I'm not sorry, Commander," she said simply, closing the box.

"Yeah, Catnip, I know," he replied heavily. "The hair matches the temper."

Catnip smiled at the old joke they'd always shared, then caught herself. Nodding, she headed for the compartment door. Jason watched as it closed behind her, then turned back to face a glowering Andrea.

"Let me guess, you'd like to claw her heart out right after you get my eyes?"

Andrea opened her mouth, then stopped. Pressing her lips into a thin line, she shook her head.

"I'm being a bit of a cow, aren't I?" she asked quietly.

Jason gave her a look of mock horror.

"Aargh, it's the 'no right answer' gambit! Nooooooo..." he replied mockingly, throwing up his arms as if to ward off a blow.

Andrea laughed at him, a response that quickly led to a fit of coughing. Jason took her into his arms, concerned as she fought back a retch.

"I'm...okay..." she gasped. "Just laughing starts all sorts of trouble."

"How about you have a seat at the desk while I start boxing up Slush's stuff?" Jason replied.

"Fine, but start with her knick knacks," Andrea said. "I don't think Slush would be happy if you started going through her panties."

Jason turned and looked at Andrea in shock.

"You didn't think about that, did you?" Andrea replied with a slight smile.

"No, not at all," Jason said, horrified at the thought. His wife's grin grew broader.

"Now you know why I'm here," she said triumphantly. "Just like you hope you never end up in an accident without clean underwear, a woman's mortified at the thought of her boss going through her unmentionables regardless of whether or not she's dead."

The insanity of the situation softened the thought of his dead wingman.

"I love you," he said, laughter in his voice.

"I'm bald, about as far from in the mood as a woman can get, and can vomit at the drop of a hat if I'm not careful," Andrea responded. "If you didn't love me, I think you'd have found some way to be busy for the next week or so."

Brig
C.S.S. Kobold
1545 SST

"Mr. Martin?"

The master-at-arm's voice broke Martin from his book. Looking up with bleary eyes, he stood up and stretched.

286

"You have a visitor," the small, thin man said. As Marines went, he was the smallest that Marcus had ever seen. However, one look at his uniform told him why the man was a master-at-arms, as he had at least three martial arts identifiers that Marcus could identify and one that he could not.

Probably fights like a rabid rat, Marcus thought. *While a good big man beats a good small man, I'm willing to bet that there aren't many big men that good in this sector, let alone on this ship.*

"I'm going to guess it's not my lawyer," Marcus replied, his eyes not reflecting the attempt at humor.

"Actually I think you'll be somewhat surprised at who it is," the master-at-arms replied.

Sarah? Marcus thought, allowing himself to feel hope for the first time since he'd awoken aboard the hospital vessel. He thrust his hands into the manacle slot for the master-at-arms to bind him.

"No need, Mr. Martin," the master-at-arms replied. "You're actually a free man after you speak to your visitor."

Marcus raised an eyebrow as the master-at-arms opened the brig cell's door.

Curiouser and curiouser, he thought, stepping through. He had no belongings he was attached to back in the cell—the book had actually been a loaner from the ship's library. It would return to the electronic ether after twenty minutes or when his jailer powered down the holo-projector.

Was tired of reading about a crazy Preacher who spoke with the voice of God anyway, Marcus thought.

It was a short walk to the conference room. Marcus followed the master-at-arms through the door, realizing he must truly be free if the man turned his back to a prisoner. There was a single table in the large room, and Marcus had the impression the space had recently been cleared of its occupants. He pulled out a chair and sat down as the master-at-arms slipped back out the door. A moment later, the door hissed back open to reveal one Henrique Malinverni.

Well, I see he's done well for himself since we last saw each other, Marcus thought disgustedly. He fought the Pavlovian reflex to stand, purposefully insulting the other man by remaining in his chair. The fleet admiral's aide looked at him with thinly veiled disgust for a brief moment before making his face passive again. For his part, Malinverni's face briefly twitched as if the man wanted to smile as he pulled up the chair opposite to Marcus.

287

"Mr. Martin," he said simply, nodding. "Seems like we keep finding each other."

"Admiral," Marcus responded, his tone curt. "I would say that it's good to see you, but so far you're two for two in showing up in my life just after Murphy has kicked me in the balls."

Malinverni pointedly ignored Marcus' comment.

"I'm sorry about the current circumstances, of course," Malinverni said, his tone overly polite. "Is there anything I can have my steward get for you before we begin?"

How about a vibrocutlass? Marcus thought angrily.

"I don't know, is it the last meal for the condemned?" Marcus snapped, clenching his hands together under the table.

"Did the master-at-arms not tell you…" Malinverni asked, his face starting to cloud.

Well I see I finally punched through that faux aura of giving a shit you try to maintain, Marcus thought fiercely.

"That I was a free man?" Marcus responded, taking pleasure in interrupting the man. "Yes, he mentioned that. But based on our previous experiences, I am sure that is a temporary matter barring someone else changing your mind."

Malinverni shook his head in wonder, holding up his hand to the junior lieutenant who'd taken an unconscious step forward at Marcus' blatant disrespect.

"Lieutenant, I would not test this man," Malinverni said without turning around. "Judging from the testimony I've heard to date, he'd gut you using a table leg or bludgeon you to death with that flower vase over there."

Marcus raised an eyebrow at that even as the young Marine officer fixed him with a glare that seemed to say, *As if.*

"Oh, Senator Du, his surviving detail, and your own security personnel speak highly of you," Malinverni said. "They credit you with all the preparations that allowed the *Titanic* to hold out until the *Constitution* arrived."

Marcus felt his throat start to constrict and his chest grow heavy. Taking a moment to gather himself, he began to speak.

"Interesting considering I got most of them killed," Marcus said, his voice quavering.

"No, actually I believe your captain got most of them killed," Malinverni snapped. "*You* kept it from being a total goat fuck from what the rest of them said."

"The captain was over a goddamn barrel," Marcus snapped, his voice rising. "It was that asshole Federov who decided Section 195 wasn't worth the paper to wipe our ass with."

Malinverni smiled, and Marcus had a ball of ice form in his stomach at the look.

"How interesting," the fleet admiral replied. "I had not heard that from anyone other than Captain Herrod. Mr. Federov, at the advice of his counsel, has refused to speak to any of my investigators."

"His counsel? You mean that shit Speyney survived?" Marcus asked, incredulous.

"Why yes, it was a Mr. Speyney who was quite adamant a Major Acheros had violated his client's rights in addition to directly threatening him with harm," Malinverni replied.

There is no Creator, Marcus thought bitterly. *There must have been some damn professional courtesy between the aliens and that fucking lawyer.*

"Nevermind that the officer in question had just gotten through going hand to hand with a bunch of aliens that had been inside some compartment full of dead children," Malinverni observed.

Oh no...no...no.

"What?" Marcus asked, his voice barely a whisper.

"I don't know any more than that, I'm sorry," Malinverni said. "Although I understand there is someone who can tell you more en route from the *Memphis*."

"Just how many ships do you have out here?!" Marcus asked.

"In case you haven't noticed, the Fleet doesn't have many passenger liners," Malinverni observed drily, not quite answering Marcus' question. "Thankfully enough captains answered the *Titanic's* distress call that no one had to stay aboard the hulk."

The hulk, Marcus thought, a wave of grief washing over him. *That vessel was my home...*

"Even so, we had to spread the survivors over almost two dozen ships. Not that we've sent any away, as there is the chance more aliens might show up."

"Why haven't we just jumped away?" Marcus asked. "There's no reason to stay here."

"The *Titanic* would require a hyperspace tug, and even with that we're not sure she can jump due to the the damage the aliends did to her hull."

"So you're just going to leave her here?"

289

"She's evidence," Malinverni replied. "There is the little matter of an Admiral's Board for Captain Herrod."

"I already told you…" Marcus said, his voice rising.

"I know," Malinverni said patiently. "More importantly, so did Ms. O'Barr, Senator Du…well, just about everyone who was senior enough to know anything about the ship's daily functions. That being said, a captain is always responsible for the handling of his vessel. Plus, as stated, you are the only one who has said Federov gave a direct order rather than repeated heresay."

"So you're going to toss a man out an airlock who was operating under…" Martin began.

"I am not at liberty to disclose what I will or will not do, Mr. Martin," Malinverni snapped. "I said tribunal, not kangaroo court. Rear Admiral Moody will listen to the available evidence and then make a determination. I will serve as the impartial appeals board."

You're as impartial as I am part unicorn, Marcus thought. Seeing the determined set of Malinverni's jaw, Marcus decided to cut his losses.

"But I am not here to talk to you about Captain Herrod," Malinverni said after a few moments' of awkward silence. "I'd rather talk to you about Senator Du."

"Spartan guy, has a female asp no more than two steps behind him on most days ending in 'y,'" Marcus said sarcastically.

"Miss Eguchi does make quite the impression," Malinverni observed drily. "I understand Miss Eguchi just about attacked Rear Admiral Moody when the latter directed that she and Senator Du would be sent to separate vessels."

Marcus allowed himself a small smile without a shred of guilt.

"But I'm not here to talk to you about the Senator's bodyguard," Malinverni continued. "I'm asking you about the man himself."

"Okay," Marcus replied flippantly. "Ask away."

"It's rather odd to meet a Security Officer who expended almost two hundred thousand of his own credits flying to various arms bazaars," Malinverni started conversationally. Marcus started before regaining his composure.

"I see that you have excellent intelligence at your fingertips," Marcus responded. "Or else one of my security personnel works for Fleet Investigative Division."

"A little of both," Malinverni conceded. "Don't worry, the individual in question is no longer with us."

Marcus snorted.

"That doesn't exactly narrow it down, of course," he said, his tone heavy with sadness and frustration.

"No, it really doesn't," Malinverni retorted solemnly. "Although that's not by design."

"Okay, so I went far and wide to go shopping," Marcus responded.

"It's not the distance, but the ordinance," Malinverni replied easily. "I won't even touch the *Hoplite* suits, as the grenades, special launchers, and weapons carts alone would make any Marine detachment commander piss themselves with glee."

Malinverni gestured for his aide. The young lieutenant stepped forward, producing a map he quickly unfurled.

"I'll tell you what I think happened, Mr. Martin," Malinverni continued conversationally. "You got a tip somehow that something big was going to go down against the *Titanic*. You weren't sure what, but you knew it involved Spartans."

Martin could see where the fleet admiral was going, but decided to let the man continue.

I'll wait for him to put my options on the table, Martin thought. *While I think Malinverni has the stones to see this through, I'm not so sure I'm ready to help him.*

"Then, *surprise*, Senator Du shows up on the passenger list," Malinverni continued, steepling his hands. "Not only does he show up, but he has a large security detachment, almost fifty people strong for just he and his wife. It's at that point you decide to get loaded for bear."

There was a pause as the admiral stopped and looked at him. Marcus met the man's steady gaze as he replied.

"Largest passenger ship in the Confederation. Passenger list that looked like a who's who of 'people with families that can pay a six figure ransom.' There's a reason we were armed better than some of your cruisers, Admiral."

"Ah, but here's the rub—there was a cruiser waiting for you. A Spartan heavy cruiser."

Glad I already had this conversation with the Senator in question, Marcus thought. Malinverni looked nonplussed at Marcus's lack of reaction.

"One of those big bitches they've built in the last couple of years," the admiral continued, his voice prodding. "No entertainment facilities, half the life support, more rail guns than the *Mogami*-class, and a heavy missile battery to boot. Just the thing I'd bring if I wanted to overwhelm the largest starliner in the Confederation then quickly destroy her with no survivors."

He's got damn good intel, I'll give him that, Marcus thought.

"Seems to me that you have this all figured out, Admiral," Marcus responded. "If you found the cruiser, what do you need me for?"

"Because the *Athena* was allegedly 'in hot pursuit' when Rear Admiral Moody found her," Malinverni snapped. "Conveniently with the sensor tapes and navigational log to match. Nevermind that her jump drives were colder than an airlocked corpse and her rations were half consumed by the crew."

Well then, aren't we at a crossroads? Marcus thought unkindly.

"Funny thing Admiral, is that I still remember what you told me that last day we were in Spartan space together. You know, the day you decided I was no longer fit to be a Marine, much less have a commission?" Marcus spat, his tone like ice. "About how a man owed his greatest loyalty to those he fought and died with, not some 'stupid Spartan bitch he was screwing,'"

"Surely you're not going to let the man get away with possibly planning to kill you!" Malinverni said, slamming his hand down on the table.

"I don't know what Senator Du may have planned. What I *do* know is that when I was standing EVA on *Titanic*'s hull there was no Spartan cruiser hanging off our bow...but there was a Spartan Senator standing right next to me, and a not so stupid 'bitch' doing wonders with a *Kanabo*."

Malinverni took in a deep breath, and Marcus waited for an eruption of epic proportions. Visibly struggling, the senior officer regained control of his emotions.

"Well then, it appears that you have truly learned discretion since we last saw one another," Malinverni seethed. "I trust that I can rely upon your testimony regarding Captain Herrod and Mr. Federov? Or do you have misplaced loyalty towards both of them due to some event that I am unaware of?"

"No, I plan on telling the truth, the whole truth, and nothing but the truth as ordained by the Articles," Marcus replied, grinning broadly as he looked at Malinverni's frustration. "Seeing as how I'm a free man and all, perhaps your steward could get me all the rum he can find so I can forget all that shit you are 'unaware of.'"

Malinverni went as pale as he could possibly get, and Marcus saw the tendons in his neck standing out.

292

"Lieutenant, why don't we show in Mr. Martin's next visitor," Malinverni bit out, every word like a shot. "Maybe then he can determine what I am 'unaware of' before he gets good and pissed."

"Yes Sir," the young Marine said, stepping out.

"I understand that we have some...*difficulties* from our previous interactions with one another," Malinverni glowered. "If you think Du wants you less dead because you happened to spend a couple of hours killing aliens, then you can be damned when that man finds you."

"Admiral, you made it very clear that you hoped I got to enjoy some time south of the proverbial Styx almost a decade ago," Marcus snapped back. "If you can't figure out enough evidence to hold against Du, there's nothing I can give you that will stand up in your tribunal anyway. The fact that Spartan cruiser doesn't have a prize crew aboard her and a spaced captain tells me the good Senator apparently has twice the balls you do."

Malinverni was about to respond when his aide opened the door.

"Sir, Mr. Martin's guest will be with us shortly. There was a false alarm among the pickets that delayed her shuttle."

Right. I'm sure that's **exactly** what happened, Marcus thought.

"Very good," Malinverni replied. "Looking forward to seeing you in a couple of days, Mr. Martin."

"Likewise, Admiral," Marcus responded.

The two men left, leaving Marcus alone with his thoughts. Completely uncomfortable with that situation, he sprang to his feet and began pacing the room. Thankfully the door opened before he'd worn a hole in the deck. He turned and felt a rush of joy as he saw the woman who stepped through the hatch.

"*Anjelica!*" he said, springing across the room. Anjelica's mouth moved wordlessly, a sob ripping from her chest as she wrapped her arms around him. He held her as her shoulders shook, tears falling from his own eyes.

"You little larrikin, I thought you'd been seen off," the older woman said once they'd finally managed to let each other go. "The last Sarah...oh Maker."

Dreading what the second set of sobs meant, Marcus started to grab Anjelica again. The woman stopped him with a hand to the chest, shaking her head.

"No, I must tell you," Anjelica said, taking a shuddering breath as she reached into her pocket. Whatever she took out, she held it in her

293

fist as her brown eyes met Marcus's green ones. What he saw in her gaze made his knees start to grow weak, the room seeming to spin.

"Sarah made it to the Purser's flat with your survivors," Anjelica said, her face anguished. "I'd already gathered 40 children there from the Nursery, and she found five more on the way there. They'd been there maybe ten minutes when the aliens passed by the first time, moving as fast they could."

No... No... No. Marcus mentally chanted, shaking his head, tears hot on his cheeks.

"Love, something happened that must have opened up the hull aft of us in E Corridor," Anjelica continued. "We heard the vacuum doors shut. The older children were frightened, and that started setting off the younger children. Sarah suggested putting the babies in the safe. In retrospect, I think she knew what was coming."

Anjelica's jaw became set, as if she was determined to finish getting what happened out of her head.

"When the aliens returned, it was chaos," Anjelica continued. "I had gone back to check on the little ones when they burst into the compartment, and Sarah was right behind me with some little tyke who didn't want to be split from his little brother because his mother would be mad."

Marcus heard the crack in Anjelica's voice and wanted to tell her to stop.

No. No you will look upon what you did, his conscience told him.

"Sarah handed the boy to me, and I rushed him back to the safe. I turned around and she dropped the hatch using the deadman's lock. With the Maker as my witness, I had no idea she knew how to use it."

Marcus closed his eyes. The deadman's lock was a device that prevented *anyone* without a Confederation Fleet code from opening a merchantman or liner's safe. It had received it's moniker for two reasons. The first was that pirates tended to treat anyone who activated one rather...*unkindly*, i.e. a laser blast to the face was at the optimal end of the spectrum. The second was that the safe, once sealed in that fashion, had a limited amount of air supply despite the oxygen rescrubbers that were required to be placed inside any secure locker of that nature.

"I turned and screamed at the door," Anjelica said. "I was pounding on it when the boy tugged at my dress and handed me this."

The small note had Marcus's name on it in Sarah's elegant handwriting. Hand shaking, Marcus took the paper from Anjelica. He unfolded it, seeing the glint of light on jewelry fast enough to catch the ring before it fell. Looking down at the engagement ring, he felt his pulse thunder in his ears. Vision blurring, sobs fighting to rise, he turned to the note. It had one simple sentence, written in cursive with tear-stained ink:

I hope it was worth me.

Marcus felt his knees give out, and he dropped to them. The note fell out of his hand as Anjelica stepped forward and grabbed him, clutching his face to her chest. He embraced her back, a wail bursting from his throat. Marcus dropped the note as Anjelica clutched him to her chest. The *ping* of the ring hitting was lost in the pain wracked sobs that echoed through the conference room.

Constitution Pinnace #1
0700 SST
25 June

"This many capital ships in one place you'd think it was a damn review," Commander Alexander muttered, staring out the pinnace's starboard window.

Captain Bolan allowed himself a slight smile. The XO was always uncomfortable in full formal uniform.

I don't like it myself, but you'd almost think he's got electrodes giving him random shocks from the way he's acting, Bolan thought. *I'm just glad Owderkirk reminded us to pack our combat suits. Nothing more embarrassing than if those damn aliens jumped into system and we were stuck sucking vacuum aboard the **Vesuvius** should she get holed.*

The massive battleship was visible in the far distance as the pinnace went into a turn to clear the battlecruiser *Golan*. A slab sided behemoth, *Vesuvius* and the other ships in her class had been nicknamed "the flying bricks" due to their heavy armoring.

"Aren't four *Basilisks* kind of useless as a patrol?" Alexander asked Owderkirk as a flight of four interceptors from the *Java Sea* passed to port, their drives glowing. "I mean, you guys thumped that cruiser with the *Thunderchiefs*, right?"

Owderkirk gave a slightly wan smile.

295

"The *Java Sea*, *Victorious*, and *Midway* are all contributing a flight of the *Basilisks* so there's actually a rump squadron up at any particular moment," Owderkirk said. "We'd hate to have nothing but *Thunderchiefs* up if the aliens jump in with their own carriers."

Left unsaid was the fact that *Basilisks* could get out of the way much quicker than *Thunderchiefs*. No one knew what else the aliens might show up with, but all of the senior officers had been read in on the massive battleship that the *Shigure* had seen off with her *Pufferfish* missiles. It was hoped that if one of those leviathans jumped in, the combined firepower of the two battleships and four battlecruisers would take care of that threat without the combined air groups getting decimated attacking it.

I feel like we're running down a darkened corridor at full speed, Bolan thought. *Any second now we're going to trip over a hatchway then go face first into a bulkhead.* Bolan listened as Lieutenant Commander Tice, stepping in for the normal pinnace pilot due to the possibility she'd be testifying, answered the *Vesuvius'* control and lined up on the battleship's landing bay. Bolan noted that the subsequent landing was one of the smoothest he'd ever experienced.

So much for her protestations about not having touched a shuttle control column in almost six years, Bolan thought. *I wasn't bringing one more person than we needed to, not with most of the junior officers having to hot bunk.*

He led the way out of the shuttle to be greeted by the shrill notes of a bosun's pipe and the *Vesuvius* honor guard arrayed for their arrival. Making his way down to the landing bay deck, he was surprised when Captain Joanna Belmonte and her Chief of Boat, Chief Gebhard Stuart snapped to attention and saluted.

Joanna's a full three years senior to me, Bolan thought. *What in the hell is she...*

"Commodore Bolan, arriving!" the average height, strawberry blonde woman said. Her face was stern as her blue eyes met Bolan's.

"Thank you, Captain," Bolan replied, then lowly where only she could hear. "Commodore?"

"You haven't read the order of the day, have you?" she asked evenly.

"No, I have not," Bolan admitted sheepishly.

"In general when one is mentioned in fleet dispatches and promoted, it's customary for his crew to pass on that little tidbit," she replied. A slight smile touched her lips. "Then again, I suspect Fleet

Admiral Malinverni's flag officer might have been a bit tardy in publishing it before you left the *Constitution*."

Bolan allowed himself a small smile of his own.

Kraken Six knows my Comms officer is aboard already, Bolan thought. *That sneaky bastard also knows I would have refused honors if he'd given me the chance.*

Several compartments away, the Comms officer in question was standing sheepishly in front of his father while coloring slightly. To his right, Lieutenant Boyles was almost beet red at Captain Herrod's gentle teasing.

"I mean, you don't call, you don't write, no 'Hey Dad, I'm in system…'. No, I find out that this stunning and obviously intelligent young lady is the only reason I got any notice that you were nearby," Abraham said chidingly. "Of course, I should have realized our Comms were down when I was having to pick up code over sensors, but I'm going to blame that on the drugs."

I will not have the memory of his last conversation with me being devoid of joy, Abraham thought fiercely. The dull ache from the quick healing nannites in his legs made the joking somewhat of an effort, but for the first time since *Titanic* had started her journey Abraham felt truly free.

"I was kind of under orders, Dad," Lieutenant Herrod replied.

"Do they not teach you anything in ethics class anymore, Charlie?" Abraham replied. "Or is 'I was just following orders' suddenly acceptable now?"

Leaving his son fighting not to smile at his garrulous tone, Abraham turned to look at Lieutenant Boyles.

"So, Naomi, I'm sorry we could not meet under better circumstances," Abraham said, then continued on before the mood had a chance to turn somber. "Charlie tells me you have two sisters and one brother. Which one is in the service?"

"My sister Madeleine is just starting sensors training," Naomi replied with a smile.

"Oh dear, following in your sibling's footsteps is always a tough one," Abraham said.

"No, really?" Lieutenant Herrod quipped.

"Oh hush, your brothers were so far ahead of you I doubt most of their instructors remembered them."

"Right. Dennis set a console on fire and Ignaas broke his instructor's arm during vessel escape training," Lieutenant Herrod said. "No, no one remembered my last name at all."

Abraham was prevented from responding by the door opening. The sour looking guard spoke brusquely.

"Mr. Herrod, you have ten minutes before your attorney gets here."

Lieutenant Herrod looked prepared to say something about the man not even acknowledging him, but a gentle touch on his arm from Naomi stopped him. The sensor officer came around the table and threw her arms around Abraham. He could smell the cinnamon on her hair as she squeezed him tightly.

"It was great meeting you, Captain Herrod," Naomi said.

I believe she really means it, Abraham thought as he hugged her back.

"Likewise, Naomi," he replied. Stopping to kiss Charlie quickly, Lieutenant Boyles walked out of the meeting room.

"The type of woman who leaves a room darker when she exits," Abraham said softly. "You did good, son."

"It wasn't planned, Dad," Lieutenant Herrod responded, his voice quavering.

"Well if you two end up getting hitched, at least something good has come of this dog's breakfast," Abraham observed

"I can't believe they're talking about executing you," Lieutenant Herrod said in a rush, anger in his voice.

"Son, I violated the Articles," Abraham replied earnestly. "People are dead because of me."

"They're dead because of that son of a…"

"I didn't raise you to insult people's mothers," Abraham snapped. "Neither did *your* mother. I don't feel like getting an earful when I get to the great beyond, be it tomorrow or twenty years from now."

"What will I tell everyone else?" Lieutenant Herrod asked, referring to his siblings.

"That your father faced his consequences like a ship captain should," Abraham replied simply. "It wasn't my personal preference to have things end this way, obviously, but this is where we're at."

"I wish…gods I don't know what I wish," Lieutenant Herrod said, and his father once again briefly saw the young boy he'd raised.

"That you'll have a long, healthy life with that beautiful woman who just left," Abraham replied. "That together you'll have healthy,

298

smart children like your mother and I did. That you'll get a chance to say goodbye to at least one of them like I'm getting a chance to now."

The tears came to Lieutenant Herrod's eyes then, and he came around the table to hug his father as well. It was a fierce hug, and Abraham wished he'd had a chance to stand and look his son in the eye one more time.

"Take care, son," Abraham said after they broke the clench. The door opened to reveal the slim, long-faced man that was his attorney. Abraham had been impressed by the lieutenant commander so far, even if the tribunal's result was almost a foregone conclusion.

Of course, he may be incredibly skilled so that no one can argue I didn't have fair representation, Abraham thought cynically. *Malinverni is no fool.*

"Goodbye Dad," Charles said. With a curt nod to his father's attorney, Charles was through the door.

Senior Wardroom
C.S.S. Vesuvius
2100 SST

Bolan was somewhat surprised that the tribunal proceedings were far more formal than marsupial. The Vesuvius Senior Wardroom, as befitting a ship of her size, had easily fit the fifty or so witnesses, a couple dozen Marines, the tribunal, and the occupants of the defense and prosecution tables with room to spare. When he'd entered to give his testimony, Bolan had noted with some shock that Herrod was represented by a military lawyer rather than the Czarina Lines' Mr. Speyney. It was only when he saw Mr. Federov seated at the second table that he'd realized Speyney representing Herrod would have presented a conflict of interest.

Moody's a bit bold charging him. The man's got connections, he thought as he sat in the first row of witnesses whose testimony was complete. To his left, Iokepa sat with a stony expression on his face. To his right sat his subordinates, the majority of whom had not been called by either side.

Always glad to waste my people's time, Bolan thought churlishly, then immediately thought how that was unfair. Rear Admiral Moody, as tribunal president, had run a brisk, efficient affair once she established to Mr. Speyney that the latter was not in a packed planetary hall of justice. An athletic, ebony-skinned woman with a full, graying head of tightly curled hair, Moody had an air about her that

299

indicated she was perfectly willing to have anyone who disrupted the proceedings flogged. Rear Admiral Cruz, commander of the *Midway* battle group, seemed content to sit to Moody's left like a silent, ancient Aztec god of dispensation. On the other hand, the *Java Sea* battlegroup's Rear Admiral Peusen regularly asked pointed questions to gain clarification as to how things had unfolded. Short and stout, Peusen was like a gray-haired bulldog determined to get to the bottom of things in both sides' cases.

There had been many tears, most of them from the passengers asked to testify. The worst had been when *Titanic*'s Purser had broken into open sobs as she recounted how the air quality had begun to fail in the safe before Major Acheros had returned to free her and the youngsters trapped with her. Following behind her, Major Acheros had recounted finding many of the lizards still attempting to break into the safe, the broken and savaged bodies of the dead scattered across the compartment. Bolan found himself almost breaking down as Acheros' clipped voice answered Speyney's cross-examination regarding the state he found the bodies in with succinct answers.

Easy to believe he finished off one of those damned lizards by choking it to death in his battle armor, Bolan thought. *He looks ready to leap off that stand and dismember Speyney with his bare hands.*

"I fail to see where you are going to arrange a defense with your line of questioning, Mr. Speyney," Rear Admiral Moody stated. "You need to get to your point or cease. There is no need to discuss just how thoroughly the aliens dissected the *Titanic*'s Hospitality Officer or whether it appeared they attempted to consume the children."

Speyney stood stock still and glared at Moody for several long seconds. There was a rustle in the compartment, as everyone expected the admiral to gesture to the master-at-arms to break out the cat of nine tails. Instead, it was Speyney that looked away from Moody's dark, cold gaze.

"No further questions, Madame President," Speyney bit out.

"Very good," Moody replied pleasantly, Speyney's vitriol rolling off her like spitballs off a battlecruiser's hide. "Do you wish to call any witnesses, Mr. Speyney?"

"No Madame President," Speyney replied.

"Do you have any other motions you wish to bring?" Moody asked airily.

"No Madame President."

"Very well, the fact finding portion of these proceedings are closed. The tribunal will now deliberate," Moody said, reaching forward and turning off the microphones in front of the trio of officers.

Gotta love Admiral Tribunals, Bolan thought as Acheros left the stand. *Expeditious justice at its finest.* He looked at the defendant's tables and was surprised to see Captain Herrod's head bowed in silent prayer.

Well that's an admission of guilt if I've ever seen one, Bolan thought, then shook his head. *What am I talking about? I don't think there's ever been a man more guilty.*

Whether Moody was keeping up appearances or there was some disagreement over culpability in some of the charges, the deliberations took forty-five long, tension filled minutes. Bolan returned from the nearest head to find Acheros had taken a seat to Iokepa's left. Both men stood to let Bolan resume his seat, but he stopped to regard them both.

"Gentlemen, if either of you ever need something from me, anything at all, do not hesitate to ask," Bolan said, extending his hand.

"Thank you, Sir," Iokepa responded, Acheros repeating the gratitude a split second later. Before Bolan could say anything more, he saw that Rear Admiral Moody was getting ready to resume the proceedings. After a couple of quick, sharp nods from Cruz and Peusen and the passing of a couple documents from each, the dark-skinned admiral took a moment to collect herself before turning her microphone back on.

"Ladies and gentlemen, please be seated," she said, her tone making it clear the "please" was more a matter of etiquette than an actual request. Once the wardroom was quiet, Moody began.

"In the matter of the hulk *Titanic*, possession of the liner and all of her equipment transfers to the Confederation Fleet as of 2359 this evening," Moody stated. "All passenger private possessions will be collated and, where not claimed by current passengers within 180 days, auctioned off with the collective proceeds divided up among the *deceased* passengers' next of kin."

That's going to leave a mark, Bolan thought with a slight bit of shock. *Usually next of kin are allowed to claim property directly.*

"Twenty-five hundred or so dead? That's a shitload of stuff going on the block," a female voice muttered somewhere behind Bolan.

"Worse than you think," a deep baritone answered her. "Czarina is either going to have to buy the stuff from the auction house themselves or end up reimbursing every family that has to attend an auction in order to buy their favorite long dead grandmother's two thousand year old earrings back."

That comment drew a couple of chuckles. Moody favored Bolan's section with a hard look as the tribunal waited for the chief petty officer preparing the official transcript to finish concluding the judgment. After taking a moment to double check his work, the heavy set man pressed a button to send Moody's ruling to Fleet Admiral Malinverni's staff aboard the *Vesuvius* sister ship, *Etna*.

Have to make the appeals process as quick as possible, Bolan thought with a grimace. Not that I think the next higher authority is going to have a great deal of mercy. Had Fleet Admiral Malinverni chaired the board himself, the next higher authority would have defaulted to the Confederation's Minister of War. Given that the latter was married to a member of the Czarina Lines board, Bolan understood why Malinverni didn't want any decisions second guessed and had worked the system to be the final reviewing authority.

I'm thinking Minister Bloodworth is going to shit a brick when he figures out Malinverni purposefully sidelined him, Bolan thought. *Still, Fleet Admiral Malinverni is definitely going to get his point across about Section 195.*

"With regards to the matter of incurred indemnities against Czarina Lines for crew deaths and loss of property, Czarina Lines shall pay no less than five years standard salary plus a stipend of one million dollars apiece for those crew members who are confirmed dead or are still missing," Moody continued. "In all cases, death certificates for the missing shall be issued within seventy-two hours, with Czarina Lines to settle all claims within thirty days of the appeal process being complete."

There was a murmur across the wardroom at Moody's statement, and Bolan noted Federov looked positively apoplectic.

"For those surviving members of the crew, all current employment contracts are held to be null and void," Moody stated crisply, her tone killing most of the chatter as if she'd thrown a switch. "Czarina Lines will pay each surviving member a total of three hundred thousand dollars or double their negotiated severance package, whichever sum is greater. Surviving crew, with the exception of the captain, are held to be free of all further liability or indemnities."

One thousand five hundred crew, Bolan thought, shaking his head. *Less than two hundred survivors, most of whom I'd say are going to need some serious therapy.*

"Czarina Lines will also be held liable for continuing all medical coverage for these employees for a period no less than ten years," Moody continued as if she was reading Bolan's mind. He watched as Federov began speaking animatedly to Speyney, the menace in the man's voice clear even if his words were inaudible. Moody stopped, her face sphinx-like as she stared at the table. Finally having had enough, the admiral spoke.

"Is there something your client would like to share with us, Mr. Speyney?" Rear Admiral Moody asked. "I am sure it must be of dire import to interrupt these proceedings prior to sentencing."

"Your hon..." Speyney began, sweat beading on his forehead as he realized his mistake. "Madame President, as the senior representative of Czarina Lines, Mr. Federov protests the punitive measures being brought against his line due to the negligence of a singular employee."

The murmuring inside the wardroom grew louder, and Moody swiftly banged her gavel on the table. Bolan looked to where Captain Herrod sat stone faced without any reaction.

Nothing like your boss stabbing you in the back in front of the Maker and several dozen witnesses, Bolan observed.

"There will be order in this room," Moody barked, and a pall fell back across the room. Once there was quiet, the admiral turned and looked at Speyney. Even though the gaze was not directed at him, Bolan fought the urge to squirm in the chair.

"Perhaps your client would like to wait until *I am done* to begin raising objections," Moody replied. "In addition, I strongly suggest neither he nor you disrupt this court again."

The look Federov gave Moody was pure venom.

"Do you have any idea..." he spat while beginning to stand. Speyney grabbed him before he could finish rising, and the man stopped speaking as Moody started to gesture towards the master-at-arms. Stopping her motion, the Rear Admiral cocked an eyebrow at Speyney and Federov.

If ever a look said, 'Do I really need to whip you in front of all these witnesses?', Bolan thought. While he'd never actually seen someone get a "visit from the dead cat" during a tribunal or court martial, such an occurrence was hardly uncommon.

*If memory serves, Moody wasn't exactly hesitant on using the lash when she commanded the **Vikrant**,* Bolan thought. *I'm not sure I'd press my luck were I him.*

303

"With regards to prize money, this tribunal finds that the *Titanic* was under alien control when boarded by the *Constitution*. As such, the crew of the *Constitution* will receive prize money for the *Titanic* and two alien cruisers. They will split a third cruiser with the crew of the *Shigure*, with the build costs for the C.S.S. *Mogami* being used in three cases," Moody said, her voice crisp.

Bolan took a deep breath as he stood to be recognized by the Rear Admiral Moody.

"Yes, Commodore Bolan?" Moody asked, her tone indicating that his movement was not unexpected.

It takes a matter of years to build a ship. It takes centuries to build a tradition, Bolan thought.

"For the widows and orphans, Ma'am," he said simply, amazed that emotion did not make his voice crack as he thought of Leslie.

"The board recognizes that the *Constitution*'s wardroom vacates the vessel's claim to their half of the cruiser for the *Shigure*'s next of kin."

Bolan saw Federov roll his eyes and fought down the urge to stride over and strangle the man.

"You may be seated, Commodore Bolan," Moody said. "The *Shigure*'s crew, to include attachments, will also receive the proceeds for an alien capital ship, with the *Kirishima*'s build costs being used to determine the appropriate outlays."

*Wow. Looks like most of the **Shigure**'s crew and her casualties' survivors just became millionaires*, Bolan thought, hearing Iokepa inhale sharply at the news. It was rare that a destroyer would be given single credit for destroying a capital ship, much less a vessel with *Shigure*'s reduced crew.

"Now for the matter of the Section 195 violation," Moody said. There was another brief moment of sound as the gathered personnel shifted. Bolan looked across at Herrod and saw that the man had ceased his prayers, sitting ramrod straight in his chair.

"Captain Abraham Ebenezer Herrod, this tribunal finds you guilty of violating Section 195 of the Spacefarer's Code, with your actions resulting in the death of over four thousand passengers, crew, and Confederation personnel. For your crime, this tribunal sentences you to death. Does the condemned have anything to say?" Moody said flatly.

Although there had been little doubt as to the outcome of the tribunal, Moody's pronouncement still caused a mild ripple through the wardroom. To his credit, the *Titanic*'s captain allowed Admiral Moody's glare to quiet the room before responding.

"No, Madame President," Captain Herrod replied, his voice strong and clear.

He's going to his grave like a spacer, Bolan thought with grudging respect.

"Then may the Creator have mercy on your soul," Moody said, gesturing for the Marine detachment to take the man away. There was a palpable energy coursing through the courtroom as Captain Herrod was pushed out in his hoverchair, his defense attorney close behind.

As the detail reached the door, Bolan saw Federov's military lawyer rising and gesturing for his two companions to do the same. The executive's movements all but screamed a naked contempt for Moody and the panel, and Bolan could feel his pulse starting to race in anticipation of what was coming.

"Mr. Ivan Nikolai Federov, this tribunal finds you *not guilty* of violating Section 195 of the Spacefarer's Code," Rear Admiral Moody read simply. Federov looked at the panel in sheer arrogance, turning to embrace Speyney as the buzz grew louder in the wardroom.

Fucking fix was in, Bolan thought disgustedly. *Guess the panel doesn't want to see their careers come to a halt after all. Constitution*'s captain could feel the rage radiating off Iokepa and Acheros.

"We are not finished, ladies and gentlemen," Moody's voice cracked like a whip through the wardroom. Federov rolled his eyes as he turned back to face the panel.

"Mr. Federov, this tribunal does find you guilty of three thousand, eight hundred sixty counts of reckless endangerment resulting in death," Moody said. There were several exclamations amid the massive exhalation of breath that followed, but the buzz stopped almost as soon as it began as Moody continued.

"As the counts carry multiple aggravators, to include the deaths of at least two hundred minors and over one hundred naval personnel, you are subject to the Tribunal's punishment under Sections 175 and 196 of the Spacefarer's Code. Do you wish to make a statement at this time?"

Federov's response startled every individual present. After a moment of incredulity, the executive began to laugh. It was not the laughter of a person coming unhinged, but that of a man who found himself utterly amazed at another's actions. Speyney placed his hand on Federov's arm, an act that led the executive to throw the offending

305

touch off with an oath and glare. Swiveling back to the board, he leaned forward on the table.

"Yes, I have a statement," Federov said. "I have had enough of this idiocy."

Uh oh, Bolan thought as the executive leaned forward on the table.

"You stupid bitch, you really expect me to sit here and grovel when your *boss*," he said with a sneer, "doesn't even have the balls to come down here and face me himself?! I don't know who you think—"

The Marine sergeant standing behind Federov moved with a surprising suddenness. One moment the executive was winding up to what he'd surely intended to be an epic rant of defiance. The next his face was slamming down to the table, his arm behind him in a pressure hold that brought a loud, surprised cry of pain. Speyney, to his credit, made no sudden moves that might have made the other members of the Marine detail suspicious.

"Let go of me...aahhhhhh!" Federov screamed, his initial struggle having resulted in the sergeant completing his wrist's dislocation. Before the executive could finish screaming, the Marine NCO slammed his face even harder into the table again. Stunned, Federov whimpered as the Marine, grabbing his hair and continuing to twist the man's wrist, stood him back up.

"Madame President, I must protest the treatment of my client!" Speyney said in shock.

"Lieutenant Commander Dealey?" the Rear Admiral asked.

"I was not aware of Mr. Federov's intent to disrespect the tribunal," the military lawyer at the table replied, his tone neutral. Looking at Federov, his eyes wild as he attempted to breathe through his bleeding nose, Dealey continued drily, "I do not think Mr. Federov wishes to continue his statement."

Life's a bit different in the Fleet, Bolan thought, remembering his shock after attending his first Fleet tribunal as a junior officer. While the iron fist of discipline was usually concealed by the decorative glove of professionalism and élan, the gauntlet was ever present and relentless in its grip. When death for an entire ship was one problem child away, the ability to rapidly eliminate acts of defiance and delaying tactics was critical to the dispensation of justice.

"Very well," Moody replied, taking a moment to shuffle her papers as the Czarina Lines executive stood with blood streaming down his face.

I get the feeling our good admiral knew that Federov was going to make an ass of himself, Bolan thought with some satisfaction. *Indeed, I'd go to a casino on those odds.*

"This Tribunal finds Mr. Federov guilty on all counts of homicide with aggravating circumstances," Moody stated. "As there are over twenty counts, the only penalty available to this tribunal is death. Due to your previous act of disrespect, the tribunal considers you to have waived your right to a final statement."

Federov looked as if he was about to say something, but was cut off by the sergeant twisting his wrist even more forcefully to place manacles upon them. Cuffed, the executive gave Moody a glare that could only be described as murderous as he was led from the wardroom.

"Ladies and gentlemen, these proceedings are closed," Moody intoned after the hatch closed behind Federov's detainers.

Chapter 12: Absolutions and Continuity

Brig
C.S.S. Vesuvius
2330 SST
2 July 3050

Abraham took a deep breath as he heard the approaching footsteps. Rising unsteadily, he stood to face the brig's transparisteel hatch.

How fortuitous that the quick heal managed to patch me up enough that I can walk, rather than be pushed, to my execution, he thought. Abraham fought back the gibbering madness that tried to consume him at the realization he was going to die. No sooner had he gained control of his breathing than four Marines stopped outside his hatch. Executing a precise right face, the men assumed a position of parade rest, the brig's overhead light causing their black dress silks to almost shimmer with reflected light. A moment later the detail officer in charge took his place in front of the gathered men. Abraham recognized the large major from the *Shigure*, and let out the breath he did not realize he was holding.

"Abraham Herrod, you know why we are here," Major Acheros said, his stern voice filling the brig. "Step forward if you wish to go to your eternity as a man upright, unshackled, and unmarked."

The Choice of the Condemned, Abraham thought with a swallow. His mouth was suddenly dry as he slowly walked forward to the cell door, his gait labored due to his still healing legs. Stopping just short of the entrance, he held his hands out, palms upright.

"I am prepared to face my destiny and atone for my crimes," he replied, the voice sounding like it was someone else's. Acheros' eyes met his, and Abraham saw a brief moment of respect before the man's face became impassive again. The major pressed the control in his hands, and the cell door hissed upwards.

"Step forward, Abraham Herrod," Acheros stated, stepping to the door's left while the four Marines stepped backwards. Abraham stepped out of the cell, taking a deep breath as he looked down the corridor to the airlock at the far end.

Easy pick up, easy drop off, even easier step out, he thought. He had first heard the words as a young midshipman whose first job had been managing an intrasystem tour boat's confinement facilities. Now, his career at its denouement, they seemed somehow so trite yet incredibly poignant.

"Turn right, walk forward to the next white line, about face, then stand by, Mr. Herrod," Acheros instructed. Moving very slowly, with his leg muscles refusing to cooperate due to the aftereffects of the quick heal, Abraham shuffled past Federov's cell. The executive had come to his cell door and stood watching as Abraham shuffled by. Abraham noted that the man's face still looked like a raccoon, his nose puffy and still clearly broken. Captain Belmonte had given explicit orders to the *Vesuvius* surgeon to perform the minimal medical care necessary for Federov to be able to breathe. The resultant shrieks had been audible throughout the brig space, as the young female lieutenant had apparently put in place metal spacers without local anesthesia.

Strange how she kept claiming 'imminent hostilities' and the 'need to conserve medicine for those who will actually benefit' as she was performing the procedure, Abraham thought. Indeed, Abraham was glad he'd received the treatment for his legs aboard *Titanic*, as he was fairly certain he'd be getting pushed to the hatch otherwise.

"Ivan Federov..." Major Acheros began.

"I want to talk to fucking Admiral Malinverni *right now*," Federov blustered, cutting Acheros off. The major pursed his lips, and Abraham could almost sense the palpable rage radiating off the man.

"Ivan Federov..." Acheros started again.

"Did you hear me, you primate? Unless you want me to pay someone to slit your entire family's throat, you will let me out of this cage right now," Federov shouted.

Acheros cocked his head to the side, and Abraham felt his own bowels loosen at the utterly predatory look.

"Master Sergeant Bonham, have you recorded that Mr. Federov's chose?" Acheros asked quietly.

"Sir, the record shows that Mr. Federov has made the choice to be bound, broken, and battered," the tall, wiry non-commissioned Marine standing to Acheros' right intoned solemnly.

"So let it be done," Acheros replied, pressing the control at his wrist.

To Federov's credit he leaped upon his opportunity like it was the last one it was going to get. Rather than attempting to run, he sprang towards Acheros in an initiation of some martial arts maneuver. While not familiar with whatever technique Federov was attempting, Abraham detachedly realized the smoothness of the executive's attempt…right before Acheros easily blocked it and countered with a strike of his own.

The ensuing beating was all the more vicious due to its cool, almost fluid savagery. The Spartan major did not ask for nor, from Abraham's vantage, require any assistance. Throughout the beating the only sound was Federov's desperate cries, the thud of blows against soft tissue, then the cracking of both arms, the executive's collarbone and, finally, femur. With the last, the executive crumpled to the ground, attempting to clutch his shattered right leg then screaming as the bones in his arms ground together. Acheros took the opportunity to step in and kick the man full in the face, the blow twisting Federov's head so savagely that Abraham was almost certain the executive's neck had snapped.

"Sir," Master Sergeant Bonham said quietly. Acheros turned to look at the NCO, his face a mask of savagery before the Spartan regained control. Coming out of his fighting stance to stand tall again, he stepped away from Federov.

I'd say whatever fueled that is fully avenged, Abraham thought as he looked at the broken, sobbing Federov on the deck. *Perhaps threatening to kill his family was a bad idea, you idiot.*

"Detail, bind this man," Acheros said solemnly, his voice betraying no sign of the exertion he'd just undertaken.

Mercifully, Federov passed out halfway through the binding process. As it was, Abraham had a feeling the man's cries would visit some detail members' dreams in the weeks to come. With each member of the detail grabbing a limb, they began carrying the limp executive towards Abraham.

"Mr. Herrod, please turn around and move towards the red line in front of the hatch."

Abraham complied with Acheros' command, finding that watching Federov's fate had given him a surge of adrenaline which allowed him to walk faster. His stomach churning, he reached the line and stopped. Acheros moved past him to the airlock control as the detail members came to a halt on his left. With a warning tone, the airlock door opened. Looking out the window, Abraham could see the *Etna* holding station barely two kilometers away, the battleship's maneuvering thrusters briefly flaring to hold her in place against Sapphire's pull.

Guess Admiral Malinverni wants to be sure of thi, Abraham thought. *It would be a bit beneath him to be pressing the button himself…even if he probably wanted to.* Despite his current situation, Abraham could not bring himself to be angry at the fleet admiral.

310

Good men and women died because of what we did, Titanic's former master thought.

"Detail, place Mr. Federov into the airlock, then bring him back to consciousness," Acheros commanded. The four men sprang to their task, lying the bloodied executive on the ground. They then stood and began preparing the special execution harness that hung from the hatch's overhead. A spring loaded mechanism, the device had two manacles attached to a simple steel bar. Arming it, the three men lifted Federov and, as the executive groaned in unconscious pain, hung him from his arms. Satisfied their prisoner was secure, the three NCOs stepped back to allow Master Sergeant Bonham into the airlock. To Abraham's shock, the man held a stun baton.

Why didn't they just use that to get him out of the cell? Abraham thought. Then, looking across at Acheros's clenched, scuffed fists Abraham chided himself for wasting his last moments on stupid questions.

Carla I'm coming, Abraham thought, thinking of his wife. *I can't wait to tell you what our children and grandchildren have been up to since you've left us.*

Abraham watched as Benham touched the stun baton to Federov's face and activated it. The executive came awake with a scream that rose in tone and intensity as he thrashed against the restraints, thus rubbing his broken bones together. Swiveling his eyes around, he found Acheros and attempted to speak, but instead immediately began coughing on the blood that ran down his throat.

"Ivan Federov, for your crimes you will now be surrendered to space's embrace until you are dead," Acheros said as the detail left the airlock. "Do you have any last words?"

How is he going to speak? You probably broke his damn jaw, Abraham thought. To his shock, the executive proved him wrong.

"I can make any of your four unimaginably rich," Federov grumbled, desperation starting to creep into his voice. "I have powerful friends, and you…"

His words were cut off by the airlock door slamming shut as Acheros stabbed the console button. Abraham could see the executive trying to scream more bargaining, the pain from the exertion stopping him mid-sentence. Searching, his eyes met Abraham's and widened, then narrowed. The sheer malevolence Abraham saw in Federov's gaze caused a chill to run up and down his spine, but he continued to lock eyes with the executive.

311

An Unproven Concept

I'll be damned if you'll go to your grave thinking you scared me, you son of a bitch, Abraham thought, keeping his face expressionless as Acheros entered a code into the console.

The airlock alarm hooted its warning throughout the brig space. After thirty seconds of cacophony that seemed like a hate filled eternity, the outer door cycled open. In a rush that jerked Federov against his restraints, the breathable air rushed out of the space and left the executive hanging with his mouth open in a final scream. The last act was a mercy, as it sped the process of hypoxia that flung Federov into unconsciousness after roughly half a minute. Sixty seconds after that, Acheros stepped forward to the hatch and produced a small laser. Shining it in each of Federov's eyes to see if the man's pupils reacted, Acheros gave a short nod to Master Sergeant Bonham. The senior NCO stepped to the controls, entered a code, then pressed the console's execute button twice. Silently the execution device swung and released its manacles, imparting Federov's body with sufficient force to flush it from the airlock. Floating with an almost perverse gentleness, the battered and bruised cadaver moved out past the outer hatch.

Well let's get this over with, Abraham thought, closing his eyes as Bonham pressed the button again to recycle the airlock. A few moments later, the door swung open. Before Acheros could order him, Abraham stepped forward into the space then turned around to face the door. He was surprised at his calmness as the detail placed his hands into the manacles.

"Abraham Herrod, do you have any last words?" Major Acheros asked crisply.

"I am truly sorry for the pain I caused," Abraham said, feeling tears come to his eyes. "I love my children and grandchildren, and hope that this act will satisfy others' desire for revenge."

Abraham swallowed, and Acheros waited for him to go on.

"I miss and love you, Carla," he finished. Looking at Acheros, he met the man's eyes. "Please tell my family that I died as a captain should, answering for my actions."

"I will do so," Acheros said solemnly. With that, he closed the inner hatch. As the warning claxon sounded, Abraham forced himself to slow his breathing, but did not stop it.

No point in holding my breath, Abraham thought. *Vacuum always wins.*

Constitution
1159 SST
Bath Works
Rumpelstiltkin System
10 July

The shrill notes of the bosun's pipe jerked Commodore Bolan out of his private reverie. Watching as Chief Dunn called the welcoming detail to attention, Bolan took one last glance over his gathered crew. He dwelled briefly on Lieutenant Higginsworth, his new communications officer.

Guess I can't blame Herrod for resigning his commission, Bolan thought sadly. *Something about "the Fleet Admiral tossed my father out an airlock" probably kills the motivation.* Looking to Higginsworth's right, he gave a slight prayer of thanks that Boyles hadn't followed her boyfriend out of the service.

Fleet Admiral Malinverni exited the shuttle hatch, ducking to ensure he didn't bash his head. Bolan came to attention and saluted the man, the gesture being quickly returned.

"Welcome aboard the *Constitution*, Fleet Admiral Malinverni," Bolan said simply. "The vessel is ready for your inspection."

"Commodore, after the last few weeks I think this ship is ready for anything," Malinverni said with a grin. To Bolan's surprise, the expression actually touched the man's eyes.

You know, it'd probably be best for any elderly individuals or small children if you grinned as little as possible, Bolan thought as he gave a slight smile in return. *Or maybe it's just the fact I now **know** you're absolutely ruthless that has me a little jumpy.*

"Thank you, Sir," Bolan replied. "Do you have any preference on where you would like to begin?"

"Let's start with the air wing since we're already here," Malinverni replied.

Four hours later, the fleet admiral and commodore stood in the *Constitution*'s "flag country." So named as its compartments normally have housed an admiral and the officer's staff were they using the battlecruiser as a flagship, Bolan had directed his surviving officers to take the spaces over due to the severe damage done to their quarters. Opening the door to the admiral's day cabin, Bolan entered first

313

followed by Fleet Admiral Malinverni. The latter turned as his aide started to follow.

"Lieutenant Boyne, why don't you knock off for a couple of hours?" Malinverni asked, his tone making it clear that it wasn't a question. "I'm sure Lieutenant Colonel Nishizawa won't mind you making an appearance in his wardroom."

Boyne came to attention.

"Aye aye, Sir," the young lieutenant replied, looking at his chronometer.

"Lieutenant, do you need help finding the Marine wardroom?" Bolan asked.

"No Sir, I have a map of the ship," Lieutenant Boyne replied confidently. Bolan nodded, then let the hatch slide closed.

"I'm going to let him find out the hard way that the Marines are now splitting a wardroom with the air group," Bolan said after a moment.

"It'll do him some good," Fleet Admiral Malinverni replied, his tone weary. "Holy shit, Mackenzie, you took a lot more damage than it sounded like in your official report."

"Sir, most of what you saw was cosmetic and did not affect the ship's combat capability," Bolan replied. Malinverni gave him a look as if he was waiting on more.

Guess I better come clean, Bolan thought.

"I also did not want to give this vessel's detractors any opening to denigrate the concept," Bolan finished.

"I think you definitely proved the concept as valid, Commodore Bolan," Malinverni said with a smile. "If anything, the only issue you had was with the power conduits. Which, between you and I, will not be a problem going forward."

Bolan must have had a look of surprise on his face as Malinverni continued.

"The *Essex* will have to be modified at her first refit, but I've already got BuShips going over safety practices for her until that happens. *Scharnhorst* and *Queen Mary* will have to be modified on the slips to take two extra fusion bottles."

"I'm sure the folks from Bath loved that," Bolan said. All service discovered shortcomings, if noted by the accepting crew on trials, are the responsibility of the shipbuilder to fix.

"I informed Mr. Freyling," Malinverni said archly, referring to the CEO of Bath Shipyards, "that I suspected there was going to be a great many more ship building contracts let in the immediate future.

You can build five destroyers in the capital slips just as well as you can build the vessels they're designed for."

I get the feeling that was a less than pleasant conversation for Freyling, Bolan thought. *Not just because of the relative profit differential involved, either.*

"Sir you want anything to drink?" Bolan asked, kicking himself for forgetting his manners. Malinverni gave him a smile that indicated he hadn't thought of refreshments either.

"You still dismiss your steward when not underway, don't you?" Malinverni asked. Bolan looked at him with slight surprise.

"Every captain has habits, Mackenzie," Malinverni said. "I make it a point to know what they are before I go troubling them on their ship."

"Understood Sir," Bolan said. "I just wonder how you have eyes everywhere."

Malinverni gave him a pensive look, then a slight smile.

"You'd be amazed how much enlisted and junior officers talk," Malinverni said simply. "I don't have spies, per se, but I usually find senior enlisted will clue you in on the latest scuttle butt. Then again, I believe I'm talking to Hercules about cleaning stables."

Bolan chuckled slightly about that one.

"Sir, I just treat my people with respect," Bolan replied. "They certainly don't give me a back brief on every officer aboard ship."

Then again, I guess Chief Dunn did warn me about the CAG and XO problem, Bolan thought to himself.

"To answer your original question, I'll take some coffee mixed with whatever alcohol you have," Malinverni said.

Five minutes later, Bolan resumed his seat after handing the fleet admiral his coffee. He'd left Malinverni to regard the cabin while he'd gone the next compartment over to make both their cups. The older officer was regarding the holopicture on Bolan's desk, the black bunting in the corner a somber reminder of what had happened to the subject.

"You know Captain Gadhavi's initial report on your actions was rather scathing," Malinverni stated. "If ever there was a man who probably wishes he'd taken a couple extra days to prepare his message before hitting send."

Well getting one's command cut short and reassigned to the Fleet G-1's office tends to indicate a superior's displeasure rather well, Bolan thought. *I'm not sure if the orders actually stated 'relieved for lack of aggressive spirit,' but I think the message was received by everyone sitting in a captain's chair.*

"He had a point," Bolan replied aloud. "I was rash, and we were lucky Contact Bravo decided turning around towards *Titanic* was his best option."

"You were aggressive, not rash," Malinverni said, shaking his head. "I take it you haven't seen Mr. Martin's report."

"No, I hadn't," Bolan replied. "Mostly to make sure my testimony to the tribunal wasn't tainted, then because we were getting ready to jump out of system."

"It makes for an interesting read," Malinverni replied. "Apparently your Marines showed up just in the nick of time in order to keep the aliens from disabling *Titanic*'s engines. "

Malinverni gestured towards the picture.

"As I told Minister Bloodworth when I rendered my report, I think if either you *or* Leslie had waited any longer things would not have turned out as well."

Cold comfort, Bolan thought to himself.

A cloud crossed Malinverni's face. Taking a look around the compartment, he placed his cup down.

"Minister Bloodworth is not pleased by my actions, by the way," the admiral continued.

Bolan hoped that his disgust did not show on his face.

"Minister Bloodworth is not merely upset because his wife is, to quote him, 'convinced I am a barbaric murderer' for tossing both those idiots out an airlock," Malinverni said, holding up his hand as if to forestall Bolan from saying something unprofessional. "He thinks that my measures against Czarina Lines were also excessive."

"Perhaps Mrs. Bloodworth would have liked to write the necessary letters home," Bolan seethed. "Or dealt with the smell of burnt flesh."

Malinverni grimaced at the last.

"In any case, while he's not so foolish as to say something publicly, he's made it clear that he does not agree with my actions. Indeed, if he could have done so without igniting a political firestorm, I'm pretty sure he'd have relieved me."

"So he'd prefer that any future captain can potentially start an interstellar war and say, 'oops, my executive made me do it' when it comes time to pay the piper? Especially if said executive had had the good courtesy to die during the tragedy rather than surviving just long enough to threaten some Marine prior to going on his last spacewalk?"

Malinverni gave Bolan an appraising look before speaking.

"Why Commodore Bolan, it would appear that you understand exactly why I refused to commute the good Captain Herrod's sentence. It is a shame that your Comms officer and his brothers saw differently."

"I'd be rather heated if someone killed my father for choosing incorrectly between the rock and the hard place," Bolan replied. "Still, maybe it's best for all parties concerned if they could not be professional."

"Unfortunately Captain Herrod's life purpose was to serve as a warning to others," Malinverni stated. "Considering how much of the original *Titanic*'s history Czarina Lines forced down their throat, he should have learned from E.J. Smith's mistake rather than trying to do the old man one better. At least in this case, Mr. Federov got to share his passengers' fate."

Some of his passengers, anyway, Bolan thought.

"On a better note, the engineering folks managed to finish stitching *Titanic*'s keel back together two days ago," Malinverni continued after a sip of coffee. "The Vestal should be able to jump her out of system, at which point we can get the Fleet focused on defending what we have rather than waiting for something to fold into a distant, uninhabited system."

Bolan grew pensive.

"Sir, if you don't mind me asking, is defense our plan? It's the number one question I keep getting asked by all my folks. People are scared…"

Malinverni started guffawing at that last, causing Bolan to stop midsentence.

"Sorry, I nearly replied 'well holy shit, so am I,'" Malinverni said after thirty seconds, his eyes moist. "Then I realized that's not exactly an inspiring message to tell some nineteen year old member of the black gang whose best friend just got electrocuted."

Bolan found himself starting to give a gallows grin despite the topic's seriousness.

"No Sir, I guess not," he replied. "Then again, you know how many ships we have in commission and coming out in the next few months and how many systems they have to cover."

"Not nearly enough," Malinverni said. "Which is why I'm not pressing our luck."

With that the Fleet Admiral stood, looking all the world like a man attempting to shoulder a massive boulder.

"The 'plan,' if I can keep Minister Bloodworth under control until the Senate regains a quorum, is to mass what we've got into task

317

forces of either two carriers and a battleship or two battleships and a carrier," Malinverni said. "We'll tell the systems it's their responsibility to hold for at least seventy-two hours, which will give us enough time to shift the task forces as necessary."

Bolan inhaled deeply, the air whistling as he did so.

"I have to think there's a bunch of systems that will not be happy about that," the *Constitution*'s master said.

"The fact that some systems have been skating by on making adequate defensive preparations is not my concern," Malinverni snapped. "For years the Fleet's inspectors have been telling system governments that they needed to make defensive improvements and investments to no avail. Pardon me if, now that creatures that will *eat them alive* have shown up, I am completely unsympathetic to loosened bowls and weak bladders."

Well that may be, but once the Caliphate, Anglo-Saxons and Australasians provide replacement senators you may have your mind made up for you, Bolan thought. *Then again, even with Bloodworth hating your guts, there's still that little matter of Senator Kimura heading the War Committee. Neither the Eurasians nor the Spartans are going to want to hear any whining about saving poorly defended systems.*

"You look lost in thought, Commodore Bolan," Malinverni said.

"I'm just having the mental image of six senators trying to convince four that just because their constituents thought defense was a luxury item before their systems shouldn't be left out to dry," Bolan replied. "It's going to come down to the Transvaals before things go to the Commons, isn't it?"

"Either way, I don't have time to wait on the politicians to figure it out before I start issuing orders," Malinverni said. The Fleet Admiral then reached into his jacket and pulled out a sheaf of papers. "Speaking of which, here are your new ones."

"Sir?" Bolan asked, perplexed as he took the orders and began scanning.

*Holy shit, he's taking the **Constitution** away from me,* Bolan thought as he continued reading. He snapped his eyes up from the paper, opening his mouth to protest before Malinverni forestalled him.

"I remind you, Commodore Bolan, they're called *orders* for a reason," Malinverni said, his voice flat. Bolan shut his mouth, lips pressed into a thin line.

"As you started to point out, the Bath workers say that it will be almost eight months before *Constitution* leaves the yard," Malinverni

318

continued. "Post-repair trials, even if I were willing to accept an accelerated rate after the goat fuck Bath made of the initial shakedown, would add another sixty days."

Malinverni gestured at their surroundings.

"So give me one logical reason why I would let you sit aboard a crippled ship for ten months? Because last I checked there's only one officer who has fought alien vessels and survived," Malinverni said.

Bolan started to look at Leslie Hawkins' picture then caught himself.

"Sir, I'm not sure I'm cut out for BuShips," Bolan replied. "Not to mention Vice Admiral Gordon…"

"Was so distraught at his son's untimely death that he said some things he shouldn't have within an embedded reporter's ear shot," Malinverni snapped. "Which is why he's taken the newly opened position of Chief Marshal, Eurasian Partition's Defense Force."

For the second time in five minutes, Bolan found himself looking up in total shock.

"Feldmarschall Seeger has had a degenerative heart condition for the last two months," Malinverni said. "She had been about to announce her retirement when she received news regarding the *Titanic* and the death of Senator Haenraats and Tran. She was in the middle of organizing the Eurasian Partition's forces when she dropped dead of a massive coronary."

Bolan could see and hear that Seeger's death had personally affected Malinverni.

I can't remember if they were classmates or just good friends, Bolan thought.

"Whatever his son's faults, Chad Gordon is a good man," Malinverni said. "While I would love to give him a mulligan, I cannot in good conscience have the press floating the impression my flag officers will embark on acts of vengeance, no matter how justified the officer may have felt in his remarks."

"Sir, I stand by Commander Owderkirk and Lieutenant Commander Tice's actions," Bolan said flatly.

Malinverni fixed him with a steady look.

"Obviously so do I, or Owderkirk wouldn't be pinning on captain and overseeing air group certification in about six months, nor would Tice be in line to be CAG-*Scharnhorst*," Malinverni stated. "Neither of them know about those promotions either, so keep that under your hat."

"Sir you're not leaving much of my...*the* wardroom aboard," Bolan protested. "Whomever's taking over is going to have to basically build their team from scratch minus the XO."

"The medicos tell me Lieutenant Owderkirk probably should consider another line of work unless she likes getting bone nannite treatments. I think she can do wonders for engineering plant development while her husband's training the next generation of idiots," Malinverni replied. "You'd almost think I try to figure out how to best benefit officers and the Fleet."

Bolan heard the mild rebuke in Malinverni's voice.

Time to take that exit off the highway to hell before I end up Fleet liaison to a prison planet, Bolan thought.

"I didn't think Lieutenant Owderkirk had gotten off as easily as CAG and Doc had hoped," Bolan sighed.

"Well from her test scores and fitness reports, she's probably best in research than operations anyway," Malinverni replied.

"Understood Sir, it just seems as if my wardroom's getting torn apart," Bolan replied, then mentally kicked himself.

Malinverni gave a slight chuckle that lacked any real mirth.

"Take more than your fair share of objectives, and you will be given more than your fair share of objectives to take," Malinverni said. "You of all people should know that success can earn you a ticket to perdition, just in a nicer car."

Why do I hate the way that sounds? Bolan thought to himself.

Malinverni's communicator beeped before Bolan could say anything aloud. Looking at the screen, Malinverni frowned.

"Well Commodore Bolan, I apparently have a priority message from Minister Bloodworth and you have a visitor," Malinverni said. "Looks like we'll have to cut this short."

The Fleet Admiral stood, and Bolan rose with him.

"Those orders take effect in thirty days," Malinverni said. "The rest of the personnel orders will be following within the next twelve hours, and your replacements will arrive in fourteen days."

"Understood, Sir," Bolan said, still perturbed.

"I think you'll find BuShips is not the hell hole you think it is," Malinverni stated with a smile. "Plus I will need good ships and I'll need them fast, and I suspect you of all people will make sure the Fleet is not getting shafted in the bargain."

As he said the last, Malinverni opened the door just in time to startle a tall, lithe woman with olive skin, brown eyes, and black hair on the other side. Dressed in a skirted formal uniform that looked expertly tailored, the woman wore the silver diamonds indicating she was a commander on her shoulder and a black arm band with a silver 'S' in the center. She had been extending one well-manicured finger towards Bolan's door console when it opened to reveal Malinverni, a black attaché case gripped in her left hand. Stepping back and coming to attention in one graceful motion, the woman regarded them both with an expression that indicated it was not unusual to run into the Fleet's senior officer.

"Fleet Admiral Malinverni, Commodore Bolan," the woman said evenly.

"At ease, Commander Fletcher," Malinverni said gently. The woman's face briefly exhibited a moment of shock that the Fleet Admiral knew her name, but she quickly recovered as Malinverni continued. "I'll let you get about your business and find my aide."

Bolan started to bring up his communicator but stopped as Admiral Malinverni held up his hand.

"I'd like to roam a little bit, Commodore," Malinverni said. "I'm reasonably certain whatever Minister Bloodworth has for me can wait."

I get the feeling he's making the Minister wait for the hell of it, Bolan thought as he watched the Fleet Admiral move off. *Which means he hasn't told me everything that's going on.* Malinverni was many things. Petty wasn't one of them. Nor was needlessly vindictive.

"Sir?" the commander asked in a soft contralto, breaking Bolan from his thoughts. He saw that her eyes were slightly wet even as her face betrayed calmness.

"Sorry Commander Fletcher, I realize you're on Shiva Detail," Bolan said, gesturing towards the black armband. "Tell me who you're here for and I'll put you in touch with their division head."

Shiva Detail. The one job no officer wants, to travel the galaxy carrying out your comrade's final wishes, Bolan thought as the officer gathered herself.

"Commodore Bolan, I'm here for you," Commander Fletcher replied.

*Oh. **That** Commander Fletcher*, Bolan thought stupidly, feeling slightly light headed.

"I'm sorry, Anna, you don't look anything like the picture Leslie had of you," Bolan heard himself saying. It was if his voice was coming from far away, the words hanging in the air as Commander Fletcher looked at him with a wan smile.

"It's the hair, Sir. That and the twenty years I've been shouting at her to stop using that picture. 'Oh, so you want me to keep a good

321

picture of you so I can lose it if I have to abandon ship,'" Fletcher said, the last in a mocking impression of Leslie Hawkins' voice.

Bolan found himself fighting hard not to laugh at Fletcher, a thin smile making it through the lid he'd held on his emotions for the past couple of weeks.

"Sir, there are some things I have for you to sign and a holographic message," Fletcher said crisply, the muscles around her dark brown eyes twitching. Bolan recognized the flatness for what it was, an attempt to maintain her emotional control. He felt his own throat constricting and swallowed hard.

"This way," he rasped, gesturing back into the appropriated day cabin. Clearly not trusting her voice, Commander Fletcher nodded.

"I've..." Bolan began, his voice quavering. "I've sent my steward..."

"...away because you're in port," Fletcher finished for him. The tears came then, rushing down her cheeks in a flood. Frantic, the commander put the attaché case down and grabbed a handkerchief from her pocket.

"I'm sorry Sir, I'm..." she started to say, her voice shaking. Bolan quickly stepped in and wrapped his arms around Fletcher, his own eyes burning as the commander sobbed quietly into his chest. They stood that way for several long minutes, until with a deep, shuddering intake of breath Fletcher gently extricated herself.

"I saw her right before she left," Commander Fletcher said, her voice hollow. "Major Acheros gave Leslie her orders at Battle Station *Malta*, so when I heard the *Shigure* had been destroyed at Zed-815, I figured there had been an error."

Well yes, there should be no way a destroyer can jump that distance...unless she's got a Herbert drive, Bolan thought bitterly.

"I wish there had been," Bolan replied thickly.

"If I'd known that was going to be last time I saw her, I'd have said so much more," Commander Fletcher said softly. "Her memorial service is in two weeks on White Isle."

Bolan nodded.

"I think I've got some time freed up," he said. "*Constitution*'s going to be in the yard for awhile and I'll be transitioning to my next assignment."

"I hope to see you there, Sir," his visitor stated. "Ashlea will be glad to get a chance to talk to you again."

Bolan closed his eyes, forcing back the urge to pound the desk in anger.

Leslie's mother is a great woman, Bolan thought. *Who didn't deserve to lose her only daughter.*

"I wish I'd been the one to tell her," Commander Fletcher continued. "But we were riding herd on that Spartan cruiser all the way back to Diasporan space. Either they've lied about the hyperspace capabilities on those new engines of theirs, or that captain needs to avoid any casinos for about the next century due to using up all her luck."

*If that big Spartan bitch was able to keep pace with the **Golan** we may be in both better and worse shape than I thought as a species*, Bolan thought. *Must have been hell on the life support though.*

The commodore watched as Fletcher finished setting up the holographic projector, made one last check of the power supply, then pressed the button starting the recording. Touching the controls in his chair, Bolan dimmed the day cabin's lights.

After a couple moments, a miniature Leslie Hawkins appeared in the air above the day cabin's desk. To Bolan's surprise, the woman's hologram was dressed in a bright green formal gown, it's cut far more revealing than the version in the holopicture on his desk but obviously by the same designer. Bolan felt his heart lurch, the dim emptiness that had been lurking in the background of his mind coming fully forward.

"Ha!" the miniature Leslie said, her tone playful. "Right now you're looking at the picture on your desk, then looking at me, then looking back and wondering when I got this dress made. Anna, meanwhile, is looking all serious and sad."

Bolan looked across the desk to find a startled look suddenly supplanting the melancholy one on Anna's face. The two of them simultaneously laughed as the holographic Leslie looked back and forth between them.

"See, that wasn't so hard, was it?" the little figure asked.

God she knew us so well, Bolan thought as "Leslie" cracked a small smile.

"So to nip this in the bud, no the boffins didn't figure out some way to get me bundled up in a tiny escape pod or teleport my essence across the galaxy," Leslie continued brightly. "If you're watching this, Mackenzie, I'm well and truly dead or at least long enough missing that Anna is carrying out my last will and testament."

Bolan looked over at Commander Fletcher and saw the hologram's brightness reflected in the wet streaks down her cheeks. His own eyes began to sting as Leslie continued.

An Unproven Concept

"Well I probably completely fucked up and never sent you the message Anna and I always talked about, and one of the advantages of likely being space debris is I can say this now without fear of messing up either of our careers," Leslie said, her eyes seeming to look into Bolan's. "Mackenzie William Bolan, I love you. I love you, I love you, I love you, I love you, I love you, and, just to be sure you understand, I love you."

The words hit Bolan like a runaway hovertank as Leslie continued, her tone sorrowful yet somehow sounding as if a great weight was off her shoulders.

"Maker, I should have said on that damn island, I should have screened it to you as soon as the Senate testimony was over, I should have said it before I invited you to my change of command, and I should have came to you taking over the *Constitution* and screamed it to everyone at the ceremony."

Holographic Leslie took a deep breath, dabbing at her eyes.

"Turn it off," Bolan rasped, feeling his chest compress.

"Anna if you touch those controls I will wake the twins up every single day you're on Shiva Detail," Leslie's hologram turned and snapped, stopping Commander Fletcher in her tracks. "I told Jessica about this message, so I'd suggest you think long and hard about it. You know she believes people can reach back across the veil."

Fletcher's hand stopped, and she gave Bolan an apologetic shrug. Taking one last extra second to glare at her friend, Leslie turned back towards Bolan.

"Mackenzie, you big, lovable oaf, your problem has always been, and probably will always be, that you think if you just shelter your heart hard enough then you'll never be vulnerable," Leslie said. "Unfortunately you seem to have a habit of attracting women who let you give them 85% of yourself as it beats the hell out of most men's 100%."

Bolan gripped his chair arm rests like a man being electrified, knowing that if he hit stop on the hologram now he'd never replay it.

I won't disrespect Leslie like that, no matter how much this hurts, he thought, choking back the urge to sob.

"Well, I'm one to talk about relationships, but the great thing about being dead is I get to be utterly honest," Leslie continued with a wry smile. "Honestly you are too great and wonderful a man to be alone, Mackenzie. I wish we'd been stuck on that island forever, not just long enough to make sure some angry Spartans didn't kill us before we could give our testimony. I wish I'd had a chance to love you and be married to you forever."

The last was said with a winsome smile that was the final crack in Bolan's dam. Great, convulsive sobs came from his chest as the miniature Leslie paused, then raised her hand as if she knew what was going on.

"Anna, if he's actually stopped being Mr. Duranium Soul, could you hold him for me?" Leslie asked softly. Bolan dimly registered the sound of Commander Fletcher's heels on the deck, then felt her arms go around him.

"As for you, Mackenzie, I would ask, as my last request, that you just let someone in," Leslie said plaintively. "Grieve for me if you're going to, but don't let me be the reason you put another inch of metal around your heart. I hope you always remember that I loved you, and I hope whomever you find next is willing to share because I'm going to be waiting for you if there's anything on the other side."

With that last bit, the message stopped, leaving Leslie with her hand stretched out towards him. Taking a long, last shuddering breath, Mackenzie gave Commander Fletcher a final squeeze then reached inside his desk for a handkerchief.

"Thank you, Commander," Commodore Bolan said, his voice quavering.

"You're welcome, Sir. Leslie said in my message I could not listen to the message before I showed it to you," Commander Fletcher replied, fighting back her own tears as she smiled. "Now I see why, that little imp."

Bolan shook his head.

"She did have a mischievous streak," he thought, his memory going unbidden to a bikini clad Leslie walking nonchalantly up behind him.

"Sir, forgive me for prying, but what did Leslie mean when she said 'the island'?" Commander Fletcher asked, startling Bolan.

I see she took secrecy as serious as I did, he thought. *If she didn't tell her best friend…*

Bolan took a deep breath, standing from the chair and walking compulsively to the hatch before he realized he was being silly.

It's the admiral's day cabin, he thought. *Not only is that door soundproofed, there are active countermeasures to prevent eavesdropping in the corridor and ceiling.*

"Sir, if you don't want to tell me," Commander Fletcher said rapidly, her voice anxious.

"I think, when it's us, you can call me Mackenzie," Bolan replied with a smile. "I mean, I nearly blew snot bubbles all over your uniform, I think we're past formalities. You are...*were* Leslie's best friend, and deserve to know. You want something to drink?"

Commander Fletcher raised an eyebrow, then shook her head and giggled.

"Sorry Sir, bad experiences with senior officers," she said, drawing a sympathetic glance from Bolan. "I'd love a soft drink, whatever you have."

Five minutes later, they had resumed their seats around the holographic Leslie. Although neither of them said anything, Bolan had the sense that by mutual understanding they each wanted to feel as if she was there with them.

"To fallen comrades," Bolan said softly, raising his glass. Commander Fletcher did the same, settling in as he began.

"You know all about us blasting the Spartan Separatist station and being immediately ordered back to the nearest base. You may also recall that the *Vincennes* disappeared for sixty days, to the point where there was a rumor we'd been intercepted by Spartans and the Fleet was trying to keep a lid on things."

Commander Fletcher nodded, her face grim.

"Si—Mackenzie, I thought the shit was hitting the fan," she said. "I was in Eurasian Space on the *Darwin* when the Separatist task force exited hyperspace over Dokken."

Not much worse than being on an **Atlanta**-*class when there's about to be a railgun fight*, Bolan mentally winced.

"Yeah, well, things weren't much better on a heavily damaged cruiser that Fleet kept having jump to keep our location secret," Bolan replied wearily. "We skipped around for a week, when suddenly we got coordinates that had us meeting up with a tug, a freighter, and ten chartered liners."

Bolan's face grew distant for a moment, and he took a long pull of his drink.

"Fleet Headquarters came up with the insane, albeit effective, plan to wholesale replace the crew of the *Vincennes* with that of the *Nagasaki* then scatter all of us to the four winds," Bolan continued. "It wasn't well received by either crew, but we got forty-eight hours to put all of our personal effects on the freighter, then divvy the crew up among the ten liners."

"Oh shit, I can imagine how that went over," Commander Fletcher replied.

"It got better," Bolan continued. "Once on the liners, we found out that we were all to be separated and sent to random worlds based solely on the luck of a draw and random computer. The rear admiral in charge nearly had us draw again when Leslie and I ended up on the same planet, as he didn't want to simplify the 'Spartan assassins' job' as he put it."

"I do wonder if someone was supposed to kill you," Commander Fletcher said grimly. "Hell, if Senator Modi hadn't shown up with half the remaining Spartan forces and threatened to open fire on the Separatists things might have gotten very interesting."

"Yes," Bolan replied. "But I didn't find out about that until after three ship changes and a shuttle later when Leslie and I were dropped off at a honeymoon cabin in the Transvaal."

Commander Fletcher's eyes nearly bugged out of her head at that one. She looked at the hologram, her mouth open.

"You little bitch, you are so lucky I can't shake you right now," she said, the heat lost in the look of utter shock on her face. "All this time I thought you guys had never ever…wait, I'm making an idiot of myself."

Bolan couldn't maintain the stern face, a smile finally cracking his visage.

"You're getting as bad as her," Anna said, then crestfallen continued. "Or bad as she *was*."

Bolan stared at his glass.

"You don't know the half of it," Bolan replied. "Nor am I going to tell you. I agree with her, it was the best month and a half of our lives…and when that shuttle came back for us we mutually decided that it would be best if we acted like it never happened. Especially given the allegations made against us by Du prior to the Senate testimony."

Fletcher's face clouded.

"I hope that man rots in Hell," the woman stated fiercely, her face coloring slightly.

"If Leslie hadn't rushed in and damaged one of the cruisers or I'd been a little slower off the jump, you'd have your wish granted," Bolan replied softly.

Commander Fletcher's chronometer chimed, and she cursed at the device.

"I thought I'd shut that alarm off," she said, fussing at her wrist. The glance down obviously triggered her memory, as she reached down and opened the attaché case.

"There was one more thing I was supposed to give you," she said. Reaching in, she pulled out a black box that was slightly larger than a softbound book. Passing her hand over the front of the box,

An Unproven Concept

Commander Fletcher simultaneously flicked down an internal stand. After a moment's hum, the front of the box grew transparent and revealed itself to be a holopicture frame. The first picture to present itself was of a familiar looking ancient Terran paperback cover. Seeing it, Bolan began to laugh. Commander Fletcher looked at the picture, then back at Bolan, then back at the holopicture again.

"While there's a slight resemblance, I'm obviously not getting the joke," Commander Fletcher said, watching as the picture shifted to another paperback cover. "And none of those four men look anything like you either."

Bolan smiled as the titles kept cycling through.

"It's an inside joke," Bolan replied, feeling both incredibly loved and massively sad at the same time. "I'll have to tell you about the classic works of men's action adventure and 20th century authors' fascination with dystopia at a later date."

Warhawk Wardroom
1130 SST
11 July

"Well either Peaches has you well trained or you're truly worried about her eating that pound cake," Lieutenant Commander Tice observed archly. "Because every other male in this place is having to put his eyeballs back in thanks to that commander who just walked in."

Jason steeled himself as Andrea paused with her fork halfway to her mouth. Every aviation wardroom had its traditions, and the Warhawks' was that everyone, regardless of rank or station, got a callsign the first time they ate in the compartment. As it was generally considered impolite to bring guests into an aviation wardroom until a ship was officially on her first cruise, Andrea had not taken a meal there before *Constitution*'s fight with the three alien cruisers. Thus, "Peaches" was shorthand for "Peach Fuzz," the nickname bestowed upon her by Bulls Five.

Please don't go catastrophic...please don't go catastrophic... Jason thought as he studiously looked at the Warhawks' livery and heritage items lining the black and gold bulkheads around them. Andrea's moods had been somewhat mercurial, which was a standard side effect of the radiation treatments. Finding out the night before she was effectively done being on warships hadn't helped her disposition.

328

"Come now, Catnip, surely you're not upset at having to actually share the male attention for once," Andrea replied evenly, then popped her cake into her mouth.

Tice smiled, and Jason was pleasantly surprised it actually reached the woman's eyes.

Those two seem to have warmed up over the last couple of weeks, Jason thought to himself. Must have been Tice helping Andrea out with all the casualty detail paperwork during their watch. With the dramatic thinning of available watch officers, *Constitution*'s XO had been forced to shuffle things around to ensure there were senior department heads available at all hours for the Bath Yard workers. Jason didn't think it was coincidence that had seen Commander Alexander place Andrea and Tice on the same shift.

"You will note that not all of us are as unprofessional as that young *Basilisk* driver two tables over," a male voice interjected, causing Jason to look behind him.

Speak of the devil, he thought as the XO slid into the empty chair to his left while Tice stood up to correct her wayward pilot. The young officer visibly colored as Tice chewed on him, her tone low but her facial expression harder than diamond.

"Of course, some of us realize that not only is the lovely Anna Fletcher married, her tastes run more towards the lovely Lieutenant Owderkirk or Lieutenant Commander Tice," Commander Alexander continued. He waited until Commander Fletcher had finished placing her order with the steward manning the food replicator and turned towards the room. Waving, he caught the woman's attention.

"Aren't you going to warn her about the..." Jason started, but realized he was too late as Fletcher stepped over the broad, bright yellow line painted on the rubber matting just before the dining area. Commander Fletcher jumped as a loud, raucous siren sounded from the room's back corner. Jason caught the start of a sly smile before Commander Alexander resumed his poker face.

Guess I'm the senior officer present, Jason thought, coming to his feet.

"Welcome to the wardroom of the best air group in the whole damned Fleet," he roared at the top of his lungs. The cry led to several raucous cheers from the other personnel present.

Commander Fletcher looked at him like he'd lost his mind, a flush coming to her cheeks as he continued.

"As you can clearly see, the stripe behind you says that you must stop and identify yourself before entering our hallowed halls,"

Jason said, pointing to the broad band. "Since our interloper clearly cannot read, perhaps someone present would like to suggest a name for our guest?"

"Dogmeat!" someone shouted.

"Blindman!" came another voice almost simultaneously.

"Eyesore!" was a couple moments later. Jason held up his left hand, thoughtfully rubbing his chin with his right.

"Yes, yes…Eyesore seems to have a ring to it," he replied, drawing a smattering of applause. "Welcome to the Warhawks, Eyesore!"

"Uh, thank you, Commander," Commander Fletcher replied, a stunned look on her face as if she wasn't sure what had just happened. She made her way across the compartment to their table, glaring at Commander Alexander as she sat down.

"Well Tristan, so glad you're *still* leading me into traps all these years later," the woman said. "Leslie would be proud."

The XO gave Commander Fletcher a sad grin.

"Well someone's got to take up her practical jokes," he replied. Gesturing at her armband, he gave Commander Fletcher an inquisitive look. "What brings you to the *Constitution*?"

"Seems that Commodore Bolan and Leslie were closer than I knew," Commander Fletcher said easily. She looked over at Jason, Andrea and Lieutenant Commander Tice.

"I'm sorry, we're being rude," the woman said. "My name is Anna Fletcher."

"Jason Owderkirk," Jason said, then waited for Tice and Andrea to make their introductions.

There was a stir just as Andrea was finishing telling Commander Fletcher about herself. Looking up, Jason saw that Lieutenant Colonel Nishizawa, Lieutenant Commander Iokepa, and Major Acheros had just come through the door. Looking at his watch, he cursed.

"Well I guess lunch took longer than we expected, XO," he started to say apologetically, then stopped as he saw the look on Commander Fletcher's face as she looked at Iokepa and Acheros. Feeling her gaze on them, the two men both simultaneously turned towards Jason's table, the scarred Iokepa stopping mid-sentence.

"Excuse me for a moment," Commander Fletcher said, pushing back her chair. To Jason's surprise, the trio greeted each other with obvious mutual respect. He watched as Commander Fletcher took the time to continue talking to *Shigure*'s former XO and Acheros.

I get the distinct feeling there's a story there, Jason thought.

"Eat you idiot," Andrea said sharply, drawing a smile from Tice. Jason dug in while making a note to ask how the three of them knew each other.

"I think I'm going to look forward to working in propulsion research," Andrea said quietly, resting her hand on Jason's arm as he wolfed down his food. He nearly choked on the bite in his mouth, reaching for his water glass to get the particle out of the way.

"Okay, who are you and what have you done with my wife?" Jason asked, looking at her incredulously. He noticed that Tice and Alexander were both studiously looking elsewhere.

"I nearly killed her," Andrea replied simply. "Maybe it was just finishing up the last of the casualty kits after I got the news, or it's the belief that everything happens for a reason. Ten minutes difference and it'd been me getting sifted into one of those radioactive containers and shot towards the system primary."

Jason turned to look at Andrea. He saw pain in her eyes as her hand gripped his arm. She leaned in closer to his ear.

"Plus if I'm going to be dirtside, maybe we can start working on screwing for keeps rather than just enjoying the practice," she whispered throatily. He turned to look at her, a look of pure mischief on her face.

I really hope I don't have to stand up right now, he thought. Little minx.

Biko
0800 Local Time (2245 SST)
12 July

As he walked along the peat covered sea bluff, the cold onshore wind just barely held outside by his coat, Marcus pondered the meaning of his life.

I feel like I should be muttering about slings, arrows, and luck, he thought bitterly, gazing out over the dark green expanse of Biko's ocean. At roughly eighty percent water and with only one functioning space port, the planet was quite possibly one of the most remote locations in the entire Confederation outside of a prison planet. Which suited Marcus just fine, as he was somewhat sick of people in all their various forms.

Three false identities and almost five hundred thousand credits later, I think I may have finally bought my solitude, Marcus thought. *Freedom on the other hand may be a bit more difficult...or it's only a*

331

few steps away. Walking up to the low retaining wall, he leaned over and glanced down at the swirling depths below.

Hamlet was a piker, he thought, the banality of his quip bringing a bitter smile to his face. *That's at least three hundred meters, so one lean and I'm reasonably certain they'd never find my body.* Biko's ocean life made the term "apex predator" seem somewhat quaint and archaic, so even if he somehow survived the fall it'd probably be mere seconds before something finished off what gravity had not.

"Contemplating existence or just enjoying the view?" a female voice called out from behind him. Turning away from the wall, Marcus looked at his interlocutor as his hand gripped the energy pistol in his pocket. The woman stood roughly ten yards away, wearing a coat that looked only slightly less bulky than his own parka. He could not tell what color her hair was underneath her tightly closed hood and the green balaclava underneath it, but the woman's hazel eyes were somehow familiar to him. Although it was hard to tell what her body looked like through the layers of clothing, Marcus got the impression the woman was either a swimmer or grappling martial artist.

"Maybe a bit of both," Marcus replied honestly. The woman walked up to the retaining wall, looked over, then shook her head.

"There's got to be easier and quicker ways," she said flatly. Listening to her accent, Marcus had trouble placing it in the high winds coming off the ocean.

"I've seen worse," Marcus replied wearily. The woman glanced at him, and Marcus could have sworn he saw a flicker of concern on her face.

"I would say I can't think of much worse than having my leg ripped off by a thirty foot fish, but your face tells me I might need to get out more. My name's Gruoch," the woman said, the moniker rhyming with hooch.

Marcus felt a nagging feeling in the back of his mind, but pushed it aside for a moment.

"Marcus," he said, shocked at himself for telling the woman his actual name.

To his pleasant surprise, the woman's eyes never broadened or otherwise gave any indication she'd recognized his first name.

"Well Marcus, I'm going to keep on my walk," she said. "If you don't decide to see what Biko's oceans have to offer first hand, my place is about three kilometers behind you. I just got here yesterday."

Marcus heard the implied question in her statement but chose to ignore it.

"Actually I'll walk with you," Marcus replied. "It'll be nice to have some company for once and I'm actually just a couple of kilometers beyond you."

As the two of them walked, Marcus found that Gruoch had come to Biko due to her mother's recent death. The woman was estranged from her father, and Marcus got the impression she blamed him for her mother's passing. While he was curious to ask for details, he figured more information would be forthcoming. As for his part, Marcus gave minimal answers as they walked, simply letting out that he was in between jobs and currently comfortable enough that he could avoid working for awhile.

"Well here we are," Gruoch said brightly. Quickly looking over the cabin, Marcus could see no outward sign her story didn't pan out. He'd walked or ran by the structure at least a half dozen times and noticed its lack of inhabitants, so Gruoch's timeline seemed to be legitimate.

Besides, it's not like I'd really care about dying at this point, he thought. *If Death's a big sleep I don't give a fuck, just as long as the nightmares stop.*

As Gruoch stepped up the walk in front of him, Marcus was surprised to find himself at least having the thought of checking her out even if it didn't get much beyond the thinking phase. Stepping through the door, she turned to look at him.

"You coming in or we having coffee out there?" she asked nonplussed. Shrugging, Marcus stepped through the door…and leapt back out it, energy pistol coming out of his pocket as Aimi Eguchi stepped into view across the cabin's single open room.

"Please don't shoot her," Gruoch said slowly from beside him. "It'd be hell on the security deposit."

Marcus noted that Aimi kept her hands in plain view as she stood before him. The former Du body guard was dressed in a form fitting crimson long-sleeved shirt, pale blue denim pants, and black flats. Her hair, even a lighter brown than previously, hung long and straight down the front of her body. With a start, he realized the hairstyle was intended to show Marcus she was completely unarmed.

Or as unarmed as someone like her ever is, he thought. *I'm sure there's a blade on her still.*

Gruoch moved over to the old style coffee machine, inserted a capsule, then placed a cup underneath the drip device. Reaching up, she lowered her hood and took off her balaclava in a pair of swift movements. At that moment recognition hit Marcus like a ton of bricks, the dark ringlets and angular face clearly a combination bred from two people who's faces he'd never forget for the rest of his life.

Well Mei and Senator Du apparently have a good mix of genetic stew, he thought.

"I thought your name was Juliet?" he seethed. The woman looked over her shoulder at him as she unzipped her coat to reveal an outfit identical to Aimi's minus her jeans being black rather than blue.

"Juliet Gruoch Gertrude Du," the woman replied flatly. "I think you'd recognize Romeo's late lover and Hamlet's mother, but not even my closest friends recognize Lady Macbeth's first name. I don't think my father and dear old Aimi misjudged your Shakespearean knowledge that badly."

"It's been my experience that the Du family attack dog and her master tend to underestimate me," Marcus spat, noting that Aimi was still just standing in the hallway. To his surprise, Gruoch laughed at his comment.

"Aimi come!" the woman called out as she walked over to the table with her coffee mug and some sugar. Aimi fixed Gruoch with a glare so heated Marcus was amazed the brunette's curls didn't catch fire. Ignoring Aimi, Gruoch sat down and primly crossed her legs as she started to drink from her coffee.

"You may notice that Aimi doesn't respond to my commands very well," Gruoch said apologetically as she made a face then added sugar to her drink. "Indeed, she's only here to keep you from blowing my head off in a fit of rage, fear or both."

The woman looked across the kitchen at Marcus, her face tired.

" Of course, Aimi tells me that her presence would not necessarily help that cause," Gruoch said, "but my father insisted that I have company."

I cannot escape that man, can I? Marcus thought bitterly.

"So does he care that much about you because it helps his image, or because getting the genetic recipe just right for baby cake mix is a bit difficult?" Marcus said.

Gruoch's face clouded, and Marcus noted that her knuckles whitened on the coffee cup she was drinking from.

"You could actually show some respect to Gruoch," Aimi spat. "She has done…"

"I can handle Mr. Martin myself, Aimi," Gruoch snapped. Aimi gave a snort that indicated her opinion on that hypothesis, but fell silent.

"So tell me, Marcus, do you hate me just because you think I was genetically created or because of my last name?" Gruoch asked pleasantly. "Wait, before you answer, why don't you actually take that coat off? You can even take that energy pistol back out of its pocket and point it at me if it'll make you feel better."

I want to do so much more than point it at you, Marcus thought, briefly considering if he could get Gruoch and Aimi both.

"Before you keep thinking about double homicide, I would submit that *I* have never actually done *anything* to you, Marcus," Gruoch said softly. "I'll even go one better and state that if my father hadn't brought so many people along, albeit with intent to kill you and everyone aboard *Titanic*, things might not have gone as well as they did."

"*Gone as well as they did?!*" Marcus exploded. "Are you out of your fucking mind?"

Gruoch took a long pull from her coffee cup.

"I'm sorry, is this the point where we get into a chest beating contest on which one of us lost more?" she said, and Marcus saw true pain in the woman's eyes even if her face was stoic. "Because I'm pretty sure we're both out fiancées, and I don't recall *your* mother bleeding to death in a ballroom."

Marcus looked at the woman for a brief moment as he wondered who her fiancée had been.

Well at least if she's here to kill you it's probably going to be quick in order to avoid complications, he thought. Stepping to the side, he pulled the energy pistol out and placed it on the counter beside him, then shrugged out of his coat. Hanging the garment on the room's second coat tree, Marcus then put the energy pistol in the hideout holster at the small of his back before beginning to fix a mug of coffee.

"Okay, if you're not here to kill me, what brings you to Biko other than the wonderful weather?" Marcus asked evenly.

"I was not kidding when I implied I was angry with my father for my mother's death," Gruoch said, relief in her voice. Aimi came into the kitchen then very slowly and deliberately took the furthest seat from Martin at the kitchen table. "But I'm actually here to offer you a job."

Marcus was so shocked he lost track of where his hands were. The hot liquid on the back of his hand brought him back to reality, and he jumped back from the coffee machine with a curse. Recovering quickly, he spun back to the kitchen table…and found Aimi and Gruoch both staring at him with bemused smiles on their faces.

"I'm glad you both find this so amusing," he snapped.

An Unproven Concept

Aimi gave an exasperated snort, turning to Gruoch then back to Martin.

"If I or she wanted you dead, do you think maybe a rail gun round while you're taking your morning walk would have done the trick?" Aimi snapped. "I mean, you're heavy but not so damn heavy we can't get you over that cliff wall."

Marcus stopped from where he was dabbing at the burn with a wet cloth.

"Glad to see you planned out killing me in your head," he replied heatedly.

"Well I hear I'm wicked good with a *Kabano*," Aimi responded.

"Do I need to leave you two alone for a few minutes to work out your differences?" Gruoch asked, clearly irritated. "I would suggest the master bedroom, as I'm pretty sure this table's not going to hold up to that sort of pounding."

"I'd sooner sleep with whatever's out in that ocean," Marcus snapped. "Been there, done that, and I'm pretty sure the original was better than the new model."

Aimi looked at him, her mouth wide in shock.

Finally knocked her speechless, Martin thought, allowing a grin to come to his face as his opponent colored. Out of the corner of his eye he saw Gruoch fight back her own smirk.

"You insufferable pig," Aimi screamed. "We are not all alike!"

"Yeah, yeah, yeah, tell it to someone who cares," Marcus replied dismissively.

"I must say, Marcus, your hatred of genetic clones makes me glad I'm actually not one," Gruoch said quietly, drawing a look from Aimi. "She is right, you know—it's not like she came off an assembly line."

"Tell it to the woman who has an evilgasm at the thought of shoving me off a damn cliff," Marcus snapped.

"For someone who claims to know us Spartans so well, you are incredibly ignorant at times," Aimi seethed.

"Oh really? That's why you looked at me like you wanted to cut out my liver the first time I ever set eyes on you."

"For he today who sheds his blood with me," Gruoch interrupted before Aimi could respond. "Sound familiar, Marcus?"

"*Henry VIII*," Marcus responded.

"*Henry V*, actually," Gruoch said. "But the larger point is this: By Spartan custom, shedding one's blood while fighting against a common enemy alleviates all previous blood feuds between two parties

336

or groups. Diasporan law *explicitly* states this in the case of meeting extraterrestrials or non-humans."

"So in other words I didn't need to worry about this crazy chick chasing me all over the galaxy trying to tie up Senator Du's loose ends?" Marcus said incredulously.

"Oh, if you'd broken *Omerta* and informed any authorities about what the Senator had planned, yes," Aimi said, her tone only slightly less angry than it had been before.

"What?!" Marcus asked, thoroughly confused.

"Since turning Fleet Admiral Malinverni against my father would have been a hostile act, that would have reignited at least some part of your feud," Gruoch said, her tone annoyed. "Or maybe some people here just like killing."

"I do not just like killing," Aimi snapped.

"No, you are just always doing it," Gruoch replied, rolling her eyes.

"I'm thinking it might be a genetic disposition," Marcus said without missing a beat. Gruoch bleated out a surprised sound as Aimi turned her focus between her two tormentors.

"Did you bring me along so you could share in mutual sport?" the woman seethed.

"Oh, I'm sorry, where are my manners?" Gruoch said teasingly. "Heaven forbid I poke fun at the great, immutable Aimi."

"It's going to be kinda hard to tell me about this job offer if Miss Perpetually Pissed has her hands around your neck," Marcus observed, starting to grin beside himself. "Especially since I'm not pulling her off you."

"Aimi and I have previously settled our differences," Gruoch said easily. "We're not allowed to do that anymore."

Marcus looked at Aimi, her lips pursed so tightly they'd almost lost their color, then back to the slightly smirking Gruoch.

Holy shit, a Du with a sense of humor, he thought. *Or at least part of one.*

"Beat that ass, did she, Aimi?" Marcus asked.

"I wouldn't say I beat her ass," Gruoch allowed. "At least not the first three times."

"The job offer…" Aimi started to bite out.

"Oh no, I'm much more enjoying this conversation," Marcus said. "You know, I don't recall Katina ever losing hand to hand to anyone. Maybe my comment about the copy and the original doesn't just apply to…"

Aimi slammed her hand down on the table.

"If you would like to discuss my hand to hand abilities first hand, *Marcus*, we may do so any time *after Gruoch tells you why we are here!*" Aimi snarled.

There was a moment of stunned silence as Gruoch and Marcus looked at the red faced blonde. Taking a deep breath and closing her eyes, Aimi visibly regained control of her temper.

"I don't think I've seen you lose your temper like that in years," Gruoch remarked conversationally.

"I have," Marcus said evenly.

"Yes, it was a few hours before Finnegan burned to death in his armor," Aimi replied quietly. Gruoch reacted as if Aimi had struck her as Marcus looked at the woman in shock.

"Verbal jousting has suddenly lost its appeal, hasn't it?" Aimi continued. To his surprise, Marcus saw a tear start to roll down Aimi's cheek.

"You bitch," Gruoch replied, her voice quavering. "I think you've served your purpose here."

I'm guessing Finnegan was Gruoch's fiancé, Marcus thought. He hadn't realized what had happened to the man until after the tribunal. The Spartan had been wounded by the final explosion, then had the hot gases from the methane enter his *Hoplite* armor and literally cook him alive.

"I am not your servant to dismiss, Gruoch," Aimi said lowly, her voice dangerous.

"Fuck you then," Gruoch said, pushing back from the table. She turned and strode off to one of the cabin's back rooms, slamming the heavy wooden door behind her. Marcus looked across the cabin's common room to the closed door, then back at Aimi.

"You know, just because I wasn't carried in someone's belly for nine months does not mean I'm some unfeeling robot," Aimi seethed. As if awaiting some trigger, the tears began streaming down her face. "Finnegan was my friend. *Laoban* was sometimes the closest thing to a mother I ever had."

Marcus felt the urge to walk over and embrace the woman.

She seems so lost, he thought. *Fuck it.* Pushing back his chair, he strode over and put his arms around Aimi and held her. After a moment the woman's arms shot up and she clung to him with a grip of iron, tremendous cries rending from her throat as she shook against him. He ran his hand through her hair as he fought back his own urge to join her keening, his own body shaking with emotion.

Well if someone had told me that was going to happen the next time I saw Aimi, I might have questioned their sanity, Marcus thought a couple hours later as he stood back in his own cabin. The two had eventually moved to the couch where they had sat in companionable silence. It was only the pinging of Marcus' chronometer that had broken the mood, at which point he remembered that he'd left his provisions sitting on the counter awaiting his return. The two had separated with a hug, and Marcus hadn't even had the urge to check for a topical poison.

An orange and white four-legged form awaited him on the front porch.

"Well hello Mr. Boskins," he said, greeting the cabin owner's large feline. The tomcat meowed back a greeting, the sound surprisingly loud from its thirty pound frame.

No matter the size or the planet, cats seem to always still think they're gods, he thought with a smile. Reaching down he stroked the cat's ears and was rewarded with a gentle lick of its raspy tongue. Boskins had marked him as a sucker early on, and he let the cat inside to plop onto his couch. The cat watched him as he started putting the day's groceries away, tail twitching as he awaited his payment.

"Fine, fine, I'm sorry I'm late," Marcus said, handing over a slice of ham. Bleating with glee, the cat took his prize and headed for the door to be let out. Shaking his head, Marcus released the feline.

"Yeah, hey, thanks for coming by, glad to know you just use me for food," he said.

"The little monster's in a hurry because he knows he's late to our house," Gruoch said from the right of the door, almost causing Marcus to jump out of his skin. She held up Marcus' energy pistol.

Holy shit, he thought, reaching back for the hideout holster.

"I imagine Aimi and you must have really made nice if you forgot this," Gruoch observed snidely. "Or did she just pick your holster to prove she could do it without you noticing?"

"Probably the latter," Marcus allowed, startled to realize Aimi had a mischievous side. "Did you only bring it back to finish framing me for her murder?" Marcus asked.

Gruoch's face clouded.

"No. We're like sisters, for both good and bad. I'm sorry you had to see the bad," she replied.

"Evidence that Spartans are human after all?" Marcus chided gently.

Gruoch laughed.

339

"Fair enough," she replied with a smile.

"I doubt you came to find out what happened to Mr. Boskins," Marcus said. "Or just to give me my energy pistol, as grateful as I am to have it back."

"No, I came to finish our conversation," Gruoch replied, hugging herself in a manner that suggested she remembered just how the last conversation ended.

"Well come on in," Marcus replied. "I'm making breakfast although now I guess it's actually brunch."

"Sounds like a plan," Gruoch replied. "I haven't eaten since six."

As he cooked their eggs and bacon, Marcus watched Gruoch as she sat staring out his common window at the ocean. Adding vegetables and thick tomato slices, he slid the woman's sandwich over to her and sat down to eat his own.

"Were you really considering suicide earlier?" Gruoch asked as he was about to take his first bite.

Humans after all, but still blunter than the front end of a hover freight car, he thought, biting into the sandwich.

"Not exactly," Marcus replied after swallowing. "More thinking that it'd be nice to hit the reset button if there's reincarnation."

"I did," Gruoch stated flatly. "I miss Mom. I miss Raghnall. I cannot stop being irrationally angry at my father."

Not so sure that's irrational but let's go with it, Marcus thought to himself.

"You're thinking I should be angry with my father?" Gruoch asked, and Marcus cursed himself for how relaxed he'd allowed himself to get.

"The fact he and his detail did save my ass is the biggest reason I didn't tell Malinverni what I had figured out about his plan," Marcus said.

"But not the only reason?" Gruoch asked.

"I thought about Finnegan…"

"His name was Raghnall," Gruoch interrupted fiercely, pain in her voice.

"Raghnall. Rhee. Everyone else on your father's detail and how they didn't deserve to be known as would be terrorists," Marcus said. "Seemed pretty simple to me, especially when you add in just how little humanity needs to be fighting right now."

"You know my father thinks you're an incredibly honorable man," Gruoch said.

340

"I don't really give a tinker's damn if your father thinks I can split atoms with my teeth and shoot lasers out my ass," Marcus snapped, then took a deep breath. "Sorry."

"He's my father, not my deity," Gruoch said. "Even if he was, I'd tell him to go to whatever Hell he'd created."

Marcus laughed for a moment, drawing a quizzical look from Gruoch.

"Sorry, but I just had visions of your father with a long, gray beard and wearing a toga," Marcus said.

"Here I thought you were imagining what the Hell would look like," Gruoch replied.

"I get the feeling you're not here to ask me to be head of his security detail," Marcus said.

Gruoch sighed, her face maudlin.

"No, but let's be honest: You'd keep him alive if you took the job."

"It's always a bad sign when someone's flattering you before making you an offer," Marcus said slowly.

"Senator Modi would like you to serve as his military liaison," Gruoch said.

Marcus looked at her for a moment as he tried to figure out if his translator chip was defective. Seeing his confusion, Gruoch continued.

"I take the stunned look on your face to mean you did not realize I worked as Senator Modi's chief of staff?"

Marcus was sure that rather than just looking like a stunned halibut, his face now looked like the same fish that had just been introduced to the wonders of a shock collar.

"Don't Senator Du and Senator Modi despise one another? As in, if there wasn't a prohibition against members of higher office dueling one another there would have been a bloodletting by now?" Marcus asked.

"So you never rebelled against your parents as a teenager?" Gruoch asked teasingly. "Although I guess working for the presidential campaign of your father's political rival is a bit more than rebelling."

"I am amazed he still speaks to you," Marcus said incredulously.

"Being an only child has its advantages," Gruoch said with a laugh that stopped suddenly. "I'm sorry, we should probably not continue down that conversation path. I think you've dealt with enough blubbering today."

"What would being the military liaison require?"

"Senator Modi is concerned that the Fleet will take this opportunity to make all sorts of unreasonable demands on the Confederation's resources," Gruoch said evenly. "Your first job would be to make sure that Fleet Admiral Malinverni and Minister Bloodworth actually have a plan for all the resources they are about to consume."

Marcus looked at Gruoch like she was crazy.

"You are aware that I got kicked out of the Marines as a first lieutenant, right?"

"Which means you have enough training to know the fleet's organization but weren't in so long that you came to accept paradigms as the only possible way to tackle a problem," Gruoch replied easily. "Not to mention, you'd have a staff of experts."

"Why not pick one of the experts?" Marcus asked, spreading his hands in a gesture that nearly caused him to lose the remainder of his sandwich.

"I'm sorry, I was not aware expertise and leadership were synonymous in your vocabulary?" Gruoch answered sarcastically.

"Okay, why me?" Marcus asked.

"Instant credibility," Gruoch replied.

"What? Did I put the hallucinatory mushrooms on your sandwich?" Marcus asked incredulously "I meant to save those for later."

"You haven't looked at a single news vid or scanned anything since you've been here, have you?" Gruoch asked, her tone surprised.

"Wait, let's see, I could swear I was prominently involved in one of the *worst disasters in recent memory*," Marcus snapped. "So, no, I've been skipping any outside information."

Gruoch made an exasperated sound.

"The starting pay is 75,000 credits with a sign up bonus of 35,000 more and an expense account," the woman said firmly.

"I'll take 50,000 credits as a sign up," Marcus said, surprising himself. "Oh, and I answer directly to the Senator, not to you."

"I'm his chief of staff," Gruoch replied archly. "We just met, why wouldn't you want to answer to me?"

"I'm sorry, you're Senator Du's daughter," Marcus replied. "All this may be completely on the up and up, but I'm going to have enough troubles as is without having to mention your last name when I talk to people."

Gruoch opened her mouth to protest, then shut it.

"Fine. You start…"

"I start in a month," Marcus replied. "Provided I don't wake up sometime in the next 30 days with a sky full of descending lizards looking to cleanse this planet of all human life."

Gruoch gave him a grim look.

"If that happens, I trust you'll come find Aimi and I so we can flee to the mountains and start our own resistance group?" Gruoch asked.

"Sure, we'll name it after some random indigenous mammal that happens to double as a school mascot," Marcus replied.

"Yet here I was thinking we'd name it after Boskins," Gruoch replied. "I was instructed not to come back without you if you accepted the job."

"When was the last time *you* took a vacation?" Marcus asked, genuinely curious.

"Years," Gruoch replied.

"You can thank me later. Screen Aimi, cribbage is always more fun with three players."

Glossary

When writing this book, I initially assumed that readers had some knowledge of aviation and nautical terms. As such, the below list is far from exhaustive but includes the terms my beta readers most often went "Um, you drinking while writing again?" about. For further terminology, I suggest the always helpful *Wikipedia*, the online *Sea Talk Nautical Dictionary,*

Term	**Definition**
Bow	The forward part of a vessel.
Class	A group of warships built upon the same or strikingly similar plans. Vessels within a class are typically referred to as "sister ships" due to their similarities.
Confederation Star Ship (C.S.S.)	A warship serving in the Confederation Fleet. This includes system defense ships appropriated for Fleet support.
Division	Two Fleet usages:
	1.) An administrative section of a ship responsible for some primary function (e.g., Gunnery, Engineering, Sensors, etc.).
	2.) A group of like type ships

344

(e.g., destroyers, cruisers, etc.) that is placed together for tactical or administrative purposes. In most cases, efforts will be taken to place ships of similar performance into a single division.

ECM

Electronic Counter Measures (typically countermeasures). The process of spoofing a hostile sensor or system via false images, jamming, or other means requiring power (to include active, vice passive, decoys).

Flight

A group of spacecraft. Typically arranged in fours, flights are the subunits of squadrons.

Keel

A vessel's primary structural member to which all others are normally attached. In spacefaring vessels there are typically ventral and dorsal keels that are themselves attached by load bearing members. The destruction of the keel is referred to as "breaking a vessel's back," i.e. delivering a blow that either cripples or destroys the recipient.

An Unproven Concept

Master-at-arms	The senior law enforcement entity aboard a Confederation Fleet warship.
Planform	The shape or layout of a spacecraft when viewed from the dorsal perspective.
Prow	See *bow* (q.v.). Typically used when talking about the absolutely forwardmost part of the ship.
Sensor shadow	The area behind an astronomical object that is impenetrable to sensors due to said entity's reflective properties. Much like a terrestrial building will intersect a searchlight, planets, asteroids, etc. tend to block both passive and active sensors from perceiving craft on the other side.
Spacefaring Ship (S.S.)	A civilian vessel capable of interstellar travel.
Standard Spacefarer Time (SST)	A 24-hour clock used aboard all intersystem vessels in the Confederation of Man. Intrasystem tugs, shuttles, space station, and inhabited

astronomical bodies are allowed to use system / local time.

Torpedo

An unguided weapon possessing a large warhead, inertial dampener, and drive emphasizing acceleration over top end speed. Typically fired in spreads from short (<25,000 kilometer) range. Usually mounted aboard destroyer and lighter vessels.

Wardroom

The officer's mess and recreational area aboard a warship. Aboard cruisers and smaller there is typically a single wardroom that is employed by the XO (President of the Mess) and all junior officers. Confederation capital ships typically have a senior (division chiefs and above) and junior wardroom, with an embarked air group entitled to its own wardroom. Although each President of the Mess and his assistant officers (Secretary, Treasurer, etc.) is allowed to set his/her own customs, in general discussing "shop" is almost universally frowned upon. In addition, the ship's captain is typically only allowed into the wardroom when specifically

An Unproven Concept

invited.

Dramatis Personae

S.S. *Titanic*

Captain Abraham Herrod, Master

Mr. Marcus Martin, Chief Security Officer

Ms. Sarah Jones, Head of Hospitality

Ms. Anjelica Barton, Purser

Mr. Ivan Federov, Vice President Czarina Lines

Senator Geirmund Du, Junior Senator, Spartan Diaspora Republic

Ms. Aimi Eguchi, Senator Du's bodyguard

Mr. Quentin Thendaron, Grognard squad leader

Ms. Lorraine O'Barr, Deputy Chief Security Officer

Mr. Hagop Al-Madur, First Mate

Mr. Ichabod Blum, Chief Engineer

C.S.S. *Constitution*

Fleet Admiral Henrique Ocelot Malinverni, Commander in Chief Confederation Fleet

Captain Mackenzie William Bolan, Captain

Commander Jason Owderkirk, Commander Air Group (CAG), Warhawks

Commander Newton Sinclair, Gunnery Officer

Commander Tristan Alexander, Executive Officer

Commander Jiang Liu, Chief Engineer

Lieutenant Colonel Isoroku Nishizawa, Commander Marine Detachment

Lieutenant Commander Charles "Flash" Gordon, Squadron Commander No. 803

Lieutenant Commander Saburo Sakai, Chief Helm Officer

Lieutenant Commander Jacquelyn "Catnip" Tice, Squadron Commander, VF(S)-41

Lieutenant Naomi Boyles, Sensor Officer

Lieutenant Charles Herrod, Communications Officer

Lieutenant Jane Horinek, Navigation Officer

Afterword

No book comes to fruition based on the author's effort alone. Everything from making sure that the writer actually sleeps, eats, bathes and occasionally fulfills all their other commitments to giving editorial advice comes from external sources. As such, this is far from an exhaustive list, as the reader is not paying to read a telephone book of shout outs. Suffice to say, I would like to thank the nameless masses who contributed everything from a smile to a character idea without realizing it. All I ask of you as the reader is this—if you liked it, tell your friends and please rate it on Amazon. If you did not like it, please provide feedback and constructive criticism on Amazon so that the next one will be better.

I would be remiss in not recognizing my wife, Anita, for her forebearance and patience. While her numerous mutterings about "All work and no play makes Jack a dull boy..." and commentary about my glare possibly being a violation of the Geneva Convention usually get an eye roll, I know that it is often difficult dealing with someone who really, *really* wants to finish that next paragraph so the Muse will shut up and let him sleep. The complexity grows exponentially when she is busy working on her own book and would like to borrow previously allocated brainpower for a sounding board. Sorry for occasionally resembling Jack Nicholson, honey.

Next I'd like to thank my parents. While Dad made the last jump to hyperspace a few years back, I'd like to believe that somewhere he's finally glad to see all those hours of reading some ten year old's scribblings has borne fruit. "I don't think a man can carry a 350 pound missile launcher, Jamie." "Oh. Guess I should fix that." As for Mom, while Dad may have introduced me to sci-fi it was she who introduced me to reading. Or, as she says, "You didn't believe me, so I told you to go look it up yourself."

Beta readers are the lifeblood of any author. While I thanked every one of them in person, I'd like to take this opportunity to recognize them and my appreciation for them again. In everything from "You really need a glossary..." to "I can't believe you just killed [character name]...", their efforts made this much easier to finish. Any typos or grammatical errors remain mine, as in a lot of cases I was throwing a whole slew of new ideas at them. Sometimes I speak in a language that resembles English / American only in my head.

I freely admit to being a bit of a *Titanic* geek, and there were numerous "Easter Eggs" for my fellow fanatics throughout this. For those of you not familiar with the historical *Titanic*'s story other than James Cameron's movie, I highly recommend Walter Lord's *A Night to Remember* and *The Night Lives On* as starting points, followed shortly by Daniel Butler's *Unsinkable* and *Other Side of the Night*. While I freely admit to writing this book as a first contact tragedy, nothing within the previous pages can match the horrible reality of that cold April night in 1912.

Author of Pandora's Memories

James Young

Acts of War

A Novel of Alternate History

CHAPTER 1: CAREFUL WHAT YOU WISH FOR...

Follow me—You have the advantage of necessity, that last and most powerful of weapons. **Vettius Messius of Volscia.**

Thames River
0900 Local (0400 Eastern)
23 August 1942

London was burning.

Somehow I doubt that this is quite how anyone expected Adolf Hitler's death to turn out, Adam Haynes thought bitterly as he regarded the burning capital's skyline. The wind, thankfully, was blowing away from where he and his girlfriend stood at the bow of the *Accalon.* Adam had the awful feeling that if it had been blowing toward the 40-foot pleasure yacht, there would have been many, many smells he would have preferred to forget filtering their way.

*Like Guernica, only…*he started to think.

With a roar, a Junkers 52 swept low over the *Accalon*'s deck, its passage so close that the aircraft's slipstream fluttered the white flag hanging from the yacht's antennae mast. An intense, white-hot rage sprung from within him as he watched the canary yellow German transport.

I hope you crash, you bastard, Adam thought, blood rushing into his ears.

"Adam, *my hand!*" A woman's voice broke through his fury.

With a start, Adam realized that he was well on the way to breaking his companion's hand. Although such an act was always unconscionably bad form, it was doubly so when its possessor was the cousin, albeit distant, of England's king.

"God, Clarine, I'm…" Adam started, opening his hand as if suddenly realizing it held a hot brick. His face colored to the roots of his thinning brown hair, making his blue eyes all that more intense. At a shade under six feet, with shoulders broad enough to fit on a man six inches taller, Adam looked very much like a bear wearing an RAF uniform. Unfortunately, when enraged, he had the

1

strength to match.

"That is quite alright," Clarine Windsor replied lightly, doing her best to smile as she worked her hand. A small, wiry woman who stood several inches shorter than Alex in the black flats that came with her Women's Auxiliary Air Force (WAAF) uniform, Clarine was far from weak. Still, her pale face was scrunched up in obvious pain.

Holy shit, I hope I didn't hurt her, Adam thought guiltily. Seeing his worry, Clarine brought up her left hand and brushed back a stray blonde hair, her brown eyes meeting Adam's as she smiled.

"You were just having the same thought I had: wishing you could shoot the bastard," she said simply. "It's understandable, given what has happened these last few days."

Still no reason to try and convert your hand to paste, Adam thought. *You didn't drop the bomb that killed Hitler.*

"Understandable, but most unfortunate," her father, Awarnach Windsor, stated as he joined them at the yacht's bow. "Especially as his escorts would probably blow the *Accalon* out of the water."

Looking up and back toward the vessel's stern, Adam mentally kicked himself for not noticing the eight Me-410s circling roughly four thousand feet above their heads. The gray fighters were hard to see in the haze of smoke roiling off London, but that was no excuse. Smoke had been a fact of life for Fighter Command over the last two weeks, and failing to see an opponent hiding in it was just as fatal as if the assault came from more naturally formed clouds.

"While I am sure you wish you had a *Spitfire* right now," Awarnach observed flatly, "I doubt your efforts would be any more successful than they were previously."

You bastard, Adam thought, fighting to keep his emotions off his face. The tone of Awarnach's voice had far too much "told you so" in it.

"Well father, at least someone was attempting to defend our nation," Clarine observed coolly. "Since many of those who were born to it could not raise themselves from their slumber."

Awarnach turned his baleful gaze from Adam to his daughter.

"Those of us who were 'slumbering', as you put it, merely believed we should have continued to enjoy the peace we had hammered out rather than meddle in affairs on the continent," Awarnach replied. "Instead, that idiot Churchil has now managed to make us forget his idiocy at Gallipoli."

"This is hardly the same as…"

"No?!" Awarnach snapped. He turned and pointed off their port bow, to where London's East End was starting to come into view. "Tell me *that* is not more terrible than some idiotic frontal assault on the Ottomans."

The *"that"* in question was the furious blaze that roared unchecked almost as far as the eye could see. The low rumble of the fire was a constant sound beating upon their senses, but Adam had managed to suppress it by concentrating on the river itself. Now, as if Awarnach had ripped open a shade, the magnitude of Fighter Command's defeat lay before them. It was like looking into a corner of Hell, and Adam was once more glad that the wind was blowing so strongly from their back.

Once you've smelled burning flesh, you have no desire to enjoy that particular sensation again, Adam thought.

"You can't negotiate with the Germans," Adam said lowly, feeling the rage starting to creep back again.

"Oh? Well then, I am certainly glad that you have pointed this out for me, my American friend. Unfortunately, it would appear that your President and Congress feel very, very differently."

"Father…"

"No, please, I would like to hear this fine young man explain to me why we should not negotiate with the Germans when his countrymen cannot be bothered to even help us," Awarnach raged, his own face starting to color to match Adam's.

"It wasn't our President that chose to accept the armistice with Himmler after Bomber Command killed Hitler," Adam snapped.

"Oh? And what would you have had us do? Were we somehow going to invade France by ourselves? Perhaps build a massive bomber fleet like that idiot Portal wanted to and bomb the Reich's cities into rubble? Would that have satisfied your need for bloodlust? There was nothing more that could be done!"

"Yes, well, *perhaps* the people in that," Adam said, gesturing toward the burning city in front of them, "would have preferred you not giving the Germans over a year to perfect their bombing

3

techniques."

"Perhaps, gentlemen," Clarine said crisply, her hand pointing, "we should be more concerned about that patrol boat's intentions."

Adam followed the point and saw the craft she was speaking of. One of the Royal Navy's MTB-class boats, the vessel was moving away from where it had been standing off the docks and turning toward the *Accalon*. As they watched, the craft began accelerating, signal light blinking furiously.

"Conroy, come about!" Awarnach shouted back towards the wheel house. Adam felt the *Accalon*'s engines stop, the helmsman turning her broadside to the oncoming MTB.

Holy shit, Adam thought, translating the other vessel's Morse code. He was about to say something when Awarnach spoke first.

"My God," Awarnach said, his face paling. "Gas?!"

"Obviously you've never read Douhet," Adam observed dryly.

"Who?" Clarine asked.

"The Italian Trenchard," Adam continued smoothly. "He recommended using gas in addition to incendiaries on enemy population centers. Explains the no-confidence vote a little better, I think."

The patrol boat began slowing, its own helmsman swinging the vessel wide so that he could put it alongside the *Accalon*. Three men crowded the bow and, with a start, Adam realized they were wearing full hoods and rubber gloves. Seeing that no one aboard the *Accalon* was in the bulky protective suits, the man standing in the center reached up and pulled the hooded apparatus off of his head.

Well now, small world, isn't it? Adam thought, feeling a smile cross his face as he regarded Lieutenant Commander Reginald Slade, Royal Navy. Tall, almost gaunt, with a face whose left side was thoroughly scarred from the explosion of a German shell, Slade wore his blonde hair closely cropped.

"You seem to be a fair distance from the North Atlantic, Mr. Haynes," Slade shouted as the patrol boat drew smoothly alongside the *Accalon*, his face breaking in a wry grin that reached his eyes. Reaching up, the RN officer scratched the area around his left eyepatch. The motion drew attention to the damaged side of his face, and Adam heard Awarnach inhale sharply.

"Sorry, I have been wanting to do that for hours," Slade said, ignoring the man's gasp.

4

"Yeah, I can see how that might be the case," Adam replied with a small smile.

"I do hope you folks aren't planning on going any further down the Thames," Slade continued. "By King's decrees the East End is off limits to anyone not on official business."

"I'm trying to find one of my mate's wife, mother, and child. He's in the hospital or else he'd be down here himself," Adam said.

Slade grimaced at Adam's words.

"Where did he say they were living?" the naval officer asked, his tone brusque.

"His mum's apartment is in Poplar," Adam replied, raising an eyebrow at the other man's coldness.

Adam had seen the look that briefly crossed Slade's face enough times to know what was coming next. The man paused for a moment, obviously choosing his words carefully.

"Unless they were extraordinarily lucky, I wouldn't hold out much hope, I'm afraid. The Germans dropped some sort of gas that got all the way through the area, and then followed it up with incendiaries. Without anyone to put out the fires…"

The officer's trailing off said all that needed to be said. In the last couple of days, Adam had heard a word for the phenomenon that some were calling the Second Great London Fire: Firestorm. The East End had become one huge flame pit, and the *Luftwaffe* had returned for three solid days to help things spread.

"Thanks Commander Slade," Adam spoke after a few moments more of quiet. Sighing at the heavy burden that now lay upon him, he looked up again at the smoke-filled sky, hoping to catch a glimpse of the big Ju-52 again.

"Looking for that arse who came tearing through here about ten minutes ago?" Slade asked.

"Yes, actually," Adam replied ruefully.

"I think that was Himmler arriving to negotiate terms with Lord Halifax."

The disgust in Slade's tone at the latter name almost matched the venom reserved for the first.

"Who knew there was a bigger bastard than Hitler in the Nazi Party?" Adam observed grimly.

"Certainly not that bunch of flyboys who killed him," Slade shot back. "Stupid pilots, always mucking things up."

Clarine chuckled behind Adam. Looking at Slade, Adam was unable to tell if the man was serious or not.

"Heard the poor bombardier blew his brains out yesterday," Adam replied. "Not his fault any of this," he continued, gesturing towards the burning city, "happened."

Slade shrugged.

"No, it's not, but that's what happens when you drop your bombs over a capital city. Sometimes you hit things you don't intend to," Slade retorted bitterly.

Spoken like someone who's never had to jettison something in order to make the fuel equation work out, Adam thought. He'd been a pilot since his seventeenth birthday, and non-flyers' superiority complexes never ceased to amaze him.

"Still. Berlin's a big city," Adam allowed. "No way they could've known they'd drop a bomb that would kill ol' Adolf."

Slade uttered a sound that made his disagreement quite clear on that one.

"Yes, and a 500-lb. bomb makes a big mess. No matter, that bastard is dead now, Himmler took over, and our betters were dumb enough to believe that tripe the Germans were spouting about the *Fuhrer*'s loss making them recognize the error of their ways."

"Excuse me, Lieutenant Commander, but as one of those *betters*," Awarnach snapped, "maybe a better explanation was that we did not want to continue losing men such as yourself in a war that we quite clearly were not in position to win."

Slade turned and looked at Awarnach, the contempt in his gaze almost physically palpable.

"So, in order to save *my* life, you buggered the French, spat on the rest of the Continent, pissed off the Americans, and gave Himmler breathing room," Slade retorted, his voice cold as ice. "During which time he hanged Goering, blew some industrialists' heads out at a meeting, and thus apparently motivated them to build a bloody great lot of planes, bombs, gas, and submarines."

Adam watched as Awarnach's face began to color while Slade continued, obviously taking a great relish in venting his spleen.

"Of course, the bloody Krauts then proceeded to kill a whole lot more of my countrymen. Capital work, your Lordship, just capital, please do not go into anything of importance."

6

Awarnach's mouth worked in shock. Before he could reply, one of the sailors stuck his head out of the patrol boat's bridge.

"Lieutenant Commander, we have been ordered to a new location," the man called.

Slade continued locking his gaze with Awarnach. It was the older man whose stare broke.

"Would hate to keep you, Lieutenant Commander," Awarnach said, his voice strained. "I'll go back to the bridge and con us out of your path."

"Well, guess we will be about it then," Slade replied, watching the man walk stiffly away.

"So what's going to happen to you next?" Adam asked. "If that is Himmler negotiating the peace treaty."

Slade gave a sideways glance to Clarine.

"I do not share my father's views," Clarine muttered quietly. "Indeed, I think he and the rest of the House of Lords were, and remain, a bunch of fools."

"In that case, understand that this war will *not* end here," Slade said lowly. "As Churchill said before the no confidence vote, there is an entire Commonwealth that will sustain the candle attempting to hold the darkness at bay."

"You mean you're going to flee to Australia or somewhere?" Adam asked, genuinely curious.

Slade snorted.

"You'd best do the same," he replied. "Rumor has it that Himmler intends to ask for all foreign fighters to be turned over as part of the peace treaty."

"What?!"

"Well, can't have a bunch of Poles, Danes, Norwegians, and Frenchmen hanging around and possibly doing something subversive, can you? Especially not after they killed Milch while there was allegedly an armistice between Great Britain and Germany," Sloan replied grimly.

With a cold feeling in his stomach, Adam could see the government being formed by Lord Halifax agreeing to such madness. Even worse, he knew what the Nazis would likely do with the men.

"I'm flying with a Polish squadron," Adam said quickly, his tone urgent. "How do I get them the hell out of here."

Again Slade gave Clarine a look, then held up his hand before Adam could say something.

"It is not that I mistrust her," Slade said. "However, you of all people know the Nazis as well as I do. Have you heard the stories of how their Gestapo broke several of the Resistance cells in France during the last year?"

Clarine paled, looking almost physically ill.

The thought of being strapped to a metal mattress and electrocuted for hours on end doesn't appeal to most people, Adam thought. *Especially given where those bastards were placing the electrodes.*

"I will go speak with my father," she said simply. "Please hurry—I do not think he would be opposed to making you swim for it."

Taking Adam's hand and squeezing it, Clarine turned and departed.

"Get the whole bloody lot of your men to Portsmouth," Slade said as soon as she was out of earshot. He pulled out a piece of paper and a grease pen from under his rubber top. Scribbling something quickly, he handed it over to Adam.

"You have less than twenty hours," Slade said, meeting Adam's eyes. "After that, you best leave that pretty lass without any idea how to find you and disappear, as I get the distinct feeling that some of my former countrymen will be quite happy to 'help' run down foreign mercenaries."

"Thanks Slade," Adam replied, extending his hand. The Lieutenant Commander took it with both of his.

"No, *thank you*," Slade said, his voice raw with emotion. "You and the others like you tried to save us, even when we have done little to deserve it. Now only you remain."

"I'm sorry we couldn't do more."

"Well, maybe you'll have more opportunity one of these days. Hopefully your President can make people see reason soon, or else it will be too late."

"I think this," Adam said, gesturing towards the burning docks behind Slade, "will help."

"Yes, yes it will. Now get out of here, and see to your men."

With that, Slade drew himself up to attention and saluted. Adam returned the salute, then watched as the man nimbly sprang back to the patrol boat. The small craft backed away under low power, then ponderously turned its bow around. Adam sighed as he heard Clarine's soft footsteps behind him.

"Father is furious," she said softly. "Strangely, I don't give a damn."

"You know that I have to go almost as soon as we get back," Adam said. Turning, he saw Clarine's eyes were moist already.

"Yes, yes I know," she said softly. "And there's no chance father will let me out of his sight until you do so."

Adam could hear the deep tone of bitterness in her voice.

"Life becomes very lonely when you hate your parents," he said chidingly.

"I have half a mind to come with you," Clarine replied fiercely. "That would bloody well serve him right."

"Well, wouldn't be the first scandal an American has caused in this country," he said musingly, rubbing his chin theatrically.

"I am serious, Adam," Clarine retorted.

"I may not even be alive in a fortnight, Clarine," Adam said somberly. "Think about that. Do you really want to throw away your future, inheritance, and family name for some vagabond American mercenary?"

Clarine searched his face.

"Is that really how you think I see you?"

"No, but it's how your father and the rest of your social circle see me. Yes, I come from the right circles and know which fork to start with at dinner, but at the end of the day I am like some exotic animal that is best petted and left alone."

"Adam, *I love you.*"

"And I you," Adam said, fighting the urge to sweep Clarine into his arms. "So much that I will not let you ruin the rest of your life to flee with me."

"What about what I want?" Clarine asked as the *Accalon* came around. "Don't I get to decide the rest of my life, or is that solely the province of my male betters?"

Adam sighed.

Strong women will be the death of me, he thought with a deep sense of melancholy.

"Why don't you tell the truth, Adam?" Clarine continued.

9

"You're scared of what will happen to me if I try to escape with you."

"Yes, the thought of you drowning or freezing to death in the Atlantic does strike me with some trepidation."

Clarine snarled in exasperation.

"Not every event in life ends the worst way possible, Adam!" she breathed lowly through clenched teeth.

Adam turned and looked behind him at the burning London, then back to Clarine.

"Perhaps now is not the time to try and convince me of this. More importantly, Clarine, I have to look after my men."

Clarine opened her mouth to argue, then stopped.

"Then when this boat docks will be the last time we see each other," she replied coolly.

Adam felt as if someone had stomach punched him. He started to reach for Clarine, but she held up her hand to stop him.

"You seem determined to leave Adam," she said. "You are even more determined to make sure I do not leave with you in some misguided attempt to 'save' me. Perhaps it is best then, that I acknowledge you have greater experience in dealing with disastrous circumstances such as these."

The words were delivered with cold precision, and they found their mark with the same brutal finality of a knife thrust.

"I do not want us to end this way, Clarine," Adam bit out, feeling his stomach sinking to his feet.

"If you had stopped after the seventh word of that sentence," Clarine said, her voice quavering, "I might have been inclined to reconsider. Instead, I believe that I am feeling rather nauseous from the smoke and will go below. Have a safe journey, Adam."

With that, Clarine turned and began walking back towards the deckway hatch, moving quickly as she wiped at her face. Adam watched her go, his stomach in knots.

Well, at least it's an improvement from last time I went through this, he thought. Fighting the urge to curse loudly, he slowly rotated back towards the *Accalon's* bow, and then walked forward to where only the Thames could see his tears.

Red Two
North Atlantic
1000 Local (0700 Eastern)
12 September

Lieutenant (j.g.) Eric Cobb, like many aviators, did not lack for confidence. It took a very confident or very stupid man to step into a single-engined aircraft, then take off from a small postage stamp of a warship on a flight over hundreds of miles of featureless ocean. Some people, to include Eric's father, believed that repeatedly doing this was the height of idiocy. Eric, on the other hand, had developed a liking for the hours of solitude, sunlight, and beautiful ocean vistas that were only visible from several thousand feet of altitude.

Unfortunately for Eric, the 12th day of September in the year of our Lord nineteen forty-two had none of the above.

"Okay asshole, I think we're getting a little bit close to the Kraut fleet's estimated position," Eric muttered, his hands white knuckled on his SBD *Dauntless*'s stick and throttle. The "asshole" in question was VB-4's squadron leader, Lieutenant Commander Abe Cobleigh, and the soup that passed for a sky all around them made following Red One's plane a feat of concentration and skill. The conditions were making Eric's forward canopy fog and he had to fight the urge to take his feet off the rudder pedals and brace himself up to look over the top of the forward glass. At several inches over six feet Eric wouldn't have had to stretch far, but taking one's feet off the rudder in the current conditions was not a recipe for longevity. Even though the radial-engine "Slow But Deadly" was as beloved for its handling characteristics as its ruggedness, Eric had no desire to see how well he could pull out from a stupidity-induced spin.

"What was that, sir?" Radioman 2nd Class Henry Rawles asked from the tail gunner position.

"Nothing Rawles, nothing," Eric called back, keeping his voice level so the young gunner wouldn't think he was perturbed at him.

Not Rawles's fault our squadron leader is a...

Without warning, the *Dauntless* burst out of the cloud bank. Eric had just enough time to register the changing conditions, give a sigh

11

of relief, then start looking around before all hell broke loose. The anti-aircraft barrage that burst around the two single-engine dive bombers was heavy and accurate. With a seeming endless cascade of *crack! crack! crack!*, heavy caliber shells exploded all around Eric's bomber, the blasts throwing it around like backhands from a giant.

Jesus Christ! Eric thought, stomping left on his rudder and pulling back on the stick to get back into the clouds.

"Sir, Lieutenant Commander Cobleigh's been hit!" Rawles shouted.

Before Eric could respond, another shell exploded on the bomber's right side with a deafening roar and flash. Eric felt a sharp sting and burning sensation across the back of his neck as the canopy shattered in a spray of glass, the *Dauntless* heeling over from the explosion. Stunned, Eric instinctively leveled the dive bomber off and found himself back in the cloud bank before he fully recovered his senses.

With full recovery came consciousness of just how screwed he was. First Eric realized that it was only by the grace of God that he hadn't been laid open like a slaughtered animal. His shredded life vest, damaged control stick and throttle, and a very large hole in the cockpit's side were all evidence that several fragments had blasted all around him. Fighting down the urge to vomit, Eric quickly checked both of his wings, noting that the surfaces were thoroughly peppered as he fought to keep the SBD level. Fuel streamed behind the bomber, starting to gradually slow as the self-sealing tanks proved their worth.

Oh we are in trouble now. The two SBDs had been near the limit of their search arc when fired upon. Even with the self-sealing tanks working as advertised, Eric was certain that the damage to the wing tanks had just guaranteed Rawles and he would not be landing back aboard *Ranger*. Swiveling his head, he attempted to find Red One's SBD *Dauntless* dive bomber through the murk.

"Rawles!" Eric called over the intercom.

"Yes, sir?" his gunner responded.

"You see what happened to One?" Eric began, then suddenly remembered Rawles' report. "I mean after he got hit."

"Sir, there was no after Lt. Commander Cobleigh got hit," Rawles replied, his voice breathless. "He just exploded!"

Eric felt the sick feeling return to his stomach. After a moment's

12

temptation to just go ahead and vomit over the side, he fought the puke back down.

"What else did you get a chance to see?" Eric asked.

"It looked like there were at least two battleships, maybe three. Jesus they were close!"

"Okay, you need to get off a position report of those German bastards. Send it in the clear back to *Ranger*, keep repeating it until someone acknowledges, and I will try to figure out if we're going to make it back."

"Aye aye, sir," Rawles replied. A few moments later, Eric heard the Morse code starting to get tapped out. Pulling out his map, he suddenly realized he had no clue which direction he was flying. Looking down at the compass, he felt a sudden sigh of relief when he saw they were heading southwest, away from the Germans and generally towards their own fleet.

"Sir, I've got an acknowledgment from the *Augusta*. She's asking our status," Rawles said.

"Send this in code: Red One destroyed, Two unlikely to return to fleet. Will send crash location," Eric said tersely.

They broke out of the low clouds into an area of open sky, the sun beaming down on the battered *Dauntless*. Eric suddenly felt exposed and began scanning around the horizon. He heard and felt Rawles unlimber his twin .30-caliber machine guns and was glad to see that he wasn't the only one on edge.

Those bastards tried to kill us! he thought, then remembered how close the Germans had come to doing just that.

"Rawles, you all right?"

"I got nicked on my calf, but it's not serious. Are we actually about to crash, sir?" Rawles asked.

"It's about two hundred miles back to the fleet, and we don't have two hundred miles of fuel…"

"Smoke! Smoke to starboard!" Rawles shouted. Eric whipped his head around and saw the smudge that Rawles had sighted low on the horizon.

"Well, you just might have kept us from a day in the raft, Rawles," Eric said happily, grabbing the stick with his left hand. Reaching down the right side of his seat, he opened his binoculars' case and reached in. There was a sharp prick on his gloved finger, and he jerked his hand back. Reaching down more carefully, he realized that while the lid was still present on the case, the container itself was twisted metal.

"Rawles, you still have your binoculars?"

"Roger sir," Rawles came back.

"Let's see what you can see," Eric replied. "Mine are shot to hell."

There was a slight rustling in the backseat as Eric brought the SBD around to begin closing with the smoke. After a few moments, it was clear there was more than one column. About ten minutes later, it was very obvious that the *Dauntless* was closing with an entire group of ships.

"Sir, that looks like the Brits!" Rawles said. "I can't tell very well, but that looks like one of their heavy cruisers and a few destroyers heading away from us."

"Great," Eric muttered. "I get to be shot at by both sides today."

"What was that, sir?"

"Nevermind, just talking to myself. Send this location in code also, then get ready to start signaling with a lamp."

"Approaching aircraft, approaching aircraft, these are Royal Navy vessels," a clear, accented voice crackled into Eric's earpieces. "Do not continue to approach or you will be fired upon."

Eric turned the SBD away, banking to show his silhouette and national insignia. The dive bomber initially complied with the movement, then suddenly staggered and began to roll to the left. Eric fought the maneuver, but found that he was only able to hold the aircraft level with the stick pressed almost completely to the right. Looking out at his ailerons, he saw that both were in the down position.

Great, just great, Eric thought.

"Royal Navy vessel, this is a United States Navy aircraft in need of assistance," Eric said once he had control of his aircraft. "Request permission to ditch close aboard."

There was a pause of a sufficient length that Eric felt his arm starting to shake from the effort of maintaining level flight.

"American aircraft, you may ditch close aboard," came the response.

Eric heard Rawles wrestling around in the rear cockpit.

"Sir, I've got the code books in a sack with a box of ammo.

14

Want me to throw it over the side?"

"Great plan, Rawles," Eric gritted. "Get rid of the guns too, don't want you getting brained when we get out."

A moment later, Eric heard the twin machine guns bang down against the fuselage on their way over the side. Shortly after, there was a similar noise as the code books and ammo followed suit the .30-caliber tail guns. Taking a little pressure off the stick, Eric brought the *Dauntless* around in a gradual left-hand turn to see the large cruiser coasting to a stop. The five destroyers accompanying the vessel circled like protective sheep dogs, smoke drifting up from their stacks.

I hope those tin cans don't find anything. Don't feel like adding "got torpedoed" to my list of bad things that have happened today. His right arm began twitching, warning of impending muscle failure, and he quickly grabbed the stick with his left hand for a couple of moments.

"All right Rawles, I've never done this before so I don't know how much time we have," Eric said, fighting to keep his voice calm. "Stand by to ditch."

As Rawles acknowledged his order, Eric had a chance to give the British cruiser a good look. A twin-stacked, three-turreted ship, the RN vessel was painted in three tones of gray, the pattern seemingly random from above. As the dive bomber circled downward from five thousand feet, Eric realized that the captain had placed the vessel athwart the wind, leaving a relatively calm area on her lee. Eric recognized the maneuver as one occasionally conducted by American cruisers in order to recover their seaplanes.

Glad to see things aren't totally different between our navies. The *Dauntless* shuddered, and Eric noted the engine starting to run slightly rougher. Giving a prayer of thanks that Rawles had sighted the vessels, Eric resolved to put the dive bomber down as quickly as possible. Clenching his teeth, his right arm starting to burn with muscle fatigue again, Eric finished the last turn of his gradual spiral down barely one hundred feet over the water and half a mile from the stopped ship. Fighting at the edge of a stall, he pulled the nose up slightly to start killing the SBD's forward momentum.

It was an almost perfect ditching. The dive bomber stalled, the wings losing their last bit of lift barely ten feet above the ocean.

There was nothing Eric could do to prevent the nose starting to come down, with the result that the landing was not as smooth as he had hoped. The impact slammed him forward, his restraints failing to prevent his head from snapping against the instrument panel. Seeing stars, Eric slumped backward briefly into his seat and took a moment to gather himself. As he ran his tongue over his teeth to make sure they were all there, Eric felt the airplane lurch and start to settle towards starboard. The swirl of water into the bottom of the cockpit told him that he did not have long to get out of the crippled aircraft.

"Sir, you okay?!" Rawles asked, standing on the port wing by the aircraft. Eric turned and looked at him, the movement sluggish. Rawles didn't wait for an answer, reaching in and starting to help Eric unbuckle.

"Get the…" Eric started, fighting hard to get through the mental fog. "Get the life raft."

No sooner had he said that than water began pouring over the edge of his cockpit. The cold North Atlantic did wonders to clear the cobwebs, and he realized with a start that Rawles was already up to his chest in the water. Kicking his feet free of the rudder pedals and disconnecting his radio cord, Eric pulled off his shredded life vest and started to stand up. The movement didn't come off as planned as the *Dauntless* slid out from under him. In moments, he and Rawles were both swimming in the cold Atlantic, their plane a momentary dark shape underneath them before it slid into the depths.

"Guess we could've left the codebooks after all," Rawles muttered. "Damn sir, you look like someone hit your noggin' with a sledgehammer."

Eric kicked his legs to get out of the water while reaching up with his left arm. He winced as he touched the massive goose egg on this forehead.

That explains why I'm a little out of it, Eric thought, pleasantly surprised he was able to form a semi-coherent thought. *Although it would appear going for a swim in cold as hell water helps clear up getting knocked on the head.*

Worryingly, Eric could feel his arm cramps returning as he treaded water.

I'm not sure how long I'll make it without a life vest, he thought worriedly. The sound of a boat moter carrying across the waves was the sweetest sound he had ever heard. Turning, he saw that the cruiser's boat was almost upon them. Eric attempted to start swimming towards the whaleboat and realized with a start that his legs were going numb.

"Just stay there, gentlemen, we will be with you shortly!" a man in the boat's prow shouted.

Minutes later the Royal Navy lieutenant was proven as good as his word, with blankets being dropped over the Americans' shoulders and rum shoved into their hands. Rawles threw his shot back quickly, only starting to shiver once he got it down. Eric, hardly a drinker, took two swallows to get the rum into his stomach and had to fight against retching.

"My name is *Leftenant* Aldrich, medical office for the His Majesty's Ship *Exeter*," the man began as the whaleboat began returning to the cruiser. Eric saw that the man was tall and thin, his navy blue jacket hanging off him like he was a walking clothes hanger.

He must be older than he looks, Eric thought as he took in the man's youthful freckled face and dark red hair. While his voice was deep and firm, Aldrich looked like he hadn't been shaving for more than a week. After a moment's silence, Eric realized the man was awaiting similar information from him.

"Lieutenant junior grade Eric Cobb," Eric said. "This is my gunner, Rawles. Since you guys actually gave us some warning, I'll assume it's not your fleet that gunned us down."

If Aldrich was non-plussed that Eric didn't give him any more information the man did not show it.

"It would appear that you have met our erstwhile adversaries the *Kriegsmarine*," Aldrich replied. "I take it that you, then, are the aircraft who sent the position report in the clear?"

"That would be us," Eric replied. Aldrich smiled.

"Well thank you for not making my wife a widow," Aldrich said. At Eric's look, Aldrich just smiled.

"I am sure Captain Gordon will explain everything to you if he sees fit. Until then, please enjoy our hospitality. *Leftenant* Cobb, you appear to have taken a pretty good knock on the head. I'll need to check you out once we get aboard."

17

Eric started to nod, then realized that would be very foolish.

"That would probably be a good idea," he began, then belatedly added, "sir."

Ten minutes later, Eric stood watching Aldrich's finger as the young-looking officer moved his hand back and forth. The two men were standing in *Exeter*'s port dressing station, a space that was normally the petty officers' mess. When the heavy cruiser was getting ready to enter combat, the space was set aside for casualty treatment and stabilization before the unfortunate subjects were taken to sick bay below.

"You mentioned something about me saving your wife from becoming a widow?" Eric asked after a moment.

"Yes, I did," Aldrich replied.

"Sir, I can tell the ship is at Condition Two," Eric continued. "Obviously you guys are expecting a fight. I got sort of confused after getting shot up, but weren't the Germans a bit far away for you to be preparing for combat?"

"Very astute observation, *Leftenant*," another voice interjected. Eric saw the two ratings in the room jump to their feet, followed at a more leisurely pace by Rawles. Eric started to turn his head to see what they were looking at.

"I will not be able to tell if you have a concussion if you turn your head, *Leftenant* Cobb," Aldrich said, causing Eric to stop his movement. "Captain Gordon, sir," he said, nodding towards the door.

"*Leftenant* Aldrich," Captain Gordon replied. "I see you've been fishing again."

Aldrich smiled as he finished moving his finger back and forth.

"I think this one is a tad bit large to have thrown back, Captain," Aldrich said, stepping back. "We're done here, *Leftenant*."

Eric turned around, well aware of his sorry appearance in a borrowed pair of Royal Navy overalls. Rawles and he had both gladly handed over their waterlogged clothes in exchange for dry clothing, but now he felt vaguely self-conscious in meeting the *Exeter*'s master. Gordon was a man of slightly above average height, with piercing eyes and gray, thinning hair topping an aristocratic face.

"Well, I must agree," Gordon said, giving Eric a pensive look. "I suppose you play what you Americans call football?"

"I did, sir," Eric replied. "For the Naval Academy."

"Barbaric sport," Gordon said. "Can't see why anyone would enjoy watching roughly twenty men bash each other's brains out over some poor pig's hide."

Eric found himself starting to smile as he contemplated a comeback. Gordon continued without giving him a chance to defend American honor.

"But, that's not what you were talking about to *Leftenant* Aldrich, and time is short. Our mission, when you sighted us, was to gain contact with the German fleet so that we could ascertain its position."

Eric nodded, starting to get a glimmer of understanding.

"Since our own aviators believed that the weather was far too much of a dog's breakfast to fly, the task fell upon the Home Fleet's cruisers, or more correctly, what cruisers broke out of Scapa Flow with His Majesty."

"Broke out of Scapa Flow?" Eric asked, confused.

Gordon and Aldrich shared a look.

"You are aware of the armistice signed a fortnight ago, yes?"

"The one between you guys and the Krauts? Yes, sir, I'm aware."

"There was some fine print agreed to by Lord Halifax's negotiators that did not sit well with the King," Gordon continued simply. "Namely the part about turning over the occupied nations' governments-in-exile and all of their forces that had fought under our command."

"That part was not covered in our briefings," Eric replied.

Of course, we've been at sea ever since it looked like you guys were about to be knocked out of the war, he didn't add. Eric was certain the term "neutral country" would lose all meaning. if the full details of the USN's actions to facilitate Great Britain's war efforts ever came to light.

Which may explain why the Krauts turned two American aircraft into colanders.

"This breakout wasn't exactly long in the planning, *Leftenant*," Gordon replied with a tight smile. "However, this is of no matter. What is important is that the Home Fleet and a few fast liners did manage to break out. What we did not expect was for the Germans to have anticipated our decision and placed submarines in our path."

Eric fought to keep the astonishment off of his face.

The submarines were part of the reason you guys had to surrender! he thought, incredulous.

"The *Queen Mary*, carrying a large contingent of forces, was torpedoed last night," Gordon continued, either not reading Eric's brief change of expression or choosing to ignore it. "She did not sink, but her speed was greatly slowed. This morning, it was decided to offload her passengers and scuttle the vessel."

Eric looked at Aldrich and then Captain Gordon.

"I am coming to the reason behind *Leftenant* Aldrich's comment," Gordon said with a slight smile. "Before the fleet departed Scapa Flow, there were reports that the German fleet was expected to sortie in order to attempt to intercept the Royal Family and compel their return. They were believed to be another two hundred miles east of the position you radioed."

I am beginning to understand now, Eric thought.

"As I noted, our own pilots did not think the conditions were suitable for flying as dawn broke. Which is why this vessel is currently part of a picket line, and as *Leftenant* Aldrich alluded to, would have likely encountered Jerry much as you did—guns first."

Eric could hear the disdain in Gordon's voice and decided to intercede on behalf of his British counterparts.

"Sir, with all due respect, the weather *is* too bad to be flying," he said bitterly. "Our commander volunteered the most experienced pilots in our squadron, and even then he had to persuade Admiral No...our admiral to allow us to fly."

Gordon's small smile broadened.

"Lieutenant Cobb, I am well aware that you are off of the aircraft carrier *Ranger*, specifically from VB-4. I am also aware that your signal was picked up by the cruiser *Augusta* and that your commander, apparently, perished. Finally, I am aware that Rear Admiral Noyes is under strict orders not to engage in direct combat with the *Kriegsmarine* unless they cross the established neutrality line."

This time the surprise was far too great for Eric to maintain any hint of a poker face.

"Guess I could have passed on tossing the codebooks over the side," Rawles said coolly.

20

"Unfortunately, *Leftenant*, the manner by which I know all this information also means that your fleet realizes we have plucked you out of the Atlantic. That," Gordon continued, his smile disappearing, "places us in a bit of a quandary."

Gordon turned towards Rawles and the two ratings in the room.

"Gentlemen, if you could excuse us?" he asked, the tone of his voice belying the appearance of his question being a request. Eric was glad to see Rawles follow the two men out into the passageway.

"As I was saying, your presence here places us into a bit of a fix. You, *Leftenant*, are an officer of a neutral nation. More importantly a neutral nation with certain elements who would gladly seize upon your death or serious injury in order to support the agenda of keeping your nation from rendering His Majesty's government any aid. I am sure that you are familiar with the term 'impressment' as it applies to our nations' shared histories?"

Eric nodded, starting to see where Gordon was going.

We fought a minor debacle in 1812 over just that issue as I recall, Eric thought somberly.

"So, in order to avoid any discussions of that sort of thing, I have consulted with my superiors. We can hardly just stuff you in a whaleboat and leave you in the middle of the Atlantic. Therefore, I am here to offer you a choice to transfer to the H.M.S. *Punjabi*. This vessel will then be tasked with escorting the liners out of harm's way, and that is probably the safest thing we can provide at the moment."

Well, no, you could actually return me to American forces or put me on a neutral vessel, Eric thought sharply, but decided some things were best left unvoiced.

"What effect will this have on your force?" he asked instead.

Gordon paused for a few moments, and Eric could see the wheels turning in the British captain's head.

"The effects would not be positive," Gordon finally answered. The man then took a deep sigh, with the breaking of his mental dam almost perceptible.

"The division of destroyers with us is one of two that departed Scapa Flow with their actual assigned crews, full complement of torpedoes, and allotted depth charges," *Exeter*'s captain said, his voice clipped. "The size of the German force is unknown, but it is highly unlikely that our advantage is so great that we can afford to lose a destroyer before the action begins. The choice, however, is yours *Leftenant* Cobb."

The silence in the compartment after Gordon's explanation seemed to press in on Eric. At least thirty seconds passed, with Gordon growing perceptibly impatient, before the American replied.

"We were briefed before we departed Newport News that our forces were to make every effort to avoid giving the impression that we were aiding RN forces," he said, and watched Captain Gordon's face start to fall. "However, we were also instructed to respond to hostile acts in kind. Those bastards killed my squadron commander and nearly killed me. While I hesitate to give them another chance to finish the job, I'll be damned if I'll make their lives easier."

Gordon exhaled heavily.

"You do realize that when I transmit this news to Admiral Tovey your own forces are going to overhear it, correct?"

Eric shrugged.

"If I end up in Leavenworth it means no one else will be shooting at me," Eric replied grimly. "Seems to me that the situation is bad enough if I force you to take this ship out of the line, the. After what they did to London, I'm not sure I want them to catch the King or his family."

Eric saw several emotions flit across Gordon's face. The man was about to respond when the ship's loudspeaker crackled. Both men turned to look at the speaker mounted at the front of the compartment.

"Captain to the bridge," a calm, measured voice spoke. "I say again, Captain to the bridge."

"Last chance to back out, *Leftenant*," Captain Gordon said, heading for the companionway hatch.

"We'll stay, sir," Eric said, right before a thought struck him. "However, I do have one request."

"What would that be, *Leftenant?*"

"Do you think that His Majesty could consider asking President Roosevelt to give me a pardon? You know, just in case?"

Gordon stopped dead for a second, confusion on his face. Still looking befuddled, he shrugged.

"I'll be sure to pass along your request," the British officer allowed. "Even though I am unsure as to what you are referring to."

Eric smiled.

"I'm sure His Majesty will have someone who can advise him as to what I mean," Eric replied. Gordon shook his head and opened the hatch. There was a quick exchange of words with Aldrich that Eric couldn't quite hear, then the man was gone. A moment later, Lieutenant Aldrich stepped back through the door.

"What is your hat size, *Leftenant?*" Aldrich asked.

"Seven inches even," Eric said.

"I'll see what we can find in the way of a helmet for you."

Eric felt and heard the *Exeter*'s engines begin to accelerate. Aldrich's face clouded as the loudspeaker crackled again. A few moments later, the sound of a bugle call came over the device followed by the same clipped voice as before calling the crew to "Action Stations".

"Well now, it appears that our German friends have been sighted once more," Aldrich said grimly as he walked towards the speaking tube at the back of the compartment. "Either that or Jerry's bloody U-boats are at it again."

Eric suddenly thought about the implications of either of those events and didn't like what he was coming up with. Rawles and the two British seamen reentered the compartment as Aldrich began calling down to the ship's store for a helmet. Eric gave a wry smile as he saw that Rawles had already been given a helmet. The pie plate-shaped headgear looked slightly different than its American counterpart, but close enough that Eric was sure the gunner wouldn't have looked too out of place aboard *Ranger*.

"I see that our hosts have already seen to your comforts, Rawles," Eric teased his gunner.

"I'd be a lot more comfortable with a pair of guns in my hand aboard a *Dauntless*, sir," Rawles said, his voice tight. Eric could see the man was nervous, and he didn't blame him. He was about to make another comment when Aldrich's voice stopped him in his tracks.

"Right, understood, I will send *Leftenant* Cobb to the bridge with the runner while his gunner remains here," the medical officer said into the tube. "Aldrich out."

"Did I just hear what I think I did?" Eric asked, struggling to

23

keep his tone neutral.

"The captain is afraid that one shell will kill you both," Aldrich replied simply. "That would be bad for a great many reasons."

I hate it when people have a point, Eric thought. *At least, I hate it when said point means I'm about to get a front row seat to people shooting guns at me.*

"Well it's hard to argue with that logic," Eric said, looking up as a man arrived in the hatchway with his helmet and flash gear. "Rawles, try to stay out of the rum."

"Aye aye, sir," Rawles replied, his expression still sour.

"Midshipman Radcliffe, you are in charge until I get back," Aldrich said, then turned to Eric. "Given what I've been told, there's enough time to give you a quick tour of the vessel before I drop you off at the bridge. That is, if you'd like a quick tour."

"Certainly, sir," Eric said. "I did a midsummer cruise on the U.S.S. *Salt Lake City*, so it will be interesting to see how differently your side does things."

U.S.S. Houston
Cavite Naval Base
2020 Local (0820 Eastern)
13 September (12 September)

Whereas most men would have felt butterflies in their stomach prior to meeting their boss, Commander Jacob T. Morton found himself hoping that the rage and bitterness he felt did not show on his lined face. He took a deep, steadying breath as the orderly returned from inside the captain's day cabin.

"Captain Wallace will see you now, sir," the marine said, coming to attention.

"Thank you, corporal," Jacob replied, his accent betraying his Maine roots. With that, he stepped through the hatchway. Stepping forward to three steps before the desk of *Houston*'s master, he saluted.

"Commander Jacob Morton reporting as ordered, sir," Jacob said crisply. Standing well over six feet, with a tall, gangly frame, Jacob forced the short, heavyset man standing behind the desk to slightly crane his head back as he returned the salute of the *Houston*'s newest XO.

24

"When I heard they called you 'The Stork,' I wondered how someone got a nickname like that," Captain Sean Wallace observed drily, his Texas twang quite evident. "Now I see a slight resemblance to you and a crane. Please, take a seat before I develop a crick in my neck."

Jacob's expression didn't change, his green eyes continuing to hold Wallace's brown ones as he followed orders.

"Why do they call you 'The Stork,' if I may ask?" Wallace continued.

Why do people always ask if a question is okay **after** *it's already been said?* Jacob thought.

"Plebe boxing class, sir," Jacob replied. "One of my opponents stated fighting me was like being attacked by an angry stork. It stuck."

Captain Wallace nodded, running a hand through his thinning brown hair.

"Horrible class, that," Wallace replied. "I think that's probably the worst experience I've ever had in my life. I take it that you did all right?"

"I boxed in the Brigade intramurals," Jacob replied evenly. "I placed second in the light heavyweight class."

Wallace smiled.

"Well, glad to see your aggressiveness won't be a problem," he said with a smile. "Its part of the reason you're here. But before we get started, would you like me to have the mess send up something? There should be sandwiches or something available, I realize you're probably famished after coming all the way out from Pearl."

"No thank you, sir, I actually ate before coming aboard," Jacob said. "I will, with your permission, have some of that water in the corner however."

"By all means," Wallace said, gesturing towards the pitcher and glasses. As Jacob stood, *Houston*'s captain began their discussion.

"I understand that you were somewhat surprised when BuPers cut your orders."

"It's rare that an officer is requested by name, much less by someone he has never met," Jacob replied cautiously. "Serving twice as an XO is lucky, but three times is unheard of."

Wallace grimaced.

"When Captain Rooks got cancer three months ago it was a shock to the entire wardroom," Wallace replied. "Admiral Hart offered every one of the officers the opportunity to transfer to other vessels, and most of the division chiefs were reassigned throughout the fleet or sent back to Pearl. I only requested that Admiral Hart give me the most experienced XO possible, and apparently your name was selected."

Well that explains it, Jacob thought, fighting the urge to curse aloud.

"I understand you had been slated to take a destroyer in about six months," Wallace continued. "I realize that an XO tour, much less one here in the Forgotten Fleet, is hardly an equal trade, but Admiral Hart has assured me that he will personally see to it that your career doesn't suffer."

Jacob was taken aback by Wallace's frankness. Usually mere commanders were not informed of admiral and captain's personnel machinations, much less apologized to for their careers being possibly set back.

"Thank you, sir," he said, feeling a great deal of tension leave his body. Wallace gave a slight smile.

"I think, were I in your position, I would be ready to punch my captain out at the first opportunity. Given that you apparently have some experience with that, I would much prefer to clear the air before we have to work together."

Jacob smiled in return at Wallace's slight joke.

Obviously not one of those men who believes that the captain must appear as a god before all mortals, he thought. As if reading his mind, Wallace continued.

"I'm not a man to stand on protocol between us in private, especially given your seniority. I also won't beat around the bush—I expect you to be my hatchet man. All six departments on this ship are good, but I need you to make them excellent," Wallace said simply. "Especially as I think we'll be in war within a month."

Jacob gave his captain a measured look.

"I'm not saying I disagree, but what is your reasoning, sir?"

"The damn Japs are probably going to take the news out of Europe as a blank check to start 'liberating' some colonies around here, and we need to make sure they don't think the Philippines are also on the foreclosure list."

"I was told before I left Pearl that there's talk of still making the Philippines independent at the end of the year," Jacob replied. "With Great Britain's surrender, is that still going to happen?"

"Apparently that idiot MacArthur thinks that the Philippines can defend themselves with Navy help," Wallace snorted. "So, yes, it will probably happen, but that won't change any of our war plans."

"So Admiral Hart still intends to retreat to the Dutch East Indies if the Japanese attack? That was the last plan I was privy to when I was on CINCPAC staff."

"Yes, we're not staying here to absorb shells for the Army," Wallace replied.

"Instead we're going to die defending some occupied countries' colonies," Jacob replied, his voice more bitter than he intended. Wallace fixed him with a hard look.

"I will forgive that outburst XO since we are alone. But I would caution you that I will have considerably less patience if you display one iota of that opinion in front of any of our junior officers. Do I make myself absolutely clear, commander?"

Jacob reined in his temper, surprised that he had grown so annoyed.

"Very clear, sir," Jacob said calmly. "I apologize."

"It happens that I agree with you," Wallace said with a wave of his hand. "However, neither of us are in charge and the hour grows late. I notice you don't wear a wedding ring, but your personnel jacket indicated that you were married."

"My wife passed away six years ago," Jacob replied evenly. "She had a massive coronary when I was in Norfolk."

Wallace's face clouded for a moment.

"My apologies," Wallace said. "It'd be nice if the damn personnel folks had let me know that before I made an ass of myself."

"For some reason BuPers is incapable of passing that information to any of my duty stations," Jacob replied, his voice with a hard edge. "I go through this every time I have a new assignment. Thankfully to date they have never messed up Jo's file."

"Jo? You have a son?" Captain Wallace asked.

"No, short for Josephine," Jacob said with a broad smile. "My wife started calling her Jo because she swears it was quite obvious to

27

everyone that I had wanted a boy."

"I have three sons myself," Wallace said. "Trust me, in some ways daughters are easier. At least you don't have to worry about them being in harm's way."

"I wish that were absolutely true, sir," Jacob returned, his smile disappearing like morning fog.

Honolulu, Hawaii
0530 Local (1030 Eastern)
12 September

I am crazy. As in, "Welcome to the nuthouse, Josephine, we are so glad to see you" insane, Josephine Marie Morton thought for the fifth time that morning. Fighting back a yawn as she stood on the quay looking out into Honolulu's harbor, she turned to look at her three companions. Two of them loomed far above her own height even in the low heels she wore with her plain brown dress. The other was only a half foot taller than her with the athletic build of a long-distance runner. Giving a sideways glance at the trio, a thought came to her mind that nearly made her giggle.

"You're in somewhat good spirits," the smaller man said quietly. Turning to face him while simultaneously brushing back her shoulder-length brunette hair, Jo finally couldn't hold the light laugh in anymore.

"I'm sorry, Nick, but every time I see you three together I cannot help but wonder how your mother went from big, bigger, biggest to runt," Jo replied.

Nick Elrod Cobb, Lieutenant (j.g.), United States Navy, gave Jo a half smile.

You know, you could really be a lady killer if you tried, Jo thought wistfully. *However, you've made it very clear that you don't want to try with me—but a gal can dream.*

Nick, unlike his three brothers, had dark hair to go with his blue eyes. While none of the Cobbs were hard to look at, the youngest of the four sons had definitely gotten more than his fair share of handsome. Moreover, unlike the two blonde-haired grizzlies behind him, Nick wasn't so big that a woman felt she had to worry about being broken in half.

28

"I think our father figured he could get just as much manual labor for half the groceries," Nick replied, looking sideways at his two brothers.

"That's a theory…" Samuel Michael Cobb, Captain, United States Marine Corps began.

"…but probably not very valid," David Aaron Cobb, Captain, USMC and Sam's twin, finished.

Nick made a sound of frustration.

"You know, four years away from you two lugs and I'd forgotten just how fu…darn annoying that habit is!"

"You know, Nick, you really can swear around me," Jo said with a chuckle. "I promise, my father has said many, many worse things around the house, to include references to the act of copulation."

"It's not your opinion he's worried about," Sam observed, giving his younger brother a glower.

"No, it would be the fact that we wouldn't want him to ever give the impression that our mother didn't raise us to act like gentlemen around a lady."

Jo shook her head.

"Has anyone ever told you Southerners that the age of chivalry has long since passed?"

"Just because you Yankee women don't know how to demand proper behavior from your men doesn't mean that we have to stop giving it," David replied, looking out towards the harbor. "I do believe that is Patricia's vessel."

"Only half a day late," Nick observed. "Damn merchant..ow!"

Jo was amazed at how quickly Nick turned around, starting to raise his hands to punch one of his brothers then stopping to think better of it.

"Why do I get the feeling I'm witnessing a family story that has played out many, many times over the past twenty-four years?" Jo asked bemusedly.

"Because you're an astute observer of human behavior," Sam said lowly, not taking his eyes off Nick.

"In addition to being highly intelligent," David continued, also watching Nick like a hawk. "Oh, and very pretty."

Jo felt herself starting to blush and was glad for the olive tint of her skin.

Sorry boys, I own a mirror, she thought. While she didn't consider herself *fat* by any means, Jo knew she could stand to lose a few pounds. *Thankfully it seems to go to the right places, though.* Voluptuous was a fair word to describe her even if pretty wasn't.

"Yes, these two think it's funny to both pick on someone," Nick said lowly, his voice making it very clear that there'd be a fight if either brother touched him again.

"Mama raised you better than to curse in front of a lady," Sam replied simply.

The incoming vessel sounded its whistle, interrupting the brothers' discussion. A small liner, the *S.S. Hampton Roads* made a regular trip between Hawaii and the mainland. Usually it returned with mostly military dependents and those seeking to make their fortune working at Pearl Harbor or one of the various Army posts scattered around the islands. Ten minutes after sounding her whistle, the ship's crew was tossing ropes to the men gathered on the dock. Shortly after that, Jo got to see yet another member of the Cobb family.

"Will you look at the hams on that one," a man said a little too loudly to his companion as they walked by. Jo, focusing on the ship, whipped her head around to see that both men were likewise looking at the gangplank as a tall, beautiful brunette began to descend. The woman was wearing a yellow dress and a matching hat, with curly locks trailing all the way down past her shoulders.

I wonder if that's...

"Well that's a sight for sore eyes," the second man replied, "Looks like we're about to get some fresh round eye..."

The man never got to finish his sentence. One second Sam, David, and Nick were standing on opposite sides of her. The next, Nick had seemingly teleported the ten feet to the ogling duo's location. Looking at the two men, Jo could tell that they were soldiers. She couldn't have identified what clued her in about their manner or their walk, but upon a closer look it was blindingly obvious.

"Excuse me, mister," Nick said lightly, "but you wouldn't happen to be about to make a comment about that women in the yellow dress, would you?"

The two men looked at Nick, then looked at each other.

"She your wife or something, pal?" one of them asked

30

belligerently. "Looks a little young to be married."

"As a matter of fact, no," Nick replied. "She's my sister."

The two men looked at one another, then looked at Nick.

"Okay, so even if my buddy and I here were about to say something, we were having a private conversation. We doubt your sister minds."

Not only soldiers, but stupid ones, Jo thought.

"Yes, but *I* mind, and I know exactly what someone means when they start talking about roundeye," Nick continued. "I would appreciate it if you talked quieter or maybe keep your comments to yourself."

The first man looked somewhat sheepish, but his companion apparently had been having a bad day.

"Well we'd *appreciate* it if you minded your own business," the man sneered. "You'd probably like it a lot more too."

Just like that, I'm standing by myself, Jo thought to herself, as Sam and David both ambled over behind their younger brother.

"You know, we're not quite as sensitive about what we may overhear," Sam said.

"After all, with the wind blowing in our direction, you may not have realized that your comments about our sister were audible to us," David continued.

"But Nick here asked you kindly enough to maybe take your comments elsewhere, and you have refused," Sam resumed, his voice dropping lower.

"So maybe it would help if we told you a bit more forcefully to *go somewhere else,*" David finished. Jo felt the hair on the back of her neck rise at David's tone.

Never thought I'd see someone beat to death, she thought nervously. Fortunately the quieter of the two soldiers realized that his friend's mouth was about to put both of them in the hospital if they were lucky, morgue if not.

"Let's go, Matt," the man said. "I don't think that dame's going to give you the time of day if you're in traction."

"Matt" gave all three Cobbs a cold, hard look as he allowed his friend to tug him away. If he was trying for intimidation, he could have saved his breath and energy.

I think he'd have more luck scaring one of the volcanoes around here, Jo

31

thought, fighting the urge to shiver from the adrenaline rushing through her. She was about to say something when she heard a very exasperated, feminine sigh behind her. Turning, Jo saw that the woman in yellow had made a beeline towards the three glowering men, her brow furrowed and mouth in a thin line. Looking at the other woman's features close up, Jo felt a sudden, insane pang of jealousy.

No wonder her brothers are protective of her, Jo thought bitterly. *Probably had plenty of practice.*

"Well, glad to see some things never change," the woman snapped, the ice in her voice freezing the honey of her drawl. "Let me guess? Did someone make an untoward comment about my attire and you three felt the need to defend my honor?"

Jo was in shock at the transformation of all three Cobbs. One moment the trio had been clearly ready to perform carefully choreographed mayhem. The next, Sam, David, and Nick wore almost identically sheepish looks.

Holy shit, I need to take lessons from her, Jo thought.

"I am once again reminded of why I will probably die a spinster," the woman continued, her delivery rapid and tone sharp.

"We figured fleeing Alabama like a wanted fugitive two weeks before your wedding to Beau might have had a bit more to do with that," Nick responded, his face hard. Both of his brothers stepped away from him, the move so quick that it was obviously unconscious. Jo didn't blame them, as if looks could kill Nick would have simply ceased to exist.

Her eyes turned into green death rays, Jo thought, remembering a line from some dime store novel she had read as a teenager.

"The only state I am a 'fugitive' from is matrimony, Nick," the woman observed. "Don't you stand here and judge me when it is *obvious* that you do not find it very palatable yourself—or is the issue more that I jilted your guys' childhood friend?"

Nick sighed exasperatedly at his sister.

"Yes, of course, because I have had so many opportunities to meet women in my line of work. Why, just the other day the *Nautilus* stopped off at this tropical refuge where there were all these doe-eyed maidens…"

"So I suppose we'll just forget all the wonderful young women that mother tried to set you up with? At least Eric was smart

32

enough to finally ask Joyce to marry him."

"Well judging from the current situation, a 'yes' sure doesn't seem to mean...."

Jo stepped between Nick and his sister, the movement causing him to stop mid-sentence. She stuck out her hand, catching the rapidly reddening Patricia by surprise.

"Hello Patricia, my name is Josephine Morton, and I'm a friend of your brothers," Jo said calmly. "As I know Nick here likes to run his trap to excess sometimes, I thought I'd see if you were interested in seeing your room sometime before nightfall."

"My room?" Patricia asked, so shocked that her anger was forgotten. "I'm sorry, there must be some...."

"Mistake? No, not really," Jo continued. "I've known Sam, David, and Nick since they got on the island. Rather than have you live by yourself, or move in with David only to have to move out when he gets hitched to Sadie, your brothers thought it'd be nice if you had a more experienced roommate to show you around."

Patricia released Jo's hand, her expression going from angry to suspicious.

"They did, did they?" she asked, arching an eyebrow. "And what do you get out of this, Miss Morton?"

You mean, other than the chance to see your brothers more often? Jo thought, successfully keeping a smile off of her face.

"I'm living in a four bedroom house by myself," Jo replied. "My father just got sent to join the Asiatic Fleet, and it'd be nice to have someone to help with household chores."

"I have very little independent means," Patricia said. "I was hoping to find a job at the shipyard or someplace else suitable to my skills."

"What skills do you have for the shipyard?" Jo asked, befuddled.

"I worked for an architect for the past four years working on blueprints," Patricia replied. "I understand drafting ships' plans is similar work."

Jo shrugged.

"Got me, but I do know the library is looking for more staff. Seems that one of the girls up and ran off with a *Dauntless* pilot."

"I have never understood why some women are so fascinated with pilots," Patricia replied. "No offense to present company."

33

Sam and David both gave their little sister a hurt look.

"Yes, it's sort of like having a father in the Navy—I don't get impressed at the sight of men in summer whites, you probably don't find silk scarves anything other than a waste of cloth."

Patricia smiled at Jo's sarcastic tone.

"I think that your offer sounds quite nice, um, Jo," Patricia said. "Especially if you've managed to put up with my brothers this long without going mad."

"So why did we come to meet you at the dock, again?" Sam asked.

"Because you thought some random stranger might ravish me," Patricia replied simply. "Or that I'd fall in with villainous company due to a need for someone to help me with my luggage. Speaking of which, here are my chits."

Sam took the proffered claims forms, scanning them for a moment. Shaking his head, he turned to the other two.

"One would think Mom and Dad would have realized something was afoot when half their belongings disappeared. Nick, you go get the car—no need throwing our backs out."

Patricia sighed.

"If you look closer, oh dim-witted brother of mine, you will see that everything except for two chests of clothing and a container of housewares is due to arrive as a separate shipment. As to how I got everything out of the house, that will just remain my little secret."

"Like how you got the money to pull all of this off?" Nick asked *sotto voce* as he walked off. David and Sam moved off in the other direction, leaving Patricia and Jo standing alone at dockside.

"Have you always been able to get them to listen to you?" Jo asked.

Patricia smiled slightly.

"Only once I stopped being their tomboy shadow," she replied. "I think it's because I look so much like Mom now."

"Well, that and it's readily apparent they love their little sister," Jo observed.

Patricia's smile grew wider.

"Yes, that does help. Being the only girl does have its advantages."

"Like having your father wrapped around your finger so that he helps you escape Alabama?"

Patricia started, her smile immediately disappearing.

"How did you..?" she started, then stopped.

Jo grinned broadly.

"I'm an only child. I'm also Daddy's little girl. I know there's no way my father would let me marry an idiot or someone who was going to make me unhappy. From the way your brothers talk about your Dad, I think that applies for you also."

Patricia gave Jo an appraising glance.

"I think I understand why my brothers obviously like you," she said slowly.

"Yes, like the little sister they missed, not..." Jo started, then stopped with a blush.

That came out a little bit more bitter than I intended, Jo realized sheepishly.

"Not like you want them to?" Patricia finished for her.

"Well, Sam and Nick, yes," Jo replied, her face still heated. "I love Sadie."

"Ah, yes, the ever elusive Sadie. You know my mother is absolutely furious that David got engaged without her meeting his fiancée?"

"I heard that rumor somewhere," Jo allowed. "Might've been tied in with the Western Union lines melting down a couple weeks ago. I'm sure the telegram folks are going to get really, really familiar with your brothers as soon as your mother knows for sure you've turned up here."

"There are worse reasons to become familiar with the telegraph man," Patricia said, a flicker of worry crossing her face.

"Has there been any more word from Eric? The boys say all they know is that he's on the *Ranger* out in the Atlantic."

"No, none," Patricia replied. "I just hope he's all right."

"He's a Cobb," Jo replied. "Of course he's all right."

H.M.S. Exeter
North Atlantic
1330 Local (1030 Eastern)
12 September

Whether or not Eric was all right was likely a matter of opinion.

He wasn't flying anymore, as the weather conditions had started to become much worse since he'd left *Ranger*'s deck that morning. The base of the clouds had once again descended, and he estimated that the ceiling was well under ten thousand feet. At sea level, visibility was under ten miles, and an approaching squall promised to make it less than that very soon.

I don't blame the Brit pilots for nixing the thought of flying reconnaissance in this, Eric thought. *Yet for some reason I'd still rather take my chances in that soup than be on this ship right now. She's definitely going into harm's way, and fast.*

The heavy cruiser's deck throbbed beneath his feet, and the smoke pouring from her stack and stiff wind blowing onto her bridge told him that *Exeter* had definitely picked up speed.

"Sir, I've brought *Leftenant* Cobb," Adlich said, causing Captain Gordon to turn around. *Exeter*'s master had obviously been mollified by the worsening conditions, as he gave Eric a wry grin when the American officer stepped up beside him.

Whoa, it's cold out here, Eric thought. As if reading his mind, a petty officer handed him a jacket.

"We remove the windows when we're getting ready to go into action," the man said. "Lesson learned after River Plate."

"Thank you," Eric said. "I guess the windows would be a bit problematic in a fight."

The petty officer gave a wan smile, pointing to a scar down his cheek.

"Glass splinters are a bit sharp, yes."

"Your squadron commander was either a very brave man or a much better pilot than anyone I know," Gordon said solemnly from behind the ship's wheel.

Or alternatively, Commander Cobleigh was an idiot who didn't check with the meteorologist before we took off.

Eric was about to reply when the talker at the rear of the bridge interrupted him.

"Sir, *Hood* should be coming into visual range off of our port bow," the rating reported. "Range fifteen thousand yards."

"Thank you," Gordon replied. The captain then strode to the front of the bridge, stopping at a device that reminded Eric of the sightseeing binoculars atop the Empire State Building. Bending slightly, Gordon wiped down the eyepieces, then swiveled the binoculars to look through them.

"Officer of the deck," Gordon said after a moment.

"Yes, sir?" a Royal Navy lieutenant answered from Eric's right. Roughly Eric's height, the broad-shouldered man looked like he could probably snap a good-sized tree in half with his bare hands.

"Confirm with gunnery that the director's tracking *Hood*'s bearing to be three one zero, estimated range fourteen thousand, seven hundred fifty yards."

"Aye aye, sir," the officer replied. Eric heard the RN officer repeating the information as Gordon stepped back from the sight and turned to look at him.

"Well, if you want to see how the other half lives, *Leftenant* Cobb, feel free to have a look."

Eric hoped he didn't look as eager as he felt walking forward towards the bridge windows. Bending a little further to look through the sight, he pressed his face up against the eyepieces. Swinging the glasses, he found himself looking at the H.M.S. *Hood*, flagship of the Royal Navy. With her square bridge, four turrets, and rakish lines, the battlecruiser was a large, beautiful vessel that displaced over four times the *Exeter*'s tonnage. Black smoke poured from her stack, and her massive bow wave told Eric that she was moving at good speed.

"You can change the magnification with the switch under your right hand," Gordon said, startling Eric slightly. He followed the British master's advice, continuing until he could see the entire approaching British force as it closed. Destroyers were roughly one thousand yards in front of and to either side of the *Hood*. Behind her at one-thousand-yard intervals were two large vessels, either battleships or battlecruisers, with another one starting to exit the mist like some sort of great beast stirring from its cave. After a moment, Eric recognized the distinctive silhouette as that of a *Nelson*-class battleship.

"That is the *King George V*, *Prince of Wales*, and *Nelson* behind her. *Warspite* should be next."

Eric nodded at Gordon's statement, continuing to watch as the final battleship made its appearance. A moment later, Gordon starting to give orders to the helmsman. *Exeter*'s bow began to swing around to port, causing Eric to step back from the sight with

37

a puzzled expression.

"We'll be passing between the destroyer screen and the *Hood* to take our place in line," Gordon said. Eric turned back to the device, continuing to study the British battleline. A few moments later, there was the crackle of the loudspeaker.

"All hands, this is the captain speaking," Gordon began. "Shortly we will be passing by the *Hood*. All available hands are to turn out topside to give three cheers for His Majesty. That is all."

Eric stepped back from the sight, his face clearly radiating his shock. Gordon smiled as he came back up towards the front of the bridge with the officer of the deck.

"The *King* is going into battle?" he asked incredulously. "Isn't that a bit..."

"Dangerous?" Gordon finished for him. "Yes, but much like your situation, circumstances precluded His Majesty's transfer to another vessel."

"What? That doesn't make any..."

"His Majesty was apparently aboard the *Hood* receiving a briefing from the First Sea Lord when the *Queen Mary* was torpedoed," Gordon said, his voice cold. "We were not expecting the German surface units to be as close as they were, and it was considered imprudent to stop the *Hood* with at least two confirmed submarines close about. Is that sufficient explanation to you, or would you like to continue questioning our tactics?"

Eric could tell he was straining his host's civility, but the enormity of what was at risk made him feel he had to say something.

"I'm no expert at surface tactics..."

"That much is obvious," Gordon snapped.

"...but the *Hood* is a battlecruiser," Eric finished in a rush. "While I didn't get a great look at the Germans before they shot up me and my commander, Rawles saw at least two battleships."

"Your concern is noted, *Leftenant* Cobb, but I think that you will see the *Hood* is a bit hardier than a dive bomber."

Okay, I'm just going to shut up now, Eric said. *I may have slept through a lot of history, but I seem to recall the last time British battlecruisers met German heavy guns it didn't go so well. A quote about there being problems with your "bloody ships" or something similar comes to mind.* The Battle of Jutland hadn't been that long ago, as evidenced by the *Warspite* still being a front-line unit. Eric sincerely hoped Gordon's confidence was well-placed.

"Sir, we are almost on the *Hood*," the officer of the deck interrupted. Eric turned and realized that the lead destroyer was indeed almost abreast the *Exeter*, with the *Hood* now a looming presence just beyond.

"The *Hood*, after her refit, is the most powerful warship in the world," Gordon continued, his voice a little less frigid. "The *Bismark* and *Tirpitz* have only recently gone through refit, while the *Scharnhorst* and *Gneisenau* have not been in the open ocean for almost six months. There should not be any major danger."

If you're looking around the room and you can't find the mark, guess what? **You're** *the mark.* Eric's father's words, an admonishment to always be suspicious of any situation that seemed too good to be true, came back to him with a cold feeling in his stomach.

The Germans would **not** *be out here unless they had a plan*, Eric continued thinking. *Somehow I think that, much like the Royal Air Force, the Royal Navy is about to receive a rude shock.*

"All right lads, three cheers for His Majesty," The loudspeaker crackled. "Hip...hip..."

As the *Exeter*'s crew yelled at the top of their lungs, Eric studied the *Hood* in passing. The two vessels were close enough that he could see a party of men in white uniforms standing on the battlecruiser's bridge and the extraordinarily large flag streaming from the *Hood*'s yardarm. Picking up a pair of binoculars resting on a shelf near the bridge's front lip, he focused on the pennant.

"That's the Royal Standard," Gordon said after the last cheer rang out. The device consisted of four squares, two red with the other pair gold and blue, respectively. The two red were identical, forming the top left and bottom right portions of the flag. Looking closely, Eric could see elongated gold lions or griffins within the squares. The gold square had what looked like a standing red lion within a crimson square, while the blue had some sort of harp.

"What do the symbols mean, sir?" Eric asked. Gordon shook his head.

"*Leftenant*, I could probably remember if I thought hard enough about it, but I do not think that is very important right now."

Eric nodded, placing the binoculars back down as the *Exeter* continued to travel down the battleline. After *Warspite*, there were two more British heavy cruisers. At Gordon's command, the *Exeter* finished her turn, taking her place behind the other two CAs. Satisfied with his vessel's stationing, Gordon began dealing with the myriad tasks that a warship's captain was expected to perform before battle. Eric observed these with a sense of detachment, noting that the bridge crew operated like they had been there dozens of times. Mentally, he compared the men to those he had observed aboard the American heavy cruiser *Salt Lake City*.

Things are so similar, yet so different. You can tell these men have been at war for over three years, Eric thought, feeling strangely comforted by the obvious experience in front of him. The feeling was fleeting, however, as the talker at the rear of the bridge broke the routine.

"Sir, *Hood* reports multiple contacts, bearing oh three oh relative, range thirty thousand yards," the talker at the rear of the bridge said. It was if his words touched off a current of electricity around the entire compartment, as each man seemed to stiffen at his post.

"Well, glad to see that she's got better eyes than we do," Gordon muttered under his breath. "Pass the word to all stations."

Eric saw motion out of the corner of his eye and turned to see the *Exeter*'s two forward turrets training out and elevating.

"Flag is directing a change in course to one seven zero true," the talker continued. "Vessels will turn in sequence. Destroyers are to form up for torpedo attack to our stern."

Gordon nodded in acknowledgment, and Eric could see the man was obviously in pensive thought. After their earlier exchange, Eric had no desire to attempt to discern what he was thinking. Judging from the look on the man's face, it was probably nothing good. Looking to port, Eric could see the British destroyers starting to steam past for their rendezvous astern of *Exeter*, a scene that was repeated a moment later on the starboard side.

Is it my imagination, or is it getting a little bit easier to see again? Eric thought. *If so, is that a good or a bad thing?*

"Enemy force is turning with us," the talker said quietly.

*Now **that** is definitely a bad thing.*

Eric had a very passing familiarity with radar, as he had been the target dummy for *Ranger*'s fighter squadron to practice aerial intercepts. It was obvious, given the visibility, that the *Hood* hadn't sighted the enemy with the naked eye. Unless the Germans had a team of gypsies on their vessels, it appeared that they also had the ability to detect ships despite the murk.

Explains how they were able to shoot down Commander Cobleigh, Eric thought, feeling sick to his stomach. *My God, they probably knew we were there long before we came out of the cloudbank but wanted to make positive identification.*

The visibility was definitely starting to get better, at least at sea level. With only the distance of the British line to judge by, Eric guesstimated that visibility to the horizon was somewhere around twenty thousand yards.

Well within maximum range of everyone's guns, he thought. *I hope someone on this side knows what size force we're facing, as I doubt the Germans are idiots.*

"Sir, the *Hood* reports she is…"

With a roar and spout of black smoke from her side, the British flagship made the talker's report superfluous. The rest of the British battleline rapidly followed suit, the combined smoke from their guns floating backward like roiling, black thunderheads.

I can't see what in the hell they're shooting at, Eric thought, searching the horizon as he felt his stomach clench.

In truth, *Hood* and her counterparts had only a general idea of what they were engaging. Indeed, if the commander of the opposing force, Vice Admiral Erich Bey, had actually followed his orders to simply compel the Home Fleet to sail a relatively straight course while avoiding contact, there would have been no targets for them to engage. Instead, Bey had decided to close with the last known position of the Home Fleet in hopes of picking off the vessel or vessels the *Kriegsmarine*'s U-boats had allegedly crippled that morning. Regardless of his reasoning, Bey's aggressive nature had inadvertently led to his superiors' worst nightmare—the hastily organized Franco-German force being brought into contact with the far more experienced Royal Navy.

Admiral Bey, to his credit, played the hand he had dealt himself. Moments after *Hood*'s initial salvo landed short of his flagship, the KMS *Bismarck*, the German admiral began barking orders. The first was for the radar-equipped vessels in his fleet to return fire. The second was for the entire column to change course in order to sharpen the rate of closure and allow the Vichy French vessels, limited to visual acquisition, to also engage. The final directive was for a position report to be repeatedly sent without any encryption so that nearby U-boats could immediately set course in an attempt to pick off any stragglers.

"Well, looks like the other side is game," Captain Gordon drily observed as multiple waterspouts appeared amongst the British battleships. A moment later the distant sound of the explosions reached Eric's ears.

"Looks like they're over-concentrating on the front of the line though," Eric observed.

Gordon turned to look at the American pilot.

"Would you prefer they spread their fire more evenly so we can have a taste, *Leftenant*?"

"No sir, not with the shells that are being slung out there."

Gordon brought his binoculars back up.

"Still can't see the enemy yet, but that's why the boffins were aboard during our refit," Gordon said. The man turned to his talker, jaw clenched.

"Tell Guns they may fire when we have visual contact or the enemy reaches nineteen thousand yards, whichever comes first," Gordon said, his voice clipped. "Inform bridge of the eventual target's bearing so we may get a look."

"Aye aye, Captain."

Gordon turned back towards Eric and opened his mouth when he was interrupted by the sound of ripping canvas followed by the *smack!* of four shells landing between *Exeter* and the next British cruiser in front of her. A moment later, a bell began ringing at the rear of *Exeter*'s bridge. Eric was about to ask what the device signified when the heavy cruiser's forward turrets roared, the blast hitting him like a physical blow. The look of shock was obviously quite apparent, as Gordon gave Eric an apologetic smile.

"Sorry, guess I should have…"

Exeter's captain was again interrupted, except this time by two bright flashes aboard the cruiser forward of her the British battleline. The other vessel was visibly staggered by the blows, with a fire immediately starting astern.

"Looks like *Suffolk* has worse luck than we do," Gordon observed grimly. The British heavy cruiser's turrets replied back

42

towards the enemy, but it was obvious, even to Eric, that their companion vessel was badly hit.

"Guns reports target is at bearing two nine zero, range twenty thousand yards…"

The bell ringing cut the rating off, as it was followed immediately by the *Exeter* unleashing a full broadside. Gordon had already begun to swing his sight around to the reported bearing, and bent to see what his guns were up to. Eric, looking past the captain, saw *Suffolk* receive another hit, this one causing debris to fly up from the vicinity of her bridge. He suddenly felt his mouth go dry.

Someone has the range, he thought grimly.

"Bloody good show Guns!" Gordon shouted into the voice tube near his sight. "Give that bastard another…"

The firing gong rang again, *Exeter*'s gunnery officer apparently already ahead of Gordon. Eric braced himself, the roar of the naval rifles starting to cause a slight ringing in his ears. He turned to look towards the horizon, following the direction of *Exeter*'s guns.

"These will help," the officer of the deck said from beside him, handing him a pair of binoculars.

"Thank you," Eric said, turning towards the officer only to see the man go pale.

"Oh bloody hell! Look at the *Hood*!"

Eric turned and looked down the British line, noting as he turned that the *Suffolk* was heeling to *Exeter*'s starboard with flames shooting from her amidships and rear turret. Ignoring the heavily damaged heavy cruiser, he brought up his binoculars as he looked towards the front of the British line. In an instant, he could see why the officer of the deck had made his exclamation. The battlecruiser's guns appeared frozen in place, and oil was visibly gushing from her amidships. As Eric watched, another salvo splashed around her, with a sudden flare and billow of smoke from her stern indicating something serious had been hit.

"Captain, the *Hood* is signaling a power failure!" the officer of the deck shouted. Eric turned to see the man had acquired another set of eyeglasses and was also studying the flagship.

Gordon nodded, stepping back from his captain's sight and brought his own set of binoculars up to study the battlecruiser. Eric quickly handed his over before the OOD could react.

"It would appear that our Teutonic friends can shoot a bit better than we expected," Gordon said grimly.

Admiral Bey would have agreed with Gordon's assessment had he heard it, as he too was pleasantly surprised at how well his scratch fleet was performing. Unfortunately for the Germans, however, the British could shoot almost as well, their guns seemed to be doing far more damage, and they had much better fire distribution. The only British capital ships with major damage were the *Hood*, set ablaze and rendered powerless by the *Tirpitz* and *Jean Bart*, and *Nelson* due to hits from the *Bismarck* and *Strasbourg*. Among the cruisers, only the *Suffolk* had been hit, being thoroughly mauled by the KMS *Hipper* and *Lutzow*. In exchange, only the *Jean Bart*, *Gneisenau*, and *Bismarck* remained relatively unscathed among his battleline. Of the rest of his vessels, the French battlecruiser *Strasbourg* had been thoroughly holed by the H.M.S. *Warspite*'s accurate shooting, *Tirpitz* was noticeably down by the bows, and *Scharnhorst* had received at least two hits from *Prince of Wales* in the first ten minutes of the fight.

Bey's escorts, consisting of the pocket battleship *Lutzow* and a force of German and Vichy French cruisers, had arranged themselves in an *ad hoc* screen to starboard. The fact that they outnumbered their British counterparts had not spared them from damage, albeit not as heavy as that suffered by the Franco-German battleline. Moreover, while *Exeter*'s shooting had set the lead vessel, the French heavy cruiser *Colbert*, ablaze and slowed her, this was more than offset by the battering the *Suffolk* had received from the *Lutzow*, *Hipper*, and *Seydlitz*. As that vessel fell backward in the British formation, the remaining cruisers split their fire between the *Exeter*, *Norfolk*, and the destroyers beginning their attack approach.

Word of the British DDs' approach caused Bey some consternation. While it could be argued that his force was evenly matched with the British battleline, the approaching destroyers could swiftly change this equation if they got into torpedo range. Deciding that discretion was the better part of valor, Bey ordered all vessels to make smoke and disengage. It was just after the force began their simultaneous turn that disaster struck.

The KMS *Scharnhorst*, like the *Hood*, had begun life as a battlecruiser. While both she and her sister had been upgraded during the Armistice Period with 15-inch turrets, the *Kriegsmarine* had made the conscious decision not to upgrade her armor. The folly of this choice became readily apparent as the *Prince of Wales'* twentieth salvo placed a pair of 14-inch shells through her amidships belt. While neither shell fully detonated, their passage severed the steering controls between the light battleship's bridge and rudder.

The *Scharnhorst'*s helmsman barely had time to inform the captain of this before the second half of *PoW'*s staggered salvo arrived, clearing the battleship's bridge with one shell and and hitting *Scharnhorst* on the armored "turtle deck" right above her engineering spaces with a second. To many bystanders' horror, a visible gout of steam spewed from the vessel's side as all 38,000 tons of her staggered like a stunned bull. Only the fact that her 15-inch guns fired a ragged broadside back at the British line indicated that the vessel still had power, but it was obvious to all that she had been severely hurt.

One of those observers was the captain of the KMS *Gneisenau*, *Scharnhorst'*s sister ship and the next battleship in line. Confronted with the heavily wounded *Scharnhorst* drifting back towards him, the man ordered the helm brought back hard to starboard. In one of the horrible vagaries of warfare, the *Gneisenau* simultaneously masked her sister ship from the *Prince of Wales'* fire and corrected the aim of her own assailant, the H.M.S. *Nelson*. No one would ever know how many 16-inch shells hit of the five that had been fired at the *Gneisenau*, as the only one that mattered was the one that found the German battleship's forward magazine. With a massive roar, bright flash, and volcanic outpouring of flame, the *Gneisenau'*s bow disappeared. *Scharnhorst* and *Jean Bart'*s horrified crews were subjected to the spectacle of the *Gneisenau'*s stern whipping upwards, propellers still turning. The structures only glistened for a moment, as the battleship's momentum carried her aft end into the roiling black cloud serving as a tombstone for a 40,000-ton man-of-war and the 1,700 men who manned her.

"Holy shit! Holy shit!" Eric exclaimed, his expletives lost in the general pandemonium that was *Exeter'*s bridge.

"Get yourselves together!" Gordon roared, waving his hands. As if to emphasize his point, there was the sound of ripping canvas, and a moment later, the *Exeter* found herself surrounded by large waterspouts.

"Port ten degrees!" Gordon barked, the bridge crew quickly returning to their tasks.

"Sir, *Nelson* is signaling that she is heaving to!"

"What in the bloody hell is the matter with her?!" Gordon muttered, a moment before *Exeter*'s guns roared again.

"Guns reports we are engaging and being engaged by a pocket battleship. He believes it is the…" the talker reported.

Once again there was the sound of ripping canvas, this time far louder. Eric instinctively ducked just before the *Exeter* shuddered simultaneously with the loud *bang!* just above their heads. Dimly, he saw something fall out of the corner of his eye even as there was a sound like several wasps all around him. Coming back to his feet, Eric smelled the strong aroma of explosives for the second time that day, except this time there was a man screaming like a shot rabbit to accompany it.

"Damage report!" Gordon shouted. "Someone shut that man up!"

Feeling something wet on his face, Eric reached up to touch it and came away with blood. He frantically reached up to feel if he had a wound, and only came away with more blood. Looking around in horror, he suddenly realized that the blood was not his, but that of a British rating who was now missing half of his head, neck, and upper chest. Eric barely had time to register this before a litter crew came bursting into the bridge. The four men headed to the aft portion of the structure, obviously there for the man who had been screaming before a gag had been shoved in his mouth. Eric followed the litter team's path, then immediately wished he hadn't as his stomach lurched. The casualty's abdomen was laid open, and Eric saw the red and grey of intestine on the deck before turning back forward.

Oh God, he thought, then had another as he thought about the injured man's likely destination. *I hope Rawles is okay.*

"Hard a starboard!" Gordon barked. Eric braced himself as the *Exeter* heeled over, the vessel chasing the previous salvo as her guns roared back at the German pocket battleship. He noticed that the guns were starting to bear even further aft as the cruiser maneuvered to keep up with the remainder of the British battleline. Looking to starboard, Eric saw the battleship *Nelson* drifting past them on her starboard side. The vessel's forward-mounted triple turrets, still elevated to port, fired off a full salvo once *Exeter* was past, but it was clear that the battleship had suffered severe damage.

"Sir, we took one glancing hit to the bridge roof," the OOD reported, pointing at the hit that had sprayed splinters into the structure. Eric was amazed at the man's calm. "We took another hit aft, but it detonated in the galley."

"*King George V* signals commence torpedo attack with destroyers," the talker interrupted. "All ships with tubes to attack enemy cripples."

Six waterspouts impacted approximately three hundred yards to port, and Eric found himself questioning the wisdom of staying aboard the heavy cruiser after all.

"Well, looks like this ship will continue her tradition of picking on women bigger than her," Gordon observed drily. "Flank speed, port thirty degrees. Get me the torpedo flat."

Eric looked once again at the hole in the bridge roof.

A step either way and I'd probably be dead, he thought wildly. *Or worse, if that shell had it full on we'd all be gone.* Shaking his head, he turned to look off to port as the throb of *Exeter*'s engines began to increase.

"You ever participate in a torpedo attack during your summer cruise, Mr. Cobb?" Gordon asked after barking several orders to the helm.

"No sir," Eric croaked, then swallowed to get a clearer voice. "Our cruisers don't have torpedoes. I'm familiar with how to do one theoretically…"

Exeter's guns banged out another salvo, even as the German pocket battleship's return fire landed where she would have been had the cruiser continued straight.

"Well, looks like you're about to get to apply some of that theoretical knowledge," Gordon said, bringing his binoculars up. The man scanned the opposing line.

"The three big battleships are turning away under cover of smoke along with the majority of the cruisers. That Frog battlecruiser looks about done for, and that pocket battleship and heavy cruiser will soon have more than enough to deal with when the destroyers catch up," Gordon said, pointing as he talked. *Exeter*'s master turned to give his orders.

"Tell Lieutenant Commander Gannon his target is the pocket battleship! Guns are to…"

The crescendo of incoming shells drowned Gordon out, this time ending with the *Exeter* leaping out of the water and shuddering as she was hit. Once again the bridge wing was alive with fragments, and for the second time Eric felt a splash of wetness across his side. Looking down, he saw his entire left side was covered in blood and flesh. For a moment he believed it was his, until he blissfully realized that he felt no pain.

"Damage report!" Gordon shouted again. "Litter party!"

"Sir, I believe I am hit," the OOD gasped. Eric turned to see the man's arm missing from just below the elbow, blood spraying from the severed stump.

"Corpsman!" Gordon shouted angrily, stepping towards the lieutenant. The captain never made, it, as the OOD toppled face forward, revealing jagged wounds in his back where splinters had blasted into his body.

"Helmsman! Zig zag pattern!" Gordon barked. "Someone get me a damage report! Midshipman Green, inform damage control that we need another talker and an OOD here!"

"Aye aye, Captain!"

"*Leftenant* Cobb!"

"Yes sir?" Eric asked, shaking himself out of stupor.

"It might be prudent for you to go to the conning tower," Gordon said.

"Sir, I'd prefer to be here than in some metal box," Eric said. "With the shells that bastard's tossing it won't make a lick of difference anyway."

"Too true," Gordon said. "Looks like the heavy cruisers and that pocket battleship are covering the bastards' retreat."

Gordon's supposition was only partially correct. In truth, the pocket battleship *Lutzow* had received damage from the *Exeter* and *Norfolk* that had somewhat reduced her maximum speed. This had prevented her from fleeing with the rest of the screen, their retirement encouraged by a few salvoes from the *Nelson*. Realizing that she could not escape the closing British destroyers, *Lutzow's* captain had decided to turn and engage the smaller vessels in hopes of allowing *Scharnhorst* to open the distance between herself and the

British. Unfortunately, *Lutzow* had failed to inform the heavy cruiser KMS *Hipper*, trailing in her wake, of her desire to self-sacrifice while ignoring Admiral Bey's signal to retire. Thus the latter vessel, her radio aerial knocked out by an over salvo from the *Nelson's* secondary batteries, found herself committed to engaging the rapidly closing British destroyers along with the larger, crippled *Lutzow*.

The British destroyers, formed into two divisions under the experienced Commodore Philip Vian, first overtook the damaged French battlecruiser *Strasbourg*. Adrift, afire, and listing heavily to port, the *Strasbourg* wallowed helplessly as the British destroyers closed like hyenas on a paralyzed wildebeest. Just as Vian was beginning to order his group into their battle dispositions, flooding finally compromised the battlecruiser's stability. With a rumble and the scream of tortured metal, the *Strasbourg* rotated onto her starboard beam and slipped beneath the surface.

That left the crippled *Scharnhorst*, the *Lutzow*, and the hapless *Hipper*. Still receiving desultory fire from *Nelson* and *Warspite*, the trio of German vessels initially concentrated their fire on the charging *Exeter* and *Norfolk*. After five minutes of this, all three German captains realized Vian's approaching destroyers were a far greater threat. The *Lutzow* and *Hipper* turned to lay smoke across the retreating *Scharnhorst's* stern, the maneuver also allowing both vessels to fire full broadsides at their smaller assailants. The *Hipper* had just gotten off her second salvo when she received a pair of 8-inch shells from the *Norfolk*. The first glanced off the heavy cruiser's armor belt and fell harmlessly into the sea. The second, however, impacted the main director, blowing the gunnery officer and most of the cruiser's gunnery department into disparate parts that splashed into the sea or onto the deck below. For two crucial minutes, the *Hipper's* main battery remained silent even as her secondaries began to take the approaching British destroyers under fire.

The respite from *Lutzow's* fire had arrived just in time for *Exeter*, as the pocket battleship had been consistently finding the range. Staggering to his feet after another exercise in throwing himself flat, Eric looked forward to see just where the heavy cruiser had been hit this time. His gaze fell upon the devastation that had been *Exeter's* "B" turret, where a cloud of acrid yellow was smoke pouring back from the structure's opened roof to pass around the heavy cruiser's bridge. Damage control crews were rushing forward to spray hoses upon the burning guns, even as water began to crash over the cruiser's lowering bow.

"Very well then, flood the magazine!" Gordon was shouting into the speaking tube. "Tell the *Norfolk* we shall follow her in as best we can."

Looking to starboard, Eric could see the aforementioned heavy cruiser starting to surge ahead of *Exeter*, smoke pouring from her triple stacks and her forward turrets firing another salvo towards the *Hipper*.

"We are only making twenty-three knots, sir," the helmsman reported.

"Damage control reports heavy flooding in the bow," the talker stated. "Lieutenant Ramses states we must slow our speed or we may lose another bulkhead."

Gordon's face set in a grim line.

"Torpedoes reports a solution on the pocket battleship," the talker reported after pausing or a moment.

"Range?!" Gordon barked.

"Ten thousand yards and closing.".

"Tell me when we're at four thousand..."

The seas around the *Exeter* suddenly leaped upwards, the waterspouts clearing her mainmast.

"Enemy battleship is taking us under fire!"

Looking over at *Norfolk*, Eric saw an identical series of waterspouts appear several hundred yards ahead of their companion.

"Two enemy battleships engaging, range twenty-two thousand yards."

"Where's our battleline?" Gordon asked bitterly. "Report the news to the *King George V*."

Another couple of minutes passed, the *Exeter* continuing to close with the turning *Lutzow*. Four more shells exploded around the *Exeter*.

"The *Nelson* is disengaging due to opening range," the talker replied. "The remaining ships are closing our position to take the enemy battleship under fire."

Again there was the sound of an incoming freight train, and the *Exeter* was straddled once more, splinters ringing off the opposite side of the bridge.

"Corpsman!" a lookout shouted from the crow's nest.

Okay, someone stop this ride, I want to get off, Eric thought, bile rising in his throat.

"Commodore Vian reports he is closing."

"Right then, continue to attack!" Gordon shouted. Eric winced, convinced he was going to die.

Unbeknownst to Eric, the *Bismarck* and *Tirpitz* had only returned to persuade the British battleline to not pursue the *Scharnhorst*. Finding the two British heavy cruisers attacking, Bey had decided some 15-inch fire was necessary to discourage their torpedo run as well. In the worsening seas the German battleships' gunnery left much to be desired, but still managed to force the *Exeter* and *Norfolk* to both intensify their zig zags.

Unfortunately for the Germans, the decision to concentrate on the heavy cruisers meant that Commodore Vian's destroyers had an almost undisturbed attack run. Vian, realizing that he would not be able to bypass the aggressively counterattacking *Hipper*, split his force into two parts. The lead division, led by himself in *Somali*, continued after the crippled *Scharnhorst*. The second, led by the destroyer *Echo*, he directed to attack the *Hipper* in hopes that the heavy cruiser would turn away.

The German heavy cruiser reacted as Vian had expected, switching all of her fire to the approaching *Echo* group. For their part, the British ships dodged as they closed, the *Echo*'s commander making the decision to close the range so that the destroyers could launch their torpedoes with a higher speed setting. Seeing the German cruiser starting to turn, *Echo*'s commander signaled for his own vessel, *Eclipse*, and *Encounter* to attempt to attack from her port side, while the *Faulknor* and *Electra* were to move up to attack from starboard.

Discerning the British destroyerman's plan, *Hipper*'s captain immediately laid on his maximum speed while continuing his turn towards port. Ignoring those vessels attempting to move in on her starboard side, the German vessel turned her guns wholly on the trio of British destroyers that was now at barely seven thousand yards. With a combined closing speed of almost seventy knots, there was less than a minute before the British destroyers were at their preferred range. In this time, *Hipper* managed to get off two salvoes with her main guns and several rounds from her secondary guns. Her efforts were rewarded, the *Echo* being hit and stopped by two 8-inch and four secondary shell hits before she could fire her torpedoes. That still left the *Eclipse* and *Encounter*, both which fired their torpedoes at 4,000 yards before starting to turn away. The latter vessel had just concluded putting her eighth torpedo into the water when the *Hipper*'s secondaries switched to her as a target, knocking out the destroyer's forward guns.

Pursuing the *Hipper* as the German cruiser continued to turn to port, the *Faulknor* and *Electra* initially had a far longer run than their compatriots. However, as the German cruiser came about to comb the *Echo* group's torpedoes, the opportunity arose for the two more nimble vessels to cut across her turn. Hitting the heavy cruiser with several 4.7-inch shells even as they zigzagged through the *Lutzow*'s supporting fire, the two destroyers unleashed their sixteen torpedoes from the *Hipper*'s port bow. Belatedly, the German captain realized that he had placed himself in a horrible position, as he could not turn to avoid the second group of torpedoes without presenting a perfect target to the first.

It was the *Eclipse* which administered the first blow. Coming in at a fine angle, one of the destroyer's torpedoes exploded just below the *Hipper*'s port bow. The heavy cruiser's hull whipsawed from the impact, the explosion peeling twenty feet of her skin back to act as a massive brake. The shock traveled down the vessel's length, throwing circuit breakers out of their mounts in her generator room and rendering the *Hipper* powerless. Looking to starboard, the vessel's bridge crew could only helplessly watch as the British torpedoes approached from that side. In a fluke of fate, the braking effect from *Eclipse*'s hit caused the heavy cruiser to lose so much headway the majority of the tin fish missed. The pair that impacted, however, could not have been better placed. With two roaring waterspouts in close succession, the *Hipper*'s engineering spaces were opened to the sea. Disemboweled, the cruiser continued to slow even as she rolled to starboard. Realizing instantly her wounds were fatal, the *Hipper*'s captain gave the order to abandon ship. The order came far too late for most of the crew, as the 12,000-ton man-o-war capsized and slid under the Atlantic in a matter of minutes.

"Well, the destroyers just put paid to that heavy cruiser! Let's see if we can get a kill of our own!" Gordon said, watching the drama unfolding roughly twelve thousand yards to his west. Another salvo of 15-inch shells landed to *Exeter*'s starboard, this broadside somewhat more ragged due to the heavy cruiser's zig zagging advance.

"Battleships are returning to aid us."

"About bloody time!" Gordon snapped.

When the *Warspite*'s first salvo landed just aft of *Jean Bart*, Admiral Bey had more than enough. Signaling rapidly, he ordered the *Scharnhorst* and *Lutzow* to cover the remainder of the force's retreat. Firing a few desultory broadsides, the Franco-German force reentered the mists.

Eric watched through his binoculars as *Lutzow* gamely attempted to follow Bey's orders, slowly coming about so she could continue to engage the destroyers closing with *Scharnhorst*. Barely making fifteen knots, the pocket battleship was listing slightly to port and down by the bows. Just as *Lutzow* finished her turn, several shells landed close astern of the German vessel.

"*King George V* is engaging the pocket battleship."

"Good. Maybe she can slow that witch down so we can catch her."

"*Warspite* and *Prince of Wales* are switching to the closest battleship."

Gordon nodded his ascent, continuing to watch as *Lutzow* attempted to begin a zig zag pattern.

"Destroyers are running the gauntlet," Gordon observed drily, pointing to where the *Lutzow* was engaging the five destroyers passing barely eight thousand yards in front of her. Eric nodded grimly, then brought his attention back to *Lutzow* just in time to see the *King George V*'s next salvo arrive. Two of the British 14-inch shells slashed into the pocket battleship's stern, while a third impacted on the vessel's aft turret with devastating effect. Eric was glad that *Exeter* was still far enough away that he could not identify the contents of the debris that flew upwards from the gunhouse in the gout of smoke and flame, as the young American was sure some of the dark spots were bodies.

"Looks like you got your wish, sir," Eric observed as the *Lutzow* began to continue a lazy circle to port. There was a sharp crack as the *Exeter*'s secondary batteries began to engage the pocket battleship, leading to a disgusted look from Gordon.

"Tell Guns we may need that ammunition later," he snapped. "I'm not sure those guns will do any damage, plus she's almost finished."

I was wondering what good 4-inch guns would do to a pocket battleship, Eric thought. *Especially when* **Norfolk** *is pounding away with her main battery and a battleship has her under fire.*

"*King George V* is inquiring if we can finish her with torpedoes?"

Gordon looked at the pocket battleship, now coming to a stop with fires clearly spreading.

"Report that yes, we will close and finish her with torpedoes, she may assist in bringing that battleship to bay," *Exeter*'s master stated.

"*Norfolk* is firing torpedoes," the talker reported.

Eric brought up his binoculars, focusing on the clearly crippled *Lutzow*. As he watched, one of the German's secondary turrets fired a defiant shot at *Norfolk*. Scanning the vessel from bow to stern, Eric wondered if the gun was the sole thing left operational, as the pocket battleship's upper decks were a complete shambles. Looking closely at the *Lutzow*'s forward turret, he could see two jagged holes in its rear where *Norfolk*'s broadsides had impacted. The bridge was similarly damaged, with wisps of smoke pouring from the shattered windows, and the German vessel's entire amidships was ablaze. The vessel's list appeared to have lessened, but she was clearly much lower in the water.

"Should be any time now," Gordon said, briefly looking at his watch. "Tell guns to belay my last, we're not wasting any more fish on her than necessary."

Eric turned back to watching the *Lutzow*, observing as *Norfolk* hit the vessel with another point blank salvo an instant before her torpedoes arrived. Given that the *Lutzow* was a stationary target, Eric was surprised to see *Norfolk*'s torpedo spread produce only a pair of hits. It was still enough, as with an audible groan the *Lutzow*'s already battered hull split just aft of her destroyed turret. Five minutes later, as *Exeter* drew within five hundred yards and Eric could see German sailors jumping into the sea, the *Lutzow* gave a final shuddering metallic rattle then slipped stern first into the depths.

"Stand by to rescue survivors," Gordon said, dropping his binoculars. "How are the destroyers doing with that battleship?"

The answer to Gordon's question could be summed up with two words: very well. The *Scharnhorst* had briefly managed to work up to sixteen knots, and had *Lutzow*'s fire been somewhat more accurate, may have managed to escape the pursuing destroyers. However, as with the *Hipper*, Vian's destroyers split into two groups even as *Scharnhorst*'s secondaries increased their fire. Another pair of hits from *Prince of Wales* slowed the German light battleship even further, and at that point the handful of tin cans set upon her like a school of sharks on a lamed blue whale.

Like that large creature, however, even a crippled the *Scharnhorst* still had means to defend herself. As the *Punjabi* closed in from starboard, the battleship's Caesar turret scored with a single 15-inch shell. The effects were devastating, the destroyer being converted from man-of-war to charnel house forward of her bridge. Amazingly, *Punjabi*'s powerplant was undamaged by the blast, and the destroyer was able to continue closing the distance between herself and the larger German vessel. The timely arrival of a salvo from *Warspite* sufficiently distracted the *Scharnhorst*'s gunnery officer, preventing him from getting the range again until after both groups of destroyers were close enough to launch torpedoes.

Severely damaged, *Scharnhorst* still attempted to ruin the destroyers' fire control problem at the last moment. To Commodore Vian's intense frustration, the battleship's captain timed his maneuver perfectly, evading twelve British torpedoes simply by good seamanship. Had *Scharnhorst* had her full maneuvering ability, she may have then been able to pull off the maneuver *Hipper* had attempted by reversing course. Whereas geometry and numbers had failed the German heavy cruiser, simple physics served to put the waterlogged battleship in front of three torpedoes. Even then, her luck remained as the first hit, far forward, was a dud. Then, proving Fate was indeed fickle, two fish from the damaged *Punjabi* ran deep and hit the vessel just below her armored belt. Finishing the damage done by *Prince of Wales'* hits earlier, the torpedoes knocked out the German capital ship's remaining power and opened even more of her hull to the sea. Realizing she was doomed, her captain ordered the crew to set scuttling charges and abandon ship.

"*King George V* is inquiring if any vessels have torpedoes remaining."

Gordon gave the talker a questioning look.

"I thought Commodore Vian just reported that the enemy battleship appears to be sinking?" Gordon said, his voice weary. "No matter, inform *King George V* that we have all of our fish remaining."

Wonder what in the hell that is about? Eric thought. Looking down, he realized his hands were starting to shake. Taking a deep breath, he attempted to calm himself.

Well, this has been a rather...interesting day. I just wish someone would have told me I'd get shot down, see my squadron leader killed, and participate in a major sea battle when I got up at 0300 this morning.

"*Leftenant* Cobb, are you all right?" Gordon asked, concerned.

Eric choked back the urge to laugh at the question.

"I'm fine sir, just a little cold," he said, lying through his teeth. The talker saved him from further inquisition.

"*King George V* is ordering us to come about and close with her. She is also ordering Commodore Vian to rescue survivors from *Punjabi* then scuttle her if she is unable to get under way. *Norfolk* is being ordered to stand by to assist *Nelson*."

"What about the Germans?" Gordon asked.

"Flag has ordered that all other recovery operations are to cease."

There was dead silence on *Exeter*'s bridge.

"Very well then, guess the Germans will have to come back for their own. Let's go see what *King George V* has for us," Gordon said.

Eric was struck by just how far the running fight had ranged as the *Exeter* reversed course. From the first salvo to the current position, the vessels had covered at least thirty miles. The *King George V* was a distant dot to the south, with her sister ship and *Warspite* further behind.

No one is going to find any of those survivors, Eric thought. *Especially with this weather starting to get worse.* He could smell imminent rain on the wind, and even with *Exeter*'s considerable size he could feel the ocean's movement starting to change.

"I hope this isn't about to become too bad of a blow," Gordon observed, looking worriedly out at the lowering sky. "Not with the flooding we have forward."

"If you don't mind, sir, I'd like to avoid going swimming again today," Eric quipped.

"Wouldn't be a swim lad. If we catch a big wave wrong, she would plow right under," Gordon replied grimly. "What has got *King George V* in such a tussy? She's coming at us full speed."

Eric looked up and saw that the battleship was indeed closing as rapidly as possible. As she hove into visual range several minutes later, the *King George V*'s signaling searchlight began flashing rapidly.

DO YOU READ THIS MESSAGE? DO YOU READ THIS MESSAGE?

"Acknowledge," Gordon said. A few moments later Eric could hear the heavy cruiser's signal crew employing the bridge lamp to respond to the *King George V*.

YOU WILL PROCEED TO *HOOD*. ONCE ALL SURVIVORS ARE OFFBOARD, YOU ARE TO SCUTTLE.

"*What in the bloody hell is that idiot talking about?*" Gordon exploded. He did not have time to send a counter message, as the *King George V* continued after a short pause.

YOU HAVE TWENTY-FIVE MINUTES TO REJOIN. FORCE WILL PROCEED WITHOUT YOU IF NOT COMPLETE. TOVEY SENDS GOD SAVE THE QUEEN

"God save the...*oh my God!*" Gordon said.

Eric looked at the *Exeter*'s captain with some concern as the man staggered backward, his face looking as if he had been personally stricken.

"Ask," Gordon began, the word nearly coming out as a sob before he regained his composure. "Ask if I may inform the ship's company of our task?"

Three minutes later, the *King George V* replied.

AFFIRMATIVE. EXPEDITE. HER MAJESTY'S SAFETY IS THIS COMMAND'S PRIMARY GOAL.

"Acknowledge. Hand me the loudspeaker," Gordon said, his voice incredibly weary. Eric could see tears welling in the man's eyes.

This is not good, Eric thought. *This is not good at all.* Although he was far from an expert on British government, he dimly remembered seeing a newsreel when *Ranger* had been in port where the Royal Family had been discussed. He felt his stomach starting to drop as he began to process what the *King George V* had just stated.

"All hands, this is the captain speaking," Gordon began. "This vessel is proceeding to stand by the *Hood* to rescue survivors. It appears that His Majesty has been killed."

Holy shit, Eric thought. *Isn't Princess...no,* **Queen** *Elizabeth barely sixteen?*

Eric looked around the bridge as the captain broke the news to the *Exeter's* crew. The reactions ranged from shock to, surprisingly, rage. As *Exeter's* master finished, the young American had the feeling he was seeing the start of something very, very ugly for the Germans.

I would hate to be someone who got dragged out of the water today, he thought. *That is, if* **any** *Germans get saved.* Eric's father had fought as a Marine at Belleau Wood. In the weeks before Eric had left for the academy, his father had made sure that his son understood just what might be required of him in the Republic's service. One of the stories had involved what had befallen an unfortunate German machine gun crew when the men tried to surrender after killing several members of the elder Cobb's platoon. Realizing the parallels to his current situation given the news he had just heard, Eric fought the urge to scowl.

Looks like you don't need a rope for a lynch mob, Eric thought as he reflected on the "necessity" of leaving the German and French sailors to drown. He was suddenly shaken out of his reverie by the sound of singing coming from below the bridge.

"Happy and glorious...long to reign over us..."

The men on the bridge began taking up the song, their tone somber and remorseful.

"*GOD SAAAAVEEE THE QUEEEEENN!!*"

Almost a half hour later, the *Exeter* sat one thousand yards off of the *Hood's* starboard side, the heavy cruiser's torpedo tubes trained on her larger consort. The *Hood's* wounds were obvious, her bridge and conning tower a horribly twisted flower of shattered steel. Flames licked from the vessel's X turret, and it appeared that the structure had taken a heavy shell to its roof. Further casting a pall on the scene was the dense black smoke pouring from the *Hood's* burning bunkerage, a dull glow at the base of the cloud indicating an out of control fire. The battlecruiser's stern looked almost awash, her bow almost coming out of the water with each swell, and as Eric watched there was an explosion of ready ammunition near her anti-aircraft guns.

Might be a waste of good torpedoes at this point, Eric thought. He realized he was starting to pass into mental shock from all the carnage he had seen that day.

"I'm the last man, sir," a dazed-looking commander with round features, black hair, and green eyes was saying to Captain Gordon. "At least, the last man we can get to."

"I understand, Commander Keir," Gordon said quietly. "I regret we do not have the time to try and free the men trapped in her engineering spaces."

"If we could have only had another hour, we might have saved her," Keir said, his voice breaking. It was obvious the man had been through hell, his uniform blackened by soot and other stains that Eric didn't care to look into too closely.

It's never a good day when you become commander of a vessel simply because no one else was left. From what he understood, Keir had started the day as chief of *Hood's* Navigation Division. That had been before the vessel took at least three 15-inch shells to the bridge area, as well as two more that had wiped out her gunnery directory and the secondary bridge.

Captain Gordon was right—she was a very powerful warship. Unfortunately that tends to make you a target.

"Commander, you are *certain* that..." Gordon started, then

59

collected himself. "You are *certain* His Majesty is dead."

"Yes sir," Keir said. "His Majesty was in the conning tower with Admiral Pound when it was hit. The Royal Surgeon positively identified His Majesty's body in the aid station before that was hit in turn. We cannot get to the aid station due to the spreading fire."

"Understood. His Majesty would not have wanted any of you to risk his life for his body," Gordon said.

"I just..." Keir started, then stopped, overcome with emotion.

"It is not your fault lad," Gordon said. "Her Majesty will understand."

Gordon turned and looked at the *Exeter*'s clock.

"Very well, we are out of time. Stand by to fire torpedoes."

"Torpedoes report they are ready."

"Sir, you may want to tell your torpedo officer to have his weapons set to run deep," Keir said. "She's drawing..."

There was a large explosion aboard *Hood* as the flames reached a secondary turret's ready ammunition. Eric saw a fiery object arc slowly across, descending towards the *Exeter* as hundreds of helpless eyes watched it. The flaming debris' lazy parabola terminated barely fifty yards off of *Exeter*'s side with a large, audible splash.

"I think we do not have time for that discussion," Gordon said grimly. "Fire torpedoes!"

The three weapons from *Exeter*'s starboard tubes sprang from their launchers into the water. Set as a narrow spread, the three tracks seemed to take forever to impact from Eric's perspective. *Exeter*'s torpedo officer, observing *Hood*'s state, had taken into account the battlecruiser's lower draught without having to be told. Indeed, he had almost set the weapons for too deep a run, but was saved by the flooding that had occurred in the previous few minutes. In addition to breaking the battlecruiser's keel, the triple blow opened the entire aft third of her port side to the ocean. With the audible sound of twisting metal, *Hood* started to roll onto her beam ends. She never completed the evolution before slipping beneath the   waves.

CHAPTER 2: AFTERMATH

We should never despair, our Situation before has been unpromising and has changed for the better; so I trust, it will again. If new difficulties arise, we must only put forth New Exertions and proportion our efforts to the exigency of the times.—George Washington

Cape Town, South Africa
0700 Local (0100 Eastern)
26 September

"Well now I know things have gone to Hell," a familiar voice said from just behind Adam. "There are bloody Americans here, and Lord knows they always portend something very, very bad."

Adam whipped around from his breakfast so quickly he nearly fell out of his chair. Stumbling to his feet, he made sure the speaker was whom he thought it was, taking in the man's tall, lanky frame and sandy brown hair before wrapping him in a giant bearhug.

"Braddon Overgaard, how in the hell are you doing?!" he asked. "Pull up a chair. I was just finishing breakfast, courtesy of His...*Her* Majesty's government."

"Yes, it is a bit difficult to change that, isn't it? Although, if certain individuals get their way you may be reverting back to what you started to say," Overgaard replied.

Adam stopped, fork halfway to his mouth.

"What? I sort of thought that line of succession thing was pretty set," the American said.

Overgaard had a seat at the table across from Adam.

"You can tell that you have been stuck aboard some tub for the past two weeks," Overgaard said.

"Hell, we hadn't even heard about the Battle of the Regicide until we were a couple hours out from harbor yesterday," Adam said. "What the hell else has happened?"

"The Duke of Windsor has returned to London."

Adam recognized the title but was not immediately able to recall why that was important. Seeing his perplexed look, Overgaard saved him the trouble.

"The Duke of Windsor is also known as King Edward," the South African officer said quietly.

Adam raised an eyebrow.

"I must confess I do not completely understand the Royal Family despite spending the last nine months in its employ," Adam said carefully. "Didn't he abdicate the throne because he had a similar problem to King David?"

Overgaard gave a thin smile.

"While I am sure Ms. Simpson would be flattered by the comparison to Bathsheba, that wasn't exactly what happened," Overgaard replied.

"Close enough," Adam replied around a mouthful of eggs. "Basically the man got the chop, as you guys put it, for taking up with another man's wife."

A couple of South African men at the table to their left turned and gave Adam a glance that was hardly favorable. Feigning obvliousness, Adam continued.

"I mean, I seem to recall there being an Act that basically said he wasn't the King of England anymore, correct?"

Overgaard nodded.

"Yes, but in light of recent events the Halifax government is attempting to reverse the Abdication Act and restore King Edward to the throne," Overgaard said.

Adam shook his head in amazement.

"Is that legal?" he asked.

"Well therein lies the rub," Overgaard said bitterly. "When the current sovereign is in another country that sort of prevents many people from raising a fuss."

"You know, I thought things couldn't get much worse a couple weeks ago," Adam said grimly. "Now I realize that I suffered from a large dose of ignorance."

"Well, Her Majesty is only sixteen," Overgaard continued. "There is a push from Prime Minister King for all the Commonwealth nations to recognize Her Majesty as the current sovereign with Churchill as head of a reformed Commonwealth government. But..." Overgaard said, then stopped suddenly and shrugged as if to say he had no idea what would happen. Their conversation was interrupted by the waitress, a rather plain-looking brunette, interrupting to ask Overgaard if there was anything he'd like to eat.

"So how did you get back here?" Adam asked after the woman had left Overgaard water and gone to make him his eggs benedict.

"Caught a liner back," Overgaard said simply. "The Germans accorded us non-belligerent status."

"What?!"

"Prime Minister Halifax, for all his faults, negotiated a decent treaty. Between you and me, if you've read that bastard Hitler's book you'd realize that France and England were a sideshow to the Nazis," Overgaard said, taking a sip of his water. "Hitler only attacked us to clear his backside before he went east. Hell, he didn't even technically attack us—just went after Poland."

Adam made a face at that one.

"Sorry mate, but as much as I know you love those Polish blokes you flew with, it's not like either us or the French really kept their promises to them," Overgaard said. "I mean, between the Germans and that bloody bastard Stalin, I'm not so sure the men who got away should not just consider themselves lucky and call it a day. Realistically, there is probably nothing worth going back for, and even if the rest of your countrymen decide to grace this war with their presence, it is highly unlikely anyone will be prying Poland from the Germans and Soviets anytime soon."

"Would you leave someone like Himmler or Stalin in charge of your home?" Adam asked incredulously.

"There comes a point when you have to accept reality," Overgaard said. "My grandfather fought against the English during the Boer War. His commando swore they would fight until the death. Well, you notice the Boers aren't in charge and my grandfather is still out on my family farm."

"The English never compared to anything the Nazis or Soviets have done," Adam snapped.

"Really? Remind me again where the term concentration camp comes from?" Overgaard replied easily.

Adam felt his face warm.

"The English *never* did what the Nazis have just done," he seethed. "They didn't even do something as horrible as Guernica."

"But would they have if they'd had the capability?" Overgaard asked simply.

Adam opened his mouth to protest, then stopped.

He has a point. Unfortunately… Adam mentally conceded as the waitress returned with Overgaard's order.

"Now the difference is the English would not have gassed or burned about forty thousand people *today*," Overgaard continued after taking a bite of his eggs. "Well, at least they would not have until a couple of weeks ago. Which is part of the reason Himmler and Halifax were able to come to an agreement, albeit one that is probably going to make you Yanks a bit upset."

"I haven't even seen a newspaper talking about this treaty yet," Adam said. "So please, do tell."

"That's because Prime Minister Smuts is studiously avoiding starting any discussion of it in Parliament," Overgaard replied quietly. "You are probably not aware, but my government was split on whether or not we should enter the war. There are those among us who do not necessarily disagree with the Nazis' philosophy regarding a master race."

Adam put his fork down, suddenly feeling sick to his stomach.

"Thankfully the number of those who absolutely feel that way is relatively small, but I think that was part of the reason Himmler allowed for the immediate release of all Commonwealth forces," Overgaard said. "The man does not want to give Her Majesty's government any assistance by upsetting Australia, New Zealand, Canada, or South Africa."

"What about any forces from the Occupied countries he could lay his hands on?" Adam asked bitterly. "I suppose they were shot out of hand?"

"Strangely enough, no. Himmler offered them a choice—they could basically serve in the Nazi armed forces for three years or be imprisoned for six," Overgaard replied.

"What?!" Adam exclaimed.

"You'd be surprised how many takers the Germans had," Overgaard continued. "Not many Poles, of course…but there were a fair number of so called 'Free French' who seemed to be a whole lot less willing to spend the next six years in a German prison camp rather than three years someplace else."

"Can't blame them, really," Adam sighed. "His Highness and Halifax persuading Churchill to call for a truce sort of screwed the French. Add on shooting up their fleet back in 1940 and I would start to wonder just how good of allies the British were."

"There's only so much that one nation by herself can do. It's not like you Americans were giving any indications of coming into the war anytime soon."

"Too many people still think we did enough last time," Adam replied. "In their mind, we don't need dead Americans cleaning up Europe's mess again."

"If your country waits much longer, they will be facing all of bloody Europe," Overgaard said resignedly. "Or at least a large European coalition led by Germany. But I'm obviously preaching to the choir."

"Yes, and this particular singer is thinking it might be a good idea to keep moving along," Adam said.

"Well you're about nine months too late for China," Overgaard observed. "At least, not unless you want to be shooting up Warlord A so that Warlord B can take over his territory then proclaim his fealty for the Nationalists."

"Yes, well, no one saw the Japanese leaving. I wasn't following that close enough to know what in the hell happened there," Adam observed. "One minute it looks like we're getting ready to go to war with them last December, Churchill sends four more battleships to Singapore, and next thing you know they go and attack the Russians."

"In retrospect I think they would like to have that decision back," Overgaard observed wryly.

"Getting an entire army annihilated will do that," Adam observed. "What did the Russians say they were going to call Manchuria, Manchukuo, or whatever it was?"

"I don't remember," Overgaard said. "I just remember that one minute they were on the offensive against the Russians, then four months later that Soviet general's accepting their surrender in South Manchuria."

"Zhukov was his name," Adam said. "Looks like he studied *blitzkrieg* at the same school the Germans did."

"I don't care if he learned it from Mars himself, he sure used it to kick the Japanese right out of China. My father told me just the other day that there was some rumor their entire cabinet committed suicide over the loss of face," Overgaard replied, putting a fork of eggs in his mouth.

"Well, I lost track of the situation about the same time you did, and for the same reasons," Adam replied, his voice haunted. "Something about the *Luftwaffe* trying to kill us."

Overgaard nodded grimly as he chewed on his eggs.

"So where do you think you'll go then?" the South African asked after swallowing.

"According to the consulate here the isolationists are talking about stripping all of us of our citizenships," Adam replied. "There's even some poor bastard who the Germans shot down over the Atlantic that they're trying to have banned from ever reentering the country."

H.M.S. Prince of Wales
Halifax Harbor, Canada
1000 Local (0900 Eastern)
26 September

So this is how an ant feels in a room full of elephants, Eric had time to think to himself as he walked into the admiral's day room of the H.M.S. *Prince of Wales*. Scanning the room, he saw more gold braid and stars than he had ever witnessed in his life in one place. That the civilian dignitaries present made the aforementioned constellation seem rather dim by comparison was more than enough to make a junior officer pray for invisibility.

"Speaking of Leftenant Cobb, here he is right now," Vice Admiral John Tovey, commander of Home Fleet, stated.

Oh look, the ant is now expected to play the trombone for everyone, Eric thought as all eyes turned towards him. There were five individuals in the large compartment besides Vice Admiral Tovey. Eric immediately recognized Secretary of the Navy Frank Knox and Admiral Ernest J. King from the pictures that *Ranger*'s captain had required every one of his officers to memorize prior to coming aboard. The other four star standing with them, on the other hand, Eric had no clue about. The tall, dark-haired man regarded Eric with a neutral expression, as if he was weighing and measuring the aviator. The other civilian in a dark blue suit similar to the one worn by Secretary Knox was standing beside the mystery full admiral.

Lastly, sitting in a chair next to the four standing Americans was none other than Winston Churchill, the man puffing contentedly on one of his trademark cigars with one hand, the other clenching a tumbler of some amber liquid.

Okay, now I'm really starting to worry, Eric thought as he came to attention.

"Lieutenant Cobb reporting as ordered, sir," he said to Secretary Knox as the highest ranking man in the room. In actuality, it had been Tovey that had requested his presence from the officer's barracks ashore one hour previously. Eric had been rather surprised at the summons, as the American ambassador to Canada had conveyed, in no uncertain, terms that neither Rawles nor he was to set foot aboard another British vessel until further notice. As that particular missive had been delivered in the presence of Captain Gordon before *Exeter* had even pulled up to the dock to unload her wounded, Eric had a feeling Admiral Tovey was well aware of it.

Knox gave Admiral King and the mystery four star a bemused look, then turned back to Eric.

"At ease lieutenant, you're not here for a court-martial," Knox said easily. "We just want to hear what happened to you in your own words."

What the hell? Didn't anyone get my after action review? Eric thought to himself. His surprise must have showed because the unknown admiral spoke up.

"Son, we know you already prepared a report for Lieutenant Colonel Gypsum," the man said, referring to the American military attaché to Canada. "However it's important that Secretaries Knox and Hull hear your story for themselves."

"What Admiral Kimmel is actually saying, in polite terms, is that he bloody thinks we altered your report!" Winston Churchill thundered.

Okay, there's a little tension here, Eric thought. Tovey stood stonefaced as Churchill took a puff of his cigar, daring any of the Americans present to deny his accusation.

"Mr. Churchill is correct," King responded, venom in his voice. "There are those in Congress and elsewhere in the United States government who have come to wonder just how coincidental it would be that you and your squadron leader just happened to blunder into the German fleet at a time when the British had been forced to dispatch cruisers to make contact with it."

"Permission to speak freely, sir?" Eric asked quietly.

"Go ahead, Lieutenant Cobb," King snapped, glaring steadily at Churchill.

"The reason why we just happened to be there is Commander Cobleigh convinced Rear Admiral Noyes that the best *Dauntless* pilots could establish a search even in that weather."

King snorted, his nostrils flaring.

"Yes—and of the twelve of you who launched, only six recovered successfully," King snapped.

Eric fought to keep his face expressionless.

Some of those men are, or maybe **were**, *my friends*, he thought grimly.

"Lieutenant Cobb, why don't you tell us what happened?" Kimmel broke in. Admiral King pivoted as if he was about to snap a response when a stern look from Secretary Knox stopped him in his tracks. "Come on over here to the plot if that will help."

"We started the day at 0300..." Eric began. He spent the next thirty minutes recounting his role in the Battle of Regicide, or as the British fleet was calling it, the Battle of the Remnants. As he talked, Eric realized just how lucky both Rawles and he had been to have survived. By the time he had stopped, he realized that his hands were slightly shaking while he stood at parade rest.

"How long until the *Exeter* is back in action?" Admiral Kimmel asked thoughtfully. "From what Lieutenant Cobb described, she sounds almost a total wreck."

"Six months," Admiral Tovey replied. "She'll be sailing for Sydney within the fortnight."

"What? You don't have any facilities closer?" Secretary Knox asked, shock clear in his voice.

Churchill and Tovey shared a pained look. After a moment, the former Prime Minister spoke.

"There is some discussion among the Commonwealth nations as to whether they will agree to be bound by the Treaty of Kent," he said solemnly.

"It appears that the former king returning to claim the throne threw a monkey wrench in your plan to continue to fight if England fell," Admiral King observed.

Eric could tell from the shocked looks on every other American's face that he was not the only one horrified by King's bluntness.

"Another 'monkey wrench' was our belief that a certain nation's assistance would go beyond fine words and promises," Churchill said after a moment's pause.

"What Admiral King meant," Secretary Hull said, his tone making it quite clear that nothing good would come from King contradicting his next words, "is that it does not seem as if the possibility of England's fall was discussed among the Commonwealth during the truce period."

"Of course not," Churchill sneered. "No one wanted to consider the fact that the Germans might resume hostilities. Hell, I had a hard enough time persuading Parliament to continue producing the items already authorized. No one wanted to believe that bastard Himmler was just playing for time to strengthen the Luftwaffe."

"Having your agents attempt to kill Heydrich in Prague and a Free Frenchman blow up Alfred Rosenberg might have had something to do with the Nazis resuming the war," Admiral King observed, gaining him a look of sheer venom from Hull and Knox alike. Eric watched Churchill's face start to redden and he opened his mouth to speak only to be cut off by Tovey.

"Perhaps you would be more interested in the present situation than a discussion of the past, Admiral King?" he asked, his voice colder than the gusts blowing through Halifax Harbor.

"Actually, gentlemen, We would be very interested in hearing about the present situation as well," a calm woman's voice observed from the hatchway behind Eric, causing him to turn and observe a slender, short brunette in a black mourning dress. Out of the corner of his eye Eric saw Churchill and Tovey both whirl away from the map, then come immediately to attention.

"Your Majesty, we were not expecting you for another three hours," Churchill said evenly as the woman strode into the compartment followed by two very large men in the bright red tunics and bearskin caps of the British Army's Guard Regiments. Eric was somewhat shocked to see that both men carried Thompson submachine guns. Judging from Admiral Tovey's face going pale, he was not the only one. While both men ensured their weapons were not pointed at anyone, Eric could feel the tension rise in the room.

"My...Our apologies, Lord Churchill," Queen Elizabeth replied, her voice genuine. "The meeting with the new Air Minister took far less time than expected. Admiral Tovey, for your information Captain Leach was given direction from me not to interrupt your meeting. We are the ones off schedule, not you gentlemen."

"Your Majesty, all of us appreciate that you made time in your busy schedule for us," Secretary Hull began. "It is a difficult time for both our nations." Behind him, Eric saw Secretary Knox give Admiral King a look that could have blistered paint.

I'm not sure I want to be in the same room with men who can silence a full admiral just with a look, Eric thought quietly. *I'm reasonably certain that Secretary Knox will relieve him on the spot if there is another outburst.*

"Thank you, Secretary Hull," Her Majesty replied. "My father considered the United States to be our strongest friend even if not strictly an ally."

Pointed comment there, Eric thought, seeing Admiral King starting to color somewhat.

"There are those in our nation, even now, who do not realize that the Nazis intend to conquer the entire world," Hull replied.

"Well, let us discuss how we will stop them from doing that, shall we?" Queen Elizabeth stated firmly.

"Your Majesty, I want to be perfectly clear—I do not have the power to negotiate a treaty and, to be frank, President Roosevelt does not anywhere close to the votes in Congress for a declaration of war."

Queen Elizabeth II regarded Secretary Hull with a gaze that radiated determination.

"I am certain that, sooner or later, Nazi Germany will provide you with no other choice than to go to war. At that time, the Commonwealth will stand with you even if England proper does not."

"That is part of the reason we are here, Your Majesty," Secretary Knox interjected smoothly. "There has been no public information regarding just what is involved in the Treaty of Kent. All we have in Washington is rumor, and some of them are so wild as to hardly be believable."

"You may find that some of the agreements Lord Halifax and my uncle have made are as terrible as you imagined," Queen Elizabeth remarked. Once again, Eric was struck by her composure.

Is it just me, or does it seem like the teenager in the room is dealing better with the world turned upside down than all the men?

"Naturally I am sure the United States' primary concern is the disposition of our fleet units," Queen Elizabeth continued. "I believe your isolationists have been roaring with full throat about President Roosevelt's folly in lending us aid when the 'bulwark of the Atlantic remained even if England did not,' correct?"

Eric had to struggle not to wince at the cold politeness in Queen Elizabeth's tone. Looking over at Secretaries Hull and Knox he could see that the young sovereign's words had stricken home.

"President Roosevelt intends to lend whatever aid he can..." Secretary Hull began.

"Yes, of course," Queen Elizabeth snapped, her reserve slipping for the first time. "That is precisely what he told Lord Churchill aboard this very vessel in August of last year. Strange then, is it not, how my nation lies prostrate and my father slain yet your 'political exigencies' still seem to prevent action."

Eric watched Admiral King's face start to shade red as the Queen had started her response. By the conclusion of it, the man's face was almost purple.

"Admiral King, why don't we go get some fresh air?" Secretary Knox said. King whirled and was about to respond when he suddenly realized that his superior was not actually making a request.

When the Secretary of the Navy asks you to step outside, you **step** outside.

With a slight neck bow to the Queen, Secretary Knox gestured for Admiral King to lead the way out of the compartment. Eric noted that Admiral King pointedly did not render any honors to the Queen on his way out of the compartment.

"Perhaps it would be best if Leftenant Cobb and the other two gentlemen left as well," Admiral Tovey stated.

"Those two gentlemen have been given direct orders to go with Her Majesty everywhere she goes," Churchill snapped. "While I trust we have nothing to worry about from anyone in this room, it would be best if we not set the precedent now."

"Leftenant Cobb may stay," Her Majesty said, favoring Eric with a small smile. "Given his luck so far, this will probably be yet another thing he can tell his grandchildren about."

Assuming I survive the next six months, nevermind long enough to marry Joyce, Eric thought. *That is, if she got my letter. Hell, I don't even know if* **Mom** *knows I'm still alive. I think I'm going to end up missing Patricia's wedding next month at this rate.*

"Please proceed Admiral Tovey," Queen Elizabeth continued.

"Your Majesty, Secretary Hull, at this moment the Commonwealth controls the majority of our ships. The only exceptions are four battleships, two carriers, a dozen cruisers, and twenty destroyers," Admiral Tovey said.

"What do you mean by 'control'? There are hardly that many ships here in Halifax," Admiral Kimmel asked.

Tovey and Churchill shared a look, then the latter answered.

"By 'control,' we mean ships that are not currently answering the orders of the Halifax Government or pledging allegiance to the Duke of Windsor."

Queen Elizabeth's nostrils flared at the last.

"My uncle renounced all of his titles the minute he set foot in London to usurp my throne and authority," she snapped.

"Your Majesty…" Churchill began.

"Lord Churchill, that topic is not open for discussion," Queen Elizabeth continued, even more forcefully

Eric saw several emotions flitter across Churchill's face, but there was no mistaking the steel in Queen Elizabeth's voice.

I would not want to cross this woman, he thought.

"Your Majesty, I for one would like to know what he should be called then," Secretary Hull said quietly. "If you allow our newspapers to come up with a name, they may choose something which gives the Halifax government the very legitimacy you seek to deny them."

Queen Elizabeth turned her gaze from Churchill to Secretary Hull.

"The Commonwealth government will refer to my uncle as The Usurper," Elizabeth said coolly. A look of surprise briefly flitted across Churchill's face so quickly that Eric was fairly certain no one else noticed it due to their focus on the Queen.

"Back to your original statement, Admiral Tovey—how did these vessels end up outside of your control?" Admiral Kimmel asked.

"*Anson, Howe,* and *Lion* are just completed," Tovey responded, his tone somber. "The remaining vessels either are not Home Fleet,

72

were recently damaged, or were en route to Great Britain and could not divert due to their fuel state."

"Why didn't the crews scuttle their vessels?" Kimmel asked, his voice disgusted.

"Because the Germans threatened to resume hostilities if there were any more incidents," Churchill snapped. "To be more specific, that bastard Himmler threatened to rip up the Treaty of Kent and lay scourge to every city within Southern England."

"So what will be the vessels' ultimate disposition?" Hull asked, his voice conveying that he was already resigned to what the answer would be.

"The Germans expect to face you sooner or later and intend to use the vessels until their three new battleships are complete. Anson and Howe have apparently already been dispatched to Wilhelmshaven along with several of the destroyers. Lion will be sent within thirty days. It is expected that they will take six months to be in German service." .

"So you're saying the Germans just got three modern battleships gift wrapped and dropped off at their door?" Kimmel asked, his tone one of disbelief.

"Are you familiar with the effect of nerve gas on unprotected civilians, Admiral Kimmel?" Queen Elizabeth asked quietly. "I can place you in touch with several officers who can tell you exactly just how agonizing a death it appears to be."

"No one is suggesting that your government should have called Mr. Himmler's bluff," Secretary Hull said smoothly, giving Admiral Kimmel a hard look. "Admiral Kimmel is understandably upset, as this will affect our own strategic calculus."

"We understand your concerns, Secretary Hull," Queen Elizabeth said. "However, given your upcoming construction we do not see cause for quite that level of alarm."

"Do not understand the reason for that level of alarm?" Admiral Kimmel asked unbelievingly, his Kentucky drawl getting more pronounced due to his anger. "How about those are two modern battleships that we will now have to account for in order to maintain open supply lines to Iceland? Or that we will have to destroy in order to return you to your throne?"

"Again, Anson and Howe will take at least six months to be

worked up with German crews," Admiral Tovey snapped. "I doubt that they will be anywhere near as experienced as your own."

"You're making the assumption they will have German crews," Kimmel said seethingly. "Our intelligence indicates that the Halifax government has not necessarily ruled out supplying 'volunteers' in exchange for concessions."

"That is a ploy to ensure that we continue grain shipments from Canada," Churchill observed, nostrils flaring slightly.

There was a moment when Kimmel and Hull both looked at him in shock.

"From your response you make it appear that you are thinking about continuing to do so," Hull said after a moment, his voice heavy.

"We will not starve our subjects," Queen Elizabeth said flatly.

"Perhaps you do not understand the gravity…" Secretary Hull started to say.

"I will not be lectured like I am some ignorant child, Secretary Hull," Queen Elizabeth snapped, her icy demeanor finally cracking. "You have the audacity to tell any one of us that we do not understand the gravity of the situation? Tell me, Mr. Secretary, when was the last time your home was bombed? Your capital burned? Your father murdered?"

Hull bit back a response, taking a deep breath.

I know a thing or two about willful women, Eric thought. *I'm pretty sure all of you underestimate this woman at your peril.*

"The American people will find it hard to understand how on one hand you can consider your uncle a…usurper yet you continue to supply grain to the people who follow him. There will be those who wonder if you are prepared to do what is necessary to regain your throne."

If looks could kill… Eric thought as Queen Elizabeth stared venomously at Secretary Hull for a brief moment before regaining her composure.

"Our government has done what is necessary throughout this conflict, Secretary Hull. We do not think the same can be said of yours," the monarch replied, her tone almost making Eric shiver from the intensity it contained.

The proverbial pin drop would have echoed like thunder in the compartment.

74

"Perhaps, Your Majesty, a break is in order," Churchill suggested after a moment, his voice neutral.

"That sounds like a wonderful idea, Lord Churchill," Queen Elizabeth replied, her lips pursed.

"Gentlemen, let us return in fifteen minutes," Churchill said briskly, looking at the clock on the far bulkhead.

"I will have a steward bring some coffee for our guests," Admiral Tovey said, heading for the watertight door.

"Lieutenant Cobb, we should probably get you ashore," Admiral Kimmel spoke from behind Eric. "A detachment should already be at your guest quarters collecting your gunner, and they should have transportation for you to return to the *South Dakota*."

I recognize an order wrapped in a suggestion when I hear it, Eric thought. Not that I mind—an ant does not need to be standing around when elephants are dancing.

"Yes sir," Eric replied, turning for the hatch.

"Leftenant Cobb," Queen Elizabeth called after him, causing Eric to stop dead in his tracks.

"Yes Ma'a...Your Majesty?" Eric said, tripping over himself.

"Thank you," Queen Elizabeth said simply.

"You are welcome, Your Majesty," Eric said, giving a slight neck bow. He stopped to wait for Admiral Kimmel to go out the hatchway, but the senior officer gestured for him to lead the way. Five minutes later, Eric found himself standing with Secretary Knox along with Admirals Kimmel and King next to the *Prince of Wales's* gangway. The fleet's service launch approached the battleship, bobbing in the choppy harbor water from the stiff wind.

"Lieutenant Cobb, I think it goes without saying you are to not to speak about anything you saw or heard today," Admiral Kimmel said quietly.

"Yes sir," Eric replied.

"Especially anything having to do with your senior's behavior," Secretary Hull snapped, staring directly at Admiral King.

"I will not be lectured by some teenaged skirt with delusions of grandeur," Admiral King snapped as he took a heavy draw on his cigarette. Eric watched Secretary Knox's face start to color as he looked to make sure no one was in ear shot.

"The British lost," King continued. "They left the Germans a

75

pretty sizeable portion of their fleet and we don't have the necessary power to go smash up Scapa Flow like they did the frogs when France fell. So pardon me if I don't get all wrapped up in protocol when I'm thinking about all the American boys who are about to die because some overwrought girl wants to avenge her daddy."

King looked out over the side as he flicked away his cigarette, and suddenly Eric could have swore the admiral aged five years right before his eyes.

"I've got six girls of my own, and I don't think anyone's going to ask several thousand boys like Lieutenant Cobb here to die if I end up on the wrong end of some German shell."

"Your personal opinions aside, I need to know if you can control yourself, Admiral King," Secretary Knox seethed.

"Gentlemen, I'm not sure now is the time…" Kimmel attempted to interject soothingly, only to be cut off by King.

"Mr. Secretary, if you think I'm incapable of fighting this war perhaps you need to go ahead and send me back to the General Board," Admiral King said lowly. "Especially if that job requires treating the people in there as equal allies who are bringing as much to the table as they're taking off of it. I took an oath to uphold and defend the Constitution, not cater to the Queen of England."

Secretary Knox took a visibly deep breath.

"We will discuss this further when we return to Washington," he said, his voice heavy with emotion. "For now, I think Lieutenant Cobb has a boat to catch."

Eric came to attention at the top of the gangway, saluting his seniors.

"Good luck, Lieutenant Cobb," Secretary Knox replied, returning Eric's salute.

"Thank you, sir," Eric replied, then started making his way down to the launch.

I have a feeling I just saw something that's not going to end well, he thought as he stepped into the small boat. The coxswain let him sit down, then began the small launch's journey back towards shore.

Ewa Air Station, Hawaii
1800 Local (0000 Eastern)
30 September (1 October 1)

"So I hear the new admiral's a real nutcracker," Sam said as he worked the ratchet in his hand.

"Is this why you stay late, Sam?" his brother asked disgustedly. "So you can gossip while you're helping to service a freakin' engine?"

There was a muted guffaw as one of VMF-14's enlisted mechanics struggled not to laugh. Master Sergeant Schwarz, VMF-14's chief mechanic, looked up from the other side of the engine to fix the offender with a baleful glare. While Sam and David had been strenuous in their declarations that they were just there as handymen and observers, Schwarz was not about to let one of his young Marines abuse their hospitality. Sam had developed the distinct impression that the tall, wiry gray-haired master sergeant sometimes enforced discipline with a bit more than his sharp tongue and gaze that would make a gorgon proud. While he hadn't brought the topic up with David in the three months the twins had been with the squadron, he doubted his brother had seen anything that would contradict that impression.

He reminds me of ol' Deputy Guston who used to oversee the chain gang back home, Sam thought grimly. *Nice man, polite to his peers and betters, but hell on wheels to those under him.*

"No, I stay late so I learn how my airplane works," Sam replied to David. "I'm just trying to make conversation."

"Well, whether the man's a nutcracker or not, he's already got Colonel Benson hopping," David said lowly, referring to Marine Aircraft Group Twenty-one's commander. "It's not like the man was a bump on the log in the first place."

Sam double checked his handiwork then went on to the radial engine's next cylinder head. Examining it closely, he raised an eyebrow and gestured for Master Sergeant Schwarz to take a look.

"This looked cracked to you, Master Sergeant?" he asked, reaching up to angle the shop light so the enlisted man could have a look. Schwarz leaned in close, squinting, then cursed.

"Yes, sir, it does. Guess we know why this aircraft was such a dog yesterday," Schwarz said, his annoyance clear.

"Better to find the fault now rather than end up going for a swim later," Sam replied.

"Attention on deck!" someone shouted, causing a rustling inside the hangar bay. Sam released the light as he stepped out from behind the engine to face the door, David close behind. Seeing the visitor, he felt the blood drain from his face as he snapped to attention.

Okay, Mom always used to say if you speak the devil's name he shall appear, but this is absolutely ridiculous, Sam thought.

Striding into the hangar was a man who looked, to quote one of their squadronmates, "older than Moses." Tall and broad shouldered, with an erect gait that made his stature seem even larger, Admiral Hank William Jensen was the newly minted Commander in Chief Pacific Fleet (CINCPACFLT), having been assigned when Admiral Kimmel had been tapped for CINCATLFLT. The senior officer's wizened features and wispy hair made him look a full decade older than his sixty years, but looking into his dark brown, almost black eyes was enough to show that age had not affected the man's mental abilities one bit. His dark, bushy eyebrows showed what color the few wisps of combed over white hair on his head had once been.

Standing beside Jensen was a rear admiral that Sam immediately recognized.

Holy shit, that bastard Bowles really does look just like his old man, Sam thought, thinking of one of his squadron mates.

Vice Admiral Jacob Bowles Sr. was a man that looked like an older Clark Gable, but with green eyes and a full head of brown hair. As he stepped away from the *Wildcat,* Sam noted the submariner's dolphins on the right side of the man's uniform shortly before Admiral Jensen started to speak. Three more men, two captains and a full commander, accompanied the admiral.

"Who is the senior man here?" Jensen thundered.

There was a moment's pause as all of the enlisted men looked at Sam and David, who in turn looked at each other.

"Sir, I am," David said, stepping around Sam to stand beside him. "Captain David Cobb, VMF-14."

"Why are you out of uniform, captain?" Jensen snapped, showing no sign of surprise at being presented with twin Marines.

"Begging the Admiral's pardon, Marine regulations clearly stipulate that when conducting services personnel are allowed to wear coveralls as their duty uniform," Sam replied evenly.

"That regulation only applies to enlisted personnel!" Admiral Bowles snapped. "Do not correct Admiral Jensen ever again."

I see being an asshole is a family trait, Sam thought quietly.

"Yes , sir," Sam replied. "Then, begging the admiral's pardon, the regulation in question is not rank specific."

Sam heard David's sharp intake of breath and watched as Bowles face started to color. Before the admiral could unleash a tirade, the hangar door opened again.

"Captains Cobb, two ea..." Major Max Bowden started to bellow, then stopped as soon as he realized that the squadron had company. A short, stocky man with thinning blonde hair and blue eyes, Bowden had so far proven to be quite capable as a squadron leader. He was also the third commander VMF-14 had had since Vice Admiral Bowles had arrived in Hawaii.

Someone is trying to do his damndest to get their son a squadron commander slot early, Sam thought bitterly.

"Good evening Admiral Jensen!" he said loudly, immediately recognizing CINPACFLT. The reason for his extra volume was apparent a moment later as Colonel Benson walked in followed by a man in civilian clothes.

"Good evening, sir," Benson said solemnly, coming to attention as he removed his cover. "Welcome to Ewa Air Station. I would have prepared a tour if I had known you were coming."

He looks tired, Sam thought as he looked at the group commander. An older man with a shock of gray hair and blue eyes, Benson had been a Marine aviator long enough to have seen action in several of the Banana Wars throughout the Caribbean. At just a shade under six foot normally, Benson seemed to be bowing under the weight of command that had descended upon his narrow shoulders.

"That's quite all right, Colonel," Admiral Jensen said. "Captain Cobb was just informing me of the finer points of Marine regulations."

There was a moment when both Benson and Bowden gave the Cobb brothers looks which clearly signified they doubted the junior officers' sanity. Before either man could speak, the chaplain politely cleared his throat.

"Admiral Jensen, I hate to interrupt, but I have some urgent news for both Captains Cobb."

"And you are?" Bowles thundered.

"Rear Admiral Bowles, I am Chaplain McHenry," the man replied evenly. "Specifically, I am *your* staff chaplain. We met six weeks ago when you took over as Chief of Staff. I understand if you do not recognize me—while I saw your son at church last week, I had not seen you recently. It is a large congregation, of course."

Whoa. Talk about soft answer turneth away wrath, Sam thought, watching as Bowles' mouth worked a couple of times in shock. McHenry turned away from the man and backed to Admiral Jensen.

"I apologize Admiral, but I am covering for MAG-21's chaplain," McHenry continued. "I just received a telegram that I need to deliver to Captain Cobb. Both of them."

*Oh no...*Sam thought.

"I think that the message..." Bowles began.

"Go ahead, chaplain," Admiral Jensen said, cutting his chief of staff off. "As a matter of fact, why don't you step outside with the two captains for a moment?"

"If you gentlemen will follow me?" McHenry said.

Feeling numb, Sam began following the chaplain out the door. There was never a good reason for a chaplain to come deliver a message.

"Who is it?" David asked as soon as they were standing outside the hangar.

"Your brother Eric is fine," McHenry replied quickly. "However, he was shot down by the Germans on September 12."

"*What?!*" Sam and David asked simultaneously. McHenry held up his hands.

"Easy, easy, let me finish then I will answer what questions I can," McHenry said. He quickly told both Cobb twins what their brother had been up to for just a little more than a fortnight.

"That's all the information I, or for that matter, anyone else here in Hawaii has," McHenry finished. "I'm sure there is additional information, but the communiqué mentioned your brother hasn't been fully debriefed and that the other information was classified."

"Holy shit," Sam breathed, then caught himself. "Sorry chaplain."

"Captain Cobb, I think if I just found out my brother had been in Canada for a fortnight after nearly getting killed by the Germans I'd probably be using some blue language as well."

80

"Has anyone informed our brother, Nick?" David asked.

"Rabbi Howe, the Submarine Force chaplain, was hoping to make arrangements after I informed him of the telegram. I received the news courtesy of a friend of mine who is on Admiral King's staff," McHenry replied. "He indicated that the Navy had only informed your mother your brother was 'missing' yesterday."

"Oh Jesus," David breathed. "Mom is going to be *pissed* at Eric."

"In your brother's defense, I suspect that he was either ordered not to contact your family or that someone held his mail," McHenry replied evenly. "The poor young man is already more famous than he is probably going to like."

"What do you mean, Chaplain?"

McHenry looked at both men.

"Neither one of you read the newspapers, do you?"

Sam and David both looked sheepish.

"No Chaplain," Sam replied.

"The Germans are rather incensed and are demanding Lieutenant Cobb's incarceration upon his return to the United States," McHenry replied evenly. "Secretary Hull has pointed out that the German Navy did open fire on a neutral aircraft so they are hardly the wronged party."

"You know, he always had a knack for finding trouble," Sam muttered.

"This is a bit different than stealing peaches from Widow Fitzsimmons," David drawled. Turning to look at his brother, Sam could see that David was obviously more upset than he was.

"Well he's safe now, and he's headed home," Sam replied evenly. "I'm pretty sure he'll have one hell of a story to tell Mom."

Singapore
1700 Local (0500 Eastern)
4 October

I almost feel sorry for the man, Rear Admiral Tamon Yamaguchi thought as he stoically regarded the fuming Englishman in front of him. Of average height, with close set, almost catlike features and a stocky build, Yamaguchi had once been likened to a gregarious catamount by one of his Princeton classmates. Like that predator, he remained almost perfectly still except for his almond eyes that tracked the tall, lanky, and clearly agitated British officer in front of him. Almost casually, he dropped his hand to the officer's sword on his left hip. He could see his superior, Vice Admiral Chuichi Nagumo, similarly tensing in front of him.

There are only three of them in this room, Yamaguchi thought. *I would not think they were so foolish as to cause an incident, but I know what path I would take in this situation.*

"I will tell you what is *reasonable*, Admiral Ciliax," Lieutenant General Arthur Percival hissed through his two protruding front teeth. "*Reasonable* is that I be advised that your nation had no intention of taking possession of this colony, but rather intended to turn it over to this bunch of barb...*gentlemen. Reasonable*..."

"I demand that you would not speak of the Reich's allies as if they are not standing here, General," Admiral Otto Ciliax thundered, both his hands on Percival's desk. "We are not, in any way, *negotiating* terms. The Treaty of Kent is clear, and the fact that you or your staff remain here is merely a formality and courtesy."

Percival glowered at his German opposite number, his face reddening around his clipped moustache.

"I have three divisions of troops under my command..." the Englishman began, only to be cut off again by Ciliax.

"Field Marshal Kesselring has over three *thousand* aircraft poised like a dagger at England," Ciliax said coldly, his accent growing thicker with emotion even as he casually waved. "How many women and children are you willing to kill with your pride?"

Percival opened his mouth then shut it again. Taking a deep, shuddering breath the man turned and looked at Vice Admiral Nagumo, then back at Ciliax.

"Then I will be damned if me or my staff will stay here to help some *Jap*," Percival spat. "For men who talk of the white race's superiority you seem to be awfully willing to do the slant eyes' dirty work."

Yamaguchi felt a rush of blood to his face even as he tried to keep his features impassive.

"Perhaps now would be a good time to tell you that Vice Admiral Nagumo will be the *Kriegsmarine*'s outside representative for inspecting the Royal Navy's indemnity payments for the loss of the *Scharnhorst*, *Gneisenau*, and damage to the *Bismarck* and *Tirpitz*?"

Percival's eyes narrowed.

"What the devil are you talking about?" he snapped.

"I am sure you will find out soon enough," Ciliax replied icily. "I believe you were taking your leave?"

Yamaguchi was as perplexed as General Percival. Even as he watched the British officer and his staff storm out of Singapore's command post, he found his mind alive with questions.

What outside representative? How is Nagumo-san going to inspect warships in Europe? Yamaguchi thought, confused.

"Gentlemen, I am sorry that you had to deal with…that," Ciliax said stiffly.

"His attitude is typical," Vice Admiral Nagumo replied, his English somewhat slow and stilting. "All of the West has long considered us inferior."

Ciliax gave a thin grimace at that.

"Despite that idiot's claims, the Fuhrer does not share that view," Ciliax replied, as a gradually building hum could be heard. "Indeed…who is flying those aircraft?"

The headquarters windows were vibrating with the roar of piston engines by the time that Ciliax finished his question.

"Admiral Yamamoto thought it best if we prepared some additional persuasion," Yamaguchi replied, his face still blank other than a slight narrowing of the eyes. "Just in case General Percival misunderstood our relative positions."

Ten thousand feet over Rear Admiral Yamaguchi's head, Sub-Lieutenant Isoro Honda gave his *Zero* some gentle right rudder to follow the maneuvers of Lieutenant Commander Shigeru Itaya, *Akagi's* fighter squadron commander. Looking back at the two other aircraft in his *chutai*, the IJN's typical three-plane formation, Isoro allowed himself to feel a small degree of pride. Their configuration was perfect, Warrant Officers Watanabe and Yoshida moving as if they were extensions of his own aircraft. The nimble, responsive *Zeroes* were weaving four thousand feet over the assembled strike aircraft of the *Kido Butai*, the Imperial Japanese Navy's strike force of six heavy carriers.

I only hope the British are stupid enough to start a fight, Isoro thought with grim satisfaction. *It will be nice to face worthy opponents again after three years of killing Chinese.* The Chinese had been like schoolchildren armed with rocks set upon by a horde of samurai, and the eight kills he had scored felt almost shameful given the Zero's superiority.

Not that the Russians were much better, Isoro thought bitterly. *Perhaps if the Army had actually managed to slow the Russians down then we might have gotten to test our mettle against them some more. Or maybe if we had been given a chance to fight those foreign mercenaries down in the south…*

Shaking himself out of his reverie, Isoro sighed as he continued to scan the skies around his aircraft. Several wingmen had often made fun of him for his tendency to always move his body in the cockpit, nicknaming him "Sea Snake" due to the undulations of his long, gangly frame. His nickname had taken on a decidedly different connotation when he started being the first to spot, then kill hostile aircraft. He turned back forward just in time to see a red and green flare arcing out from the lead torpedo bomber below.

No trade for us today, Isoro thought, shaking his head in disappointment. *It would appear that the British are going to accept the Germans giving us Singapore after all.* There had been rumors in the ready room that the Germans had not only ceded Japan Singapore but Malaya as well. If so, it was a gesture of goodwill that had Isoro reconsidering his view of Japan's alliances.

"Akagi fighters will land ashore," his headphones crackled with Lieutenant Commander Itaya's voice. "All others will return to carriers."

Well, well, looks like Lieutenant Commander Itaya wants to be the first to see Japan's latest colony, Isoro thought. *Hopefully the women will be friendlier than the Chinese were…or at least the Army dogs won't have time to make them hate us.*

U.S.S. Houston
Manila Bay
1434 Local Time (0134 Eastern)
6 October

Jacob looked thoughtfully at the chart spread out on the table before him, then back across at the captain of the U.S.S. *Houston.*

"So, Admiral Hart has decided that we are going to ally with the Dutch and attempt to keep the Japanese from the East Indies?"

Jacob asked incredulously.

"Yes, XO," Captain Wallace replied. "I take it you do not approve."

"The damn Japs have Singapore," Jacob said, incredulous. "That's like trying to close off a flooded compartment when the overhead's been blown away."

Captain Wallace regarded him calmly for several seconds, then replied.

"How much oil is there in the Philippines?"

"None, sir," Jacob replied, instantly seeing the light.

"Exactly. Just as there is none in Japan, which is why it is widely believed the East Indies is one of her primary objectives if war breaks out. I don't see the Germans trying to maintain convoys from Iraq during open hostilities, do you?"

I still can't believe we're just letting the Krauts sail tankers right by us, Jacob thought. *What's the good of having a navy if we're afraid to use it?*

"But that's not what our war plan states we are to do," Jacob replied. Captain Wallace smiled benignly.

"War Plan Orange is somewhat vague on what we're supposed to do, actually," Captain Wallace replied evenly. "Other than die bravely, and if I'm going to do that I want it to be for some other reason than General MacArthur's pride."

"I'm not sure I follow, Captain," Jacob replied.

"The fate of the Philippines is directly linked to that Army bastard's reputation, his 'place in history' as he's always telling Admiral Hart," Captain Wallace said, the disgust veritably dripping off his words. The man paused to take a drink from the coffee mug at his left elbow.

"Should the Philippines fall, General MacArthur would be disgraced. Especially since he has been spending so much to train the Filipinos over the last year."

Captain Wallace jabbed his finger at Lingayen Gulf.

"MacArthur sees our fleet as something to hurl against the Japanese transports to disrupt them when they land here," Wallace sneered. "He doesn't comprehend that the Japs will probably bring up battleships to blow this vessel out of the water."

Jacob nodded at that statement.

Trying to explain to an Army officer that 8-inch guns aren't all that heavy is like trying to explain to a toddler that the bath water isn't all that hot, he thought bitterly. *It's all a matter of scale and experience.*

"The Commonwealth commander, Admiral Phillips, just spent the last two days guaranteeing Admiral Hart that Her Majesty's Navy will fight for the Dutch East Indies," Captain Wallace continued.

"Be nice if he'd had some of that fighting spirit for Singapore or Malaya then," Jacob observed, doing his best to keep his voice matter-of-fact. Captain Wallace's glare told him that he'd succeeded only enough not to be immediately relieved.

"Rumor has it that admiral the Krauts sent out here basically told the Brits they'd gas London again if they tried to put up a fight. Given that Percival still answered to King Edward, he really didn't have a choice. Phillips, on the other hand, answers to the rightful Queen."

Jacob nearly laughed at that, but stopped himself.

Rightful Queen?! He says that as if she's ours, he thought as Captain Wallace continued.

"Admiral Phillips, per previous agreement with the Dutch, will set out from Sydney for Java if hostilities appear imminent. There he, and we, will combine with the Dutch East Indies fleet and deny the oil fields to the Japanese."

"Sir, that's suicide with the little bastards owning Singapore," Jacob replied in disbelief. "Hell, they can row small craft from there to Sumatra, never mind bring any fleet units they station in the harbor! How will we fight under enemy air cover?"

"We won't," Captain Wallace snapped. "With the amount of air power the Dutch and Commonwealth will have concentrated in the Dutch East Indies, intelligence estimates that the Dutch and Brits have the Japanese air force outnumbered two to one. Factor in their advantage in quality, and it's probably going to be a rout. Air superiority is a two-way street."

Looking at the charts in front of him, Jacob found himself slightly mollified.

Yet the Japanese aren't stupid, he thought. *I have to imagine some little yellow son-of-a-bitch is staring at his own charts right now.*

"You seem unconvinced, Commander," Captain Wallace observed.

"Sir, I can't help but think that the Japanese have to have figured this out as well," Jacob said slowly. "They picked a fight with the

Russians and got their heads, hands, and feet handed to them before they slunk back to Tokyo to lick their wounds. A thorough beating tends to make a man introspective."

"Commander, there's a natural order of things," Captain Wallace replied. "A bunch of people who were in the Dark Ages less than eighty years ago aren't going to beat us, the Brits, and the Dutch. That's why they backed down back in '41, and if they don't remember what's good for them we'll give them a beating that will make the Russian fight seem like a love tap."

"What about the Philippines?" Jacob asked.

"If the Japanese don't take the East Indies, they can hold this place until Judgment Day—they won't be getting any oil through to their Home Islands, German or otherwise. Six months to a year of that and we'll be able to sail right into Tokyo Bay."

Captain Wallace stepped back from the map.

"But enough talk of fighting in the Dutch Indies," the man said, looking at the clock. "What's our status?"

"Well, when it comes to a fight, I think we're as ready as we can be," Jacob stated firmly. He pulled out a small notebook in which he had written notes to himself.

"All departments completed their last checks early yesterday, and we finished taking on ammunition about an hour ago," he said. "I still think our damage control is shaky, but it's getting better and I've drilled as much as possible without asking for the *Boise* to shoot us with a live shell."

"I don't think having his cruisers shoot one another is what Admiral Hart intended when he stated we needed to conduct realistic training," Captain Wallace replied sardonically. "Admiral Hart is conducting a captain's call at his quarters in about an hour and a half. Set a skeleton watch and get the men some liberty—I get the feeling we're about to start training with our new allies."

"Aye aye, sir," Jacob replied.

"Oh, and Commander—not a word of our discussion to any other officers," Wallace warned. "We don't need talk getting around about what our plans are. General MacArthur has many connections. I don't want some fat, dumb, and happy senator in Washington deciding this vessel is expendable after all, just as long as precious Dougie doesn't get hurt."

"Understood, Captain," Jacob acknowledged.

"Until then, I'm going to my cabin to get cleaned up." With that, Captain Wallace turned from the chart table and headed for the hatch leading from his day cabin to his quarters. After he left, Jacob took another look at the map.

It's going to be one hell of a fight if it comes to that, he thought. *It's almost as if everyone is just waiting for a reason to go to war.*

24966294R00248

Made in the USA
San Bernardino, CA
13 October 2015